The Automobile Club of Egypt

Alaa Al Aswany's first novel *The Yacoubian Building* was longlisted for The International IMPAC Dublin Literary Award in 2006 and has sold over a million copies worldwide. He is also the author of *Chicago* and the short story collection *Friendly Fire*. His work has been translated into 29 languages and published in over 100 countries. Al Aswany was named by *The Times* as one of the best 50 authors to have been translated into English in the last 50 years. He speaks Arabic, English, French, and Spanish.

The Automobile Club of Egypt

※ Alaa Al Aswany ※

CANONGATE

This paperback edition published by Canongate Books in 2017

First published in Great Britain in 2016 by
Canongate Books Ltd,
14 High Street, Edinburgh EH1 1TE

www.canongate.tv

First published in English in the United States
in 2015 by Alfred A. Knopf, a division of
Penguin Random House LLC, New York

Originally published in Egypt as *Nady Alsayarat*
in 2013 by Dar El Shorouk, Cairo

British Library Cataloguing-in-Publication Data
A catalogue record for this book is available on
request from the British Library

ISBN 978 0 85786 221 1

Typeset in Minion by Scribe, Philadelphia, Pennsylvania
Designed by Betty Lew

Printed and bound in Great Britain by Clays Ltd, St Ives plc

MIX
Paper from
responsible sources
FSC
www.fsc.org   FSC® C018072

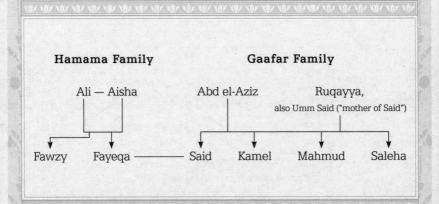

Hamama Family

Ali — Aisha

Fawzy   Fayeqa ——————— Said

Gaafar Family

Abd el-Aziz   Ruqayya,
                also Umm Said ("mother of Said")

Said   Kamel   Mahmud   Saleha

My wife finally understood that I needed some time on my own ...

I left her the big car and the driver so that she would be able to get around with the kids. I drove the smaller car to our chalet on the north coast, a three-hour drive alone with my thoughts and the voice of Umm Kulthum streaming from the cassette deck. At the gate, the security man checked my papers. In winter the resort management stepped up their security to prevent burglaries. A cool, refreshing breeze blew in from the sea. The place was completely empty and had the air of a fairy-tale town whose inhabitants had fled. All the chalets were locked and the streets deserted except for the lampposts. I drove past the main square and then turned up the street leading to our chalet. A new Japanese car suddenly appeared, driven by a man in his fifties and with a beautiful woman somewhat younger in the passenger seat. As they overtook me, I looked over at them ... they must be lovers, come to the resort to get away from prying eyes. That had to be it. For such blushing languor and loving serenity are not typical of married life. The door of the chalet squeaked as I opened it. I followed my wife's instructions to the letter. I started by opening the windows, plugging in the fridge and removing the covers from the furniture. Then I took a hot shower and went into the bedroom to unpack and hang up my clothes. I prepared my seat in the sitting room next to the balcony. I telephoned to order food from the only place open in winter, and perhaps owing to the sea air wolfed down the food and nodded off. By the time I woke up, night had already fallen. I looked out from the balcony at the empty resort. It was dark except for the strip of lampposts. I felt a little strange and then a worry came to my mind:

I was now completely alone and hundreds of kilometers from Cairo. What if something were to happen? If I had a heart attack, for example, or if armed robbers set upon me, would I be able to cope with any of those situations we read about in the newspapers?

My death would make a sensational headline: "Well-Known Novelist Murdered in Mysterious Circumstances!" I made an effort to pull myself together. Three kilometers away there was a new, well-equipped hospital I could get to if I suddenly fell ill, and there was no chance of a burglary with the security having been heightened at all the entry gates and even by the sea. The guards, all local Arabs familiar with the coastal region, patrolled twenty-four hours a day. But what if the guards got themselves together and started burgling? I decided that only happens in cheap detective novels. I took another shower. That was how I usually got rid of unwanted thoughts or feelings. Whenever I stood under the tap and felt the hot water pouring over me, I could calm myself down and clear my mind. Thus refreshed, I made myself a cup of coffee and set to work.

I connected my laptop to the printer and loaded a whole ream of paper. I had already proofread the novel a few times, but I resolved to go through it a final time. It would take me three hours, and I would end up not changing a single word, perhaps a comma or a period here and there. I closed the file on the laptop and went out onto the balcony, lit a cigarette and stared out at the empty street. I knew it would be hard to bring myself to print out the novel, that I would put off that singular moment as long as I could, but then, with a click, my novel would be born; it would come out into the light, suddenly transformed from the hypothetical text composed in my imagination into a finished, tangible thing with a real and independent existence. The moment of clicking on the print button always gave rise to strange and powerful ambivalence—a combination of self-satisfaction, gloom and anxiety. Self-satisfaction for having finished writing the book. Gloom because taking my leave of the characters has the same effect on me as when a group of friends have to depart. And anxiety, perhaps because I am on the verge of delivering up into other people's hands something that I treasure. It will be the same with my daughter—for as happy as I shall be at her wedding, the thought that I am no longer her everything, as I deliver her into another man's hands, will rip me apart.

I got up to make another cup of coffee, but no sooner had I stepped into the kitchen than, lo, another surprise. I could hear footsteps. I could not believe my ears. I ignored the sound and busied myself with the coffee, but the sound was getting clearer and louder. I cocked my head to focus my hearing, and I was sure of it. I was not dreaming. They were the footsteps of more than one person. I was glued to the spot. No one knew I was here, so who could these people be, and what might they want? The footsteps came closer and closer, and then the doorbell rang. They were outside, standing in front of the door. There was nothing to do but deal with the situation. I quietly opened the kitchen drawers one after the other until I found a long sharp knife and then laid it on the shelf opposite the door, within easy reach. I turned on the outside lamp and looked through the peephole. I could see a man and a woman, but I could not make out their features in the weak light. I opened the door slowly, and before they could utter a word, I said, "Everything okay?"

The woman answered in a cheerful voice, "Good evening, sir."

I kept looking at them. The man then spoke in the tone of someone addressing an old friend, "We are very sorry to bother you. But we have come to see you on a serious matter."

"I don't know you."

"Actually, you know us very well."

She smiled as she said this. I noted the confidence in her voice and responded, "Excuse me. I think there is some mistake."

"There is no mistake," she said, laughing. "You know us well."

The situation became even more curious. The man smiled and said, "Don't tell me you don't remember seeing us before?"

I started to feel afraid. I was having an odd sense of déjà vu. The man and woman did in fact look familiar, as if I had seen and spoken to them before, as if my previous meeting with them had lain buried in my memory and then suddenly resurfaced. In a loud voice, I said, "I don't have time for riddles. Who are you and what do you want?"

With disarming calm, the man answered, "Are you going to leave us standing at the door like this? Let us in and then we'll speak."

The strange thing is that I obliged. I stood aside and let them in as if I had suddenly lost control of my own actions. I could hear what I was saying and see what I was doing, as if I were another person. They came in slowly, walking around as if familiar with the place. They sat next to each other on the sofa, and I could finally see them in the light. The man was in his late twenties. Large but not flabby. Olive-skinned. Handsome. The woman was just over twenty, beautiful, winningly lithe of figure with fine facial features to match, glowing brown skin and beautiful green eyes. Her elegant outfit was straight out of the forties. The man was wearing a lightweight white sharkskin suit, a white shirt with a starched collar, a tightly knotted blue tie and spats. The woman was wearing a tailored blue outfit with a white collar and buttons and white hair clips and a straw hat on her plaited hair. They exuded a sort of vintage aura, as if they had just stepped out of an old photograph album or a black-and-white film. I had no idea what to think. I could not take in what was happening and thought that I must be hallucinating, no longer sure that the man and woman sitting in front of me were real.

The man opened a pack of red Lucky Strike cigarettes. He held one with two fingers and then tapped it on the back of his hand, before putting it in his mouth and lighting it with a small lighter. He took a deep drag and said, "I am Kamel Gaafar, and this is my sister, Saleha Gaafar."

"You can't be!"

He laughed and spoke slowly, "I know that this is a difficult turn of events for you to absorb, but it is true. I am Kamel Abdel Aziz Gaafar and this is my sister, Saleha."

I stared at his face and, suddenly angry, I snapped, "Listen. I am not going to let you waste my time."

"Please stay calm until I have explained everything to you."

"I don't want an explanation, thank you very much. I have work to do."

The woman smiled and said, "But we are part of your work," and the man added, "Actually, we are your work."

I could not answer. A shiver went through me. I could feel my heart racing. I was sweating and thought I was going to lose consciousness. Almost sympathetically, the man gave a friendly smile and continued, "Sir, please believe me. I am Kamel Gaafar, and this is my sister, Saleha. God alone knows how much we like you. My sister and I are products of your imagination and have come to life. You dreamed us up for your novel. Your imagination led you to write down the details of our lives, and at a certain point as you outlined our characters, we came into being. We have moved from the realm of imagination into that of reality."

I could not answer. I carried on looking at them. The woman laughed and said, "I can guess just how much this surprise has affected you, but this is the truth. We have come from the realm of your imagination to meet you."

I remained silent, and the man carried on speaking amicably, "We have to thank you. It's our good luck to be your characters. I can only admire your dedication to your art. You spend years writing a novel, and it is so rare to find novelists who put so much effort into it."

"Thank you."

I uttered those words sotto voce while absorbed with the thought that I was getting used to the strangeness of the situation. I looked at each of them in turn. Saleha smiled and spoke in her mellow voice, "Please don't look at me as if I were one of the wonders of the world. You're a great writer, and you know that there are many inexplicable extrasensory phenomena. You sweated blood and tears to create living characters. And now we are actually alive and in front of you. Isn't that what you wanted?"

In a loud voice, I said, "Let's assume that you are speaking the truth, and even that you are Kamel and Saleha Gaafar; what do you want from me?"

Kamel smiled broadly, tapped the ash from his cigarette into the ashtray and said, "Ah. You see, sir. We have come here in all seriousness to stop you from printing out the novel."

"By what right?"

"The novel is really rather good, but it is lacking a few things."

"Such as . . . ?"

As if by some prearranged plan, Saleha smiled and chimed in, "Some of our thoughts and feelings are absent from the novel."

"I have expressed the thoughts and feelings of my characters quite well enough."

"You have expressed them from your point of view."

"Naturally. I'm the author."

"Why don't you let us speak for ourselves?"

"No one has the right to interfere with my work."

Kamel remained silent for a few moments, as if he was looking for the right words, and then said gently, "Sir, please trust us. We know just how much effort you have made, but you can't describe our thoughts and feelings by proxy."

"That's what all authors do."

"But our case is different. We have come to life. It is our right to be able to speak for ourselves. We have got some important elements that need to be added to the novel."

I rose from my seat and shouted forcefully, "Listen. It's my novel. I wrote it from my imagination and experience. I will not allow anyone to add a single word that I haven't written."

Saleha also stood up and moved closer to me. I recognized that she was wearing "Nuit de Paris" perfume. She said, "I don't understand why you are getting so upset, sir. We only want what is best for you. If the novel is published before we have a chance to add our thoughts and feelings, it will be a great loss."

There was nothing left to say. I made up my mind, walked over and opened the door and told them, "If you don't mind . . ."

"Are you asking us to leave?" cried Saleha, giving me a look of rebuke. Her green eyes were strangely affecting. "We haven't done anything to deserve such heartless treatment."

"Please leave the house immediately."

Kamel got up first, followed by Saleha, who said, "You insist on humiliating us. All right. We'll leave. But I want one thing from you."

She opened her travel bag, took out a CD in a transparent cover and said, "This is a version of the novel in which we have recorded everything that happened in our lives."

"For heaven's sake, I am the one who wrote the novel!"

"You might have written it, but we are the ones who lived it."

There was no point discussing the matter any more. I was almost at the end of my tether and on the point of doing something stupid. Saleha was standing there, smiling, her hand stretched out with the CD, but when she realized that I was not going to take it, she carefully set it down on the small table. They left, shutting the door gently behind them. I had no idea what to do. I lit a cigarette. Good Lord, what is going on, and who were these people? Were they con artists or simply mad? What were they up to, and how could they know the names of the characters in my unpublished novel, which no living creature apart from me had read? Could fictional characters really come to life? There is a whole science called parapsychology that seeks to explain otherwise inexplicable paranormal phenomena. The worry I'd had earlier resurfaced. I might be ill. Was I mentally disturbed and suffering from hallucinations? If I had been a drug user, I could have solved the matter with one drag of hashish. I had tried it once, but it left me feeling so dim-witted that I have avoided it ever since, and I have no idea how some authors manage to write at all while under the influence.

In my case, writing demands total concentration. I returned to my senses and realized that the two visitors must have been real and that, overwhelmed by the shock of it all, I had treated them badly. I should not have told them to leave. I should have made them stay until I had got to the bottom of things. I should have overcome my sense of amazement and listened to them. I opened the door and ran down the steps. Maybe I could catch up with them. I would apologize and bring them back to the chalet. I had to find out what was going on. They could not have gone far. I strode down the garden path, but when I reached the street, I became completely befuddled. Had they gone left or right? If I went the wrong way, I would lose them forever. I noticed one of the security guards, in his distinctive blue uniform, sitting on a wicker chair on the opposite pavement. I rushed over to him, and he stood up. I asked whether the man and woman who had just left my chalet had gone toward the sea or the desert road. To my utter astonishment, the guard said that he had not seen anyone.

I described them to him, but he reiterated that he had been sitting there for hours and had seen no one go in or come out of the chalet. I stopped trying to contradict him and started looking around, but I was only clutching at straws. I hurried off toward the sea, and then I returned and rushed off in the opposite direction, hoping that I would catch sight of them. But they had completely disappeared. I knew that my efforts were futile. I went back to the house, panting, and slowly walked up the steps, overcome by an unexpected anxiety. I must be sick. I was suffering from hallucinations. People were appearing before me whom no one else could see. I could feel the sweat dripping down my forehead and almost hear my heart beating. It occurred to me that there was only one way to find out whether this was merely a vision or reality. I unlocked the door and flicked the switch on the wall, flooding the sitting room with light. I blinked hard and looked at the table. The CD was there. Exactly where Saleha had left it. I relaxed. With trembling fingers, I removed it from its cover and slid it into the laptop. It took a moment for the laptop to recognize it, and then I started to read.

1

The story started when a man called Karl Benz met a woman called Bertha.

In the only extant photograph of him, Karl Benz appears distracted, his mind so preoccupied by something other than the details of daily life that he has forgotten to do up the buttons of his jacket as he stands for the camera. His face appears to show a deep-grained sadness, a look of despondency left by a hard childhood. His father, a railroad engineer, had died in a terrible accident when Karl was just two, and his mother fought hard to provide him a good education. Still, he had had to start working at a young age in order to help support his siblings. The photograph shows his intelligence and determination, but it also portrays him as somewhat distant, as if he is looking at something on the far horizon that only he can see. Bertha's photograph, on the other hand, reflects a special type of beauty, one not sensual but brimming with maternal tenderness. Still, the captivating graciousness and angelic modesty of her features cannot hide a steely determination of her own and a readiness to sacrifice herself for duty.

It was July 20, 1872. In the German city of Mannheim, the church was full to the rafters with men and women in their Sunday best, so many people having been invited that some had to stand during the ceremony. Despite rebukes and reprimands, the children kept babbling and fidgeting. The smell of the freshly painted church walls permeating the hot air did nothing to relieve the stifling heat as the women muttered and rapidly fanned themselves with their patterned silk fans. Suddenly, cries of joy went up, along with scattered clapping, as Karl Benz appeared in his elegant white suit, arm in arm with his bride, Bertha, who glittered in a beautiful gown of green French lace encrusted with small clusters of diamanté, the gown glistening and the deep round neckline showing off her exquisite skin. It was pulled in tightly to highlight her fabulous waist and below that puffed out in a bell shape like a ballet dancer's costume. The couple walked slowly up the aisle to the altar and then repeated the marriage vows uttered first by the corpulent priest, who, due to the heat, took a sip after every sentence from a glass of cold water placed near him and wiped the sweat from his brow with a large white handkerchief.

Karl held Bertha's hand and spoke his vow in a staccato and rasping voice, as if he was reticent about the words. When it was Bertha's turn, her face reddened slightly, her breath becoming irregular, and the words came out in the disjointed fashion of a schoolgirl reading out a difficult text for a demanding teacher: "In the name of our Lord Jesus Christ, I take thee, Karl Benz, to be my lawfully wedded husband. To have and to hold, from this day forward, for better, for worse, for richer, for poorer, in sickness and in health, to love and to cherish, till death do us part."

A dinner for the family and some close friends followed the ceremony. Just before midnight, Karl opened the door to their new house, and Bertha paused before walking across the threshold. She thought about how one part of her life was coming to an end and a new one was beginning, and she whispered a prayer to God to bless their life together.

The bedroom was upstairs. Bertha had only ever permitted Karl to give her a few furtive kisses. Her vigilant Protestant conscience only allowed her to give her body to him after a licit marriage in the house of God. Thus, their first act of physical union took on a unique and celebratory dimension, every last detail of it to remain imprinted in her memory forever. Bertha, her whole life long, never forgot those first spontaneous, confused, eager, feverish yet delightful moments—their attempts at conversation on a scattering of subjects, the speechlessness which struck them both, how Karl edged toward her and started kissing her gently, his warm breath smelling of cigar and alcohol and the feel of his prickly mustache and the fresh aroma of his white silk pajamas mixed with that of his body. She would always remember how she almost passed out from shyness as she whispered to him to turn out the light, the string of kisses that made her body gradually relax until she felt she was swimming in a wide-open void and then the way their bodies clave to each other in a strange yet familiar way, causing her at first a little pain, which soon gave way to the wonderful feeling that they were now truly joined together for life.

Bertha would always recall those days with a smile of satisfaction and tenderness. Those first days of marriage were a period of utter contentment. She did everything she could to make her husband happy, in the hope that they would create an upright Christian family that would be like a fruiting tree in the Lord's garden. Unfortunately, though, clouds started gathering and obscured the sun. Bertha quickly found out that her husband was more eccentric than any other man she had known or heard about. He was different from her father and brothers and the husbands of her friends. He sometimes appeared so unpredictable that he could almost be two different people in one body.

The gentle, mild-tempered and affectionate Karl whom she loved and married could be suddenly beset by demons and turn into another person, absentminded, irritable, nervous, ready to quarrel over the slightest matter. He could be curt in a way that she had never expected. He could become unfathomable, shrouding everything he did with such secrecy that she started to wonder whether she really knew anything about him.

She knew that he was an engineer at a workshop and that he had set something up with a partner in order to earn a living. One day he came asking her to lend him a sum of money to buy out the partner. She did not hesitate for a moment but handed over the amount from her own savings, with Karl kissing her hands in gratitude. He said excitedly that he would never forget her kindness, but within a few days he had gone back to his odd ways. He told her that he had rented the cellar of the Millers' house in the next street as a workshop. There, he said rather brusquely, he would be able to finish what he had started in the workshop. Then he avoided answering any of her questions, smiled cryptically and left the house.

Karl started spending long hours at the cellar, refusing to allow Bertha to see it, and when she asked him who was cleaning the place for him, he pretended not to hear. As the days passed, his behavior became more erratic. He would settle himself down in the far corner of the sitting room, smoking a cigar and saying nothing, completely aloof from everything around him, when suddenly he'd jump to his feet and rush out of the house as if he had just remembered some urgent chore. He would be gone for hours on end and, when he returned, would carry on as if nothing was awry.

One night when they were in bed, their bodies joined in the passion of lovemaking, Bertha opened her eyes and, in the glimmer of light coming through the window, she saw his face. Karl, in their most intimate moments, looked distant and distracted. He was with her in body but his mind was elsewhere.

That night Bertha realized that she had lost him forever. She agonized over having a husband who seemed to be thinking of something else when making love to his wife. Then it came to her in a blinding flash: Karl must be in love with another woman. This was the only way to explain things, but who was the other woman? Was she more beautiful than Bertha? How and when did they fall in love? Why did he not marry her instead of deceiving Bertha? Could she be sure that he had used her money to start a business of his own, as he claimed, or might he be spending her money on that other woman? Could she even be sure that he was using the cellar as a workshop?

The Miller family, known for their greed, might well turn a blind eye on adulterous activities in their cellar provided they received a decent rent.

Bertha was wracked by such doubts when one night she woke up to find Karl was not lying there next to her. She sprang out of bed and found him in his study, smoking and writing something on a sheet of paper, but the moment he saw her, he tried to cover it up. She asked him about it, but he tucked it away, saying, "I've got some work to finish tonight."

She stood there looking at him. Did he have so little shame as to leave his marital bed to write a letter to his girlfriend? She thought of lunging forward and grabbing the paper from his hand, come what may. But she hesitated and then just went back to the bedroom.

She lay awake wondering why she had not confronted him and why she had not snatched the letter away, the proof of his guilt.

Deep down, she was afraid of confronting the truth. Anxiety over her adulterous husband had been gnawing away mercilessly at her soul, and there was only the most remote possibility of his innocence. What if she were to confront him and he confessed to adultery? What would she do then? Should she tell her family, walk out on him? She had to think it through properly first. She decided to play for time while preparing to have it out with him, remembering that once you start out on the road downhill, there is no stopping.

One morning after breakfast, as he was about to leave for work, she was standing by the door to see him off and was surprised to hear him say, avoiding her gaze, "I won't be home tonight."

"For what reason?"

"I've got some work that I can't put off, so I am going to work through the night in the cellar."

Now, for the first time, Bertha could not control herself. She exploded, and her voice could be heard throughout the house, "Just stop it, Karl. I can't continue putting up with your lies. What work would make you spend the night out of the house? What do you take me for? I am neither a child nor a fool. I know what has been going on. You're cheating on me, Karl. But why live a life of lies with me? Leave me and go to her, if you're in love."

She said all of this, standing with her hands on her hips, her hair disheveled, a look of fury on her face and her greenish eyes exuding bitterness and anger. She was raging, ready to fight it out, but then she burst into tears. Karl looked at her calmly, in a state of incomprehension. He knitted his brows and said nothing but tried to embrace her. She pushed him away forcefully, sobbing, and she shouted, "Get away from me!"

Then, suddenly, he grabbed her hand and pulled her toward the door as she cried out, "What are you doing?"

"Come with me."

He grasped her hand more tightly and pulled her outside.

The autumn sky was dull, overcast and threatening rain. Karl strode forth while Bertha tried to wriggle out of his grasp, almost falling a few times; they were such an odd sight that some passersby started giving them sidelong glances. When they reached the Millers' house, he led her down to the cellar and unlocked the door with his right hand while keeping hold of her with his left. The door screeched open in response to his kick. He pulled her inside, finally letting go of her hand to turn on the lamp.

Rubbing her now freed wrist, she looked around. The space was full of strange objects, machines great and small, bicycles of various sizes lying on the floor, a large blackboard covered with scores of equations, technical drawings hanging on the walls, a wooden workbench with engine parts on it with countless nails and screws in containers nearby. Karl sat her down on the only chair, and he leaned against the old wall covered in flakes of paint as he started to explain. As she listened to him, she started to put the whole picture together, and her sullenness turned into astonishment. When he'd finished explaining, she asked him a few questions, to which he gave straightforward and complete answers. Finally, there was nothing left to say, and a pregnant silence fell over them. Karl knelt down beside her, kissed her hands and knees and said, "Bertha, I love you. I will never love another woman. I am so sorry that my work has kept me away from you, but I have been working for years to achieve the dream I have been living for. I am trying, one day, to invent a horseless carriage. A carriage driven by a motor."

She flung her arms around him, pressing her nose into his hair, and whispered, "I love you too."

That night she gave herself to him as never before. Unfurling like a rose refreshed by the dew, she threw herself at him as if he had just returned from a long voyage, kissing him all over, cradling him like a child, as if her long mistrust of his faithfulness had turned, in an instant, into feelings of guilt, unleashing a torrent of affection. Thereafter, Bertha understood how to love her husband for what he was and not to wish to change him. She no longer cared if his mind wandered elsewhere when he was with her or if he spent the whole day outside the house. Now that it was clear he was not an adulterer but a devoted, industrious and upright Christian, nothing worried her any more. She could want no better. If he had things to do that took up most of his time, so be it. At least he would not be drinking, gambling or wandering, as many other husbands did. Bertha was happy and bore him four children. They took up most of her energy, and he carried on spending most of his time in the workshop, obsessed with his work.

One evening, as she was busy making dinner, the back door flew open, and Karl stood there with oil-spattered hands. "Bertha," he cried, "drop everything and come with me!"

She had no idea why, but the overwhelming joy on his face was contagious, and so she dried her hands, undid her pinafore and went off with him. The moment she entered the workshop, she beheld something very strange indeed: a giant bicycle the likes of which she had never seen before, with three large wheels, two at the back and

one in front, and a seat wide enough for two people. Behind the seat was a metal cylinder from which hung a black leather drive belt.

Karl looked at her, gave a shout and clapped his hands. He threw his arms around her and lifted her up as he showered her with kisses. "Bertha!" he cried. "This is the greatest day in my life. I have made the first motor carriage in history." He went over to the carriage, took hold of the leather strip and explained, "Look. It doesn't need a horse to pull it. It is propelled by an engine!"

As the significance of what he was saying dawned on her, she exclaimed, "Oh that's wonderful. Thank God."

"Tomorrow," Karl said dreamily, "I'm going to register the patent in my name. I'll find investors for a factory. It'll be called the Benz carriage, and we'll sell thousands of them and earn millions."

A thought came to Bertha's mind, and she asked gently, "But, Karl, do you really think that people would buy this carriage?"

"Certainly. They won't need horses anymore. They'll drive my carriage. The Benz carriage."

"Karl, I don't know if it's that simple. It's hard to get people to change their ways, and I don't think that they'll spend their money on something they don't know anything about."

Then, as Karl looked at her pensively, she got up slowly and walked toward him with a look of determination. She took his head in her hands, planted a kiss on his forehead and whispered, "Karl, I am just as happy as you about your invention. I'm proud of you. But our work isn't over. It has just begun."

The next day Bertha set to work on her plan.

She invited Mannheim's most famous photographer, Tom Miesenberg, to the workshop. He was a tall, slim man in his seventies with completely white hair. His clothes were as shabby and creased as if he had slept in them. As usual, he was drunk on arrival and insisted upon receiving payment in advance. Then he spent the whole day taking pictures of the carriage from various angles. When he had developed the images, Bertha chose the most dazzling one for distribution in the local newspaper, accompanied by a paid advertisement, which appeared in the Sunday edition with the following text:

"The engineer Karl Benz is pleased to announce to the people of the city of Mannheim that, after long years of strenuous effort, he has invented the Benz carriage, the first motor wagon in history. This carriage requires no horse to draw it but is driven by a small gasoline-powered engine. This astonishing new means of transport promises a great improvement to our way of life. Karl Benz will offer a demonstration of his motor wagon this Sunday, May 15, in front of his residence, at exactly one o'clock. All are invited to attend."

The advertisement caused a great stir in Mannheim and the neighboring localities, with controversy raging around the new invention: most people were simply dumbfounded and wondered how a carriage could move without being drawn by a horse. Some scientifically minded enthusiasts thought such a thing was theoretically possible while others publicly mocked Karl and his claim of a horseless carriage. His fiercest and most outspoken opponents, however, were the conservative Christians, who insisted that "the notion of a horseless carriage is impossible. The Lord did not create the universe in vain, and horses he created for us specifically to draw our carriages. This eternal truth cannot be altered by Karl Benz or anyone else."

The fundamentalists went all over Mannheim furiously uttering their imprecations: "You who believe in Jesus! This new carriage is not an invention but a trick sent by Satan, who will not rest until he has tempted the faithful and shaken their belief in God. Karl Benz is neither a man of learning nor an inventor. He is a swindler who, along with his wife, summons evil spirits. But Satan's snares are weaker than a spider's thread, as the Lord Himself has confirmed, and you will see for yourselves how these tricksters will meet a terrible end, in time the same punishment of all those who sell their souls to Satan."

The hubbub about the Benz carriage only grew until the naysayers and the yea-sayers, together with the merely dubious, were all swept along in a storm that engulfed all other topics of conversation in Mannheim.

By the appointed hour, Karl and Bertha had prepared everything meticulously. Karl had cleaned and polished the carriage until it gleamed all over, and the two then brought the carriage out of the workshop and set it in front of their residence. The whole street filled with onlookers, thronging the roads leading to the Benz residence until there was so much pushing and shoving that the police had to come and restore order. At one o'clock exactly, Karl Benz appeared accompanied by his wife. He was wearing a light-gray suit with a white shirt and a deep-red bow tie. Bertha was wearing an elegant sky-blue dress, bought especially for the occasion, and a matching blue hat with white ribbons.

The whispers started to turn into a clamor as the couple edged their way through the assembled throng toward the covered vehicle. Then with one flick of his hand, Karl pulled off the tarpaulin. Some shouts and nervous laughs rang out from the spectators. Karl stood looking at the crowd, as if he were about to speak. When the crowd had quieted down, Karl spoke out in a shaky voice:

"Ladies and gentlemen! I would like to thank you for coming here today, and I should like to confirm that you are about to witness the beginning of a new era, a moment that will change the world. One day you will tell your grandchildren that you saw the first Benz motor wagon. Here is a carriage that has no need of a horse and is propelled entirely by means of a rear-mounted engine. It is also easy to handle, as you shall now see for yourselves."

Karl placed his right foot on the step attached to the undercarriage and climbed into the driver's seat. There was almost total silence as people jostled forward to see exactly what would happen. They held their breath and stared at Karl, who struggled to keep smiling as he held on to the steering handle with his right hand and grasped the black leather drive belt with his left hand. He gave the latter a violent pull, and the carriage gave out a loud, angry roar, puffing out thick smoke and then lurching forward. The crowd shrieked in unison as if they were aboard a wildly swaying ship sinking into the ocean, and as if, until that moment, they had been absolutely convinced that what was happening in front of their eyes was real. The carriage set off down the street, the crowd running after it, shouting and clapping and cheering, with Karl in perfect control of the machine, steering it easily and capably like a masterful rider bending his steed to his will. As the carriage sped forward, Karl steered it onto the main road, the people still running along behind it. Karl was doing so well that a triumphant smile appeared on Bertha's face as she watched.

Karl managed to follow the road until he came to a large tree, where he pulled on the metal brake arm. He gave it a few sharp pulls, but unfortunately, it did not respond. Karl was struggling to control the steering handle, but the vehicle, now moving at full throttle, as if in defiance, started to meander wildly before mounting the sidewalk, where it crashed into a tree and overturned. Thus ended the excursion, with the carriage upturned and its wheels hissing and turning as the motor whined and blew out thick smoke. The carriage looked like a giant nightmarish insect lying on its side, unable to right itself. And Karl was stuck underneath it, choking from the smoke and coughing loudly. He finally managed to wriggle free, his face, hands and elegant suit all covered in oil. There was complete and utter silence. The stupefied onlookers needed a few moments to absorb what had just happened, but their feelings, momentarily suppressed, all burst out at once, and they started shouting, jumping and laughing like madmen. Karl left the carriage where it lay and, with his head downcast, walked back to his house with Bertha following him as he endured the mockery raining down on him from all sides like poisoned darts.

"Oy, Mr. Benz! At least a horse doesn't overturn our carriages!"

"You want us to give up our horses and ride a carriage of death?"

"Thanks for the comedy show, Mr. Benz. You should do it in a circus!"

"That's your due for challenging God's laws."

"Tell your spirits to make you one that doesn't flip over next time!"

The following days saw the couple subjected to more grief and gloating. Benz's carriage became a laughingstock in Mannheim, and no sooner had the newspapers expressed encouragement for the invention than their tune changed to trenchant sniping. Karl felt unable to go out in public. Worst of all were the drunken layabouts who would fill up on wine in the tavern and then, having nothing else to do so early, go to Karl Benz's house to gawk at the carriage. Some plucked up the cheek to knock on his door and pretend to want to see the horseless carriage as a serious customer thinking of buying one might do. Karl realized that they were probably nothing of the kind, but on the slightest chance that they were, he would lead them to the workshop anyway, and no sooner would he start describing it to them than they would start bombarding him with stupid questions and comments. Only when dead certain that they were making fun of him would he walk to a chair in the corner, where he would sit quietly until they had had their fun and left. Karl bore all of these travails, and Bertha did her best to ease his anguish either with sincere words of consolation or else by ignoring the subject and carrying on as usual. But his disappointment was like a heavy black cloud casting a shadow over the couple wherever they went.

One hot August day, Bertha suggested that they take their supper in the garden. She had prepared Karl's favorite dish of roast chicken, and they drank a bottle of chilled, refreshing rosé. She tried to make the dinner enjoyable, or at the very least ordinary, by speaking about anything other than the carriage and the failed demonstration. Everything was going well until a man in his late forties in a white shirt and blue trousers suddenly appeared at the garden gate. They wished him a good evening, whereupon he said in a loud voice, "Excuse me, sir. Are you Karl Benz, who invented the horseless carriage? If it's no trouble, I'd like to see it."

Karl said nothing for a moment and in a deep voice replied, "I'm very sorry, but there's nothing to see."

"What do you mean? I'd like to see the carriage you invented."

Karl looked down for a moment and then raised his head toward the man before quietly repeating his response, "There's nothing to see."

The man kept looking at him and then with a bow politely said, "All right, Mr. Benz. I'm so sorry to have disturbed you. Have a nice evening."

That night, the couple lay stretched out near each other in bed, in the dark, saying nothing. Bertha put her arm around him, and as if on command, he shifted his body a little and laid his head on her chest. She asked him gently, "Why wouldn't you show the carriage to that man?"

He said nothing for a few seconds, then sighed and in a weak voice, as if speaking to himself, replied, "I'm just tired of being taken for a fool, Bertha. I just can't stand any more of those skeptical glances, the preposterous questions and the gloating laughter."

"They are the fools. They have no idea of the value of your invention."

"Stop it, Bertha, my darling, I have failed. That's the truth of the matter, and I have to face up to it. I have been building a castle in Spain, chasing a chimera."

He said nothing for a little and then continued in a whisper, "Bertha, please swear as God is your witness that you won't talk to me about the carriage ever again."

His head was still on Bertha's bosom. They fell back into silence, and she felt his body start to tremble. Her Karl was weeping. She thought her heart would break, and she held him firmly. They stayed like that, clinging to each other, until she heard his breathing become regular, and she could tell that he had fallen asleep. Gently, she placed his head back on the pillow.

She stayed sitting up in bed, wide-awake and musing away in the darkness. By the time the first glimmer of light came through the open window, she had made up her mind. She tiptoed to the wardrobe and took some clothes out in the dark, went downstairs and got dressed in the sitting room. She then woke up her two sons, Richard and Eugen, who were fourteen and fifteen years old, respectively. She asked them to get washed and dressed as quickly as they could. When they asked her where they were going, she thundered back, "I'll tell you later."

She carefully opened the front door to avoid its squeaking and then stopped as if she had just remembered something. Leaving the children standing there, she went to the kitchen and on a large piece of paper in large letters she wrote, "Karl. Don't worry about us. We've gone to visit my mother. Back tomorrow."

She pinned the note where he would see it when he woke up. Then she went out and locked the front door. Holding her children by the hand, she walked them to the workshop, where the three of them pushed the carriage onto the street. Then she helped them in, sitting between them on the seat. She grabbed the leather drive belt with both hands and jerked it as hard as she could. At that moment, the motor growled and gave off a puff of smoke, and the carriage lurched forward.

2

The morning call to prayer sounded, and Ruqayya opened her eyes and whispered the profession of faith. Then she slid out of bed and shut the bedroom door quietly behind her in order not to wake up her husband, Abd el-Aziz Gaafar. She went to the bathroom and lit the boiler, then walked to the kitchen. She prepared a tray with breakfast for the guests and made sandwiches for the children to take to school. By the time she went back to the bathroom, the water was hot, so she laid out her clothes for the day and took her morning shower as she had done every morning since getting married.

At that time, she was living in Upper Egypt with her mother-in-law (may God have mercy on her soul), who used to observe whether she took a shower in order to know if she had had sex with Abd el-Aziz the night before. From then on, a morning shower was Ruqayya's way of covering up her private life. Over time she just got used to starting her day with the feeling of being refreshed. After showering, she would carefully dry herself and put on a clean, ironed galabiyya, go upstairs carrying the breakfast tray covered with a napkin and put it down outside the guest room on the roof, which was reserved for relatives who had come to Cairo from Upper Egypt for one reason or another—for medical treatment, to get some official papers or on business.

The guest room was spacious and had a sink, a toilet and a separate staircase. Abd el-Aziz's house was always open to relatives, and he considered putting them up just as much his duty as he did taking care of his own children. Ruqayya would then set about waking up the children. Mahmud, the difficult one, would always require a few attempts because he would just go back to sleep each time. She was patient with him, forgiving whatever mischief he'd get up to. Some months after his birth, she had noticed that he was a bit sluggish and had taken him to a renowned doctor in Aswan who told her that the boy would have developmental problems. Thus it was no surprise that Mahmud kept having to repeat a year at school. At the age of seventeen, he was big and bulky, since he spent all his free time and energy lifting weights.

After her first attempt to wake Mahmud, Ruqayya would go and wake his older brothers, Said and Kamel. Kamel was stick thin, and the moment he felt her touch on his head, he would open his eyes, sit up and kiss her hand. Then he would wake up his brother Said. Ruqayya liked to leave Saleha until last, to let her have a little more sleep. After the children washed and dressed, they would sit around the table. Ruqayya always tried to make them a delicious breakfast: eggs, cheese, fava beans and fresh bread with tea and milk. Then she would sit cross-legged on the sofa with her left hand holding the string of ninety-nine prayer beads as her children lined up and bowed to her one after another. She would place her hands on their heads and utter a Quranic verse over them to keep them safe.

She would not let them leave the house together for fear of the evil eye. People might look at them and say, "There go the Gaafar children," and some disaster or illness might strike them. She insisted that they leave the house one by one, none setting out until the one before had reached the end of the street. Said would always wriggle out of taking his sister, Saleha, to school, whereas Kamel willingly walked with her to the Suniyya school and then took a bus to the university.

Mahmud was always the last to leave. His mother would make him swear by the holy Quran that he would really go to school and not go off to play football in the street or to the cinema. He never argued with his mother. All her children had inherited the light-brown Gaafar skin tones except Mahmud. He was coal black, like a Sudanese. At school when students teased him for being a dullard and for the color of his skin, he would fight back and beat them up. On those occasions, he hardly knew his own strength. The previous year he had been in two fights, splitting the brow of the first boy and breaking the arm of the second. This led to the headmaster's warning Mahmud's father that the next fight would mean expulsion. That was a day from hell. Abd el-Aziz gave Mahmud a good beating, shouting at him, "It's not enough for you to be too stupid to get anywhere at school, but you have to go around strutting like some tough. I swear by God Almighty that if you touch another student I'll come to school myself and show all your friends how I beat you."

She never forgave her husband for doing that. Poor Mahmud. He was simpleminded and needed to be handled gently. Every morning, before he left the house, she would kiss him, say a few providential words of prayer over him and give him the same advice, "If someone upsets you, don't start a fight! Just walk away from him and say the *fatiha* in your head."

Mahmud would agree and embrace her. Feeling the power of his muscles, she could not help but be a little proud. After her children had left, she had time to herself until nine o'clock, when she had to wake up Abd el-Aziz. During her free time, she would prepare herself a cup of mint tea and sit by the window. She would listen to the cries of the hawkers and the sounds of the cars in the street below, as well as the voices of the children and office workers. But on this particular morning, she was exhausted. She had not slept well the night before. She sat staring out the window without seeing anything. She did not even notice the taste of the tea. She realized that in two weeks' time she would have lived in Cairo for five years. Good Lord, how quickly it had passed. The day she left Daraw for Cairo had been a great event. People said that, apart from the time that the great nationalist leader Sa'ad Zaghloul famously made a visit to Upper Egypt, the train station at Daraw had never been so crowded as on the day she and her four children left for Cairo. On that day the people come to bid them farewell clustered both inside and outside the station, at the entrance, in the station hall and on the platform. All the important families of Daraw had members to bid her farewell: the Mahjubs, the Abd el-Maquds, the Oways and Shayba families, even the Balams in spite of the tense relations with the Gaafar family due to an ongoing dispute over some date palms to the east of the town—their sense of duty had overcome past bitterness, and they sent ten men with their wives and children to take part in the farewell formalities. They were all fond of her. Her husband and first cousin was Abd el-Aziz Gaafar, one of the foremost residents of Daraw. He had inherited property and money from his father and was renowned for his decency and respectability, always doing his utmost to help out his relatives, neighbors, in fact anyone from the town. Alas, his debts had started piling up, and he had to sell off his land bit by bit. Now, over forty years old and almost penniless, he had to move to Cairo in search of whatever work he could find. There was great sympathy from the people of Daraw, since whenever they had needed money, Abd el-Aziz had given them loans from the goodness of his heart, as well as helping them in other ways. They all felt partially responsible for his bankruptcy. Ruqayya saw expressions of deep sympathy and love on the faces of those who had come to see them off. To them, she was the very model of an authentic Upper Egyptian woman, sticking by her husband come what may, supporting him with the same determination in good times and bad.

All those feelings were present on the day of their departure, like a large cloud casting its shadow on the scene. Ruqayya got out of the carriage with a big beautiful smile on her face, a smile of fortitude and complete acceptance of her fate and what more might come. The younger children, Saleha and Mahmud, were clutching the hem of her black outer coat, and the two older boys, Said and Kamel, walked along behind her. Each of them was carrying a suitcase and a basket on his head. The largest suitcase was being carried by her brother Bashir on his shoulders. The people thronged toward her, surrounding her, and she started greeting them and thanking them one by one. She shook the men's hands and embraced and kissed the women. Some of the women were crying, while others gave Mahmud and Saleha honey and sesame sweets. Mahmud ate them up straightaway, but Saleha, more clever and with better manners, waited until her mother gestured her permission. Then she took out one of the sweets and said in a clear voice, "Thank you, uncle!"

Ruqayya was making slow progress. The moment she finished shaking one hand, more hands appeared. Then they started addressing her in the traditional manner, as the mother of her eldest son, "We hope all goes well, Umm Said!"

"Have a good trip and come back safe and sound, in sha Allah!"

"Give our regards to Abd el-Aziz!"

It took Ruqayya ages to reach the platform, where the train was already waiting. She made her way with her children trailing behind her and her brother scurrying along with the suitcase on his shoulder. She pulled herself together amid the well-wishers and caught sight of some women from the Balam family. She made her way toward them and embraced them warmly, and still holding the hand of the clan leader Abd el-Al's wife, she said loudly so all could hear, "Thank you so much for coming. It means so much to me."

Abd el-Al's wife was so overcome by Ruqayya's kind words that she embraced her again, looked her in the face, and with her voice full of feeling, she said, "God knows how much I love you, Ruqayya."

"And I love you too."

"You Gaafars are the cream of our town."

"No, you Balams are the ones who have done the most for us all. It was Satan, may God curse him, who came between us. May God guide us all. Kith and kin may have squabbled with each other, but blood is thicker than water.

"May God preserve and look after you, Ruqayya."

At that moment, Bashir came over to his sister, Ruqayya, and whispered something in her ear. She nodded and carried on talking to Abd el-Al Balam's wife. It would not have been right for her to bring the conversation to an abrupt end. She knew that her every gesture with Abd el-Al al-Balam might be misinterpreted and could reignite the family feud again.

She carried on talking to the woman for a few minutes more and then moved off to greet some other people. This time, however, Bashir, almost hauled her by her galabiyya toward the train whose angry whistle and thick smoke augured its imminent departure. The onlookers all started shouting, and Ruqayya grabbed Saleha and Mahmud, and with Said and Kamel and Bashir following behind, she started running as fast as she could.

Ruqayya sipped her tea and a smile appeared on her face as she remembered how, due to the throngs of well-wishers, she missed the train that day. Whenever she recalled that to her neighbor Aisha, she would laugh heartily, joking about the stupidity of the Upper

Egyptians. Bashir had to reserve new tickets for them on the next day's train and then had to go around to all the houses in Daraw asking them not to come to the station again. All complied except for Abd el-Barr, son of her cousin Oways, who insisted on coming to see them off again. When her brother tried to dissuade him, he flushed with anger and said, "Just as she is your sister, Ruqayya is my cousin. I swear to God that even if she were to miss the train a hundred times, I would go to the station to see her off."

Abd el-Barr indeed went to the station again, and Ruqayya was grateful to him for that. They had grown up together, and there had even been talk of marriage, but fate is fickle, and she knew that his insistence on seeing her off was not entirely innocent. Abd el-Barr might still have been in love with her after all this time, but she did not even dare to think about that out of respect for her husband, Abd el-Aziz, who meant everything to her. After twenty-five years of marriage, she could still recall her wedding as if it had happened the day before. That night there had been a huge feast, and celebratory gunshots had reverberated all over Daraw. The feasting went on for a whole week, and people commented enviously that the camel carrying her to her husband's house was groaning from the weight of all the gold that her bridegroom had given her. It was a sight to remember. In Daraw she had a large house with a spacious sitting room, a garden with date palms, servants, jewelry, horses, camels, cattle and poultry, and, most important, a wonderful husband. He never behaved badly toward her or beat her. He never put her down, and she knew that he would never cheat on her. When at first she could not get pregnant, his mother (may God have mercy on her and forgive her) started urging him to take a second wife. She would say to him, within Ruqayya's earshot, "You're a man. You have to produce a son. Take another wife alongside Ruqayya. It is what God commands."

Any other man would just have taken another wife. Had he done so, no one would have blamed him. He refused, however, and announced that he would have only Ruqayya, even if she could never have children. How could she forget such magnanimity? When his mother asked Shaykh Mash'al to make an amulet to help her get pregnant, Abd el-Aziz received him coolly and said, "You can keep your amulet. I will not do anything the Prophet forbids. Whether we have children, live or die, or manage to support ourselves—they are all matters over which we can never argue with God."

He fell silent for a short while and then added sarcastically, "If you are such a good friend of the genies, Shaykh Mash'al, why don't you ask them to cure the rheumatism eating away at your bones?"

After two years of trying, they were blessed by God with six children, of whom two died, leaving them with four. Then came the great ordeal of her husband's bankruptcy. Praise be to God. The Lord chooses some men to receive his bounty and exposes others to catastrophes. Who ever thought that she would end up starting a new life in Cairo? Abd el-Aziz worked his fingers to the bone to provide them with a decent living: he rented a spacious flat in al-Sadd al-Gawany Street in the Sayyida Zeinab district. It had four rooms and a sitting room, plus a room on the roof with a separate entrance and staircase. The rent was high, and the needs of their children cost a fortune, not to mention the cost of looking after the ever-present guests, as well as the expenses of food, tobacco and clothing from time to time. God gave him strength, and somehow he managed to find enough money and to cope with his menial job—even though his whole life long he had been a property owner in Daraw. When he handed over to Ruqayya his first set of work clothes, a yellow uniform with brass buttons, to be ironed, he just said, "I work as a storeroom assistant, and this is my uniform."

At that time she made a huge effort to hide her feelings. She prattled on about inconsequential matters and laughed as she carefully ironed his uniform. She folded it into a small case, said good-bye as he went out the front door and then burst into tears. Would Abd el-Aziz Gaafar, a man from a decent family, have to do a menial job for all eternity?

God be praised for everything. She stopped daydreaming, glanced at the clock in the sitting room and noticed that it was after nine. She rushed into the bedroom, opening the door quietly, and looked at Abd el-Aziz's face as he slept. How she loved this man. She loved him for his strength, his determination and his pride. How could he cope with all these ordeals? Many other men would have given up the ghost, but Abd el-Aziz was a believer and accepted whatever God dealt out to him. She shook him gently to waken him, and he got out of bed. He took a shower and made his ablutions before saying his morning prayers and getting dressed. As he was sitting down to his breakfast, she set her plan into motion. She sighed and said, "May God give you the strength to support us all, dear Abd el-Aziz. May he grant you sustenance so you can sustain us."

There was silence. Abd el-Aziz carried on carefully cracking his boiled egg, and as he laid the pieces of shell on his plate, he asked her calmly, "Is there something you want?"

Ruqayya sighed and whispered slightly apologetically, "The ration book for the cooperative shop . . ."

"At the end of the week, God willing. Anything else?"

"By God, I'm a little ashamed to mention it. You know how troublesome Said can be, but he has set his heart on buying a new shirt."

"Whatever."

He finished eating, lit a cigarette and sipped his coffee. Ruqayya seized the opportunity and moved the subject on a little. She smiled and said, "I have a request, my darling Abd el-Aziz, and please, I beg you by the Prophet, don't embarrass me for asking you."

"Well?"

"I want to sell two of my bracelets and buy a Singer sewing machine. You know I have always loved making clothes. I could buy a sewing machine and do some piecework. Even if I don't earn a fortune, at least I will be sitting respectably in my own home, and every extra piastre will help us."

Abd el-Aziz looked at her. He gave her that familiar look of someone who does not like what he has heard. He responded in a tone of sour derision, "You want me to come home from work and find you busy with customers?"

"A bit of work never hurt anyone."

"So the Gaafar house will become a seamstress's workshop for all eternity?"

She knew he would never agree, but she did not lose hope.

"All right. Let's forget the sewing machine. Now, Saleha . . ."

"What's the matter with Saleha?"

"If she were to leave school and stay at home, we'd save the school fees."

"Shame on you, woman. So I should work my fingers to the bone to pay the school fees for Mahmud, who is stupid and keeps failing, and we should keep our brilliant and clever Saleha at home and throw away her future?"

"Her future is to get married and have children."

"As long as she wants to keep studying, that's what she must do."

"I've got another thought."

"You've been doing a lot of thinking lately, Umm Said!"

He spoke the latter words as he stood up and unhooked his tarboosh from the peg, and as he was straightening it on his head, he said, "Don't worry, Ruqayya. We'll see, by the grace of God. I'm certain."

3

It was sheer madness.

From where Bertha Benz lived in Mannheim, it was more than a hundred kilometers to the town of Pforzheim, where her mother lived. How could she ever have imagined that she could cover this distance in the carriage? After all, what did she know about this machine she was driving? Just a smattering of information she had gleaned from Karl. She had only seen him drive it once—when it had moved forward some small distance and overturned with him in it—and now she was planning to cover a hundred kilometers nonstop. There was no thinking it over. She had been so moved by her husband's despair that she was now rushing headlong into an act of folly. She was as sure to fail as the day is long. She was on her own now. She tried to control the accursed carriage, with her sons on either side fighting off sleep, perplexed at what their mother was doing. As she drove, Bertha discovered that the steering lever was not finely tuned, so there was a delayed reaction whenever she tried to move it left or right. She also noticed that the carriage was quite light in weight and bobbed up and down like a boat on ocean waves. Quite a few times, it shuddered and almost toppled over. Each time, she shouted at the boys to keep tight hold of the front rail. Then she discovered that the carriage ground to halt at the merest hint of a gradient. At every hill, she and the children had to get out and push. Then the fuel ran out.

She left the boys in the carriage and rushed off to the nearest pharmacist's shop, where she asked for ten bottles of gasoline, which at that time was only used for domestic cleaning. The old pharmacist's curiosity was aroused, and as he was packing the bottles into a bag, he asked, "I feel certain that madam must live in a very large house to need all this cleaning liquid."

Bertha smiled shyly and answered, "Please come with me for a moment."

The pharmacist hesitantly came from behind the counter, smiling with astonishment, and followed her into the street.

"I'm using the gasoline as fuel for this."

He had heard about the invention and showed great curiosity and enthusiasm, inspecting the carriage as if it were a recently landed creature from outer space. He insisted on helping her. She opened the fuel cap, and he slowly poured the gasoline into the tank until it was completely full. Bertha climbed back up onto the seat and tugged on the drive belt. The carriage gave off a screech and the usual puff of smoke. The pharmacist clapped his hands in delight, and Bertha called down to him in gratitude before the carriage lurched off.

Then it was the turn of the cooling system to break down: the water ran out, and the engine became red hot. Bertha turned it off and, leaving the boys behind in the carriage again, set off on foot with Karl's special rubber can to find a public tap in the park. She hoped that would be the last disaster, but it was far from it. The car soon shuddered to a halt again. Bertha got out and discovered that the carburetor was blocked. After a few moments' thought, she took out one of her hairpins and, with the tenacity of an ant, used it to give the carburetor mesh a good poking. But this time when she tugged on the drive belt again, the motor did not respond. She pulled it again and again before it finally started turning, and the carriage set off. Ten full hours later, during which all sorts of problems and delays had occurred and after bouts of hopelessness, frustration and despair, Bertha drove the Benz carriage into the town of Pforzheim. Before going to her mother's house, she stopped at the telegraph office. In her haste, she left the engine running and ran in to send the following telegram to her husband, "Today, the Benz carriage has traveled over a hundred kilometers from Mannheim to Pforzheim. Karl, we have done it. We are proud of you."

The following day, Bertha drove the carriage back to Mannheim. Profiting from the previous day's mistakes, this time she brought a large pitcher of water and a number of bottles of gasoline. She borrowed needles from her mother for unclogging the carburetor. All these preparations cut two whole hours from the journey. Words cannot describe the state Karl was in when Bertha and the children got home. He was standing in front of the house, and as soon as the carriage appeared in the distance, he started calling out and clapping. When Bertha proudly stepped down from the carriage, he rushed over to hug her and shower her with kisses. Karl would write in his diary, "At some point I was so alienated from everyone that I started to doubt the value of what I was doing. But one person's faith in me never wavered. One person who deserves the credit for everything I achieved. My wife, Bertha."

The news from Mannheim and Pforzheim spread all over Germany and then to Europe and the world beyond. Karl Benz was soon flooded with offers, and he started manufacturing automobiles, slowly and cautiously at first, but then he began churning them out. A large part of public opinion was still fundamentally opposed to his invention, whether out of religious scruples or ignorance or because of the noise and smoke that the vehicles produced. Some, especially in the countryside, would run along behind the automobile, swearing at the driver, throwing rocks or hurling enormous tree stumps in its way. Those were the last desperate efforts in a battle whose outcome had already been decided.

Automobiles started to spread at an astonishing rate. On September 13, 1899, the first automobile fatality occurred. An American man named Henry Bliss was crossing the street in New York City when an automobile ran him over, crushing his skull. His death engendered real fears and a far-reaching controversy about the dangers posed by the new invention, but popular enthusiasm for it did not die down.

A great leap forward was made by the American Henry Ford, who started mass-producing cars. His strategy was to reduce the profit margin but increase the volume of production and sales. This was based on a simple conviction—that the employees of his own factory should be able to afford an automobile. And so the automobile went from being a toy for the rich to an accessible means of transport that changed people's lives and way of thinking completely. Great distances were no longer daunting. An automobile owner could work far away from home; he could take his family to the beach and have them home in the same day. The automobile established man's sense of independence and individuality and confirmed him as master of his own destiny.

Egypt, at that time under British occupation, was no different. In 1890 Egyptians saw their first automobile. It was a French De Dion-Bouton, imported by Prince Hassan, a grandson of Khedive Ismail, who loved adventure and innovation. He exposed himself to great danger when he drove his automobile, with two friends in it, from Cairo to Alexandria along an unpaved agricultural road. The trip took ten whole hours and cost a fortune, as the vehicle damaged many fields of crops and hit quite a few cows and donkeys. The prince handed out cash to the peasants on the spot. Egyptians fell in love with the automobile. In 1905 there were 110 in Cairo and 56 in Alexandria. By 1914 Egypt had imported 218 automobiles. The ever-increasing numbers proved the need for an automobile club to deal with all related necessities, such as issuing licenses, surfacing roads, setting speed limits and creating driving instruction and vehicle maintenance manuals. After repeated efforts over the course of twenty years, the Royal Automobile Club officially opened in 1924.

The Club's founders were all foreigners or members of the local Turkish aristocracy. The first chairman was Prince Omar Toussoun, and King Fuad consented to be the patron. Elections were held for the administrative committee, and an Englishman, James Wright, was appointed managing director. Everything was done to make it a carbon copy of the famous Carlton Club in London. The building itself was an architectural jewel of traditional elegance.

When the administrative committee sat down to draw up the Club's rules and bylaws, two problems arose. First: Should the Club allow Egyptians to become members? This idea was rejected by a majority, led by the Englishman Mr. Wright, who declared, as he lit his pipe, "I should like to make clear that our job in this Club is to ascertain a policy for automobiles in Egypt. Egyptians in general, even if they are wealthy and educated, are not qualified to make such

decisions. The automobile is a Western invention, and it is Westerners alone who should decide policy. I don't expect Egyptians to do
more than buy them and ride in them."

After many frank expressions of opinion, an Italian member who
spoke Arabic warned them that they were in danger of raising a stink
in the Egyptian press, which in turn would affect automobile sales in
Egypt. He said, "National sentiment in Egypt is inflamed against the
British occupation. At any moment this sentiment could change into
xenophobia and the declaration of a commercial boycott. We don't
want that. I think we all want to see Egyptians buying more and more
automobiles." The words reverberated in the boardroom, and other
members took heed.

After a long discussion, the committee members agreed to accept
Egyptians provided that they could furnish letters from two members of the administrative committee to second their applications for
membership. Foreigners who provided proof of automobile owner-
ship would receive membership automatically. Thus the committee
could prevent Egyptians from becoming members, inasmuch as was
possible, in a manner that would not provoke public resentment.

The other issue was that of the staff. The committee members
naturally hoped to employ Europeans. When they studied the matter, however, it became clear that the cost of employing foreign staff
would be astronomical. Facing this insurmountable problem, some
committee members suggested staffing the club with Egyptians.

"They're dirty. Stupid. Filthy. Liars and thieves." These words were
spoken by a French committee member, but they expressed the opinion of the majority.

The issue of staff continued to be discussed for weeks without
resolution. At one of the weekly Tuesday meetings, the managing
director, Mr. James Wright, arrived carrying a large manila file.
He stood at the head of the board table and announced formally,
"Gentleman, members of the administrative committee! I have put
together a perfect plan for staffing the Club. I shall present it to you
now and then take note of your reactions."

SALEHA ABD EL-AZIZ GAAFAR

I still have my photographs from when I was a child.
When I look at them now, I find that they reflect an inner peace.
How happy and content I appear. I was blessed with an undeniably
happy childhood, and except for the irritations caused by my brother
Said, I do not remember any childhood traumas. I was the only girl,
and everyone spoiled me. I had no worries or frustrations until we
left Upper Egypt for Cairo, and it seemed like we were going to live in
a better place. Two incidents stand out indelibly as important mark-
ers in my life. I was taking a shower when a trickle of blood started
flowing down the lower part of my body. I screamed and ran to my
mother for help, but to my astonishment, she did not seem particularly bothered and just proceeded to show me how to deal with the
bleeding. When I finished my shower, she embraced me and told me
that this would happen every month, and it meant that God had now
made me into a woman capable of having children.

The second incident happened when I was a student in the second year at the Sunniya high school. During the last lesson, as Mr.
Ma'mun, our Arabic teacher, was busy explaining how to use the
adverbs of time and place, the classroom door suddenly opened,
and Miss Sawsan, the deputy headmistress, came in. We stood up for
her, and she smiled, greeted us and gestured to us to sit down. She
whispered a few words to Mr. Ma'mun and then walked to the center
of the classroom and announced, "Those girls who hear their name
called out are to come with me . . ."

She read out three names from a piece of paper: mine and those
of Khadiga Abd el-Sattar and Awatef Kamel.

We had no idea why we had been singled out, but we all felt quite jolly when we left the classroom for the cool air outside. We walked along behind Miss Sawsan, who, as usual, was marching along in an almost military way, with ne'er a look behind her. Soon, we started skipping, and Khadiga was imitating her walk. I exchanged glances with Awatef, and we could hardly contain our laughter. It was rather strange that I got on so well with Awatef, since I usually did not like her. She was pretty but unbearably arrogant. Our classmates used to make comparisons between us—which of us was prettier? I hated those discussions, even though I was sure that I was prettier. I used to list to myself the features of my body that I was proud of: my ink-black hair, the greenish eyes I inherited from my grandmother, the prominent line of my upper chest and my slim thighs. I even loved my small feet!

We followed Miss Sawsan to the office of the headmistress. It was gloomy in there except for a patch of light from a reading lamp by which she was reading over some papers. I detected the smell of old wood and another pleasant odor, though I could not tell where it was coming from.

Just standing there in front of her was enough to fill us with dread. We were silent until she raised her head, looked at us with a smile and then, as if she had practiced them, quickly uttered the following sentences, "You are the only girls in the second year who have not yet paid the second installment of your school fees and this was due two months ago. According to school regulations, we cannot allow you to sit the final examinations until the fees have been paid. I am sorry, girls, but the regulations from the Ministry of Information have to be followed."

She handed us unsealed envelopes containing letters addressed to our parents. Then, in a firm tone but not one without a hint of compassion, she said, "Off you go now. Good-bye. You are not to attend school until you bring your parents and the fees."

The bell rang for the end of the school day. We had to go back to the classroom to pick up our bags before going home. I started to feel a bit odd. It felt like my body was walking along on its own, uncontrolled by my mind, as if some external power was driving me along. Some of the girls stopped us to ask why we had been called to see the headmistress. Awatef said there had been some sort of problem with our names that needed to be corrected before they could fill out the forms for the end-of-year exams. At that moment we felt a sort of solidarity, a silent collusion. We had a secret that united us. Strangely, we did not talk about what had happened. We just chitchatted about other things.

Suddenly, with no one else near, Awatef said angrily, "The school has no right to stop us taking the exam just because we haven't paid the fees. I'm not speaking about myself. My family is quite well off, thank God. We don't have a problem with the fees. I'll pay the amount due tomorrow, but what if one of us was really poor or her family was having a hard time. Would she lose her whole future just over a few Egyptian pounds?"

I knew that she was lying, but I made no comment. I was still trying to take in what had happened, and what the headmistress had said kept echoing in my ears: "We cannot allow you to sit the final examinations until the fees have been paid." I went through the motions of giving Khadiga and Awatef a hug and a kiss, picked up my bag and went out of the school gate, where I found my brother Kamel waiting to walk me home as usual. He smiled, hugged me and then put his hand on my shoulder and asked me, "How was your day?"

I did not reply, having a hard time controlling my emotions.

Kamel, now a little worried, said, "What's the matter, Saleha? Did something happen at school?"

Because of his gentleness, my tears welled up, and I could taste their saltiness. I handed him the letter. He read it quickly, then folded it again and put it in his pocket.

"Don't worry about it."

On the way home, Kamel stopped at the juice seller on the square and bought me a big glass of the guava juice I loved. He patted me on the shoulder, smiled and said, "You are too sensitive. It's a very simple matter. Our father has been busy with his work and forgotten to send the school fees. Tomorrow morning, please God, I'll go to school with you and give them the fees."

I nodded and tried to smile. I wanted to make him happy. I was certain that he was lying, but I pretended to believe him.

We went home, and I took off my school clothes, had a shower and put on my housedress. Kamel took my mother into the kitchen, and when she came back, I noticed that she looked dejected and was avoiding my gaze. After lunch I told her that I had a lot of homework, and she said I did not have to help her with the washing up. I went to my room and shut the door. I lay on the bed, just wanting to be left alone. For the first time, I felt I did not know what was happening: If my father was really so busy, why hadn't he sent the school fees along with Kamel? Couldn't he afford it?

As far as I knew, we were not poor. I knew that our father came from a great and wealthy family. I still had wonderful memories of my childhood in Daraw, and of when our father sold his land in Upper Egypt and went to Cairo, he did so to provide us with a better education. That's what my mother said, and with great pride, I used to repeat to my school friends, "My father has a senior position at the Automobile Club, and he meets the king a lot and speaks to him."

How could it be that my father worked with the king but could not afford my school fees? The king must have paid his staff high salaries, so what could have happened? Had there been some incident with my father? Had someone stolen his money or bullied him into handing it over? What would we do in a crisis like that? Thank God I always sailed through school with flying colors and never had to retake any classes like my brothers Said and Mahmud. My marks were good in geography and languages, and I always came top in mathematics. Suddenly, my thoughts turned elsewhere. I started feeling guilty. Perhaps I was the cause of the crisis. How many times had I nagged him to buy me new clothes or take me to the cinema? Had I known he was going through difficult times, I would never have burdened him. All the things I had asked him for now seemed like wasteful trifles.

A little later, when my mother came into my room, she found me covered up in bed. I muttered that I was worn out and feeling ill. She put her hand on my forehead and sounded worried. "We will have to get the doctor to see you."

"No . . . I just need to rest. I won't go to school tomorrow."

She gave me a baffled look. "If that's how you feel."

Thus I pretended to be ill to give my father the chance to raise the school fees. That was the only way to avoid embarrassing him. I did not dare ask him for the money or even discuss the matter directly. I could not bear to see him in a bind even for a moment.

My mother brought me a glass of hot lemon juice and left. After a while, I heard my brother Kamel, who came in and sat next to me. "Hello, Saleha!"

I repeated my symptoms to him, but he can always see right through me. He completely ignored what I was saying and smiled. "Don't worry. Within two or three days at the most, we will have the fees paid."

I was about to try to convince him that I really was ill, but he gave me a little bow, planted a kiss on my forehead and left the room.

4

"Alku." The name itself is a pharyngeal groan sounded through tightly pursed lips. In Nubian it means a leader or important person, but at the Club it took on mythical dimensions. It called to mind some great and legendary winged beast, the subject of fantastic tales passed down over the generations, until one day the monster suddenly takes flesh and casts its toxic shadow over everything. Alku was just such a creation. His full name was Qasem Muhammad Qasem, and he was a Sudanese Nubian in his sixties. When not speaking Nubian, he spoke heavily accented Arabic, mixing up the masculine and feminine suffixes. He could converse fluently in French and Italian but could barely write them. Alku had two jobs: those of servant and master. He'd first been taken on as the king's valet, and as part of his duties as master of the wardrobe, he dressed and undressed the king. Alku was the palace's head chamberlain and the most senior servant, and he enjoyed the confidence of His Majesty.

His relationship with His Majesty greatly overstepped the boundaries of his position. Alku was present at His Majesty's birth, and he held him in his own hands when the king was just a suckling, and observed with sincere joy his first crawl, his first tottering steps and his first words. When His Majesty was a child, Alku accompanied him on hunting and bicycle trips and horseback-riding lessons. He was the only one who knew whether His Majesty was feigning illness in order to skip torturous lessons with his strict teachers. It was Alku who purloined desserts from the palace kitchen and smuggled them into His Majesty's suite when his English governess had imposed a harsh dietary regimen upon the boy to make him lose weight. It was also Alku who, with complete discretion, organized His Majesty's first trysts with beautiful women of the upper class, this to relieve all the adolescent fervor that was affecting his concentration and state of mind. When His Majesty went off to school in England, he insisted upon taking Alku with him, though it was less than two years later that, following his father's sudden death, the king returned to accede to the throne of Egypt. At that point, Alku gained unprecedented and overwhelming influence at the palace. All royal correspondence, however confidential or important, was opened personally by Alku, who would read it aloud to His Majesty every morning as the latter lay naked in his hot bubble bath, with Iliana, the Greek pedicurist, taking care of his feet, shaving him and trimming his mustache and eyebrows. His Majesty would listen and offer a word or two of comment at most. "We agree" or "later" and so forth. Sometimes, if His Majesty was worried or anxious, he would flip over in the bathtub, and his enormous body would create a huge wave, like that of a great fish. Then he would wag his finger and say, "Qasem Alku! You'd better behave yourself!"

During such periods, Alku would answer the urgent correspondence as he saw fit. He would write instructions in French, not without grammatical errors. Alku, thus, was the true gateway to the king and much closer to His Majesty than any other individuals of the court or the palace administration. A story has been passed down that serves as a perfect example. When Dabagh Pasha, the prime minister of Egypt, wanted an audience with His Majesty, Alku asked him about the purpose. The prime minister's face flushed with rage. He found it highly impertinent that he, an Oxford graduate, should have to provide an explanation to a servant. In a delicately sneering patrician tone, he told Alku, "Who has the right to question the prime minister of Egypt when he requests an audience with the king?"

The next day the king summoned the prime minister and deliberately kept him standing. The king gestured toward Alku and said, "I hope that you understand, Pasha, that this man represents Us. Treating him with respect is the equivalent of treating Us with respect."

The prime minister lowered his head deeply and uttered some words of apology. Thus the supreme status of Alku in the palace was confirmed, and ministers and politicians all continued to curry his favor despite deep resentment that they struggled to hide. For them, Alku was no more than a black servant, a simple valet, ignorant, vulgar, riffraff, but they were careful to keep on his good side due to his endless ability both to create mischief and to be useful. Alku, at will, could cause anyone to gain or lose the king's favor. He held the keys to the king's personality and could read his state of mind at any moment. Moreover, Alku had enormous life experience as well as a sharp, instinctive brain that enabled him to see right through people with one glance. One might go so far as to say that his manner of presenting facts and personages to His Majesty should be taught in diplomacy courses. He had only to look at the king to know whether his thinking was going to be clear or muddled, and Alku would appropriately choose to present or withhold matters from him accordingly.

Alku could carry out His Majesty's orders for days without conferring with him, and at other times he knew by experience that he should ask the king for his opinion. In making his report to the king about a particular person, for example, he never spoke in a straightforward manner but discreetly dropped a fact here and there and repeated certain other people's views in such a way that the king always ended up reaching a decision that Alku desired. Alku practiced all these skills with the ease and self-assurance of a talented soccer player kicking the ball at the goal from an angle he had practiced a thousand times—and scoring. His role overseeing the king was one side of Alku's duties, and he had another no less important job: he also oversaw all the servants in all the royal palaces. Second only to God Almighty, he was the sole controller of their lives, their earnings and their fates.

If the palace needed more servants, Alku would send men dressed in the local galabiyya to Aswan and Nubia in the south of Egypt to scour the area for men who fit the bill: intelligent, in good health, fit and of good name. The promising candidates would then be shipped off to Abdin Palace in Cairo, where Alku would look them over and either take them on or order them to be sent back. Just from looking them up and down and having a few short words with them, Alku could spot an impertinent or angry type, a nervy, obstinate reprobate or one addicted to alcohol or hashish, each of which were enough to rule a man right out. The surviving candidates would spend a few months in the two-story school building in the garden of Abdin Palace, learning how to serve in the palace—"l'art du service," as Alku used to call it in his supercilious French accent. Their training consisted of four rules:

First: Personal hygiene

A shower must be taken daily both in summer and in winter, the body scrubbed with particular attention to the neck, the nape and the armpits. Deodorant must be used. Everyone must be clean shaven. Teeth must be brushed with toothpaste morning and night. Hair must be washed and worn with a part. Careful attention must be given to the heels, and nails, both finger and toe, must be kept trimmed.

Alku imposed the hygiene regulations with such severity that they gradually became second nature to the servants. At any moment he might carry out an inspection, ordering a servant to open his mouth or to show him his neck or fingernails. He would often tell a servant to remove his shoes and socks to check his feet. And woe betide him if Alku thought his toenails too long or if his feet were dirty. He would order that man beaten immediately but not before roaring at him, "How can you serve the king with filthy feet, you animal!"

Second: Attire

All work clothes, whatever their type or color, must be clean and well ironed. A chipped button, a wrinkled collar or a spot would result in punishment. Socks must be clean and new and worn uncrumpled. Shoes must be cleaned and polished to perfection. Daily.

Third: Service etiquette

Possibly the most important lesson: service requires a capacity for subservience in the face of opulence, an ability to accept that you matter not a whit, to allow yourself to be ground into dust. For a true servant, such is a matter of pride, his essence summed up in the words, "Yes sir," as any further discourse with his master is impertinent. There is no such thing as an exchange of opinions between a servant and his master; there is no right or wrong but only what the master wants, what he orders or even what he is hoping or thinking about. That is how things are, without exception. In the palaces, ladies putting on low-cut nightgowns should not hesitate at all to summon a male servant to their rooms.

As far as ladies are concerned, a servant is not a man. He is a servant, much too lowly to become excited or tempted. The true servant is like a silent letter. It is present in the word but has no value. A servant must not draw attention to himself. He may not, for example, wear a fine watch or a gold chain. He may wear nothing that singles him out. His master must never be aware of him unless he needs him. The enormous distance between the master and his servant reflects a universal truth as undeniable as the sunrise or the orbit of the moon. It will never change. Very occasionally, the master, when in a good mood, cheered by some news or after a glass too many, might partake in some chitchat with a servant. At that moment, the servant must do no more than concur with his opinions, extricating himself from any further intimacy. He should bow, light his master's cigar, change the ashtray, clear the table. That is, he must carry out some act that signals his awareness that each condescension from his lord is a fleeting act of grace.

Alku taught the servants when to say "Your Excellency" or "Your Honor" and the difference between a prince and a royal relative or a pasha and a bey. He taught them to speak to their master with a low and submissive voice and a small ingratiating smile, to bow and to avoid the unthinkable gaffe of walking alongside his master. He should walk two or three steps behind, never more or less. except in one particular circumstance—when the master asks the servant to direct him somewhere. Then, a servant may take a step forward to advise, but as soon as the master grasps the directions, the servant must step back again, keeping his usual distance.

Members of the Automobile Club could always request a servant who was guilty of some wrongdoing to be punished in the manner brought over from European clubs. The member was entitled at any moment to request the complaint book to register a servant grievance. These complaints were brought immediately to Alku, who would unleash a torrent of anger against the guilty servant. Ordinar-

ily, it was enough for a club member, unhappy with a servant, simply
to ask him to bring the complaint book, at which the servant would
make a profuse apology begging the member to withdraw his complaint. Most members would show mercy, but there were some who
were unforgiving and would insist that the servant be punished.

Fourth: Royal protocol

Dealing with royalty was also part of the servants' syllabus, and only
when a servant showed proficiency in it could he graduate and be
given work. This particular mode of behavior was Turkish in character and carried out only in the presence of a member of the royal
family. A servant must leave the royal presence bowing continuously
as he backs out of the room, the crucial point being that he never
turn his back on a royal highness. This piece of etiquette required
alertness and concentration and could only be attempted after much
practice, as the servant might have to walk backward at any moment
and without care might trip on something, bump into someone
standing behind him or knock something over. What an unseemly
sight that would be!

Alku told his students time and again that proficiency in leaving
the royal presence demanded the eye of a hawk, the gait of a gazelle
and the cunning of a fox. Anyone undertaking it must have the details
of the room engraved in his mind, so he might picture the exact path
backward to avoid this chair and walk around that table, steering a
path through the empty spaces, away from clusters of guests, until he
safely reached the door. Properly performed, this particular act was
considered one of Alku's crowning glories. From his youth, he had
been able to navigate the largest and most crowded salons backward
in a most brilliant and unrivaled manner, as skillfully as if he had eyes
in the back of his head.

When Alku was satisfied that a servant had perfected the royal
protocol, he would assign him places of work. The rules stipulated
that those with dark complexions would work in close proximity to
their masters in jobs such as waiters and valets. Those with light-
brown skin would be sent off to work in the kitchens or as guards or
gardeners. It was considered that a servant with a coal-black com-

plexion showed off the true gentility of his master. This might have been a notion inherited from the days of slavery, or maybe it was that a light complexion was too similar to that of the master and thus ran the risk of their appearing indistinguishable at a distance. After a servant had been allotted work, Alku continued to rule over everything he did. A servant was not allowed to keep tips. He had to hand the cash over immediately to his superior, who, at the end of the day, would put it in the tips box. A servant was not allowed to carry any money in his robe, the smallest coin in his pocket subjecting him to harsh punishment. Alku took half of the tips for himself and split the rest among the servants according to seniority. This system was called the "trunk" and was written in stone. Woe betide anyone who infringed it.

The trunk did not include the head servants. Rikabi the chef, Maître Shakir, Bahr the barman and Yusuf Tarboosh the casino manager all earned large amounts directly through their positions. From their extra earnings, they handed Alku a portion, which was called the "bonus."

In exchange, Alku also provided them staff flats in the Abdin district. Bachelors lived three or four to a flat, and separate flats were provided for married servants with families. Alku oversaw all the minutiae of their lives. He knew everything about them, including the names of their children. Alku never overlooked a detail. He saw to their needs, married them off and often even involved himself in settling their marital disputes. If a wife was being mistreated by her husband, Alku would listen to both parties, pass fair judgment and see that it was carried out. He might then pay them a surprise visit to check on how they were generally getting on with each other. Alku's word was absolute law, his decision final, brooking no exception or appeal. From time to time, the servants would grumble to one another about Alku's severity, although the plaintive, emotional and miserable tone of their whispers spoke of pain tinged with pleasure, in the manner of a wife satisfied in the most wonderful way sexually who complains about her husband's brusqueness, never letting on that she rather enjoys his rough ways.

The supreme authority that Alku wielded over the servants would suddenly invert itself in the presence of foreigners. He could be standing like a crowned king among the servants, but the moment he saw a foreigner, he would rush over and bow, opening the door of the salon or lift with his own hands. He would show complete deference, even veneration, to any foreigner, which was most sincere, as he believed firmly in the superiority of the white race. He would always tell people, "The foreigner is always better and cleverer than we are, and whether you are Arab or Nubian, you must treat him with more respect." His submissiveness to foreigners actually served to augment his prestige, as if he were declaring to the servants, "I am the servant of His Majesty the king and of foreigners, but to you I am lord and master."

It was almost five o'clock in the afternoon when a black Cadillac cruised down Qasr al-Nil Street and stopped in front of the Automobile Club. The driver jumped out, bowed, and opened the door and Alku stepped out regally. He was dressed in his valet's suit of green broadcloth, a zouave-style waistcoat with bullion embroidery, gold epaulets, and across his whole chest were gold aiguillettes, which swung gently whenever he moved his arms. He was wearing an elegant tarboosh and holding a cigar from which he took a puff from time to time, exhaling thick smoke, which obscured his face, the aroma mingling with his French eau de cologne.

Behind Alku scurried Hameed, his right-hand man, who carried out the punishments he decreed for the servants, which ranged from slaps on the feet to the lash in the case of major infringements. Hameed was a chubby black man in his twenties whose every movement made his corpulent frame shudder like a soft, blubbery mass unrestrained by bone or sinew. He had a fixed expression of sullenness and exuded a generally sour aura. His supercilious, repugnant gaze was ever watching for the slightest blunder. There were dark rumors. People said that Hameed was Alku's illegitimate son by a belly dancer Alku had fallen in love with and that although Alku refused to acknowledge his paternity, he had secretly looked after him and paid for his upbringing, before finally taking him on as his closest associate at work. It was also said that one of the servants had abused Hameed as a child and that he had grown up to be a homosexual. For according to the Upper Egyptian folklore so ardently believed by the servants, a tapeworm had come to live in his dark, dank sphincter, feeding exclusively on the semen of the men who screwed Hameed, and that whenever the worm was hungry, it would gnaw so ferociously at him that he had to rush around looking for someone to sodomize him just to soothe the pain. This was how Hameed came to be a queer who craved hairy chests and strong thighs and who quivered like a woman at the sight of an erect penis. It was this lustful inclination that, in the opinion of the servants, explained his delight at humiliating men and the glee with which he administered a beating. Some of the servants swore by God Almighty that they had seen with their own eyes how, after a good flogging, he ran his hand over the weals on the servant's naked back and bit his lower lip to suppress the waves of pleasure coursing through his body.

Most likely these stories were merely calumnies invented by the servants, who enjoyed swapping them surreptitiously out of their dread of Hameed, whom they detested no end.

The moment Alku set foot in the Club, everyone knew at once, the servants asking each other in terror where he was headed and what he wanted. Had he come on a routine inspection or to investigate something reported to him by one of his ubiquitous spies? These questions always remained unanswered. Alku's inspections were one of the vicissitudes of fate from which no one felt safe. One never knew how far they would reach, and so when they occurred, the servants would always pray to God for protection. No matter how skillful or experienced a servant might be, as in a game of roulette, he could never predict when his number would come up. For Alku, good and evil were completely random matters. He might spend a whole day checking the rims of the lift doors for traces of dust as his gaze darted over to old Mur'i the lift attendant, who would stand there quaking. He might then take the lift and head to the bar where Bahr the barman would rush over to him and say in Nubian, "Good afternoon, Your Excellency. To what do we owe the honor?"

Alku did not answer greetings from servants, except a wave of his hand or a slight nod if he was in a good mood. If in a foul mood, he would raise his eyebrows almost imperceptibly or just ignore the greeting completely. Alku walked into the empty bar with the servants scurrying behind him and gestured to Hameed to open the wooden drawer with the previous night's receipts. Reaching into the drawer, Hameed gave them a fleeting glance before flinging the slips into the air and, in a voice choked with anger, crying out, "Your tabs are really floating now, Bahr!"

Bahr was about to respond, but a piercing look from Alku shut him up and made him lower his head. Alku did no more than register this impertinence before turning and walking out of the bar.

A little explanation is needed here. The "floating tab" was a well-known system used by barmen to manage their receipts. Rather than ringing up an item such as two beers or two whiskeys again and again, a barman would put enough money to cover the tab into the till and would then present the same bill to another member who ordered the same thing. This time the barman pocketed the money. Hence it was called a floating tab as the same bill bobbed around from customer to customer.

Alku then headed to the restaurant, but just as he reached the door, at the very last moment, he turned and headed for the casino, the servants still hurrying along behind him. He strode up to the farthest table in the room, next to the window, rubbed his hand a few times on the underside of the table and then slowly lifted his fingers up to his eyes. The waiters stood around him, almost breathless from fear. It would be an unmitigated disaster if Alku saw the slightest trace of dust on his fingers. But thank the Lord, there was not an atom of dust on the underside of the table. What happened then is proof of Alku's second sight. As he was waiting for the lift, he spotted Idris the waiter in the distance. He turned to look him over, and then, like a cat that has just seen danger, he tensed his muscles and arched his back as if bracing for a fight. Gesturing toward Idris, Alku harrumphed and shouted, "Bring that one here!"

Idris froze on the spot, with an ingratiating smile. Hameed grabbed him and dragged him so roughly by the sleeve of his robe that he almost fell over. Alku uttered another phrase that hit Idris like a lightning bolt, "Search him."

At this, Hameed was to take the suspect to the servants' changing room on the roof. There they stood, surrounded by servants trying their best to hide any sympathy for their colleague. With an ugly and vengeful smile, Hameed told Idris to take off his caftan, which he searched carefully. Then Hameed inspected Idris's baggy undertrousers, causing Idris to utter a low moan that soon turned into a loud gasp as Hameed extracted two twenty-five piastre notes from Idris's sock.

"Thief!" shouted Hameed and then, like a hunting dog, turned to present the notes to Alku, who asked in a low and deliberate tone, "How long have you been thieving, Idris?"

"Forgive me, Your Excellency," he wailed, almost in tears. "I'll never do it again."

Alku shook his head once, whereupon Hameed took his cue and gestured to two of the servants to grab Idris by the arms. This served two purposes, forcing the colleagues of a guilty servant to witness the beating while also enlisting them to prevent him from dodging any of the lashes. There was no such thing as friendship for anyone who broke the rules. It made them understand that it could happen even to one of their oldest colleagues. It was no use feeling upset at his disgrace and pain, as the guilty had no rights.

Hameed went up to Idris, now restrained, and started slapping him. Hameed had a singular technique, which was to raise his hands on either side of the servant's face and then slap him with each hand in turn. Occasionally, he would deliver a resounding slap with both hands. This achieved the highest degree of humiliation and pain. After the first round of slapping, Idris received another one, and as Hameed started to get carried away with himself, his face flushed, his eyes bulging and teeth grinding. By some additional bit of bad luck, Idris suddenly cried out, "Enough! Shame on you."

Hameed was startled. He stepped back, and panting with exhilaration, he said, "Shame? I'll teach you the meaning of shame!"

Hameed looked toward Alku, who made an almost imperceptible gesture, such as an impresario might give the musicians to ready them for an encore. Springing forward, Hameed showed himself surprisingly agile for his large frame. He picked up a short, rough stick and started waving it. The two servants holding Idris knew what they had to do. They pulled him roughly and pushed him down onto a bench, taking off his shoes and socks. Then as they held Idris's legs, Hameed pursed his lips and grimaced before raising the stick as high as he could and bringing it down with full force on the soles of the surly servant's feet . . .

KAMEL ABD EL-AZIZ GAAFAR

At that time, my emotions were in turmoil, and I was reeling from one extreme to another. I could feel overwhelmingly happy and optimistic and full of self-confidence, and then suddenly, for no reason, I would lose my enthusiasm and a sense of gloom sapped my will to do anything at all. I would withdraw into myself, alone in my room sprawled out on my bed, reading, smoking and giving myself over to my restless imagination. I imagined myself performing deeds of chivalry and self-sacrifice, saving an innocent girl from a gang of evil men or helping a stricken friend so generously that his eyes welled up with tears of gratitude. I saw myself as the hero of some tragedy who displays nothing but generosity and courage to all with a steady gait and a steadfast heart as fate lies in wait to drag him to meet his destiny. Sometimes I thought of our house as a theater. I would watch my siblings coming out of their bedrooms and walking around as if they were actors performing their roles. It was like watching them from behind a glass partition. Sometimes I felt that I was experiencing a life that I had already lived, as if everything around me was already hidden away in the recesses of my memory. With all such emotions burning inside me, I felt the power of poetry for the first time. I wrote a poem, which was published in the magazine of the College of Law and for which some of my fellow students expressed their appreciation.

When suffering my own ups and downs or lost in my untrammeled imagination, I felt sad about what was going on in our house.

My mother had admitted the truth to me: our father had come from Upper Egypt after losing all his money and was working as a storeroom clerk to support us. As if he were living with chronic pain, my father's face was holding something back. Even when laughing or speaking about something cheerful, his expression was still dark and ominous. I felt bad that he was going through this ordeal. I wished I could help him and thought about looking for some work in addition to my studies. But when I suggested this to my mother, she responded firmly, "Your only job is to study and graduate."

My feelings of responsibility to my family weighed on me heavily. I could not let them down. I was their emissary to the future, the focus of their unshatterable hope. I can never forget my first day at university. I had had a haircut, shaved and put on some aftershave as well as a new suit. My father got up early to wish me well, and seeing me off, he smiled and said, "Good-bye, professor! May God keep your every step safe."

It seemed to me that he was fighting back tears. The responsibility I felt spurred me on to study as hard as possible. I was always on time for lectures, seated in the front row and taking meticulous notes, which I would study thoroughly. I received outstanding grades for my first-year examinations. My father's face beamed with joy, whereas my mother, concerned to avert the evil eye, made me walk seven times through smoke issuing from an incense burner. I started my second year enthusiastically, longing to graduate so that I could work and share the burden with my father.

My brother Said, who was two years older, was a different sort altogether, and we almost never agreed with each other on any subject. Said never thought about anything but himself, and furthermore, he had a supercilious nature. One day he came into our bedroom, sat down in front of me and, in a tone of derision, asked me out of the blue, "Does your father still think that he's a landowner in Daraw?"

"You should have some respect when speaking about our father!"

"Can you explain to me what is going on in this house?"

"What have you got to complain about?"

"Look, we are going through hard times. There's hardly enough money for food and our school fees, but all the same, your father keeps on paying for hordes of jobless Upper Egyptians to stay here."

"Those Upper Egyptians are our relatives, and they are not jobless. They are in Cairo to arrange some things."

"Are you trying to convince me that our father is responsible for the whole population of Daraw?"

"He is."

"How ridiculous. He should be spending his money on us first."

"The duty to look after your own people is obviously too honorable for you ever to understand."

"It's exactly those delusions that have bankrupted our father."

"Shut up."

"I'll say what I want."

We were always quarreling like that. Said felt aggrieved that his younger brother had been accepted at university whereas he was at a technical college, and he blamed our father for his own failure—it is always easier to blame someone else. It was hardly our father's fault that Said neglected his studies and had to repeat two years at school and even then received poor marks on his secondary-school certificate. Said's sense of persecution turned into aggression. Except for our father, no one at home was safe from his outbursts. He would argue with me, boss around our mother and hit Mahmud for no reason, and when it came to poor Saleha, his rage was boundless. Just last week, she left the door of her bedroom ajar and was lying on the bed in her nightgown, reading a textbook. Said made a huge fuss, wiping the floor with her, accusing her of having no manners because she was lying on her stomach with the bedroom door open. He screamed in her face until she started shaking and would have hit her had I not grabbed his hand. I deeply resented the endless bickering, but I do not dislike my brother Said.

These were the focal points of my life: university and home, our rocky finances and my father's struggle to support us, my fertile imagination, my repressed desires and my forays into poetry. Never for a moment did I doubt that I would one day graduate, get a job and support my family. My life stretched out before me like a long road, but I could see where it led. Then, suddenly, it changed course. It is strange how that can happen unexpectedly due to some small matter or a passing word, going down some street at a particular hour or turning right instead of left or appearing late for work and bumping into someone—any such thing has the potential to change everything.

It was a Wednesday. I will never forget it. Our professor had canceled a lecture, so I decided to go home for lunch before the afternoon classes. As I was leaving the lecture hall, some of my classmates stopped me and invited me to go and hear a talk by Hasan al-Mu'min, chairman of the Wafd Party at the university. Politics did not really interest me, and I begged off, but one of the students taunted me, "Pull yourself together, Kamel. Are you afraid of being arrested?"

I was almost provoked into giving an answer, but I said nothing. Another student grabbed me by the arm, and I went along with him, telling myself that I would stay for a while and then sneak off. When we reached the courtyard in front of the auditorium door, standing there was Hasan Mu'min, with his svelte body, his handsome face and his large, dreamy eyes, but at that moment he looked like a different person. He managed to captivate the students completely. He started by discussing the political situation and explaining how the king was colluding with the English. Then he turned to the occupation. His voice echoed through the hall: "Students! Generally, we associate rape with physical violence. That is wrong. Rape in essence is the violation of our will. The British occupation means to subdue Egypt, and the English want to break our will. The occupation is rape. Egypt is being raped on a daily basis. Does it bother you to see your country being violated?"

A murmur arose from the students and then shouts of "Long live Egypt! Long live Egypt! We'll free Egypt with our blood!" The strange thing was that I found myself gradually joining in with them, shyly at first and then full-throatedly. I was swept along in a spiritual and mysterious way. I became one with the crowd and forgot that I had been planning to slink out.

After a few moments, Hasan Mu'min made a gesture with his hand, and the clamor gradually died down. He then raised his voice anew: "You, Egyptians! University students! There is no point in negotiating. Britain will not leave Egypt over a few words. Britain only understands the language of force. They occupied our country by force, and only force will make them leave. You, sons of Egypt! You are the country's greatest hope, and all eyes are upon you. This is your day. The English soldiers are raping your mothers and sisters, and what are you doing about it?"

Pandemonium broke out. The students surged toward Hasan Mu'min and lifted him above their heads. One voice started calling out, "Egypt, we'll save you!" until the chant was picked up by everyone. I saw some students so moved that they were crying like children. The university guards had closed the main gates from outside so that the demonstration could not spill out onto the street, but the crowd pressed against them until they swung open. I walked along in the demonstration, shouting the slogans enthusiastically. As we approached the overpass, we found the military police waiting for us. They charged at us in waves and beat us with sticks, blows raining down on our heads and bodies haphazardly. People were screaming, and some were bloodied. The secret police surrounded the square to arrest us as we fled. I saw the danger and concentrated on finding an escape route. I darted this way and that until I got to an alley I knew next to the College of Engineering and ran as fast as I could down the small streets by the zoo.

By some miracle, I made it home without being stopped. That night I did not do any studying. I sat smoking and reviewing the day's events in my mind, becoming increasingly emotional. The comparison of the occupation to rape had filled me with anger. I opened the window and looked outside. An English military patrol was heading down al-Sadd Street toward the square. I stood there watching them, becoming ever more incensed. Those pale-faced Englishmen with their blue eyes and white skin had come to rape our country. I imagined an Englishman trying to violate my sister, Saleha, and could hardly contain myself. I slept fitfully that night and woke up still overwrought. I got dressed quickly and returned to the university to look for Hasan Mu'min, finding him in the cafeteria with some students, going over some papers. He greeted me as calmly as if he had been expecting me. When I whispered that I would like to see him privately, he got up immediately. I had prepared what I wanted to say, but the words just disappeared from my mind. I stood mutely in front of him as he looked at me with a friendly smile. Then I blurted out, "I want to do something for Egypt."

My voice was emotional and shaky, and I shuddered as I pronounced our country's name. Hasan Mu'mim was a true leader. He said nothing but nodded as if he completely understood. After asking me a few questions about my group of friends and where I lived, he invited me to a meeting of the Wafd committee at five o'clock that day in the garden of the College of Agriculture. The committee was made up of students from various colleges. At the meeting, I was introduced and immediately made a committee member.

When the meeting was over, Hasan pulled me aside and said, "Welcome, Kamel. I want to reassure you that there are many people who love Egypt. We have a broad front made up of nationalists of all political hues. We are everywhere, and by the will of God, we will be victorious."

Hasan took to charging me with various duties, all of which I carried out to the best of my ability. I translated some articles from the English press to be published in the Wafd's magazine, which was distributed for free at the university. Then I helped him to set up a Wafd marquee in Sayyida Zeinab. Day by day, my duties increased, and three months after I had joined the committee, Hasan Mu'min surprised me by calling for an early morning meeting—which was highly unusual. I found him, on his own, waiting for me in the garden of the College of Agriculture. He was holding a black briefcase and smoking voraciously, lighting each new cigarette with the butt of the last. He appeared nervous and agitated, pallid and with bags under his bloodshot eyes. He looked around and then whispered under his breath, "In a few days, the British foreign secretary is coming to Egypt. We have prepared a pamphlet protesting his visit and listing the crimes perpetrated by the occupation."

I looked at him in silence, and he put a hand on my shoulder.

"I want you to distribute this pamphlet in Sayyida Zeinab."

I did not answer. Things were happening too quickly. I said nothing and just looked at the grass under my feet. I could hear the shouts of the students playing football near us and became aware of Hasan whispering to me again.

"In all good faith, I have to tell you from the outset that what you are about to undertake is considered a crime under the law and punishable. If the authorities connect you with the pamphlet, they will arrest you, put you on trial, and you could spend years in prison."

Alarming thoughts rushed through my mind. I could see myself in prison, my broken-hearted mother in tears and my sad father looking at me, crestfallen.

Hasan continued, "Kamel, you are a nationalist and a brave man, but I would beg you not to rush this decision. I'll give you some time to think the matter over. If you decide to refuse, I will understand."

Deep silence hung between us. I calmly held out my hand to take the briefcase. He tried to say something, but I took the briefcase firmly from his hand.

5

People in al-Sadd al-Gawany Street consider it their moral and religious duty to settle quarrels between married couples. The moment a husband and wife on the street start arguing, be it day or night, their neighbors rush over, listen carefully to the facts from both sides and try to suggest a solution based on the Quran and the traditions of the Prophet, not leaving the couple alone until the storm has died down. There was one exception to this rule: the arguments between the grocer Ali Hamama and his wife, Aisha. No one ever tried to keep them apart during a quarrel. Perhaps that was because, in spite of the ferocity of their arguments, they never resorted to physical violence or attempted to kill each other or commit suicide as other couples did. In fact, their arguments had a somewhat festive and entertaining character, with Ali Hamama and his wife exchanging hilariously filthy curses. As far as the people who lived in the street were concerned, Uncle Ali Hamama and his wife, Aisha, were not quite based in reality. They generally behaved like ordinary people, but they had this other side to them that was close to the rough-and-tumble of street puppet theater.

Ali Hamama! The name on his birth certificate was actually Ali Muhammad Hanafi, so how did he come to be known as Ali Hamama? There were many explanations. People said that when he came to Cairo as a ten-year-old from his village (Ashmoun in the governorate of Menoufiya) to work for Yunus the kebab man in Sayyida Zeinab Square, he was noted for his ability to run faster than anyone else, and so they called him Hamama ("the pigeon").

A competing story was that the nickname was owing to the blue pigeon-shaped tattoo that had been inked on his temple when he was a small boy, as is traditional among the rural people. After being teased mercilessly about it by the people in Cairo, he went to a tattoo parlor and had it removed, but the nickname stuck. There was a third much more enthralling story claiming that when he was young, he used to carry out circumcisions on boys, and the name arose because in Egyptian folklore, the pigeon symbolizes the male member. He used to carry the tools of his trade in a briefcase and go from village to village in the vicinity of Cairo, offering his services, negotiating his fees and carrying out the procedure on the sons of poor peasant farmers.

One day, completely stoned from having smoked a bit too much hashish, he set off to circumcise a child in Qalyubiya, disguising his telltale bloodshot eyes with some eyedrops. The house was decked out with lamps and little flags in celebration of the child's circumcision. The moment Ali Hamama stepped inside, he was met with a storm of ululation from the crowd of women who seemed to be everywhere—in the hallway, on the roof, in the bedrooms and in the living room, where Ali slurped down a glass of rose sherbet before being led to the room where the boy was waiting. After the women left the room, the father and uncle placed the little boy on the bed, and although he struggled hard to get away, they managed to remove his shorts and spread his legs apart, exposing the pertinent area to Ali Hamama, who, as always before carrying out the procedure, uttered the phrases, "In the name of God, the Most Gracious, the Most Merciful" and "There is neither progress nor might except through Allah," and then positioned himself in front of the child. He took the boy's penis in his left hand, and the sharp blade glinted in his right. He pulled the penis toward him, but due to the effects of the hashish, instead of removing the foreskin with one deft cut as usual, Hamama accidentally cut directly into the penis. The boy let out an ear-splitting shriek as blood spurted out like a fountain onto the bed and floor. All hell broke loose as word of the dramatic bleeding spread to the boy's relatives standing outside, and they rushed into the room in a panic, the women howling and wailing as if the boy had died.

Ali Hamama made some reassuring gestures, but then he sighed, smiling broadly, and nodded as if this were absolutely normal. Trying to sound cheerful, he said, "By the way, the boy has a rosy future. His foreskin is off. Do you know what that means?"

"What does it mean?" asked the boy's father, scowling with worry.

Hamama forced out a laugh and said, "It means that the kid will grow up to have a thick one that will drive women crazy. For sure!"

He shook his head in jest, but no one smiled at his attempt to mollify them. The child's screams reverberated through the air like an incessant siren, and rivulets of blood kept streaming down his thighs. Ali Hamama noted the grim faces on the relatives crowding around him and realized that their anxiety would soon turn to fury. Calmly and politely, he asked them to fetch him coffee grounds from the kitchen to staunch the wound while he nipped out to purchase a special cream from the nearby pharmacist. When they suggested that one of them could go and buy it, Ali Hamama insisted that there were a number of preparations with the same name, and they might end up buying the wrong one. Then, having made sure to allay their suspicions and having purposefully left his case of medical instruments behind, Ali Hamama set out toward the pharmacist. He walked with a slow and steady gait in case anyone might be watching from the window, but the moment he was out of sight, he started running as fast as his legs could carry him until he reached a taxi stand, where he paid a driver to take him to Cairo (throwing away money as never before and never since). He thanked the Lord and his lucky stars that the family of the victim had not come looking for him, though perhaps they had expected him to take the train and went in pursuit to the railway station. Moreover, they knew neither his full name nor where he lived.

After that sorry episode, Ali Hamama never again carried out a circumcision, instead setting himself up in the small dark grocer's shop he bought opposite the tram stop at the beginning of al-Sadd Street. He would work all day behind the dilapidated counter wearing his old tarboosh with its slightly battered top and, over his striped galabiyya, a khaki raincoat that made him look like a plainclothes agent from the Ministry of the Interior. He owned three striped galabiyyas, because he believed, for some reason, that striped cotton was the last word in style. He could sit there for hours saying nothing except when absolutely necessary, for as is typical with serious hashish users, he was more inclined toward introspection than any form of movement or activity. His sullen face never bore any expression. As he sat there, his narrow eyes would blink incessantly, and on occasion he would open them wide and try to make out what was going on around him (there was a rumor that he had lost his spectacles years ago and that, as he was too cheap to buy a new pair, his eyesight had become even worse).

Despite his taciturnity, his poor sight and shabby appearance, Ali Hamama was always aware of what was going on. Like a dormant microbe, he lay in wait, saving his energy for the right moment, watching everything in his shop, as customers reeled off orders and as products were fetched, weighed, wrapped and handed over. He watched as money was exchanged and put in the drawer, as the women living in the flats above called down and lowered their shopping baskets on a rope from their balconies and as the serving boy grabbed the money from the baskets and replaced it with their purchases and their change. Ali Hamama watched all this activity with a sensory perception that made up for his poor eyesight. If an argument broke out, he would intervene immediately. What naturally made him angriest was when a customer tried to ask for credit, since, in order to avoid a misunderstanding, he had hung a sign over the doorway that read, "Do not ask for credit as a refusal often offends." He found that a troublesome customer did not generally make his intentions known from the outset but rather would order, for example, a quarter pound of cheese or a halvah sandwich, and once the items were in hand, he would grin idiotically and say, "I'll pay you tomorrow, please God."

At that moment, the normally taciturn and placid Hamama would suddenly spring into action, shocking the customer by barking, "Oh no you won't. You'll pay now or never, buster! Goods exchanged for payment only."

At that moment, the well-trained shop assistant would grab the package from the customer's hands. If the customer was the sort of lowlife who tried to argue, he would find Ali Hamama inching toward him to settle the matter by other means.

Ali Hamama was renowned as a miser and an unusually brusque one. He never uttered pleasantries or took account of people's feelings, and even though he went to pray regularly at the mosque, he never missed an opportunity to cheat his customers in the weight or quality of his merchandise. He had doctored the scales and used a particularly thick and heavy type of reinforced paper to weigh out the cheese and *basturma,* significantly adding to the cost. These deceitful practices made the people in al-Sadd al-Gawany Street dislike him and hope deep down that some evil would befall him.

Completely unlike Ali Hamama, his wife, Aisha, was enormously popular in the street. Just the mention of her name put a smile on people's faces, and their eyes would light up with affection and admiration. As far as the men were concerned, Aisha radiated the allure of sinful and debauched delights, and even though they all tut-tutted in public about her behavior, they secretly wished their own wives possessed something of her femininity. The women, on the other hand, loved Aisha because she expressed what they could only dream about and never dared utter. Aisha's most salient feature was that she knew no shame. She loved to prattle on in her hoarse voice and with her insouciant smile, in great detail, all about her conjugal practices. The women would cluster around her, hanging on to her every word, now and then letting out little shrieks of mirth or hiding their faces in embarrassment. She would declare that sex was the most beautiful thing in all creation and describe how she bathed and beautified her body every night, how she would perfume herself and lie in bed, waiting for her husband, in only her nightdress.

One of the women listening asked her, "Don't you feel cold going to bed without your underwear on?"

Then, as part of the show, she would give a little cluck of denial, and wiggling her pursed lips from side to side to imply the hopelessness of the questioner, she would pause like a seasoned actor, waiting for the laughter to die down, before telling the woman flatly, "It's what a husband gives a wife that warms her up. And let me tell you that without that particular thing a woman will never know the meaning of happiness."

Vulgar talk was Aisha's favorite pastime, just as some men like collecting stamps or playing chess. She would chat away to men and women with equal frankness. She used to hang out the laundry from the window at the back of her apartment, which overlooked a student residence, having first made sure that the top two buttons of her galabiyya were open. Thus, as she stretched forward over the line to pin out the clothes, her breasts would be exposed to any student standing on the balcony opposite, and she would pretend not to notice the scorching hot looks she attracted. One time, when a student plucked up his courage and uttered a comment about her beautiful cleavage, she was not angry nor did she scold him but started lecturing him about why a woman's breasts need to be caressed during sex. She went into such detail that the teenage student became red and short of breath, whereupon he cut the conversation short so that he could dash off to the bathroom to ease himself. As if guessing what he was about to do, Aisha cackled and leaned over to pick up the empty laundry basket and flounced away from the window. In all fairness, she was not seeking a sexual encounter with the student. She just liked talking about sex. Nothing more, nothing less. The same way as any soccer fan enjoys talking about his favorite goals. Let us just say that Aisha enjoyed talking about sex as much as she liked the act itself, although, truth to tell, it was not quite clear whether she had ever cheated on her husband.

There was one ugly rumor claiming that Ali Hamama had amassed his fortune principally from hashish and had got his start working for a big dealer, who was nicknamed Mr. Handsome because of his stunning good looks. The gossips said that Mr. Handsome was in the habit of spending each evening at Hamama's flat, where he and his host smoked so much hashish that Ali Hamama would drop off to sleep. At that point, Mr. Handsome would crawl into Aisha's bed and spend the night with her. The people from the street who disliked Ali Hamama, and they were numerous, claimed that he only feigned sleep and would receive payment from Mr. Handsome in the form of favors, cash and free goods. God alone knows the truth. It should be noted, however, that Fawzy and Fayeqa, Ali and Aisha's son and daughter, did not resemble each other at all. Fawzy was as dark skinned and unsavory looking as his father, whereas Fayeqa was beautiful with the gleaming white complexion of a Turk. Some people naturally inferred that Fawzy was his father's son but that Fayeqa was the product of an illicit relationship between Aisha and the dealer, Mr. Handsome. Residents from the street were not inclined to repeat this calumny, however, because a person's honor is a taboo subject, and when all was said and done, they loved Aisha too much to wish her any harm. They loved her not just for her outrageous manner and her saucy talk but because she also had a serious side, which revealed itself in times of crisis. When there was difficulty at hand, her feckless smile would fade, the vulgar joking would cease and her face would turn pensive as she listened intently to people's problems and handed out heartfelt and considered advice. She never sent anyone away or put off helping a neighbor, whether it was in joyful times such as at a birth or marriage or in times of grief such as sickness, divorce or death.

The previous day, just after midnight, Ali Hamama had come home as usual after closing the shop. He wolfed down the dinner Aisha had prepared and was relaxing with his mint tea, when she took the opportunity of his good mood to raise a slightly thorny, sensitive and complicated subject: she wanted some money to buy their son, Fawzy, a suit.

The request took Ali Hamama by surprise, and he gawped at her but quickly straightened himself up and regained control. He uttered his brusque and peremptory refusal before slurping his tea as if to confirm the answer, but Aisha did not despair. She could get around him in various ways: she could butter him up, tell him how she prayed for his health and long life, point out that God Almighty had granted him a good living because he was a devoted father who never failed to provide everything for his family. She then moved on to describe Fawzy's urgent need for a suit. What would people say if they saw the son of Hagg Ali Hamama, a man of such repute and who had made the pilgrimage, walking around in rags and tatters? But her argument, however strong and persuasive, had no effect whatsoever on Ali Hamama.

He would not budge and gradually started to take umbrage at Aisha's insistence. Finally, she was obliged to use her biological weapon: she stood up, sighed deeply and sat down next to him on the sofa, right next to him, thigh against thigh, with her heady perfume filling his nose and letting him feel the heat of her body. He realized that, as usual, she was completely naked underneath her galabiyya. Not stopping there, she started to caress his lower abdomen. Ali Hamama sensed the blood pulsing in his veins, his heartbeat quickening and his vision blurring in the heat of passion. He almost put a hand on his wife's warm and supple breasts, but he knew that submitting to her seduction would come at a serious financial cost. He got up and stepped away from the source of heat and sat down in the armchair in the opposite corner of the room.

Once he had collected himself, he started his rebuttal: "He has more than enough clothes already. Even if they are a bit worn, you can mend them! That's the way to bring up a man. A child should know the value of money. Frittering it away on juvenile whims is the quickest way to go broke. And remember, Fawzy is a dunce, a good-for-nothing, useless! He's seventeen and still at school. What does he need a new suit for? A reward for failure?"

Aisha looked at him and asked, "So we just let him run around in shabby clothes like a beggar?"

"If he keeps failing at school, he can go to hell for all I care."

Hamama spoke those words calmly, avoiding Aisha's glance.

She threw out a final challenge: "So, what's your decision? Are you buying him a suit or not?"

"No," Ali Hamama answered without hesitation.

Aisha growled, got off the sofa and stood in the middle of the room, shouting, "Shame on you! You'll be the death of me. If you go on like this, I'll have a stroke! Your son, the fruit of your loins, wants to buy a suit and you'll pay. You should have some fear of God in you."

"Oh, it's God who told us to throw our money down the drain?"

"That's just like you. Heartless. Are you a Muslim or a heathen?"

"Muslim, praise be to God!" retorted Ali sneeringly.

Aisha let out a long sharp wail, which was, in the language of international law, a declaration of war, and Ali Hamama in his turn uttered some unintelligible grunts, which could be interpreted as a confirmation of his refusal and reiteration of his come-what-may attitude. Then he withdrew into himself, shrouded in taciturnity, staring into space as if the discussion was no concern of his.

Aisha walked right over to him and then gave him two almighty slaps on the face, shouting, "May God punish you! What a miserable marriage! I was warned from the outset that you were tighter with money than Yazid's dog!"

"Then why did you marry me? Were you forced into it?"

"I was young and stupid. The day I met you was the worst day of my life!"

Ali answered calmly, "Don't worry your pretty face. If you want, we can end it and each go our separate ways."

"Chance would be a fine thing. If you were a man, you'd divorce me."

"Then give me back your wedding jewelry first!"

Aisha took a deep breath and then let out an audible snort as she waved her finger in the air in that recognizable gesture of insult as if to an imaginary audience, as she shouted, "What are you saying? What bloody jewelry, you useless man?"

"The bloody jewelry I provided upon our marriage. Give it back and I'll divorce you."

"I'd rather flush it down the drain, you miserable bastard."

Aisha rushed off to the bedroom and came back with a velvet box containing the gold necklace that was her dowry. She shrieked as she threw it onto his lap, "Take it, you piece of filth! And I hope you're happy with it!"

Ali grabbed the box, opened it and checked its contents, almost sniffing it, as if he were receiving goods for his shop. Then he gently shut it and carefully placed it beside him on the sofa, pondering ruefully aloud, "I dragged you up from nowhere. I wonder how it feels to have nothing again."

Aisha was now working herself up into a froth of anger, and as she shrieked yelps of fury, she let her galabiyya slip to the floor, leaving her standing there completely naked. She started beating her fists against her thighs and declaring, "Just so you know—you were right, Mama! He is such an upstanding man that I hope God sends him downward to hell!"

"Oh, so now you want to keep me from going to heaven, you piece of vermin?"

She went for him. She clasped her hands together and brought them down on his chest. He pushed her away, jumped up and darted away from her reach. Clutching the jewelry box under his arm, he rushed out of the room with the sound of her curses ringing out after him.

6

Every night Bahr the barman would stand behind the bar in the dim light. Behind him were various bottles and shelves with downturned wineglasses. A man in his fifties, in his gleaming suit, white shirt and red bow tie, he looked for all the world like a born barman. Indeed, the few times that some of his customers saw him outside the bar, walking in the street and out of uniform, he seemed somehow out of place.

Bahr plied his profession with the precision and absorption of a concert pianist. He would take an order, bow and smile, and then prepare the drink. If a customer ordered a cocktail, he would make a performance out of its preparation. He would twirl around on one leg as he lovingly mixed the ingredients. He did this little dance as he shook the cocktail shaker and then poured the drink into the glass, serving it with another small bow, which he held for a few seconds as if waiting for applause. Patrons in the bar would look at him with amazement, and he was seldom denied a "Bravo. Well done, barman!"

Every day until one o'clock in the morning, Bahr would see to it that service in the bar was entirely up to scratch. He would scour all the corners of the bar, watching the staff like a hawk as they served drinks to the members. At the first sign of a mistake, his face would start to twitch in a way the staff noticed immediately. Then in the same code, a signal only the staff understood, he might scowl, raise his eyebrows, shake his head or gesture with his hands, and his men would put things to right. If he was gesturing hurriedly, they would speed up, and if he was indicating to the contrary, they would slow down. He might have been a conductor beating out the tempo with his baton. When it came to the customers, Bahr showed them utmost care and sensitivity. Drinkers could be fickle and their mood highly changeable, but Bahr knew exactly when a customer needed to talk and when he needed to be left in silence, when Bahr should offer a pleasant anecdote or keep his distance. He could uncannily tell from the very first moment if a customer was drinking to forget his sorrows or to celebrate or simply out of habit. He could discern with one glance whether the lady sitting with a customer was his wife or mistress, and he knew immediately whether a drink would further improve a customer's good nature and generosity, or in the case of a foul-tempered man, only make him more aggressive. Bahr was never upset by the slights uttered by drunkards, as he knew that they were no longer in control of themselves, and in fact he would always tell his staff, "Never be offended by a drunk . . . You must look after a drunk!" If someone was completely out of control, Bahr would follow a strict professional protocol, refusing to serve the man any more or in a pinch giving him a glass of ice water with a drop of whiskey in it for a touch of color. Bahr would then help the drunk out by summoning his driver, or if none was waiting, Bahr would prevent the drunk from getting into his car, and then he would call a taxi, paying the fare in advance so that the club's patron would not be fleeced.

Unlike most of the other staff, Bahr the barman showed no humility. He did not consider himself a servant. His work was on a different level than simple cleaning or carrying out orders. It cannot be denied that he too was subject to Alku's authority along with the other staff, but he felt himself a professional. He was the master of a sophisticated craft, and his pride in this enabled him to uphold his dignity. He could put up with all sorts of drunken antics, but he would not countenance slights from sober customers. These he would answer with certain effective and safe acts of retribution—effective because they were a satisfying form of vengeance, safe because they could not be interpreted as anything other than acts of politeness. For example, Bahr might take a long time to respond to an order from an offensive customer, apologizing as he served him with obvious insincerity in his voice, thereby registering his resentment but providing no pretext for complaint.

Another way of getting even was to treat the customer with the utmost respect but call him by the wrong name, a method that caused even more chagrin if the customer was in the company of a lady who was not his wife! If the customer failed to notice that he was being wrongly addressed, Bahr would repeat himself until the customer corrected him, whereupon he would apologize profusely but too late since the message would have already been delivered—that the customer was a man of such insignificance in the Automobile Club that the barman did not even know his name.

The third method was to make a big show of welcoming the customer and bowing to him, but as soon as the customer looked at him, he would look back with an expression of disgust for a fleeting moment before carrying on with the unctuous welcome as if nothing were amiss.

Finally, there was a fourth method, which Bahr had only resorted to once. This had happened two years ago during a visit from Abd el-Al Pasha Hafiz, minister of justice, who was known for his sharp tongue and for the enjoyment he derived from humiliating anyone who worked for him, whether of high or low rank. Bahr tried as hard as he could to avoid any conflict, but in vain. The pasha treated him from the first with sneering arrogance. Bahr served him a chilled bottle of beer, and when Abd el-Al Pasha finished it, he called out in a voice so loud that everyone in the bar could hear him, "When I finish my drink, you are supposed to come and ask me if I would like another one. Am I supposed to do your job? You're not a barman. You're a bloody donkey!"

Bahr could not remember ever having felt as humiliated as he did that night. Suddenly, an idea came to him. He grabbed a bottle of beer and left the bar. He crossed the hallway, making sure that no one saw him, and still clutching the bottle, went into the toilets, returning quickly to the bar and putting the bottle back on the shelf behind the bar. When the Pasha ordered his third bottle of beer, Bahr served him and watched with some pleasure as the bloated Abd el-Al Pasha Hafiz, minister of justice, drank beer that had been diluted with the barman's urine.

To be fair, that event was an exception, a small blot on Bahr's otherwise unstained escutcheon. Usually, Bahr took pleasure in honoring his customers, and his name was often mentioned in expressions of praise reserved for those at the peak of their professions. Perhaps the most fabled example was the visit of Colonel William Caldwell, an English aristocrat and close associate of Field Marshal Montgomery. Colonel Caldwell had a particularly pompous and abusive manner hidden under a veneer of forced politeness. The moment he sat down at the bar, Bahr knew that he was a tricky customer and started serving him with the utmost care in order to give the colonel no chance to get the better of him or create any problems. Colonel Caldwell drank a gin and tonic, then put his pipe in his mouth and, in his upper-crusty English stammer, asked Bahr an obviously supercilious question, "You there, barman. Do you know how to make cocktails?"

"Yes, sir."

"Which cocktails can you make, then?"

"Any, sir."

"Are you sure about that, barman?"

"Yes, sir. Can I get you something?"

The colonel reflected for a moment, puffing on his pipe, and with the stupid expression of a child at play, he said, "All right then. Make me a One Ball."

He pronounced the name of the cocktail deliberately, as if delivering a killer tennis serve. Then he turned away without following the tennis ball, so convinced was he of his shot's effect that he did not need to see his opponent miss it. Bahr betrayed no more effort than if the colonel had just ordered a glass of water. He reached for a bottle of champagne, uncorking it with a flourish. Applying himself with total concentration, he poured a measure of it into the cocktail shaker, added the other ingredients and shook them for the requisite amount of time. Then he emptied the contents into a glass of ice. The colonel turned back to watch him carefully and with some astonishment. He took the glass from Bahr, and as he sniffed and tasted it, the pomposity disappeared from his face, and his tone changed utterly as he asked Bahr, "Where did you learn to make this cocktail?"

"In Egypt, sir."

"Do you know why it is called a One Ball?"

"It is a reference to Adolf Hitler, sir."

"How so?"

"Because he was born with only one testicle."

The colonel's eyebrows rose. He laid his pipe on the bar and stretched out his hand to pat Bahr on the back. When it came time to pay his tab, he left a whole pound tip for Bahr.

For all Bahr's professionalism, the question still remains whether he ever cheated his customers. The answer depends upon one's concept of cheating. Bahr resorted to a number of ruses in order to increase his income. He used the floating tab by which he extracted multiple payments for the same bill. Another ruse depended on the Club administration's charging Bahr according to an expectation that he would sell twenty glasses from one bottle of whiskey; by always pouring slightly less than the specified full drink's measure, he could stretch a bottle to twenty-six glasses, pocketing the difference. Bahr carefully chose the customers so served: those who got drunk quickly (and who would not notice the diminution in their glass) and those so trusting that they never checked their tabs. Thus, in cahoots with Morqos the accountant, Bahr was able to reap a tidy profit from the bar, though he did not consider this to be theft by any stretch of the imagination but merely the usual creative license of the barman trade and completely licit, provided the customer was kept satisfied. In return for his profit from the bar, Bahr would pay Alku the monthly amount called the "bonus."

That night, Bahr was worried because Alku had rebuked him and accused him of theft in front of his colleagues, which meant that Alku was up to something. "God help me," thought Bahr, who did not consider himself one of the serving staff but rather one of the Big Four, comprised of the chef Rikabi, the maître d' Shakir and Yusuf Tarboosh, manager of the casino. All were managers and received special treatment. Alku never punished them with a flogging, choosing instead to dress them down, and when he accused one of them publicly of theft, it meant that he wanted more money from him. Bahr knew that much from experience.

There were still a few days until the first of the month, when the bonus had to be handed over, but Bahr put the usual amount in an envelope, placing it in a drawer in the bar ahead of schedule. He carried on supervising his staff halfheartedly and in a state of apprehension. At midnight, he announced, "I am off to see Alku."

They knew from his expression that the matter was serious, and one of them rushed over to stand in for him behind the bar. Bahr put the envelope in his pocket and took a taxi to Abdin Palace. Midnight was the best time to see Alku. That was when His Majesty the king was otherwise engaged, in the casino of the Automobile Club or out with his friends at the Auberge des Pyramides. At Alku's office, Bahr was greeted by Hameed, who looked at him quizzically. Bahr cringed with a smile and said, "Mr. Hameed, I would like to see His Excellency Alku."

"Wait there."

Hameed pointed quickly at the chair in the far corner. After half an hour, Hameed returned and said tersely, "His Excellency Alku will see you."

Hameed used the words "will see" rather than "is waiting for," as it did not befit Alku to wait for anyone. Bahr sprang up from his chair, quickly checked in the mirror to make sure that his shoes were shined, that his bow tie was straight and his jacket spotless, and then walked into Alku's office, bowing deeply as he said, "Good evening, Your Excellency."

Alku was sitting at his desk, holding a cigarette, which gave off thick smoke. He was wearing his embroidered chamberlain's uniform and gold spectacles as he read over papers lying in front of him on the desk. He left Bahr standing in front of him for a full minute before he raised his head to look at him. Bahr smiled politely, bowing again, and then came forward two steps, placing the envelope on the edge of the desk. The envelope was unsealed, and the banknotes were visible. That was the usual method of handing over the bonus to Alku, who normally did not even look at it but would just make a gesture of dismissal. This time Alku looked at the envelope and, appearing offended, bellowed, "What is this?"

"A small gift for your goodness, Your Excellency."

Alku screeched, "Take it and get out."

Bahr turned pale, and his face showed great consternation as he tried to speak, but Alku's voice echoed around him, "Get out. Get out of here!"

Bahr picked up the envelope and hurried out.

7

James Wright would rise at six in the morning, wash his face, brush his teeth and enjoy a cup of tea with two of his favorite chocolate cream biscuits. Then he would pick up his tennis kit and leave his villa on the Nile in Zamalek, walking the few minutes that it took him to reach the Gezira Club to play for an hour. After that, he would go back home and take a hot bath, eat a proper breakfast and dress before making his way to the Automobile Club, where he had been managing director since its establishment. He would work in his office from nine o'clock until four in the afternoon. Then his chauffeur would drive him back to the Gezira Club, where he would drink two or three whiskeys as he read the English newspapers or played a game of cards with his friends. At exactly seven o'clock, he would arrive back home for dinner with his wife, Victoria, and his daughter, Mitsy. Mr. Wright's life was lived at such measured intervals. At any given moment, it was possible to know where he was and what he was doing. Like most people, however, he also had something to hide. Two or three times a week, after his chauffeur dropped him off at the club, Wright would go into the bar and knock back a drink. Then he would stroll along the corridors as if taking his constitutional and sneak out of the back entrance. After a long while, he would return and climb into his car to go home as usual. Where did he go on these secret trips?

The story starts two years ago, at the Automobile Club's annual New Year's Eve party, which was attended by the British high commissioner, ambassadors, ministers, VIPs and princes of the Egyptian royal family. His Majesty the king surprised the guests with a gracious appearance just after one o'clock in the morning. He wished all those present a happy new year and then took his seat at the green baize table and played cards until dawn. The party, as usual, was an occasion for the guests to display the latest fashions, evening dresses, furs and smoking jackets. One of the female guests caught Mr. Wright's attention: a petite white woman in her forties with jet-black hair cut in a bob, smoking nonstop and wearing a plain blue dress completely inappropriate for the occasion. Wright kept eyeing her with astonishment, wondering how a woman could dare to appear at a society soiree in a dress that would hardly do for a tea party. The strange thing was that she was chatting away and laughing with the guests as naturally as if she had no idea how out of place she looked. This only heightened Mr. Wright's curiosity, and he finally asked Maître Shakir about her.

Maître Shakir bowed and whispered, "That is Madame Odette Fattal, sir."

"Is she related to Monsieur Henri Fattal?"

"She is his daughter, sir."

Curiouser and curiouser. The millionaire Henri Fattal was one of the largest cotton dealers in Egypt. Why would his daughter turn up looking that way? Any secretary in her father's office would most certainly have worn something more formal. What was she up to and why were all the guests overlooking her faux pas? Wright could not contain his curiosity and ordered another drink, quickly downing it. Having thus overcome his inhibitions, he walked over to her. As she looked at him, he bowed and said, "Bonsoir, Madame. Please allow me to introduce myself. James Wright, managing director of the Automobile Club."

As he kissed her hand, he noticed the softness of her skin and her light and captivating perfume. She smiled and said, "I am Odette Fattal. I am a teacher at the Lycée Français. *Enchantée!*"

He felt encouraged by her smile, and as he reached for another glass from the tray of a passing waiter, he said, "May I ask why we have not had the pleasure of seeing you here at the Club before?"

"I don't like the Automobile Club."

"I'm sorry to hear that."

"If it wasn't for my friends, I wouldn't have come tonight either."

"Then I am most grateful to your friends."

"Please don't be upset with me. I am just being honest."

Wright continued looking at this strange creature, who, in spite of everything, was not lacking in a certain charm. He said, "May I ask why you dislike the Automobile Club?"

"Because it is such a deceitful and artificial environment. Full of sharks."

Odette said this in a straightforward manner. Wright raised his eyebrows and gave her an uneasy look, but she paid no heed and carried on speaking, "Here, in the Automobile Club, the thieves don the finest clothes, douse themselves in cologne and then disport themselves in a sort of pantomime of respectability."

"When you say thieves, to whom are you referring?"

"Everyone here. Aren't those pashas the cream of the Egyptian upper classes? Just mention the name of anyone here, and I'll read you his charge sheet."

In all his sixty-one years, James Wright had never had such a bizarre conversation. He knew that he was in the presence of a woman unlike those he saw day in, day out. Despite her eccentricity, she had a certain allure. They chatted on, until the guests who noticed them together started whispering amongst themselves. At six in the morning, he dropped her off at her building, and the following day he rang to check on her. They went out together three more times, and on the fourth occasion he invited her to dinner at the Mena House Hotel, afterward dropping her off at her apartment in Zamalek. As she stepped out of the car, they were exchanging their usual good-byes when suddenly she leaned over and planted a quick kiss on his lips. Trying to control his excitement, he pulled her into his arms and covered her with kisses. That night they slept together for the first time.

Even after a whole year, his feelings of wonder had not dissipated at all, though for all the happiness that he felt with her, she remained an object of mystery. As things continued, all sorts of unanswerable questions arose in his mind. Often he would stand in front of the mirror, looking at his wrinkled and furrowed face and the small strip of gray hair around his bald pate, and he would try to fathom how the beautiful Odette could be attracted to such a plain-looking man twenty years older. Did she have an Electra complex; was she looking for the father she had lost? Why had she moved out of her father's mansion in Maadi and rented a small place in Zamalek? Why was the daughter of the millionaire Fattal forced to earn her living as a teacher at the Lycée? Why not work in one of her father's numerous concerns, if at all? And what about her Lebanese husband, who lived in Paris, about whom she refused to speak? Why were they not living together? At various moments he had thrown all these questions at Odette, with each, her beautiful face turning ashen before she answered him tersely, "I grew apart from my father years ago. I do visit him occasionally, but I don't let him interfere in my life."

"How did you grow apart?"

"We are different in every way."

"Had my father been a millionaire like yours I would never have grown apart from him." He let out a laugh and then asked her why she did not live with her husband or ask him for a divorce.

Odette smiled and answered calmly, "James, do you love me?"

"Of course."

"Then love me for what I am. Don't keep on asking me about my life."

He acceded to her wish. Odette would remain mysterious, but he loved her more than he had ever loved his wife. He could not imagine his life without her. He had never been a devoted husband to Victoria, never feeling any pangs of conscience all the times he had cheated on her. At the same time, he was always ready to forgive his wife for her predictably regular outbursts. He considered marriage necessary in order to produce offspring, but beyond that he deemed it a flawed and useless institution. The odd extramarital affair simply helped to keep a husband and wife together. It was his style to have a fling and then go back and try harder at keeping his wife happy. He had always felt the same about his mistresses, but with Odette, it went somewhat deeper. She had shown him true happiness. It was as if she were the first woman he had ever known. She excited him so much that, even at this stage of life, he started to wonder about his sexuality. It was her boyish appearance that excited him so much. Had she grown her hair out, worn high heels, plastered her face in makeup and acted more feminine, he would not have been so attracted to her.

The most beautiful thing about Odette was something that was almost masculine. She had an instinctive and visceral roughness about her. Her serious talk and her revolutionary ideas were also alluring, expressed in her distinctive way of speaking. She spat out her consonants and emphasized things with small nods of her beautiful head. Wright couldn't help but smile whenever he thought about her. What a wonderous creature she was. She had been offering her body to him for a whole year now and had asked for nothing in return. No presents, no money, no privileges—although she did once intervene on behalf of a peon at the Lycée to help his son get a job at the Automobile Club.

For her birthday, Wright bought her a gold necklace. She leaned toward him, and they lost themselves in a kiss. Then she pulled away slightly but with her arms still around him, smiled and said, "I hope you don't mind, but I won't wear this necklace."

"Why not?"

"Actually, I don't wear gold."

"You are probably the only woman in the world who has something against it!"

"I don't base my opinions on their popularity."

Her strange and surprising notions always produced a mixture of shock and admiration. He asked sharply, "May I know what you have against gold?"

"People run after gold because it represents wealth, but in itself it has no value. It's valued only for its rarity and price, and, personally, I think it looks awful."

Wright closed the box with the gold necklace in it, and in a tone of barely suppressed anger, he said, "I'm so sorry that I have upset you with this gift."

"No. I'm the one who has upset you with my bizarre reaction."

She smiled and looked at his face as if to make sure that he was not still upset, then grinned wider and said, "Even so, I reserve the right to be given a present."

A few days later, she took him to a small shop in Soliman Pasha

Street and picked out a silver chain with an ankh. It was not expensive, but she was thrilled. Wright gave the gold necklace to his wife, who naturally was delighted with it.

The day before, he had arrived at Odette's apartment before her and let himself in. He poured himself a glass of whiskey and stretched out on the sofa, savoring it. When Odette turned up, he became a slave to his passion and for the first time showered her with kisses before they'd even spoken a word. After making love, they simply lay together on the bed. He loved it when she rested her head in the hollow between his arm and his chest. He could feel her hot breath and leaned to kiss her smooth hair.

After a short while, she roused herself, gave him a quick kiss and then looked at him and asked, "You seem a little distracted this evening . . ."

"Do I?"

"What's wrong?"

"Problems at work . . ."

"Tell me about them."

"It's nothing specific. It's just that from time to time I carry out surprise inspections of the staff at the Club, and I always find some gross violations of policy."

"What a fine general manager you are!"

"Yes. I always think that the Egyptian's capacity to work as well as his moral values are completely different from our own."

Odette pulled away from him slightly and gave him a disapproving look.

"I can't believe that is how you think."

"Why?"

"It's racist."

"I'm not a racist. I'm just speaking the truth. Egyptians are lazy, dirty and liars too."

"Well, if they're so awful, why do you live among them? Why don't you go back to clean and efficient England?"

"My work obliges me to live in Egypt."

"Oh, really! How terrible that must be for you! How can you put up with the villa you live in with your family, your grand car and your fabulous salary?"

"Odette, don't mock me. Obviously, my job does afford me some perquisites, but were it not for that I wouldn't be able to bear life in this country for a single day."

"I just don't understand why Europeans come here to pillage the country and suck the blood out of the Egyptians, all the while despising them. You sound just like Winston Churchill, who considers the British occupation of Egypt to be a moral duty."

As she ranted, he turned red with anger. He sat up against the headboard, looking rather odd as he, still completely naked, lit his pipe. With some anger in his voice, he retorted, "Well, if you insist on ruining our night, let me tell you that I am in complete agreement with Churchill. Britain, or any civilized European country, is making a huge sacrifice in sending its military to a backward land like Egypt or India. I don't know how much longer Britain will consider it a duty to bring civilization to the barbarians."

"It really infuriates me that a decent man like you can believe that. The British are simply robbing Egypt and stealing its resources. That's the truth of the matter. The British are thieves."

"Can you deny that the British occupation has helped to modernize Egypt?"

"The only modernization the British have carried out is that which helps them to fleece the country. The British built the railways to transport troops and to filch Egyptian cotton. Their administrative systems enable them to control all economic activity. Do you know how resolutely Lord Cromer opposed the establishment of the Egyptian University? British colonial policy will never change and can be summed up in two words: organized theft. And I can cite plenty of facts and figures."

He gave her a look of irritation and then said sarcastically, "I don't understand how you can defend Egyptians so enthusiastically. Do you consider yourself Egyptian?"

"I was born in Egypt, but I have French citizenship. It was my grandfather who moved from Lebanon to Egypt."

"So you're Lebanese?"

"Does everyone have to belong to a particular country?"

"I can't imagine a person with no nationality."

"Nationalities are a fascist way of thinking aimed at forcing people into a narrow and stupid sense of belonging. It makes some people feel superior to others and perpetuates hatred and war."

"But at the end of the day people need to belong to one country or another."

"That's pure fantasy. I pay no heed to nationality or religion. I was born Jewish, but I am a total atheist. I am neither Egyptian nor Lebanese nor French. I am just a human being."

"Well, I am a British citizen."

"The Britain you belong to has committed terrible atrocities in Egypt, India and Africa. Britain's victims number in the thousands."

"Well, you can't pin that on me personally."

"You don't even see the contradiction. When your government does something good, you are proud of it, but when it commits a crime, you wash your hands of it."

"I have always been proud of being British."

"Hitler was proud of being German too, and he had the Jews incinerated."

Wright seemed on the verge of completely losing his temper and shouted, "I'm fed up with your lecturing. All right. Britain has committed some awful crimes against the people in her colonies, just as Hitler carried out the holocaust against the Jews, but what are the Jews doing to the Arabs in Palestine? What are the Haganah gangs doing to Arab women and children? Are they tossing flowers at them?"

"If you could only believe in humanity, it would help you to see things. As a human being, I condemn the holocaust just as much as I condemn the slaughter of Arabs by the Haganah gangs."

They sat in silence for a long while, the only sound that of Wright puffing on his pipe. Finally, he put it down and took Odette's hand, kissing it and whispering, "Can't we end this argument?"

He smothered her hand in kisses and then started for her neck.

She pulled away from him, whispering almost dejectedly, "I don't know how I ever got involved with someone so dyed-in-the-wool!"

Still embracing her, he whispered, "I may be dyed-in-the-wool, but I love you."

KAMEL

I threw myself straight into the job. I did not think of the consequences. I was like someone who shuts his eyes and jumps in at the deep end. I decided to distribute the pamphlet in the dead of night. Until three in the morning, the streets of Sayyida Zeinab would still be swarming with people and the denizens of the coffee shops, and I knew that plainclothes police would be out and about. After four o'clock in the morning, the first clusters of people would appear on their way to morning prayers. I decided to go between three and four in the morning, starting with our own street. I went from building to building, climbing to the top floor and then leaving a pamphlet at each door as I descended. I completed a number of buildings in our street and then continued to another.

I avoided going into any building with lights on. I must have done at least twenty buildings and was so absorbed in my task that I did not notice time pass until I reached into my bag and realized there were only a handful of flyers left, which I decided to leave in front of the closed Cinema al-Sharq. I had just one copy left in my bag. That was my single error. I crossed the street by the police station and walked in front of the Sayyida Zeinab Mosque as I made my way home. Just before the end of the mosque wall, a number of British officers appeared out of nowhere, accompanied by an Egyptian policeman. They were carrying out a surprise inspection at a spot in the square that was impossible to avoid or slip around. I was rattled. I was certain that the officers had seen me. If I were to throw away the pamphlet, they would arrest me immediately, and if I carried on walking toward them, they might notice my alarm and start questioning me. They would certainly frisk me, find the pamphlet and arrest me. That's how I found myself doing something so strange that I still do not know how it occurred to me. I carried on walking, and a little before I reached the officers, I stopped and put my right foot against a wall. I bent over and pretended to tie my shoelace. I untied it and then tied it again as if distracted by some thought, with not a care in the world. It took me about a minute to tie my shoe before I calmly walked toward them.

The English officer asked me, "What's your name?"

"Kamel Abdel Aziz Gaafar."

"Where do you work?"

"I'm a student at the College of Law."

"Where are you going now?"

"I'm on my way home."

I made a show of nonchalance. I tried to make my voice sound completely normal. The officer looked at me for a moment and then stepped back, clearing the way for me, and said, "Off you go then."

God in heaven. I was safe. When I recall what happened, I can still hardly believe it. I mouthed the first sura of the Quran, thanking God for rescuing me . . . I returned to my bedroom to find my brother Said sleeping. I put the remaining pamphlet in my desk drawer, got undressed and went to bed, falling quickly into a deep sleep.

The moment I opened my eyes that morning, I found Said sitting on the edge of my bed. He was already dressed and wearing an ominous expression. He said contemptuously, "Good morning, Mr. Kamel!"

"Good morning," I responded, still half-asleep.

"And where were you last night until dawn?"

I sat up in bed and asked him, "What's it got to do with you?"

"I'm your elder brother and have the right to know where you were . . ."

"I'm not a child, and I don't need you to look after me."

Said got up, leaned toward me and brandished the pamphlet.

"Has this got something to do with you?"

"How dare you go through my things!"

"I didn't go through anything. I found it on the desk."

"Liar. It was in the drawer."

"In the drawer or on the desk. It's all the same. What's this all about?"

I resolved to come clean.

"Read it yourself and you'll understand," I shot back at him.

"You tell me!"

"It's a statement protesting against the British occupation."

"It's not a statement. It's a pamphlet."

"So what?"

"Do you know what they do to people who distribute pamphlets?"

"I do."

"Are you crazy?"

"No. I am an Egyptian whose country is being occupied."

Said let out a guffaw and said, "So you are the one who is going to liberate Egypt?"

"I'm doing my duty."

"The only thing that will accomplish is that you'll go to prison! Do you think that the English will be so scared of your pamphlet that they'll evacuate Egypt?"

"We have to fight the occupation with all the means at our disposal."

He laughed again, and his face turned ugly.

"So Professor Kamel Gaafar will defeat Great Britain by means of pamphlets?"

"Patriotism is something greater than anything you can understand."

"Patriotism does not mean you throwing away your future and ending up in jail."

"If everyone thinks like you, we'll never liberate Egypt."

"Oh, when are you going to stop dreaming?"

"That's mine to know." Then, almost exploding with anger, I told him, "You are the one who could use a bit of brotherly guidance."

Now giving me a look of great irritation, Said replied, "You've always been ill-mannered."

"You should have some self-respect!"

He pushed me with his hand, and I caught hold of him by his shirt, and we started fighting. He was stronger, but by the sheer force of my anger, I shoved him so hard that he fell onto the bed. He got up again and tried to punch me, but it only landed on my shoulder. That's when our mother ran into the bedroom screaming. I leaned into his face and whispered a warning, "If you say a word to our mother about the pamphlet, I'll tell her what you get up to on the roof."

8

Every day, upon first arriving at the Automobile Club, Abd el-Aziz Gaafar would go upstairs to greet the staff, who at that hour were busy cleaning. The cleaning staff were all Upper Egyptians who knew very well the repute of the Gaafar name. They felt sympathy for Abd el-Aziz as someone from a good family who had fallen on hard times. He was one of those landowners who, at an advanced age, had been forced into service in order to support their children. The staff looked up to him all the more because his position had nothing to do with their tips. They would seek out his advice, and after considering the matter, he would come up with a measured opinion. He was the most approachable, unintimidating and just authority that they could imagine, and they treated him accordingly. No sooner would Abd el-Aziz appear than everyone would shout out a greeting, rush toward him with a chair, a cup of tea or a glass of ice water, and then chat with him as they carried on cleaning.

Abd el-Aziz loved these morning chats with the staff, and he would often bring some Upper Egyptian delicacies, such as flaky pastry *feteer meshaltet* or savory *qaraqeesh* to share with everyone. He really enjoyed listening to their stories and jokes and would laugh as heartily as if he were sitting with his friends after evening prayers in front of his big house back in Daraw. And so it was unusual that that day, when Abd el-Aziz arrived at the Club, he did not go up to greet the staff. He did not have the energy to see anyone. He just wanted to be left alone. He came in through the main entrance of the Club, crossed the hallway that led to the administrative offices and headed straight for the storeroom. He turned the key and the door creaked open. The air was heavy and musty and smelled of wood.

The storeroom was a large, dark space with a high ceiling like the wings of a theater, a gloomy and forgotten backstage world away from the limelight of the Automobile Club. It was an enormous room with piles of everyday and unusual things, things you would expect and things you would not, cases of whiskey of all brands, the best cigars, imported soap, bottles of hand soap for the members' washrooms, toilet paper, tablecloths, roulette chips, electrical devices, spare parts for bathrooms, plates and glasses of varying size and design, and most important, two categories of playing cards—luxury cards for the members and the royal cards with gold-leaf edges, reserved for His Majesty. His Majesty never used a pack more than once. At the end of the month, all the used royal decks would be gathered and incinerated in a special furnace in Abdin Palace, the ashes removed with the palace rubbish. The destruction of the royal cards was a serious matter, whose execution was supervised by Alku himself. Should one of the royal cards ever make its way to a popular café and be used by the hoi polloi, what would become of the king's dignity?

Only once in the history of the Automobile Club did a staff member attempt to purloin some of the used royal decks, and it caused a tremor that shook the Club to its core. The culprit was tracked down and dragged off to the office of Alku, who snatched the *kurbash* down from its hook on the wall and thrashed the living daylights out of the villain. Then the police were notified. They carried out an investigation, and the man stood trial and was sentenced to three years in prison. The message was clear: the gilded royal playing cards, like the "royal" bright red used on the royal automobile fleet, like His Majesty's special claxon, which could not legally be used on an automobile by anyone else, these all constituted a red line. If anyone dared to cross it, he would be crushed.

Abd el-Aziz changed into his yellow uniform with the shining brass buttons. He made himself a cup of tea and sat on a small seat at the end of the storeroom under the tires hanging from the ceiling. In that gloom and quiet, he felt at ease, and as he breathed deeply, he started to reminisce. He remembered how, whenever he had come to

Cairo years ago, it had been a much anticipated and exciting occasion. After his date harvest, he used to come just to get away for a while. He would stay at the Union Hotel in Ataba Square and spend a few days enjoying the delights of the capital. A smile came back to his face as he remembered those times. He asked God for forgiveness and praised Him again and again for having enabled him to carry out the duty of making the hajj before he fell into penury. Perhaps God Almighty had already forgiven him his old transgressions, and what a huge difference between the old days and now, when he had been living in Cairo for five years. He was now a storeroom assistant and was now one, furthermore, reduced to begging in order to pay for his children's education. Oh God, what had he ever done to deserve this ordeal? He could not complain about God's judgment, but he did wonder when these travails would end. A man could cope with catastrophe in his younger years, as God might later recompense him with some prosperity, but that he should find himself in such misery in his fifties! But if it was his lot that this ordeal should continue, he prayed that it should at least end sooner rather than later. God forgive him, he concluded that death would be more honorable.

After lighting another cigarette, he took a drag and felt such a splitting pain in his head that he dropped the cigarette into the ashtray and grasped his head in his hands. Armies of ants were crawling up his forehead and making their way to the back of his head. He had had headaches like this before. They came every day now, and he had been putting off going to the doctor, not because he was trying to ignore them but because he was terrified of the unknown. These were bad times, and nothing good could come of it. He shuddered to imagine that moment when the doctor would take the stethoscope out of his ears and with a grave expression tell him the bad news as delicately as he could. What would Abd el-Aziz do then? Who would support his children? The best thing would be for him to carry on as he was, a few months longer, until Said got his technical diploma and could find a job. Then if Abd el-Aziz succumbed, at least the family would have some means of support.

Abd el-Aziz heard the door opening and then the heavy footsteps of George Comanus. George was a Greek-Egyptian from Shubra. He was fat, jolly and garrulous and loved telling jokes. All the staff liked him because he never bossed anyone around and had never offended a soul. He had been the storeroom manager ever since the Club was established, spending the last twenty years in this large, dark room. It was part of his life. He had always insisted that he did not need more than one assistant and had worked for years with Beltagi, who was from Sohag. He was a good, hard worker, but God had called the lad to Him. When Comanus needed to find a replacement, some of his friends recommended Abd el-Aziz, and Comanus took a liking to him. He found him a respectful and polite man dressed in neat, clean clothes.

The two got on perfectly from the very first. Abd el-Aziz never once let Comanus down. He learned the ropes quickly and then took on further responsibilities: he started writing down the contents of the storeroom and checking it against the actual inventory. Comanus was pleased with this system, as it enabled him to have up-to-date stock information at any moment. Over time, spending all day together, speaking man to man and sharing personal details, Comanus and Abd el-Aziz became friends. But Abd el-Aziz never mixed work and friendship. They might be sitting having a friendly chat, but the moment someone came with a request, Abd el-Aziz would spring to his feet and wait for his boss to give him orders. Comanus considered this ability to separate working and socializing to be a mark of civility, and it made him grow even fonder of Abd el-Aziz.

One evening, he invited Abd el-Aziz to dinner in the Union Restaurant, opposite the Rivoli Cinema. Comanus was surprised to see Abd el-Aziz order the escalope in breadcrumbs and then eat it using a knife and fork. Abd el-Aziz noticed his astonishment and remarked, laughing, "Don't be so surprised, boss! Even though I'm an Upper Egyptian, I've had treatment for it and can now use cutlery!"

Abd el-Aziz regaled him with stories of his visits to Cairo when he had been well off. Comanus started inviting him for dinner from time to time, and Abd el-Aziz would return the invitation whenever he could. One time, he invited Comanus for kebab in the popular Hussein district. He also started bringing in food cooked by Umm Said, which they would share in the storeroom. She would send *mulukhiya* with rabbit, or roast duck stuffed with onion and served with creamy baked savory rice.

Today, as Comanus entered the storeroom, Abd el-Aziz sprang to his feet as usual. Comanus greeted him, took off his jacket and pulled on black satin protectors over his shirtsleeves. There was some heavy lifting to be done. Abd el-Aziz went up to the bar and brought back a crate of empty beer bottles. Then he took a crate of whiskey to the restaurant. When he returned to the storeroom, he stood examining the list of instructions Comanus had written up for him.

"What's wrong?"

"Nothing."

Comanus asked him to make two cups of tea, and when Abd el-Aziz brought the tea, Comanus told him to sit down and offered him a cigarette. Abd el-Aziz sipped the tea and took a drag of his cigarette. Comanus returned to the subject: "You don't look yourself. Please tell me what the matter is."

Abd el-Aziz leaned back in his chair and replied in a faint voice, as if talking to himself, "I'm a bit overtired, boss."

Comanus looked somewhat worried. "What has brought this on?"

"Finding the money to keep my children in school is proving a bit of a yoke around my neck . . ."

"I told you so at the beginning, but you didn't listen to me!"

"God knows, I have done everything within my power."

"You rent a large apartment that costs a quarter of your salary. You could have chosen a smaller, affordable one. Just do what you can afford, and things go easier."

"Boss, our house in Daraw was four hundred meters over two floors, not to mention the date orchard and guesthouse. After living like that, how could I coop up my children in one room?"

"We all have to live through our share of ups and downs."

"I couldn't do that to children who bear the name Gaafar."

Comanus fell quiet and appeared to be thinking. He felt for Abd el-Aziz. He looked at him, and in his straightforward and well-meaning way, he made a suggestion, "Listen. I can give you an advance on your salary, and you can take as long as you need to pay it back."

"That's very kind of you, but I need your help for something else."

"If it's anything I can do, just tell me."

"I want some extra hours. After the storeroom closes, I could go work in the bar or the restaurant. Every extra piastre would help."

Comanus scratched his beard and said, "It's not so easy. You would need the authorization of Mr. Wright."

"Then I can go and see him."

"Mr. Wright is not particularly fond of Egyptians, and even if he were to give you the authorization, there's still another problem. In the restaurant or the bar, you'd be working under Alku's supervision, and he is very tricky."

"Well, that would simply be a work relationship."

"You don't know Alku! He likes to humiliate anyone under him."

Abd el-Aziz remained silent for a moment, then raised his head and asked Comanus, "Please, boss. Give it a try."

SALEHA

The following day, I stayed in bed. My mother brought me endless cups of hot mint tea with lemon as well as laxative pills that I could hardly get down. She made me a piece of poached chicken and a green salad for my lunch and urged me to eat something. By the end of the day, she had stopped asking me how I felt but still came into my bedroom from time to time for a quick chat. I felt that she knew I was feigning sickness and was putting me to the test.

In the evening, Kamel came in and kissed my head. He smiled and told me, "I've paid your school fees today. Here's the receipt. You can go to school again tomorrow."

He put the receipt on the bedside table and got up to leave, but I grabbed hold of his hand and said, "Kamel. Just a moment."

"All right."

"What is going on with our father?"

"Everything's fine with him, praise be to God."

"Why didn't he pay the fees?"

"I told you already. He must just have forgotten."

"Kamel. Please tell me the truth."

I burst out crying. The tension was more than I could bear. Kamel placed his hand on my head to calm me. I kept on asking him, and he nodded and said quietly, "The fact is that our father is going through a financial crisis."

"Isn't our father a rich man?"

"Of course he is, but this year's crops didn't sell well."

I kept looking at him in silence. He said gently, "Don't worry about such things. They happen to everyone."

"Oh, but it must be so hard on our father."

"The crisis will pass, please God."

"Isn't there something I can do to help?"

"If you want to help him, then look to your studies. What will help our father the most is to see us doing well."

I looked at him and tried to smile. He leaned over, planted another kiss on my forehead and left the room.

The following day, when I went to school, nothing was the same. Everything had changed. My feelings toward myself, toward my girl-friends, the way I dealt with the teachers. I felt as if I was hiding the truth from everyone, as if I had a secret life apart from the open life with my schoolmates. I felt inferior to all of them, even those I disliked or considered ugly or at the bottom of the class. They were all better than me because they had not had to stay home until their father paid their fees. I started sleeping fitfully and became completely absentminded and could no longer follow what the teachers were telling us. After two weeks of aimlessness, I started to really worry about my behavior. If I carried on like that, I would end up having to repeat the year, and I kept remembering what Kamel had said to me, "The thing that will help our father the most is to see us doing well."

I decided to throw myself into my studies. Prayer helped me to get over my melancholy. The moment I did my ablutions, I would feel a sense of calm, and I regained my focus. I set myself a serious and methodical study schedule. Math was like falling off a log for me. For as long as I could remember, I had always loved numbers. They were real and definite, whereas a word could be ambiguous. The number five was always the number five. It meant the same for everyone. As a child, whenever I was on the tram, I would amuse myself by seeing how many numbers I could spot through the window. I tried to memorize all the numbers I saw on license plates and houses. As time went on, I realized I could do complicated sums in my head. I can't remember not getting top marks in math, and my mother used to beg me to refrain from showing off in front of my classmates so they wouldn't get jealous. I was always ahead of them, astonished that they could not grasp the relationships that to me seemed totally obvious. Whenever I would sit down to solve a problem and then checked the solution at the back of the book, I was always thrilled to discover that I had not made a single error. I often think of my life in terms of mathematics. If I were to draw a graph of my childhood, I would find that it went along a straight path and then veered sharply. The straight line represents the carefree time. I was the only daughter, spoiled by everyone. It was as if I grew up snuggling in my mother's lap inhaling her familiar smell. Then my dream world vanished. We were poor, and our father had difficulty making ends meet. I studied harder.

My mother and Kamel were very supportive, but my brother Said was jealous because I was getting good marks, whereas he had ended up in a vocational school. He would cause all sorts of problems in order to stop me from studying. He would accuse me of not doing enough around the apartment, of lacking manners, and would invent excuses to punish me. He would rant and rave because I gave myself a manicure or curled my hair in ringlets. He would tell me off for lying on my stomach and reading with my bedroom door open. When he tried to slap me, Kamel and my mother would always intervene. Thinking about Said, I would always become sad and fearful. Why did he resent me so much? His feelings toward me hurt much more than any physical pain he inflicted.

After every argument, when I was crying, I felt that Said became a little more relaxed, as if he had achieved his aim. His physical presence filled me with dread, particularly when Kamel was out at university. The moment I heard Said's voice, I would lock my door. Complaining about him to our father was out of the question, as he did not need any more problems. He was already going through enough for our sakes. Contrary to his intent, the war Said was waging against me only made me more determined in my studies. Unfortunately, no sooner had the matter of the fees been decided than I found a new problem waiting for me at school. I wasn't the only one of my classmates to be taken by surprise when Miss Suad, the physical education teacher, told us we had to buy white ballet shoes.

We did our gym classes in sports shoes, which had always done the job, but Miss Suad, in one of her fickle moments, had decided that ballet shoes were what we had to have. Some of the girls resisted, telling her that our regular rubber-soled gym shoes were cheaper and sturdier than ballet shoes, which were not only expensive but so flimsy they would only last a few classes. But such efforts were in vain, and Miss Suad declared with finality, "You girls will simply have to purchase ballet shoes. Any girl who comes without them will be punished."

I was torn. After the school fees, I did not dare ask my father for ballet shoes. And I was overcome by guilt. If only I had saved the money I frittered away on the cinema and unnecessary purchases, I would at least have been able to contribute toward the cost. There was a small hope that Miss might forget the matter. But she did have her moods the following week, when I turned up in my regular gym shoes and stood at the end of the row, hoping that she would not notice. She said nothing until a few minutes before the end of class; then Miss came up to me and said in a hard voice, "Saleha! Where are your ballet shoes?"

I apologized and said that I had forgotten to bring them. "Bring them next week or you'll be in serious trouble. Understood?"

I nodded and promised not to forget, but then I showed up next time in my rubber-soled shoes anyway. I was the only girl in class with the wrong shoes. Miss was as good as her word. She pulled me out of the class, stood me in the yard as my classmates continued their exercises and threatened to march me off to the headmistress if I did not bring the ballet shoes to the next class. I felt trapped. Could I simply skip school on Saturdays in order to avoid her class? That would mean missing some other important classes. In the end, I had to tell my mother. She put her arms around me and said, "Why didn't you tell me from the beginning?"

"I don't want to be a burden on my father. He has enough to worry about."

It was the first time I had spoken frankly with my mother, rather than going along with the rosy picture she always painted. She replied in a serious tone, "I'll tell your father. He'll manage."

"I need the ballet shoes before Saturday; otherwise, I won't be able to go to school!"

"Don't worry, Saleha. We'll get them for you, God willing."

"What do I do if my father doesn't have the money?"

This last question seemed to weigh heavily on her. She shook her head and left my bedroom looking worried. That evening, the moment I saw my father, he said, "Saleha! I'll take you to buy the shoes on Friday."

I looked at him and smiled, but it must have been a somewhat despairing smile, as he added, "Don't worry. I promise you. We'll get them on Friday, God willing!"

I tried to speak, but no words came out. I wanted to tell him that if it were not for Miss Suad's stupid obstinacy I would have given him no more worries. I wanted to apologize for ever having nagged him to buy me little treats in the past, to tell him that I loved him and thank him with all my heart and say I was sorry for all the grief we were causing him. When Friday arrived, I put my prettiest clothes on. I always loved going out alone with my father. I loved holding his hand and walking alongside him in the street. It gave me a sense of security and pride to be protected by my father, and, in turn, I was proud of him. This time, my feelings were a little different. I felt sorry for him, and embarrassed, but at the same time, I was worried about what could happen to me if I did not buy the ballet shoes. The thing I feared most was being made fun of by my classmates when they learned that my father was too poor to buy ballet shoes.

We started looking at the shops on Soliman Pasha Street. Most of them had the right shoes. I looked at my father, and the moment I saw him hesitating in front of a shop window, I said, "This shopkeeper is a thief. Miss Suad told us that the shoes should cost much less than that!"

Miss Suad had mentioned nothing of the sort, but I was trying to save my father from feeling embarrassed. For this purpose, I lied freely without feeling any guilt. I just could not bear to see him admit that he couldn't afford the shoes. We went into every shop in the street, but the shoes were a fortune in every one. Finally, I said, "These shopkeepers are all thieves. I don't think you should buy anything from them. I know you could afford to pay double what they cost, but why should we let ourselves be robbed?"

But my father only became more agitated, and I regretted speaking so thoughtlessly. He took my hand and said, "Come on. Let's go to Sayyida Zeinab. They have the same goods at half the price!"

We went to a shop in front of the mosque and then to another after that, but there were no ballet shoes to be found. At last my father found some blue shoes that looked similar, and he asked me to try them on. I hesitated a little, but when I got them on and they fit, he got up to pay. I did not have the heart to mention that I was supposed to get white ones. He walked over carrying the shoes with a smile, "I know you were supposed to get white shoes, but don't worry. We'll fix them!"

I could hardly object. Anything I said at that moment would have shattered him. When we got home, my mother was waiting. Her kind voice had some worry in it when she asked, "Did you get them, then?"

I was carrying the bag with the shoebox. My father boomed, "Thank God! It's all sorted out now!"

I thanked him again and said I was going to my bedroom. I lay awake for a long time but then fell into a worried, listless sleep. When I woke up with a dreadful headache, my mother handed me the ballet shoes, which had been dyed white.

"Your father, bless him, dyed them after you went to bed. After all, you'll only be using them for one lesson a week."

I did not say a word. I tried the dyed shoes on. They looked awful and misshapen. They screamed, "Can't afford the real thing." On Saturday, I changed into my gym clothes and tried again to disappear among the other girls. I tried as hard as I could to keep my feet out of sight and thanked God that none of my classmates had noticed them, but just as I was drawing a breath of relief, Miss Suad swooped down like a vulture, "Saleha! Get over here!"

I moved a little toward her, but she gestured for me to come closer. Looking down at my shoes, she said, "Are those ballet shoes dyed?"

9

At ten o'clock in the morning, when the staff arrived at the Club, there would be a clamor of shouts, greetings and guffaws. It was joviality itself, perhaps because they were starting a new day or because they were simply relaxed before having to deal with their supervisors and the club members. They would go up to the changing room on the roof and get into their work clothes—old galabiyyas whose hem they hitched up and tucked in at the waist, showing their long underwear and their undershirts. Then they would fan out through the Club carrying the tools of their trade: brooms, floor rags, dusters and various cleaning liquids. They would start from the top of the building, working their way down, floor by floor. They worked together so efficiently and rhythmically that they might have been doing a Nubian dance. One would call out a snatch of song, or someone else might tell a joke in a loud voice, and they would all burst out in laughter, working without interruption all the while. They emptied all the cigarette and cigar butts into rubbish bags and removed scores of stains from the seats, the tables, the floor and the walls. Each kind of stain had its own specified treatment. Those on the rugs could be removed with cleaning fluid. The dirty tablecloths were gathered together and sent off to the laundry, but those with burn marks from cigarettes were thrown away. Sometimes they would find bits of vomit from a customer who had had too much to drink. They would cover it with a thick layer of sawdust, give it a good brushing and wash the spot with carbolic soap. They scoured the place like a team of expert mine sweepers, and they often found something valuable a drinker had left behind: a gold lighter or a diamond earring or sometimes a full wallet. They would hand over any item immediately to the office of the general manager, Mr. Wright. This was not so much out of a sense of moral duty but out of fear. Many of them, if they could have got away with pocketing something, would not have hesitated for an instant.

The cleaning took around two hours. After they had finished, they would all return to the roof, shower in turn and put on their clean and ironed work caftans and receive their instructions for the day according to where they worked in the Club, in the bar, the restaurant or the casino, the cleaning crew thus transformed into the serving staff. The Club opened its doors at one in the afternoon. The first shift ended at eight in the evening, and the second shift went on until the last guest left near dawn. It was hard work at the Club, and it usually left everyone exhausted by the end of their shifts. Not that they went straight home, most typically preferring to spend a little time at the Paradise Café, which had many advantages, being close to the Club, large enough to contain all of them and open twenty-four hours a day. Being frequented by the staff, it became known as the "Servants Café," a name that Abd el-Basit, the owner, found distasteful and worked hard to stamp out. To any customers not on staff at the Club, he offered a warm welcome, sometimes even free drinks to encourage them to stay longer. He had Ramadan calendars printed with the name Paradise Café on them, as well as regular calendars and greeting cards for the holidays of Eid al-Adha and Eid al-Fitr, which he handed out to residents of the area. He had an enormous and expensive illuminated sign reading "Paradise Café" installed above the door at great cost. All these efforts came to nought, however, as the "Servants' Café" became so well known that, in the end, the owner gave up trying to convince people otherwise. The staff of the Club took great pleasure in spending a little time at the café, with their hot and cold drinks, smoking a nargileh and playing chess, dominoes and cards.

At first, looking at each other in their street clothes they felt slightly odd, like a band of actors who had just removed their costumes following a stage performance. Gradually, though, they would get used to the way everyone looked outside the Club and would start sharing the latest news, gossiping, singing, laughing out loud and chatting with great gusto. For their own entertainment they would also launch into spectacular arguments, which always ended amicably. They had a deep need to affirm that they, like the rest of mankind, were entitled to a normal life out from under their work caftans. They especially enjoyed sitting at the tables and giving the waiter their orders, metamorphosing from servants to customers. Some of the Club staff were easygoing with the waiters at the café, overlooking their mistakes, but others would carry the meticulousness of the Club with them, handing out sharp rebukes should a waiter make the smallest mistake with their order. Sometimes, in fact, there was a silent barrier of resentment between the Club staff and the café waiters such as happens when people dislike what they see of themselves in others, much like the resentful tension that arises when two beautiful women or two film stars run into each other in the same place. Although they were just regular punters in the café, there was something about the Club staff that set them apart; there was something about their demeanor, the way they sat, their voices and their laughter. It was almost imperceptible, but it was something like an indelible sign of submissiveness, which had been stamped upon them during their work as servants in the Club.

At about three p.m. Bahr the barman arrived at the café. Greeting those who were already there, he went over to the table in the farthest corner next to the window, where the managers were seated: Rikabi the chef, Maître Shakir and Yusuf Tarboosh the casino manager. They got up to greet him, and he shook hands with each in turn before sitting down. Bahr immediately told them what had happened the previous evening with Alku.

Thinking it over for a moment, Rikabi asked, "Why do you suppose Alku refused to take the bonus from you?"

Bahr answered calmly, "Isn't it obvious? He must want more money."

The answer hit them like a thunderbolt. They sat in silence for a while before Rikabi cried out, "More money? He's already taking all the food from our children's mouths!"

Rikabi the chef was in his fifties. A short, stocky man, with a huge paunch, he was completely bald apart from a few hairs that still sprouted from the back of his enormous head, and his bushy eyebrows almost obscured his eyes. He was also permanently stoned, as he believed that hashish relieved fatigue, sharpened the senses and enabled him to create dishes he otherwise would not have thought of. He was even convinced that hashish improved his sense of taste and helped him to perfect the seasoning of his preparations. He was a talented chef but a selfish one. He would never speak of any but the most rudimentary principles of cooking. As to his best recipes, he would never divulge to his assistants the secret ingredients that gave his dishes their zesty flavor. Rather, he would mix the herbs and spices at home and bring them into the Club in jars. If he had to make an important dish from scratch, he would order his assistants out of the kitchen. If an assistant proved reluctant to go, Rikabi would give him a few punches with his puffy-fingered fist and then yell, "Get out, you bastard! I've slaved for hours learning how to do this. You think I'm just going to hand it over to you?"

Nothing in the world could embarrass Rikabi. His modus operandi was shamelessness itself. He would shout, scold, curse, argue and gesture obscenely with his fat fingers as if proud of his utter lack of discretion. His insolent indignation was that of a man who felt himself wronged, and he seemed to derive pleasure from the verbal abuse he heaped onto others. It was as if he were saying: "My life hasn't been easy. No one has ever treated me kindly or taken my feelings into consideration. I have only ever known harshness and scorn. Now it's my turn."

Rikabi was, in short, a bully. The moment someone responded in like manner, he would back down. He was from the school of hard knocks but a coward at the same time. He never went on the attack unless he was sure of the outcome, and the least opposition was enough to deter him. But if he got the better of his opponent, he would take it out on him mercilessly.

When Rikabi finished work, late in the night, he would put together a generous tray of food and send it to Bahr the barman, who would return the compliment by sending him a quarter bottle of leftover whiskey. Rikabi would wrap the bottle carefully in layers of newspaper, and with the package under his arm, he'd tell his assistants, "Good night. I'm off to ride the ferry now."

The ferry was, in fact, his wife. Rikabi was in the habit of regaling his friends and colleagues with the intimacies of his married life, giving them all the details of the frequency of his copulation and the sexual positions he favored but never once mentioning his wife by name—this he omitted out of respect for her, only referring to her instead as the ferry or the old lady or sometimes the missus.

Rikabi was equally frank with those around the table about his adamant refusal to increase Alku's bonus.

Maître Shakir plucked up his courage and asked in his usual unctuous manner, "How can Alku expect us to pay him more? It's very odd."

Maître Shakir was a man of sixty-two, a paragon of slippery ways and backstabbing, a master of deceit who specialized in fleecing the customers. He had made an art out of exaggerated shows of respect and reverence, which wore the customers down and ended with them tipping him lavishly. A customer had only to appear in the distance for Shakir to scurry over, bowing and uttering his praise and welcome, inquiring as to his health and the well-being of his children, whose names he knew. Shakir could always convince a customer of his importance at the Club, especially if the customer had come with a lady, in which case, after a lengthy welcome speech, Shakir would bow to the lady and say as if in confidence, "You know, Madame, it's my job to look after everyone here at the Club. However, as God is my witness, His Excellency the Bey is the Club's favorite member and one of our most respected guests."

How could a member then fail to give him a large tip! It was barefaced flattery but it had magical effects. Shakir was in fact so popular that before reserving a table for dinner, members would often first make sure he was to be on duty, as his presence alone guaranteed good service. Maître Shakir's comrade-in-arms was Rikabi the chef. Neither could do without the other. They got together at least once a day to consult and exchange thoughts. They understood each other and worked in such harmony that they were like two men rowing the same boat or playing musical instruments in unison. There was honor between them: they shared with each other the kickbacks they received from the grocers, the butchers and the poulterers from whom they ordered provisions for the Club. They had a very refined system for manipulating the bills from the restaurant. Sometimes, when circumstances allowed it, and with special permission from Morqos the accountant, they would run the restaurant for an hour or two for their own benefit, reaping rich rewards. There was in fact nothing that Rikabi or Shakir would stop at in order to make money. They were supremely inventive crooks. If there were specific ingredients piling up in the kitchen, they would pass them on to the customers in "operation fridge empty." Maître Shakir would announce that there was going to be an open buffet for Club members, and Rikabi would then use all his wiles to present the old food as if it were a special offering. If there was an ingredient that was on the turn, such as shrimps, Rikabi would peel them, dip them in breadcrumbs, fry them and inform Maître Shakir, who would nod his head in agreement and wait for a customer to ask him: "Shakir, what do you recommend this evening?"

The question was academic, but it afforded the customer the pretense of fine dining. A person who asked a question like this wanted only to confirm to himself and to those around him that he was an important personage and that Shakir was so devoted to him that he would indeed recommend only the finest and steer him away from the ordinary. Maître Shakir would bow his head to this sort of customer and whisper in the most tantalizing tones of conspiracy, "Your Excellency, the *crevettes panées* are excellent, but I'm not sure if chef has any left."

At this, the customer would feign dismay and press him, "Are you sure there are none?"

"Ah, I'm certain that the chef must have saved a plate or two for you, Your Excellency!"

An expression of gratitude would appear on the customer's face, and he would feel so special that he would order the shrimps. The order would be brought by the waiters, but served by Maître Shakir himself, who would whisper, "*Bon appétit,* Your Excellency. May God forgive me, but I had to lie to the other diners and tell them we were out of the *crevettes* so that chef could prepare some for our best customer."

Thus did Maître Shakir kill two birds with one stone: he got rid of the shrimps about to spoil and guaranteed himself a tidy tip.

Next to Maître Shakir sat Yusuf Tarboosh, who knew that he would have to say something. "Praise be to the noble Prophet!"

Everyone then uttered his own praise and prayer for the noble

Prophet, and Yusuf continued, "Increasing the bonus is an injustice, and injustice is forbidden because Allah has commanded us to act justly."

Hagg Yusuf was sixty-five. He was a nervous man whose wiry body never stopped shaking, so he could never hold his head still, something that made his colleagues poke fun at him when he first started working at the Club. It was for this reason that they gave him the nickname Tarboosh, because his head shook like the tassel on a tarboosh or fez. He had worked in the casino since the Club opened and eventually became the longest-serving employee. His life changed completely when His Majesty the king started spending his evenings at the Club. The king came to believe that Yusuf's presence at his side brought him luck at the gambling table. The notion became so firmly fixed in His Majesty's mind that often, when immersed in a game, he would call out in French, "Joe! *Bougez pas!*"

Yusuf Tarboosh would bow reverently as his heart pounded with joy. Whenever the king won, he pushed some of the chips toward him with the croupier's stick, saying, "*Ça c'est pour vous,* Joe!"

Tarboosh would take the chips and put them to one side, never in his pocket, as it would be unseemly to do such a thing in the presence of His Majesty. The following day, Yusuf Tarboosh would go to see Morqos the accountant and cash them in. Even on the rare occasions when the king lost, His Majesty would take the stick and rake some of the winner's chips over to Joe. That is how the money started piling up for Yusuf, slowly at first, but then in a torrent that changed his life completely. He became a man of means. He kept his scrawny and haggard Upper Egyptian wife, the mother of his children, but took as a second wife a beautiful, pale widow from Mansoura in the Delta, who was a quarter century younger and revived his licit sexual appetite. Then he had a large house with a garden built in his hometown in Nubia and bought a three-story building in Abdin, which brought in a significant amount each month in rents. Life had smiled upon him, granting him more than he had ever hoped for: a deep sense of satisfaction, a comfortable income, health and property. But can any contentment ever be complete?

Before long, Yusuf Tarboosh had fallen into a religious quandary, and his happiness started succumbing to a profound sense of having transgressed. And his sin was so enormous that he was sure he would end up in the fires of hell. All the jurists were clear about that. Would God, may He be praised, listen to his prayers and accept his fasting while he was living on the immoral wages of gambling? He was getting on a bit now and might drop dead at any moment, as happened to people all the time. One night he might just go to bed and never wake up again. At such a time what would he do, and what would he say to God Almighty on the Day of Judgment?

Yusuf Tarboosh went off to speak to some of the renowned religious scholars, and when he told them about his situation, he received various responses: one shaykh advised him to leave his job in the casino immediately, and after keeping back just enough to feed his children, give the rest of his money to charity and look for some un-sinful work. Another opined that he should leave his job in the casino but purify his savings by giving a portion to charity. A third shaykh was more comforting: until he could find a religiously lawful job that offered the same income, he might continue in the casino. Yusuf anguished over the conflicting opinions of the learned men. Feeling out of sorts and so unhappy, he performed the hajj. In front of the Kaaba, he cried for a long time, calling upon God to set him on the right path. When he returned, he felt the great sense of ease of a man who has been shown the answer. He did not leave his job in the casino nor rid himself of his savings, but he paid for a mosque and an orphanage to be built in his hometown and started sending funds to help a large number of poor families. At the beginning of each month, he would put the money in sealed envelopes with names on them and leave these with the Club receptionist. That was how he overcame his feelings of guilt. God knew that he had not chosen to work in a casino and that his advanced age and dodgy health did not allow him to look around for another job. God Almighty is forgiving and merciful, and should He call him to Himself now, all those poor people he supported would intercede to pray for him.

Yusuf also now busied himself reading religious books, and after some complicated negotiations with Alku and Mr. Wright, he managed to win their agreement to use a corner of the roof, next to the changing room, for a room where the staff could go and pray— outside working hours of course. By virtue of his religious devotion,

Yusuf Tarboosh gained some status among the staff even though they did not trust him completely, for, when all was said and done, he was still one of the managers who supported Alku against them, and the contradiction between his newfound piety and his job in the casino did not do much to help his credibility.

The moment Hagg Yusuf Tarboosh declared his opposition to the increased bonus, a new wave of objections rang out.

Maître Shakir said, "He's gone too far this time. God Himself can see how unfair it is."

Rikabi the chef was so worked up that he made an obscene gesture with two of his fingers. Then with a loud grunt, in piece with the bestial hugeness of his body, he cried out, "Brothers! It's our livelihoods and children that are at stake here. I am not going to give Alku a cent more."

Bahr was listening to them, saying nothing as he smoked a *shisha*. Suddenly, Rikabi turned on him and shouted, "What's with you, all calm and relaxed? Aren't you worried about your income?"

Bahr smiled and responded, "Rikabi, you are all hot air, and I really don't like men who run off their mouth."

Rikabi shouted back, "All right. You tell us what we should do?"

"Either refuse to pay the increase, or pay it and shut up."

They all started voicing their objections, but Bahr sat straight up in his chair, lay down the mouthpiece of the *shisha* and looked at them. "So you refuse to pay the increase?"

In a jumble of voices, they answered in the affirmative. Bahr then stood up and said matter-of-factly, "All right then. I'll go see Alku and I'll tell him."

Rikabi called out, "Wait, Bahr. Just a minute."

Bahr ignored him and made as if to leave the café. The three others at the table called out to him. Rikabi rushed after him and grabbed him by the arm to stop him. Bahr knew his colleagues through and through; their anger was just so much hot air, nothing they dared act on. Even at the peak of their fury, they made certain to keep their voices down lest the other staff members in the café hear them. It was this sort of posturing that so irked Bahr. One minute Rikabi, Maître Shakir and Yusuf Tarboosh were huffing and puffing so much that anyone would have thought that Alku could suffer a good drubbing were he to appear there in front of them. But Bahr's mere threat to go and tell Alku was enough to turn them into quivering rodents. He looked at them contemptuously and said, "Fine, I won't go. But if you are so bold, then go and tell Alku yourselves!"

They made no response, at which Bahr responded, "Just as I thought. Now shut up and go on being Alku's playthings and pay him his bonus."

That very day, just before midnight, the four managers were lined up in Alku's office, where as usual he was smoking his fat cigar and leafing through his papers. He gave them a quizzical glance, and Shakir cleared his throat, made a small bow and stated, "Your Excellency! We owe what we are to your Excellency. It was you who brought us from Upper Egypt, helped us to establish ourselves and turned us into decent human beings . . ."

Alku looked at them, his expression turning from quizzical to weary. Now Shakir took a step forward and placed on the desk a large envelope visibly stuffed with banknotes. Then, with a quaking voice, he said, "Out of gratitude to you, Your Excellency, we have increased the amount of the bonus. May God keep and preserve you. It is small recompense for all your kindness."

Alku exhaled a thick cloud of cigar smoke, which hovered around his face, and then he sat back in his chair and stared off into space as if they were not standing there. Bahr was observing the scene calmly, but his three colleagues were terrified by the thought that Alku might again refuse to accept even the increased bonus, and they would be at a complete loss. They could not possibly pay more. Perhaps Alku was angry about something else. The worst thing would be that Alku was angry over something they knew nothing about. Shakir bowed again and slid the envelope across the glass desktop as if willing Alku to take it. After an age, Alku nodded with seeming disgust and gestured for them to leave. That, thank God, meant he had agreed to accept the bonus. They left his office sputtering gratitude. The crisis had passed.

Was Alku so unreasonable for wanting an increase in the bonus? He always watched his managers very closely, and his ubiquitous spies fed him daily reports. He knew exactly how much money they were creaming off from the Club, which is why he set the bonus on a sliding scale rather than at a fixed amount. Hence, the amount of the bonus had been carefully calculated, and, after all, there were no exceptions or favoritism. Receiving the bonus always prompted Alku to go on an inspection spree, after which he would harshly rebuke the managers and have their subordinates flogged for the slightest error, all this just to remind them that payment of the bonus would neither absolve them of their responsibilities toward him nor inspire any laxity in his review of their accounts.

That was how Alku had lorded it over the staff for the last twenty years—eagle-eyed and ironfisted. There is, however, usually a gap in even the most foolproof systems.

One morning, Mr. Wright called Alku and asked him to come to his office. Alku demurred, saying he could not leave the palace before seeing to the affairs of His Majesty, who never arose before the afternoon, but Wright's insistence worried Alku, so he went to see him. Wright greeted him curtly, lit his pipe and exhaled a thick cloud of smoke, and then said, "Listen. Tomorrow a lad called Abdoun is coming to see you. Put him in the school until he learns service, and then he will work for us in the Club . . ."

It was an order. There was nothing to discuss, so Alku bowed and said, *"A vos ordres!"*

Mr. Wright said nothing more and started reading again as a signal that the meeting was over. Alku asked him whether there was anything else he might do for him. Wright shook his head without raising his eyes from the book. Alku left the office astonished. James Wright, the English general manager who treated Egyptians like muck, was now intervening personally to appoint a waiter! Alku ordered his ubiquitous spies to get to the bottom of this, and a few hours later he received a report. Abdoun was the son of the doorman of the Lycée where James Wright's lover, Odette Fattal, taught. Alku smiled and muttered to himself, *"Cherchez la femme!"*

The following day, Abdoun came for an interview with Alku. He was a sinewy boy with a mocha complexion. Tall and polite. He had wide, dreamy eyes, and his pleasant smile revealed pearly white teeth. He was so handsome that Alku detected on his assistant Hameed's part nervous tension as he brought the lad into his office. Alku gave Abdoun a cold, sullen look and said, "Mr. Wright's intervention on your behalf has clinched the matter, but you should know that there are thousands who dream of getting a job at the Automobile Club. If you show you can work hard, we will take you on."

"I shall do my utmost."

"First, you will go to our school so that we can see how much training you'll need."

Abdoun smiled and said, "I hope to live up to your expectations."

The boy seemed polite enough, but he left Alku feeling slightly uneasy. In all his sixty years, and having dealt with hundreds of servants, Alku had hardly ever erred in appraising a new servant. This Abdoun was clever, he acted politely and appeared eager, but there was something unsettling Alku could not put his finger on. He had a recalcitrant edge to his voice and was hiding something. Alku gave orders for a background check and discovered that his record was completely clean. Abdoun made good progress at the school, passing all the tests without any of the usual beginner's mistakes, and after just two months, he could execute the royal protocol so skillfully that he reminded Alku of his own younger self. All that should have left Alku feeling content, but something kept nagging him and he said to himself, "I've got a strange feeling about that lad."

Alku decided to implicate Abdoun in some misdemeanor that would lead to his dismissal, so he appointed him assistant barman. Bar work, for a new employee, was very risky. The most important personages in Egypt frequented the bar, and one slipup with them could be catastrophic. Moreover, one had to be very sensitive when serving the inebriated, because alcohol made people both fickle and tetchy. Weeks passed without Alku hearing about any issues with Abdoun, and when he asked Bahr about him, the barman only sang the boy's praises. This astonished Alku because Bahr took immense pride in his work, and his assistants hardly ever lived up to his expectations. Abdoun's presence continued to gnaw away at Alku, who finally decided to go on the attack. He went off to see Mr. Wright.

Standing in front of the Englishman, he feigned confusion and hesitancy to speak. Wright asked him to spit it out, but Alku stuttered as if from the awkwardness of a bad situation. "Mr. Wright, please do not be angry with me."

"For heaven's sake, what is it you want?"

"That lad Abdoun keeps making mistakes."

"He'll learn," Wright answered peremptorily.

Alku sighed, "I have tried and tried to teach him, but to my chagrin it has no effect."

"What are you driving at?"

Alku now had his goal in sight and so he took his shot. "In all honesty," he muttered, "that lad Abdoun is not fit for service. I could find him another job outside the Club at a better salary."

Wright shook his head and said, "No, he stays with us at the Club."

Alku tried to object, but Mr. Wright had returned to his paper, signaling the discussion was over.

Giving Mr. Wright a look of disbelief, Alku bowed, turned and walked out.

10

Some things in life seem so natural that it is difficult to imagine when they began. Such was the intense friendship between the two strapping young men, Mahmud, son of Hagg Abd el-Aziz Gaafar, and Fawzy, son of Ali Hamama the grocer. But in fact there was every reason why they should get on with each other: their age—Mahmud was just a few months older than Fawzy; they lived in the same building in al-Sadd al-Gawany Street; and they were both in their third year at the Abd el-Latif college. Beyond all that, they had an identical outlook on life. Fawzy and Mahmud were both convinced that studying was a waste of time.

Fawzy would ask his friend, "Can you tell me what use are all those trivial facts that they try to cram into our brains?"

"Yeah. It's just a load of old nonsense."

Fawzy, the more excitable, would work himself into a lather and ask, "Take calculus. If all those complicated equations don't help us with simple calculations, then why do we have to study it at all?"

At this point, Mahmud assumed a look of forbearance and mused calmly, "Anyway, calculus is a piece of cake compared to geography, with all those tedious maps and crops and precipitations. God alone knows why we should have to know the varieties of crops grown on Sumatra! We live in Egypt and we're never even going there!"

According to the boys' way of looking at things, school was simply a place set up to torment you. Whoever said that success in life depends on success in school? There were lots of wealthy and successful men who had never gone to school, whereas some spent long years studying and then could not find a job. In addition to their dislike of studying, the boys shared four hobbies. First, cutting class—they had thought up many tricks for getting out of school, from jumping over the wall to bribing the doorman, old Shazli, with cigarettes to unlock the gate for them after the first lesson. Second, playing soccer on the "triangle," a patch of empty ground in front of the Rimali Mill in Sayyida Zeinab. Third, chatting up girls, going out with them and trying to snatch a cuddle or a kiss. Fourth: weight lifting, on which they spent all their free time trying to bulk up their bodies.

That life was secret, their real life, far from the stupidity and boredom of school. Fawzy could still remember how they'd become friends. One day, he had cut class as usual and gone to play soccer on the triangle. Having left his books on the pavement, he was dribbling a bit on his own to warm up for the game. Then the ebony-skinned, svelte and muscular Mahmud suddenly appeared. In that first time the two played football together, as a result of some well-judged passes from Fawzy, Mahmud scored two out of their side's four goals. At their victory celebrations, everyone stood around drinking iced soda paid for by the losers. As Mahmud was happily sipping his bottle of Sinalco Orange, with a satisfied and grateful look that said, "I wish that I could drink it all the time," Fawzy walked over and introduced himself. They exchanged a hearty handshake and eyed each other slowly up and down like a pair of animals sniffing each other. Then Fawzy cried out, "Well done, Captain Mahmud! A great match. You were great on the attack. And those killer strikes!"

"May God keep you, Captain Fawzy. Thanks!"

Fawzy took a step closer to Mahmud and said, "Looks like you do a lot of lifting."

"As much as I can."

Fawzy reached out and felt his musculature, commenting admiringly, "Great shoulders and traps!"

"Well, I've been working on them a lot. God knows!"

"I've been trying forever but with no results. I just end up tired and then I stop."

A serious look came over Mahmud's face, and he offered to help Fawzy. That same day, Fawzy visited Mahmud at home for the first time. He greeted Mahmud's mother, Umm Said, and kissed her hand,

and then Mahmud took him off to his bedroom at the far end of the large apartment for his first lesson in how to put on some muscle. Mahmud pulled two- and five-kilo dumbbells out from under his bed, with which he demonstrated a few exercises that Fawzy tried. Next, Mahmud lay flat on the floor and disappeared under the bed, and when he reappeared he was dragging something Fawzy had never seen before: one of those big sturdy wooden poles like the one peasants used for stirring the laundry; at either end were attached two identical cans labeled "Authentic Sultan Ghee."

Fawzy looked astonished, but Mahmud chuckled and said, "Well, real metal weights are expensive. I made these myself."

"How?"

"Simple. Just get a heavy wash pole and two empty cans full of cement when it sets. You'll have a perfect set of barbells. Just watch!"

Mahmud dipped his hands into the round tin of talcum powder under the bed and got himself into position. With his feet together and his back straight, he took a few deep breaths and then gracefully leaned over, gripping the pole with both hands. He stayed in that position for a few seconds as he focused himself, before letting out a loud cry, "By the strength of God, let me do it, O mother of miracles!" In one movement he snatched the weights and held them above his head for a few seconds as his face reddened and his arms and neck bulged. Fawzy clapped and cheered, "Bravo, Mahmud. You're really something!"

Mahmud lowered the weights to the ground and let out such a loud roar of victory that Umm Said came rushing in to see what the matter was, but Mahmud simply asked her if she would bring them some mint tea with lots of *qaraqeesh* and cheese. Mahmud promised to give Fawzy a training session at least twice a week, and soon the results of organized and proper weight lifting started to show. Fawzy's biceps got bigger and his abdominals became tighter. After that, the two lads became inseparable, doing everything together. They would meet in front of the school gate in the morning, then slip away to a café far enough from school to be safe, and they would sip tea with milk and smoke a nargileh, trying to decide whether they should see a film, take the tram to the zoo and try to chat up some schoolgirls or just play some soccer on the triangle. They even tried to convince their respective families to let them do their homework together. Aisha agreed immediately, but Umm Said said she would not allow it.

"Listen, son. You are supposed to study with clever people so that you can learn from them. So why on earth would you study with that Fawzy? You're both terrible students!"

Mahmud, however, would not relent, and he whittled away at his mother's resistance. The two boys started doing their homework together every evening, preparing for their sessions as if for a party or the opera. First a long, hot bath, followed by a careful shave. Then they would slather moisturizing lotion on their bodies. With the aid of hair cream, they would comb their hair into a neat part, before dressing and dousing themselves with cologne. Naturally, all these preparations took quite a while. At whoever's flat they met in, they would greet each other as if he were returning from a long trip. Then they would prepare the theater of their drama. First they would check that the floor was spotless, sweeping it if they found even a speck of dust. Removing the clean, ironed cloth from the table, they would check the glass top underneath it for any spots.

One might ask at this point why bother over a few flecks of dust on the floor or a small spot smudged on the tabletop that was covered anyway? What had any of it to do with their homework? In truth, it went against their meticulous nature to overlook these minutiae over which they might spend a whole hour. Then they would sit down facing each other, open their books and get on with their homework. It would generally only take a few minutes for Mahmud to mutter in disgust, "Oh God, my pencil has gone all scratchy!"

At this, Fawzy would stop reading and take the pencil from his friend to check the extent of the problem. Then he would smile and say, "Don't worry, boss! I'll sharpen it for you."

Some might think it is a piece of cake to sharpen a lead pencil, but they could not be more mistaken. Sharpening a lead pencil to get the point just right is a fine art requiring concentration and expertise. Proof of this is the fact that Fawzy Hamama, for all his sharpening powers, often gave the pencil one twist too many in the sharpener, and the worst would happen: the slight cracking sound of the point breaking off. Fawzy would start all over again, while Mahmud sharpened another pencil. The boys would sit there working away until they had a good supply of finely sharpened pencils. After completing this task, which naturally took a good a bit of time, they would set about their homework again, but then, no matter whose apartment they were in, the host felt it his duty to ask the guest whether he would like to eat or drink anything. These were the inviolable rules of etiquette. The requests were usually manifold and very specific: a toasted cheese and tomato sandwich, a plate of mashed fava beans served with spices or fried eggs with pepper and cumin. That would be followed by cups of mint, delicious salep or fenugreek tea, which is known the world over for its excellent nutritional value. The host would go and prepare the food himself, but as a matter of form, the guest would go with him to keep him entertained. And so between sharpening pencils, polishing the glass tabletop, making food and wolfing it down, not to mention trying to come up with yet another new exercise for their shoulders and thighs, evenings spent doing homework passed this way. It should have come as no surprise when they got their marks at year's end that both of them had to repeat that year for the second time in a row. They were not particularly bothered by this, though they resented it when their parents cut off their pocket money for a few weeks as punishment. Fortunately, they had already put some aside for emergencies and survived on it until the sentence was served.

That winter, as the two friends were sitting the same classes for the third time, they hatched a brilliant new plan. They would meet in the early morning and each down a glass of buttermilk, before a hearty breakfast: plate after plate of fava beans, fried liver and eggs, this in order to gain the necessary energy. Afterward, they would go down onto the street in the cold, in short sleeves with the top buttons open. They would head for the Huda Shaarawy Girls School, where—as they stood with their bulging muscles and open-necked shirts show-ing off their thick tufts of chest chair, another blessing that God had granted them—the sight of them would arouse the curiosity of the girls, who, wrapped up in their pullovers against the cold, would chirrup excitedly and flock around them.

One of the girls would call out, "Look at that! They're wearing short sleeves in the middle of winter!"

Fawzy would turn to her and shrug, "What of it?"

"What of it? It's freezing out here."

At that point, Fawzy would puff himself up like a bird and say, "Fortunately, God made us tough."

During these morning struts, they got to know two pretty girls in particular: Nawal and Soraya. They even managed some snogging with them in the back row of the upper circle during the morning show at Cinema al-Sharq. It was typical that the two friends passed their days in utter contentment. In fact, they were simply confirming the old adage which says that a man's happiness comes from within. They took things as they came, unperturbed by what might bother other people. They were totally at ease, precisely because their priorities in life were different from those of the rest of mankind. A muscle that did not respond to training, a girl that turned up late for a date at the cinema, a soccer match lost on the triangle or even a zit one might get on his face—such were the matters that occupied their minds, whereas other benighted souls thought about getting good marks at school.

One week, Fawzy, the brains of the duo, asked his friend, "Mahmud! Have you forgotten our *kushari* bet?"

From time to time they would wager to see who could eat more *kushari*—a dish of rice, lentils, onions and tomato sauce. They would go to the *kushari* café in Tram Street and gobble their way through plate after plate until one of them gave up. A winner would be declared, and the loser, as per their bet, had to pay the bill.

Mahmud smiled and said, "Of course I haven't forgotten. It's always such fun!"

"Do you know that guy Sidqi al-Zalbani?"

"Yeah. I know him."

Al-Zalbani had been a classmate of theirs at the Ali Abd el-Latif School, but he had managed to move ahead and get a place at the Ibrahimiya Secondary School. Fawzy continued, "I've set a date with Sidqi al-Zalbani. Next Friday, please God, after prayers. The three of us are going to the *kushari* café to see who can eat the most. The loser will pay not only for the lot, but he'll have to give a pound to each of the others. Don't you think it's a great idea?"

The torrent of information overwhelmed Mahmud, who could only take things in slowly. A platitudinous smile froze on his dark face as he looked inquiringly at Fawzy, who went over the plan again more slowly this time: Sidqi was the son of Muhammad al-Zalbani, owner of the famous Zalbani Sweet Factory, who had heaps of money. The two friends would easily beat Sidqi in the *kushari* competition, not only getting to eat a huge amount free of charge but getting paid a pound each to do it.

Mahmud finally caught on, and his face relaxed. "Great thinking, boss!"

Friday arrived. The three contestants said their prayers in the Sayyida Zeinab mosque and then headed for the *kushari* café owned by Hagg Subhi, who, according to terms prearranged with Fawzy, had kept a table for them in the far corner, out of sight of the other customers. At the last moment, Sidqi al-Zalbani became hesitant and whispered anxiously, "Let's forget the bet. Why don't we just go to the cinema instead?"

"You're speaking like a child!" Fawzy barked back at him. "We've already agreed, so let's get on with it, or are you so afraid of losing?"

The last remark hardened Sidqi's resolve, and the three cavaliers took up their positions around the table. Fawzy asked the waiter to stay near them, "Listen, brother! We three champions have got colossal appetites. The moment you see an empty plate, clear it away and bring another one. And make sure that you don't keep us waiting!"

"At your service, Master Fawzy," the waiter answered politely, Fawzy sneering back at him, "God protect you! You look healthy enough, but by the Prophet, I'm sure that you'll trip over your long legs when serving us. Anyway, in the name of God, just keep bringing us the *kushari,* will you!"

"Would you three young sirs like medium or large portions?"

Fawzy snorted indignantly and snapped back, "Since when do big cheeses like us eat medium size? What a stupid question."

The waiter apologized for his blunder and rushed off to the kitchen, returning quickly with three large plates of *kushari.* The boys shoveled them down in a trice, whereupon Fawzy called out, "Next one!"

The second round was followed by a third and then a fourth. By the fifth round, Fawzy had expected Sidqi to throw in the towel or at least show signs of slowing down, but he was going full steam ahead as he finished off the fifth plate. In the sixth round, Fawzy managed to finish his plate with some difficulty, and he noticed the color ebbing from Mahmud's face. When he noticed Sidqi still eating like there was no tomorrow, Fawzy realized that the contest would not be a pushover.

The three sat eating in grim silence. Fawzy, hoping to get his breath, ordered a jug of water. He was about to drink it slowly in order to settle his stomach, when Sidqi poured a whole glass down his throat in one go and gave a huge belch before calling out to the waiter, "What's the matter with you? Have you gone to sleep? We're waiting for the seventh round!"

With the first spoonfuls, Fawzy and Mahmud started having obvious problems. They were chewing slowly and finding it difficult to swallow. Sidqi, on the other hand, was sending spoonful after spoonful down his gullet, in a state of complete insouciance. The sight of him shook Fawzy's morale; he felt dizzy and breathless, not to mention that ache in his distended stomach.

"This is a catastrophe!" he thought. "That Sidqi's a ringer. But if I lose, it will be even worse. I've only got ten piastres on me."

11

Aisha had such a thunderous voice that she might as well have shouted her curses through a megaphone, as her every word was audible to the neighbors, passersby and those whiling away their evenings in the coffee shop opposite the apartment building. They all regularly enjoyed a good row. The only person disturbed by it was Said Gaafar. He had put on a white shirt and gray trousers, shaved, combed his hair meticulously and dabbed lavender cologne all over his neck and hands. Then he stood by the front door of his flat, anxiously listening to the argument across the hall, his usual insouciant look wiped from his face. Said was neither brainy like Saleha nor talented like Kamel, but he was also not as dim-witted as Mahmud. He had an alert and organized mind, though he lacked the imagination to fathom anything beyond the immediate scope of his senses. He understood nothing in life that he could not translate into a number. Said saw the world as completely stark, without shadows, one-dimensional. In Said's world, life was just one enormous race for riches. Words of wisdom and tales of other people's achievements were nothing more than chimeras, distractions from the real business of life that could only bring about the sort of misery into which his father, Abd el-Aziz, had fallen. After all, while his father had gone around claiming to be the leader of a clan and a wise Arab elder, he had frittered all his money away on his relatives, only to discover that they were ingrates and not prepared to lift a finger to help him back out of penury. If only his father approached life in a more practical manner, they would not now be living through these hard times. Deep down, Said resented his father for his ridiculous behavior, all the more so since Abd el-Aziz, despite having so little, still maintained a guesthouse on the roof for all those hangers-on from Daraw. He appeared not to have learned his lesson. It was his father's spendthrift behavior that was preventing Said from going to university. Well, he could not deny there was also the matter of his having had to repeat a year at school twice and even so not quite having managed to get the marks necessary for college. But if his father had saved his money instead of squandering it on his good-for-nothing relatives, Said would have been able to afford a private college, and then he would be able to go to university like his younger brother.

Nevertheless, he knew what he had to do and had set himself some very specific goals. If life was a race, then he had to come first. He tried to map out exactly how he could get the desired results. He did everything in a calculated and meticulous way, starting with shaving: after each use he dried the razor blade and put it back in its paper wrapper to keep it from rusting. Likewise with his shoes, which he put back in their original box every night before going to sleep as if he were putting his children to bed. Then there were his savings, which no one knew about. His ceaselessly competitive spirit subjected everything to the dictates of profit and loss. Often, when meeting someone for the first time, after the usual introductions, Said would cock his head and ask, "And how much do you earn?" Usually, the person was so taken aback that he actually answered. Then Said struck with another question, "And how much do you save each month?"

This utterly gauche behavior afforded him great satisfaction when he came out on top after comparing the answer to his own monthly savings. Said subjected everything he did to the same careful scrutiny, except for his relationship with Fayeqa. It was not romantic love but rather physical attraction that made him chase after her, helplessly, like a moth to a flame. Fayeqa simply exuded femininity. It was as if her mother's flawed and aggressive sensuality had been distilled into some pure essence in Fayeqa. Nature grants women sufficient charms to attract a man so that they can bond and form a family, but, without exaggeration, Fayeqa's inherent allure was greater than the sum of its parts. Her every movement and glance could wildly excite a man. Such natural and searing femininity often became a crushing burden for a woman, an unanswered cry for help that left her troubled and overwhelmed. Taking a refreshing hot bath seemed to help. But there too: for Fayeqa, bathing was not just something she did for cleanliness but a ritual in which she celebrated her body. She would check herself all over: the fingernails that she clipped, filed, buffed and painted every day making them look like little works of art; her soft, smooth skin, her jet-black hair, her pale face with its rosy blush. As far as she was concerned, her beauty was not just a blessing but a modus vivendi, and one to be cultivated. Just as a soccer player works on his agility, a violinist practices fingering and a singer does vocal exercises, Fayeqa worked her body as her chief asset and the guarantor of a secure future. Despite her father's stinginess, Fayeqa, through all sorts of clever schemes, had managed to amass a small arsenal of beauty products, her mother's hand-me-downs, some items bought on sale and a few odd gifts in addition to a library of old glamour magazines she had bought for next to nothing from Awad the secondhand bookseller in Tram Street.

One of the most astonishing things was Fayeqa's ability to transform herself completely not only with makeup but with manners. Like a gifted actress, she could blend in to any situation. All she had to do was decide on an emotion and she could embody it. If she wanted to affect sadness, she could weep like a child, and if she wanted to appear happy, everyone would be moved by her sincere delight. Fayeqa was always quarreling with her mother, perhaps because they were so much alike. Sometimes they had violent run-ins, like wild animals disputing territory. At the same time, they were completely in sync and between themselves could communicate with a single glance.

Standing behind the front door of his apartment, Said looked out through the peephole, his mouth dry and his breathing labored in anticipation. As they had agreed, at half-past midnight, Fayeqa would carry a basket with colored laundry up to the roof. She could get away with going up there at that hour by saying that the laundry bin was completely full and that coloreds could not be hung out to dry in the sun without fading. Said was out of sorts that evening. Just a little before his rendezvous with Fayeqa, an enormous argument had broken out between her parents. That meant that he would probably not see her. He was completely crestfallen. He had started the relationship just three months earlier, but she had become indispensable in his life, and he now felt like a child told he couldn't go out to play. The moments Said spent with Fayeqa were his only escape from the daily stress. And so it came to be that he could not imagine life with her. At the end of every date, they would agree on the next one, and that prospect would preoccupy his thoughts. The argument tonight sounded so ferocious that he was sure she would not be able to elude her quarrelsome parents and reach the roof. "Why are you still waiting, Said?" he told himself. "Go to bed, and may God give you strength."

There seemed no point standing by the door. He should go to bed, but he knew his emotions would never let him fall asleep. So he remained glued to that spot, and after a short while, something surprising happened. Ali Hamama stomped out, slamming his front door in the face of Aisha spewing curses. Total silence followed, and Said's hopes sprang up anew. Had his sweetheart already gone to bed? How could she have fallen asleep with that racket going on? True, some people can sleep through anything. But even if she was awake, she would most likely be busy consoling her mother. Maybe she figured that he was no longer waiting anyway. These thoughts went swimming in his head as he stood planted by the door. But then, by God, a miracle happened. His heart almost stopped as he heard the door of Fayeqa's flat opening. He looked through the peephole, and in the dim light of the bulb overhead, he saw her, in all her beauty, with her penciled eyebrows, her cheeks dabbed with blusher and red lipstick on her juicy lips. She closed the door of her flat gently behind her and started climbing the stairs. He shut his eyes in rapture at the sound of her footsteps. After a few moments that seemed like an eternity, he slipped out. He sprang up the stairs to the roof door. It was a dark night, but he could make out her shape as she hung the wash on the line. He rushed over and hugged her tightly, but she brushed him away. That little "don't do that" drove him wild. She always tried to push him away, and he always managed to win her over, wrapping his strong arms around her and feeling the warmth of her full breasts against his body. She would whisper reproachfully, "Said! Are you mad? You'll be the end of me."

Those words, uttered so gently, only served to inflame him, and he would throw himself on top of her, kissing her all over, rubbing himself against her until he could control himself no longer. His volcano extinguished, he would lie there holding her for a while, chatting a little. They would exchange gentle kisses, which would get him so aroused that they would go through the whole performance a second time.

That night Fayeqa seemed different. She seemed a little strange and sullen. Her pushing him away had been unusually forceful. He kept his distance for a few moments trying to gather his thoughts. Then he put his hand on her and asked apprehensively, "What's the matter?"

Fayeqa gave a big sigh, which worried Said even more, and he repeated the question. She answered meekly, "I'm frightened."

"Frightened of what?"

"Frightened of God, because what we do is a sin."

"God won't punish us for being in love."

"Would you like it if your sister, Saleha, fell in love with a man who did to her what you do to me?"

He did not answer, so she shouted angrily, "Of course you have no answer. That's just like you—you worry about your sister's honor, but you don't give a hoot about mine."

As she uttered that last sentence, she burst into tears, and Said could only stand there feeling miserable and not knowing what to do.

She moved away from him and said, "I'm going downstairs now."

"Please don't go," he pleaded, stretching out his hand, but she pushed it away.

"I'm not coming up to the roof again, Said."

"But, Fayeqa, I'm in love with you."

"If you're in love with me, then treat me properly."

"I do treat you properly."

"When you treat someone properly, you meet them in broad daylight."

"What do you mean?"

"I think you know what I mean."

"I told you, I'm going to ask your parents for your hand when the time is right."

"Oh, stop it. Let me go. I'll see you again when the time is right then."

Said watched as she straightened her dress, smoothed her hair and went back the way she came. He walked behind her, in a trance, watching her as she went down the stairs. She stomped down as if to say that she did not want to be near him. Said felt as if he were falling into an abyss.

At the same moment that Fayeqa was going down the stairs back to their apartment, her father, Ali Hamama, was wandering aimlessly around the streets of Sayyida Zeinab, having fled from Aisha, still carrying under his arm the velvet box with the gold necklace that he had grabbed as he stormed out. What should he do now? Where should he go? Instinctively, his footsteps led him to al-Khalfawi tea-shop in Qalat al-Kabsh, which was open all night long. He felt he needed a little space to clear his mind. By God, his head felt like it was about to explode. He went into the tea shop, greeting the customers who variously muttered greetings in return. As soon as Ali Hamama took a seat in the far corner, the black serving boy, Abdu, with his two chipped front teeth and his squinty eye, came over. He set down a freshly rinsed water pipe, along with a tray of clay bowls stuffed with Ali's favorite tobacco. Ali Hamama leaned back against the wall, stretched out his feet as if relaxing after a long trip, took a lump of hashish out of his pocket and said wearily, "Take this, Abdu, and make me two nice strong ones so I can forget everything."

"I hope everything is fine, Hagg Ali."

"The missus is giving me hell, Abdu."

"Same with everyone, Hagg!"

Ali Hamama took the mouthpiece. Feeling so down in the dumps and in need of relief from the hashish, he took a long drag on it, making the charcoal glow. This gratified the squint-eyed Abdu so much that he let go of the mouthpiece, raised both hands above his head as if dancing and started chanting, "Praise to the Prophet! Praise to the Prophet."

The best thing about Abdu was that he did not try to make small talk with the customers. When he noticed that Ali Hamama was deep in thought, he carried on tending to him without a word more. Gradually, the hashish worked its way into Ali Hamama's head, and he could think clearly again. He went over the evening's events in his mind and felt stunned. How could things with Aisha have deteriorated to such a degree? How dare she treat him like that? Thank God he had some hashish to calm his nerves and teach him wisdom. Had he been addicted to alcohol, his nerves would have shattered and he would have killed her with his own hands. By God, that's what she deserved. What do this woman and her children think I am? That pampered and useless Fawzy wants a new suit. Of course he does. But he's not going to get one. A new suit while he keeps failing at school? When he passes his final exams, what'll it be then? A Cadillac?

With a bitter smile, Ali Hamama asked himself, "Do they think I can just print banknotes on a machine in my shop? Every day, it's 'I want this, I want that.' Does everyone think they can just help themselves to my money? Are you kids trying to get your inheritance while I'm still alive? Bloody bastards!" He smoked ten bowls of tobacco, one after the other, then got up to go and pay al-Khalfawi, the tea shop owner. His bill was less than half what it should have been, as a result of a complicated agreement whereby purchases from his grocery were set against the cost of the tobacco he smoked there. As he left the tea shop, he felt as free as a bird and as finely tuned as a perfect musical phrase. He set off slowly, swaying from side to side, but still clutching the box with the necklace. Gradually, he started to see the situation in a new light. Aisha was his wife, and he knew her only too well. She was as stubborn as a donkey, and when angry, she was the worst sort of harridan created by God, fully capable of causing considerable damage. He could never forget the day she took a pair of scissors to his beautiful brand-new galabiyya. In the end, there was no might nor power except in Allah. What was the point, then, in continuing to provoke Aisha? Her capacity to do him evil was unequaled, and her obstinacy beggared belief.

"Right. I'm going to be better than her. I'll be the noble, forgiving one."

So it was decided. He would just tell her off this time so that she would realize that she'd been at fault and not do it again. But instead of plotting revenge on Aisha, he started thinking how he could make her happy. It was actually not because he was afraid of her or feeling unusually compassionate that Ali Hamama's mood changed but because he was so aroused that it almost hurt. Hashish sent his sexual imagination into overdrive, but he could never imagine sex with any woman but his wife. For a quarter of a century, he had not been to bed with any other woman, not out of propriety but because Aisha used up so much of his energy. Her fondness for sex and her amazing skills under the covers had always kept the spark in their marriage. Ali Hamama made a half-hour detour to the Tahira sweet shop and then went home to find the light still on in the bedroom. He tried to open the door, but it was locked from the inside. He gave the door a few friendly yet persistent taps with his finger, but Aisha did not respond. He was certain that she was still awake. He leaned against the door and said quietly, "Open the door, Aisha."

She did not answer, so he tried again with a jollier voice. "Ayooo-sha. Open the door, sweetheart. Please don't do this. Let's not act childish."

"Have you brought the magistrate with you?"

Her voice was angry but also soft and seductive. Feigning surprise, Ali Hamama asked, "The magistrate? What do we need a magistrate for?"

"To divorce us!"

"Don't be so silly, my little missus. How could I divorce you after so long?"

"You don't want to divorce me, but you took my necklace? I tell you what, mister. Let's get a divorce and go our separate ways."

The indifference in her voice drove him wild with excitement. Quaking with desire, he called out, "Ayooosha. It's time to stop these foolish games. We both rubbed each other up the wrong way, but it's over now. Do you think I would take your velvet box after a lifetime of happiness? I'll buy you another. You're worth your weight in gold."

"Oh my, dear me! Do you think I was born yesterday? I'm not like you, Ali Hamama!"

She spoke that last sentence with such languor that he almost burst with anticipation and called out, "Open the door, sweetheart, Aisha. Don't do this. You can't leave me in this state. I brought you something . . . a half pound of *basbousa* with clotted cream from Tahira's. It's all for you—I already had a piece, thank God. And as for the jacket for Fawzy, well, I'll buy it for him on Friday, please God."

That was what is called, in diplomatic negotiations, a compromise with an indemnity. All it took was a half pound of the *basbousa* with clotted cream, which Aisha adored, to make her accept his substitution of the suit by a jacket. Bull's-eye! Ali Hamama heard the sound of a sigh, then footsteps, followed by the click of the door being unlocked and opening slowly.

SALEHA

"Are those ballet shoes dyed?" Miss Suad said tersely.

I looked at her in silence. I was trying my best not to cry. After a moment, Miss Suad repeated the question, louder this time, "Answer me! Those ballet shoes have been dyed, haven't they?"

Choking back my tears, I answered feebly, "Yes, Miss Suad."

She looked away and waved me off.

"All right. Get back in line."

At that moment, I hated Miss Suad from the bottom of my heart. I hated her because she kept on about a completely trivial matter. I hated her because she had made me put pressure on my father, made him even more aware of his poverty, and only then dismisses it all as nothing. Had she punished me, expelled me from the class, that would have been better. Instead, she just wanted to come across as Miss Compassionate, having already called attention to our poverty. Now, she could just let me off to take my place in the line. Back to my place I dragged my feet along in those awful dyed ballet shoes, almost falling over myself in anger and embarrassment.

After that day, being at school felt like a festering wound. I tried to forget my pain by studying as hard as I could. That was the only way I could help my father, as Kamel had said. I would be first in the class and show him that all his sacrifice had not been in vain. I would lock my bedroom door and spend hours studying, but my zeal for learning had acquired a rather bitter taste. In some way, I was taking revenge. I would do well in my lessons in order to affirm my existence. It was true that we were so poor that my father could not pay the school fees or buy the ballet shoes, but I was cleverer than all my classmates put together. I was top of the class in our midyear exams. As I handed my report certificate to my father for him to countersign, a strange feeling came over me, as if I had just run a huge distance and was now standing there panting. My father smiled as he picked up his pen. Without saying a word, he got up and put his hands on my shoulders, "Saleha! I'm so proud of you. I hope God lets me live long enough to see you teaching at university."

"Why do you think I'll end up teaching in a university?"

"I don't know. I can just imagine you giving lectures to the students."

His words touched me, and I agreed enthusiastically, "Then you will see me teaching at university one day, I promise."

I continued studying my heart out and was top of the class at the end of the year too. During the summer holiday, I didn't ask my father for pocket money or to take me on outings as I used to do. I was happy to stay at home, helping my mother and waiting for Kamel to come home at night. Then we would talk for a long time. Kamel was the person who understood me best in the whole world. I loved chatting with him. He would talk about anything with me: politics, art, literature. He used to tell me excitedly, "Egypt is a great country, Saleha, but it has not seized the moment. The Occupation has kept us all down, but if we expel the English, we can build a strong new democratic country."

He used to read classical and modern verse aloud to me. I loved to listen to him explaining the love poems. I'll never forget certain verses of Andalusian poetry. I adored the one that read:

> *If my sin is allowing love to be my master, then all nights*
> *of love are sin,*
> *I repent of the sin, but when God forgives me, for you*
> *I atone.*

Could a man love a woman so much? As Kamel was explaining the verse to me, my imagination was set loose. Should a man ever love me to that extent, I would grant him my body and soul. I would be ready to live and die for him. I was by nature excitable, subject to wild emotions and mood swings. Sometimes I felt cheerful for no reason, but mostly I just felt depressed and would lock myself in my bedroom and cry. Then I started having dreams every night, but when I woke up, I could never remember what they were. Every last trace of them would disappear from my memory, leaving me sad and gloomy. Then the same dream started recurring two or three times a week. It is strange that a person can have the same dream again and again, but it was even stranger that I could remember the details of this one. I can still recall it with astonishing clarity. It starts off with me walking between two rows of trees in a beautiful park. Wherever I look, I can see pretty flowers in all colors, the smell of jasmine every-where. I feel like I don't have a worry in the world. Then my father suddenly appears from a side path; wearing a clean white galabiyya, he looks as relaxed and carefree as he did in his youth. His white teeth glisten as he smiles and holds his hand out to me, saying, "Come with me, Saleha."

I feel enveloped in a sense of security as I take his hand and feel its warmth. He pulls me along behind him, down the side path. I am laughing, hoping that I can stay with him forever. He stops between the shadow of two trees, smiles and says,

"Look at me."

Then I notice that his left ear is missing, and I scream in terror, but he just whispers calmly, "Don't worry, Saleha. I'm all right."

I point at his missing ear and try to speak. I try to tell my father that his ear has disappeared, but I cannot get my throat to utter a sound. He puts his arms around me and leans over to kiss my head, and as I feel his lips touching my forehead, I wake up.

12

Try as he might, Mahmud could hardly finish his seventh plate of *kushari*. His eyes bulged, and his head lolled forward as he wheezed like an exhausted bull. Both Fawzy and Mahmud felt sick from overeating and both secretly regretted ever having come up with the bet. But that damned Sidqi al-Zalbani ordered an eighth round and immediately started eating it, so Fawzy and Mahmud did not have a moment to catch their breath. They continued cramming *kushari* into their stuffed bellies, desperately trying to keep up. Sidqi cleaned his plate and seemed delighted at the sight of his competitors struggling.

Suddenly, Mahmud threw his spoon down onto the plate with a clang. He let his big head roll forward and put his hands on his stomach, crying out, "Oh, my stomach. My stomach. My stomach's killing me."

Fawzy was in no better shape, though it showed on him differently. He was having difficulty breathing, he felt dizzy and rivulets of sweat were running down his face.

Sidqi just looked at the two of them and laughed. "Tough luck, guys. I've won."

"How do you know?" said Mahmud, still holding on to his stomach.

Sidqi looked at him almost sympathetically and said, "All right, Mahmud. Let's carry on with the ninth round."

"Can't," said Mahmud, giving a large groan, and Fawzy's silence confirmed their defeat.

Sidqi laughed again and said, "Well, that means you've got to pay the bill, and don't forget you each owe me a pound."

They remained silent until Fawzy cleared his throat and said in a friendly way, "Of course. We have to pay, but unfortunately we weren't expecting to."

"What do you mean by that?" Sidqi shot back at him.

"Please, Sidqi," Fawzy whined, "could you pay the bill and, God willing, we'll pay you back as soon as we can?"

"If you can't pay, why did you make the bet?"

"Don't get all uppity with us!"

"I'll get however I want with you!"

"Oh, do I have to teach you some manners?"

Fawzy was trying to turn it into an argument because he was sure that he and Mahmud, in spite of being completely exhausted and stuffed to the gills, could take Sidqi on in a fight. Then this tricky situation would be just a quarrel that sooner or later would end with a truce. There was the added complication, however, that the waiter had overheard them discussing the bill and scuttled off to tell Hagg Subhi, the owner of the café, who rushed over to them panting and shouting, "The bill, gents! You've had twenty-four large plates of *kushari*."

Mahmud said nothing, but Fawzy smiled and answered, "Of course Mr. Subhi. We'll pay the bill immediately, with a kiss on top of it."

"Forget the kiss, you waste of space. I want what I'm owed!" Hagg Subhi snarled, looking as if he was about to pounce.

But feigning a jovial air, Fawzy replied, "Don't worry. The bill is going to get paid, God willing. Believe me. Of course, you know Mr. Sidqi al-Zalbani?

Hagg Subhi glowered at them, appearing unwilling to allow the conversation to move away from the topic of the bill.

Fawzy gestured at Sidqi, saying, "Hagg Subhi. I'd like you to meet our friend Sidqi, son of Hagg Muhammad al-Zalbani, owner of the famous al-Zalbani sweet factory. Naturally, you will have heard of him . . ."

Hagg Subhi barked back at him, "Listen, sunshine! I've never heard of al-Zalbani, or al-Talbani for that matter. You owe me for twenty-four large plates of *kushari*!"

Fawzy smiled and wincing at his tone said, "Give us a moment, sir. Our brother Sidqi al-Zalbani is going to pay right away."

Sidqi had already stood up and said in a loud voice so that everyone could hear, "Listen, Hagg Subhi. Let's settle this like gentlemen."

Hagg Subhi roared back at him, "Oh, so you want to settle this like gentlemen?"

"Yes. Have I made any sort of arrangement with you?"

"No."

"All right then, Hagg. The bill will be paid by these two who made the arrangement with you. Good-bye."

Sidqi dropped this bombshell and walked away. Fawzy called after him despairingly, "Wait! Sidqi. Come back. I want to tell you something."

But Sidqi ignored him and left the restaurant.

Hagg Subhi turned to Fawzy, shouting, "All right now. You made the arrangement, you have to pay the bill."

"Mr Subhi, I'll pay it. I promise you. But please give me twenty-four hours."

"Twenty-four hours, my arse!"

That was the signal for five enormous waiters and busmen to gather around the table. They had been trained for such a situation, and they performed beautifully. The owner, Hagg Subhi, grabbed Fawzy by the collar, jerking his head back and bellowing, "Either you pay now or you'll regret that your father ever met your mother!"

In a final attempt to calm the waters, Fawzy asked Hagg Subhi to let him go with the restaurant's employees to his father's shop on al-Sadd Street, where the elder Hamama would gladly pay the bill. Hagg Subhi gave this some thought, although his glowering face did not change one iota. He gave a signal, and his men clustered around Mahmud and Fawzy, who were so large and muscular that each required three of the restaurant men to frog-march him out of the restaurant. On the street, they were stopped repeatedly by people asking them, with thinly veiled curiosity and feigned concern, "Is everything all right? What's going on?"

When the employees explained what had happened, some pass-ersby just laughed, and others dished out suggestions as to what should be done with the boys. A skinny man in his fifties wearing slippers and a faded and old blue galabiyya almost in tatters around his shoulders listened to the story with a scowl; he looked at the pair and said timidly, "What a pair of filthy swindlers!" And then, out of nowhere, he walloped Fawzy's face, to which the fettered lad responded with a torrent of obscenities as Mahmud tried to wriggle out of his captors' hold to retaliate. But they held him all the tighter, dragging them all the way to Ali Hamama's shop.

It was almost three in the afternoon, and Ali Hamama was sitting, as always, behind the shabby counter. As the group entered, silence fell in the shop, and the customers cleared a path for them. Ali Ha-mama was squinting wildly to try to make out what was happening before his eyes, and at last he shouted hoarsely, "What's this all about, Fawzy?"

Fawzy, too stunned to speak, just stood there looking rueful while the restaurant staff gripped him ever more tightly. One of the café men volunteered to tell the tale, which he did in a voice loud and clear enough for everyone in the shop to hear. Old Ali Hamama listened without showing any further emotion. His face wore that impassive expression with which he usually met the world. He stood up slowly and walked over to the group, deliberately, as if he were going to the toilet, and then, standing face-to-face with Fawzy, he gave him an enormous and loud slap on the face.

"So, it's not enough for you to fail at school and be a general dis-appointment! I just have to sit here and you go out losing me money! There's not a brain in that skull of yours, you bloody moron."

Bedlam broke out as all the customers started jostling forward to try to calm the situation. But Ali Hamama, having now slapped Fawzy and Mahmud a few times over, turned to the café employees and asked them, "How much did they eat?"

"Twenty-four large plates."

Old Ali Hamama squinted in disbelief, "How many?"

"Twenty-four—large ones."

The old man raised his hands into the air as if about to do a jig, while making obscene gestures with his fingers and crying out, "I'd like to try to understand this, please God! I wasn't born yesterday. How can three boys eat twenty-four plates of *kushari*? Explain!"

The employees tried to explain the bet to Ali Hamama, but he refused to listen and kept insisting that he simply could not believe they had eaten so much. Some arduous negotiations followed, which kept coming up against this dead end, and whereupon the customers intervened to get them moving again. At last, Ali Hamama announced that he would pay for ten plates but no more. The café men, enraged, rejected the offer, but Ali Hamama simply retreated quietly to his seat and cocooned himself in silence, leaving them to continue clamoring. Finally, he said calmly, "Either you take the money for ten plates or you can take these boys to the police station and let the law teach them a lesson." Then waving off Fawzy and Mahmud, he said, "Now, you two, get out of my sight and let me get on with earning a living."

For half an hour Ali Hamama gave no further thought to the *kushari* problem. He directed his shop assistant that business carry on as if nothing had happened. From his seat behind the counter, Ali did likewise, reeling off the items for purchase so the cashier could tally them. This retreat achieved its aim, and one of the café men scurried back to the café to ask Hagg Subhi's opinion about the offer proposed by Ali Hamama. He sped back with Hagg Subhi's consent to accept payment for ten plates, allowing that God would somehow compensate them for the rest. At this point, Ali Hamama progressed to stage two of his plan and announced that for the moment he was short of petty cash but that as a trustworthy man who put the worship of God above that of men, he would pay them in kind. There was a further wringing of hands and rumble of protestation, but eventually the café men left the shop with three small pots of honey and various packages of cheese, butter, dried beef slices and pickled cucumbers.

13

It proved to be very difficult for Abd el-Aziz Gaafar to obtain extra work at the Club. He had not the slightest experience in service, and it was out of the question for a man over fifty to be sent to the training school. Moreover, Alku, as a matter of principle, avoided hiring on the basis of a recommendation, as it wouldn't do for an employee to have a divided allegiance or a false sense of security. Comanus was aware of all that and tried a different tack. He went to see Mr. Wright, who, despite his hauteur, actually treated him decently, because Comanus was, after all, Greek and not Egyptian. Comanus explained Abd el-Aziz's difficult circumstances and how his salary hardly covered his family's needs. A half-supercilious, half-sympathetic smile appeared on Mr. Wright's face, as if he were listening to a child's prattle.

"The Automobile Club cannot help everyone who is a bit hard up. We are not a charity."

"But Abd el-Aziz is a trustworthy and hardworking man."

"Well, that's only thanks to you."

"Sir?"

"An Egyptian only works in exchange for a reward or out of fear. There is no such thing as self-motivation in the Egyptian psyche. If an Egyptian manages to carry out his duties properly, it is only because a European manager has trained him well."

"Mr. Wright. Do you consider me a friend?"

"Yes, of course."

"Well then, shouldn't friends help each other out from time to time?"

"What are you driving at?"

"I would like Abd el-Aziz to work as an assistant to Suleyman the doorman."

"Let me think it over."

"Suleyman is over seventy and needs an assistant. I am just asking you to allow Abd el-Aziz to stand with Suleyman at the entrance. The Club will not have to pay him, but he could earn a little extra in tips."

Wright thought it over for a few moments, puffed out a thick cloud of pipe smoke and said, "I'll agree, on one condition."

"What is that?"

"I don't want to hear his name ever again. If I hear a single complaint about him, I'll fire him, and you won't be able to protect him."

"I give you my word."

Wright nodded in agreement. Comanus got up, thanked him warmly and shook his hand, but just as he was leaving, he turned and asked, "Do I need to tell Alku?"

Mr. Wright stared incredulously. "If the general manager of the Automobile Club has given his word, I don't think you need to go and get the agreement of the head chamberlain," he replied.

That was just the answer that Comanus wanted. It meant that Mr. Wright would take it upon himself to inform Alku, who would not dare to disagree. Comanus, delighted at having achieved his mission, went back to tell Abd el-Aziz, who was deeply grateful. The following day, he went out for the first time to stand in the doorway of the Club. He already knew Suleyman the doorman because he came from the village of Kom Ombo, which was near Daraw in Upper Egypt. Despite their acquaintance, however, Abd el-Aziz knew from experience that working together with people one knows, even a close relative, called for a different set of rules. Suleyman gave him a warm welcome and appeared happy to have him there. By the end of the day, it was clear to Abd el-Aziz that working the door did not require any special skills. Suleyman's job was completely symbolic. He was a human salute. He would sit on a bench outside the door of the club, and as soon as a member's car hove into view, he would jump up and shuffle over, opening the door with a bow and say with the utmost deference, "It's an honor to have you here, Your Excellency."

Then His Excellency would get out of the car in a state of such high-handedness that he would hardly notice Suleyman, yet despite this distracted and oblivious state, he would still stretch out his hand to tip Suleyman, who would bow, utter some words of gratitude and call for God's blessing upon His Excellency and then shuffle along behind the man until he reached the lift.

That was how Suleyman welcomed the members, who at the start of the evening arrived in droves, and how he would see them off as they left. As soon as an esteemed Club member stepped out of the lift, he would hurry over, bowing as he went, and then rush ahead to open the car door and collect his tip, which was generally double the arrival gratuity, since by that time of night members were typically a little sloshed. As for those who were really drunk, Suleyman would help them along, and if they were being difficult, he would take charge of them firmly but politely, not letting them go until they had reached the safety of their cars. He did all that with infinite humility, even if the drunken Excellency was out of control, shouting, cursing and behaving irrationally. If the Club member was tottering about, Suleyman would hold him up with both arms, and even if he had to put the poor man's arms over his shoulders and drag him along, he did it with such aplomb that the inebriated Club member's dignity was not dented, allowing him to wake up the following morning without feeling humiliated or mistreated.

Abd el-Aziz had spent a few days observing Suleyman at work, when one day they were sitting together on the bench, and he seized the opportunity to speak, "I'm going to ask Comanus to find me a different job."

"Why, Abd el-Aziz? Has something upset you?" Suleyman asked worriedly, but Abd el-Aziz smiled and tried to reassure him.

"Not at all. But you can do this job perfectly well on your own. You don't need anyone to help you."

Suleyman insisted that he did in fact need Abd el-Aziz's help and that between the two of them they would earn more than enough tips, for God provides man's sustenance. After some further discussion, they agreed upon a new modus operandi. When Suleyman rushed over to welcome a member, Abd el-Aziz would follow him and stand a little behind him, following Suleyman's lead. He would bow to His Excellency and mutter the same words of welcome. Abd el-Aziz carried on this way for a few days, but not a single member acknowledged him. They continued dealing with Suleyman and ignored the new man completely. He was taken aback by this, and though Suleyman insisted that this was natural at the start because members did not yet know him, this treatment continued for a whole week, leading Suleyman to suggest at last that they change places. Abd el-Aziz would now rush over to the car and open the door, bowing in welcome as Suleyman stood behind him. What was strange was that most of the members continued to ignore Abd el-Aziz. They walked right past him bowing, focusing their attention on Suleyman and giving him the tip. Just why did the Club members continue to ignore Abd el-Aziz?

It might have been because of his appearance. Perhaps because of his height and his proud look. Perhaps it was because he did not give the necessary impression of being a servant, as his face did not exude the wheedling and docility by which servants got their tips. When Abd el-Aziz bowed to a Club member, he looked as if he was acting, as if he thought himself an equal and was only feigning subservience. The plan had failed, so Abd el-Aziz stopped greeting the members and went back to standing behind Suleyman. At the end of the week, Suleyman surprised him by handing him two pounds. Abd el-Aziz refused to take it, but Suleyman pushed the money into his pocket and said, "This is your money. Don't offend me by refusing it."

"My money? How did I earn it? I haven't done a thing."

Suleyman laughed and continued, "I don't do anything either. We just run to open and close doors for people."

Abd el-Aziz objected, but Suleyman told him firmly, "It's to feed your children, Abd el-Aziz. You get a third and I get two-thirds."

Thus, when Abd el-Aziz finished his work in the storeroom, he would go and sit next to Suleyman. They would chat and drink tea, and whenever Suleyman went to greet a member, Abd el-Aziz would stand behind him, and then, at the end of the week, he would take his share of the tips. It was a tidy sum, and Suleyman always treated him fairly. There was nothing about Suleyman that Abd el-Aziz could complain about, but deep inside something was vexing him. He felt a constant sense of hurt, which he would try to suppress by chatting with Suleyman and having a few laughs. But he remained distressed.

He felt degraded. He had lost his dignity. Every time he thought that he could not sink any lower, he discovered that he had to. Having lost all that he had ever owned, he had left Daraw and come to Cairo. Before he got the job in the storeroom, he had been convinced that there was virtue to manual labor, but now he had become a servant. Could he describe what he was doing in any other way? He was a servant who opened doors, bowed and stood in the street hustling for tips, little better than a beggar. What an end for a son of the illustrious Gaafar lineage. For years he had given charity to the poor of Daraw, but now he himself had joined the ranks of the needy. He consoled himself that he would not be a servant for long, that in a few months his son Said would graduate from technical college and that in two years' time his son Kamel would get his law degree. When that happened, he would be able to depend on some help from them and go back to working in the storeroom only or perhaps even retire with dignity.

Abd el-Aziz worked the door for three weeks, during which time Alku made a number of visits. It was always the same: the moment Alku's black Cadillac appeared in the distance, Suleyman would jump up. He would scurry over as fast as possible to open the car door, with Abd el-Aziz directly behind him. Alku would ease himself regally out of the car, ignoring Abd el-Aziz, giving Suleyman a fleeting and glowering glance and grunting something that passed for a greeting. One time, feeling magnanimous, he actually said something to Suleyman. It was so indistinct, but it might have been something like "Good evening" or "How are you, Suleyman." This gave Suleyman a rush of joy. Alku hardly ever spoke with the servants except to give orders or to dress them down, so any word spoken with any other intent was met like a good omen. Alku's presence never filled Abd el-Aziz with dread, as it did all the other serving staff. Abd el-Aziz would bow respectfully while telling himself, "Why should I be afraid of him? He has no reason to be angry with me."

Deep down, Abd el-Aziz felt that he did not really belong at the Automobile Club. Circumstances had obliged him to work there temporarily. He considered himself more like a passenger on a train. No matter how irritating the other passengers, he had to put up with them because he would eventually reach his destination and leave them behind forever. Not only that, but he felt that Comanus afforded him some protection because Alku, for all his arrogant posturing, went to pieces when dealing with foreigners.

Did Alku perceive this lack of fear in Abd el-Aziz? Did he feel that Abd el-Aziz had greeted him in a manner that however respectful was devoid of submissiveness? Could he see something in Abd el-Aziz's face that gave away his sense of dignity? Or might Alku have held a grudge over Comanus's having gone above him to Mr. Wright to get Abd el-Aziz the job on the door? Perhaps Alku was just in a particularly foul mood that evening.

These questions remain unanswered even though there are a hundred ways of recounting the event. It was midnight. Alku's car was met with the usual hubbub. Suleyman rushed over, followed by Abd el-Aziz. As the car door opened, Abd el-Aziz had the odd feeling that the air had become heavy. He felt as if the usual rhythm of life had been interrupted, replaced by something strange and oppressive. Alku stepped out of the car, but instead of casting a cursory glance at them and continuing into the Club, as he always did, he just stood there with fat, trembling Hameed at his side, staring at Suleyman and Abd el-Aziz. There was a tense silence. Alku started scrutinizing Abd el-Aziz as if he were looking at some strange creature for the first time, and then, gesturing toward him, he called out incredulously, "Who is this guy?"

The question came out of nowhere. It broke Alku's accustomed silence toward the servants and was a clear declaration of war. Alku knew very well who Abd el-Aziz was. He had seen him numerous times before, so why was he now pretending not to know him? Why such an angry, incredulous tone of voice? Abd el-Aziz felt a sharp pain in his head, his hands turned cold and his breathing became labored.

Suleyman was perplexed and stood there saying nothing, which led Alku to thunder at him, "Who is this guy? Answer me, Suleyman."

Overcome with fear, Suleyman could only stutter out his answer, "Your Excellency, Alku. He is your servant Abd el-Aziz Gaafar, the assistant of Monsieur Comanus in the storeroom. He also assists me at the door to earn a little extra because he is going through some hard times and has a family to support."

Alku continued staring Abd el-Aziz up and down as if he heard nothing of what Suleyman said. His anger was building, perhaps because Abd el-Aziz was not quaking with fear and had not rushed forward to pay obeisance or perhaps because Suleyman appeared so sympathetic to Abd el-Aziz, a sentiment that Alku knew could lead to insubordination. Alku gave a loud grunt, and Hameed, like a well-trained hunting dog, picked up on the signal immediately. He went right over to Abd el-Aziz, fixed him with a glower and asked in his high-pitched unctuous voice, "Have you got the key to the storeroom, you piece of scum?"

Abd el-Aziz was startled. He felt his mouth go dry at being spoken to in this way by someone who was young enough to be his son. He said nothing. Hameed took the humiliation one step further, "Are you deaf? I asked you if you've got the key to the storeroom!"

"Yes," replied Abd el-Aziz, trying to control his anger. Hameed continued to stare contemptuously and said, "Then run and get your master, Alku, a box of Havana cigars."

Abd el-Aziz remained silent. He turned quickly and started toward the storeroom. He knew where the cigars were kept and wanted to fetch them to stop the insults from being piled on him, but before he could take a single step, Hameed shouted at him, "You do know what Havana cigars are, don't you, you donkey?"

Abd el-Aziz turned around and answered firmly, "I am not a donkey. I am a human being like you."

Hameed grunted and relaxed, as if he had finally made the point. Standing right next to Abd el-Aziz, he shouted in his face, "You are a donkey, and I'm going to teach you some manners."

KAMEL

I pieced together the details of what had happened that day.

Hameed called over Labib the telephonist and Idris the waiter. The two held my father to still him as Hameed slapped him across the face, shouting, "You have no right to do that. You have no right to do that."

Witnesses to the incident confirmed to me that Hameed slapped my father until his nose bled. After Alku and Hameed had left, my father's colleagues gathered around him. They sat him down and wiped the blood from his face with a damp cloth. Idris and Labib tried to console him. They felt guilty for having held him to receive the slaps.

Idris said weakly, "Don't worry, Uncle Abd el-Aziz. We have all been through it. Alku beats the stuffing out of all of us."

My father nodded but said nothing. Idris put his arms around him and whispered, "By the Prophet, please don't be upset with me. I had no choice."

Labib then declaimed, "Sometimes Alku is harsh with us, but he has a good heart and he looks after us like a father."

He added that sentence as a precaution. If Alku came to hear about them consoling my father, then Labib would at least be able to provide a defense for himself. My father just mumbled a few platitudes about not being angry with his colleagues. He shook their hands as he got up and seemed to be in a hurry to leave the Club.

According to my mother, he arrived home at around two in the morning. He got changed, made his ablutions and said his prayers before sitting down to eat his dinner. My mother noticed that he appeared downcast, but when she asked him about it, he just said he was tired out and wanted to go to bed. My mother went into the kitchen to make him a glass of lemon juice with mint, but when she returned to the sitting room, she found him at the table, the tray of food in front of him untouched and his head lolling backward. She walked over to him, shook him gently and called his name, but he just gave a weak groan. His eyes were half open. My mother screamed and rushed outside to ask our neighbors to come and help. Aisha came immediately. She poured some ammonia onto a cloth and held it under his nose. Then she dripped some sugar water into his mouth. The ambulance arrived about half an hour later. After examining him carefully, the doctor said that there was no hope. My father died before his fifty-second birthday. He just gave up the ghost. He had struggled along with honor and pride until he was delivered a mortal blow.

I went through a period of denial, as if the news of my father's death was patently a fabrication with no basis in reality. It was a joke for him to have died like that. It went against all the rules. It was a sudden unilateral breach of trust. It was not fair that you could build your whole life around the presence of one person and then without forewarning have to face his sudden and senseless disappearance. I could not cry for my father until some months after his death. I felt a sadness greater than anything I could express. And I was caught in a slough of inaction. It takes us some time to absorb the great tragedies that hit us like thunderbolts, and it might take you years to grasp what it means when your father dies. Your father's death means that you are left alone and naked, unprotected and insignificant, with no buffer against the vicissitudes of life. You feel like a victim of a fate, which, like some enormous mythological bird, has cast its shadow over you, making you realize that death comes to one and all, sometimes sooner rather than later. It is disorientating to have spoken to your father in the morning, to have chatted and laughed with him, only to come home in the evening and find that he is a corpse for you to lower into the earth the following day. It is astonishing to find that your father, that robust being who has always been the mainstay of your life, has suddenly turned into a memory and that every time you mention his name, you have to add, "May God have mercy on his soul."

During my father's funeral, I experienced a strange *froideur,* as if I were observing everything from behind a thick glass screen. I made a point of walking with the coffin all the way to the cemetery, deliberately trying to make myself feel as much pain as possible. When I saw the gloom of his prepared grave, I was taken aback, unable to take my eyes off the dark and dank hole in the earth. This was the end of the line, the last station. This whole fierce and violent struggle into which our lives plunge us ends up here in this hole. Here, everything is equal. Happiness and misery. Poverty and wealth. Beauty and ugliness. We can only bear to live our lives to the extent that we can avoid thinking about death. If death were constantly in our thoughts, if we were constantly aware it could come at any moment, we would not be able to live a single day.

With my father's death, a chapter in our family life came to a close, and a new one began. Apart from Said, who was always in his own world, we all changed. We were fractured. We were orphaned. Is orphanhood the loss of a parent, or is it a feeling, an expression, a type of behavior, or is it all those things?

For the first few days, my mother cried unceasingly and continued talking as if she could see him, "Why have you left us on our own, Abduh?"

There was reproach in her voice, as if she was angry at him for having made his mind up to die. Gradually, my mother exhausted all her tears and became a little calmer, but her whole manner changed. She became cold and brusque. She turned from wife into widow. The loving glances she used to give us, with a twinkle in her eye, whenever she was happy, had now disappeared forever. Her beautiful brown face took on the dejected and frightened expression of someone dealt a hard blow and who was not about to let it happen again.

I came home from university that evening, and she told me, "Be ready tomorrow. We're going to the Automobile Club to claim what they owe your late father."

The next day, I went with my mother to the office of Mr. James Wright, the general manager of the Club. Our appearance elicited sincere expressions of sorrow among the staff, and I shook hands with them one by one. They all came to express their condolences: the doormen, the waiters, Monsieur Comanus, Maître Shakir, Yusuf Tarboosh. Even Rikabi the chef rushed over to us in his white uniform and toque, shaking my mother's hand and putting his arms around me. The staff's welcome and sympathy could not, however, hide the fact of tension in the air. There was something that they were not saying, but it was apparent on their faces. The most honest was Bahr the barman, who, as he pressed my hand, said, "May God have mercy upon your father. His passing is a huge loss for us. He was a true man. May God punish those who wronged him."

Mr. Wright received us in his office with calculated civility. He bowed and shook my mother's hand in condolence, then gestured to us to take a seat. He spoke slowly, articulating carefully to help us understand his poor Arabic. From the outset I felt his courtesy was mere formality. He seemed entirely without feeling, operating within his officious parameters. It was apparent that he had decided to act within some very limited parameters.

My chair was a little way from him, whereas my mother was sitting right next to him and came straight to the point: "We have come to ask you for what my late husband was entitled to."

As if expecting the question, he answered without hesitation, "You are entitled to his end-of-service payment. I will have it sent to your home within the next two days at the latest."

My mother pursed her lips and looked straight at him. "And what about my late husband's pension?"

"Unfortunately, there is no pension."

As Mr. Wright uttered that sentence, his blue eyes shot us an admonitory look. We were testing his limits.

"My late husband worked at the Club for more than five years. How can you leave his children without a pension?"

"We will pay everything we owe you."

"The end-of-service payment, however much that is, will keep us going for a few days or months. Our security depends on his pension, to which we are entitled."

It surprised me that my mother neither pleaded nor begged but rather declared her rights with her head held high. Mr. Wright's face flushed, and in a tone of growing impatience, he replied, "I would like to be able to help you, but my hands are tied by the rules and bylaws of the Club, which make no provision for a pension."

"Then the rules and bylaws are unjust."

"Well, that's as it may be, but we cannot go against them."

My mother smiled derisively. "Did they just fall down from the sky?"

Wright gave her an uneasy look. He held up a finger in warning. "I beg your pardon!"

My mother paid no heed and continued angrily, "When you die, will the Club not pay your pension to your children?"

Wright was surprised by that question, but he took it in stride. He had a harsh look and was relishing the condescension of his considered reply, "Yes. There will be a pension for my family when I die. However, in your case, there is no pension. You are entitled to his end-of-service lump sum and that is all."

"And why would that be?"

"Because the Automobile Club has no pension plan for Egyptians. Only for Europeans."

"Aren't Egyptians flesh and blood like Europeans? Don't their children need support like the children of the Europeans, of the *khawagas*?"

"What you are saying may be correct, but it was Europeans who invented the automobile and introduced it to Egypt. It was Europeans who founded the Automobile Club and who manage it whereas Egyptians only work here as menials. Egyptians and Europeans cannot possibly enjoy the same rights."

There was a moment's silence in which I felt nothing but loathing for Mr. Wright. My mother stood up and, her voice quivering with emotion, said, "I shall get my husband's pension. You will see for yourself."

"I wish you good luck."

"We will get what we are entitled to, even if it means going to court, Mr. Wright."

At that moment, Mr. Wright decided she had gone too far, and he shouted back, "Is that a threat?"

"It is not a threat. I am simply telling you what I am going to do."

My mother stormed out of the office with me behind her. In the entrance of the club, some of the staff were waiting for us. My mother told them what had happened, and they all commiserated. Some said that the management of the Automobile Club always treated Egyptians worse than foreigners. In spite of their obvious sympathy for us, however, I noticed that they spoke cautiously, some even lowering their voices and glancing around.

As well as being furious with Mr. Wright, I was in awe of my mother. I had the same feeling that used to come over me as a child when I went with her to the market and, terrified by the clamor, clutched the hem of her robe for protection. I saw her differently now—as an Upper Egyptian woman, who, under her abundant tenderness, had a core of steel and was ready to fight, heedless of the odds or the consequences. In the days following our visit, my mother carried on as usual, but it was clear from her face that she was obsessed with purpose. She seemed to be working up a plan.

A few days later, she took me to see a distant relative who was a lawyer and asked him to take on our case against the Automobile Club. I had to miss some morning classes in order to go with her to get various official forms and seals. For some reason, I felt certain that my mother would win.

Approximately a month after our meeting with Mr. Wright, she was surprised to receive a telephone call from Mr. Comanus. He said he wanted to come see her regarding an important matter. She fixed a time with him for the following day at five o' clock. We all waited for him, my mother, Said, Saleha and I. Even Mahmud put on his best clothes and waited with us in the sitting room. At the appointed hour, the doorbell rang.

14

Over the course of just a few years, the king of Egypt went from being a hardworking and upright young man—his subjects' greatest hope for a national renaissance—to a reckless and lazy man who lived for pleasure, carousing all night and sleeping all day. He spent his nights gambling at the Automobile Club or enjoying himself at the Auberge des Pyramides nightclub. He would summon dancers and chanteuses over to his table and then choose one of them to take back to the palace. As part of his obsession with sex, the king converted a chamber in the palace basement into a cinema for blue movies, imported just for him. He lived a wild, youthful whirl of relationships with women of all sorts—daughters of the aristocracy, wives of high-ranking government officials, dancers and actresses— his sexual hunger insatiable. These feverish, unfettered trysts often led to resounding scandals and sometimes even to diplomatic crises, as happened following His Majesty's involvement with the wife of the French military attaché. The soldiers of the royal guard took meticulous precautions to prevent the king from being photographed in compromising situations, often arresting the paparazzi, smashing their cameras and even roughing them up to make them hand over any film rolls they might be hiding on their persons. In spite of all these measures, the king's outrageous behavior left behind a foul odor in Egypt and abroad, particularly after Her Majesty the queen demanded a divorce, confirming to the population that all the rumors of the king's depravity were true. Newspapers around the world discovered that the king's antics were good for sales, for their readers thrilled to the adventures of an excitable Middle Eastern potentate whose life seemed a modern retelling of stories from the wondrous and captivating Arabian Nights. The question that cropped up time and time again, and that the Western ambassadors were at such a loss to answer, was how the young king had managed, in such a short time, to become a slave to his own desires.

It might be that he had come to the throne too young and inexperienced and still at school. Perhaps, some in his entourage encouraged his depravity because it made him easier to control. It might have been his way of forgetting how his world had been turned upside down when, after his father's death, his mother, giving not a whit for convention or appearances, went through men like water. He had caught her one night, in flagrante delicto, with the comptroller of the royal household. Or perhaps it was the accident: some years before, his royal car had crashed into one carrying some British soldiers. For two whole days the king lay in a coma. A renowned British surgeon, flown in from London, carried out three operations and, to everyone's surprise, managed to save his life. But it was said that the accident had an effect on the king's sexual stamina and that thereafter he could not contain himself long enough to satisfy his partner. So it might be that time spent in the company of so many beautiful women in public places was an attempt to affirm for himself and the public that his virility was undiminished.

Whatever the underlying reason, the result was the same. The king had become a debauched bon vivant, and his entourage reflected this. Most of his respectable friends withdrew, and he was surrounded by a group of pashas who were willing to do whatever he wanted, no matter how dishonorable. They were prepared to lose to him at poker, only to claw back double the amount through privileges granted by His Majesty. They were swimming in money. And as for the king's sexual conquests, they were generally linked to one name: Carlo Botticelli. An Italian in his midfifties, he was born in Shubra, and studied mechanics at the Don Bosco Institute before getting a job as an automobile mechanic at Abdin Palace. As part of the job, Botticelli always drove behind the royal fleet in case one of the cars should break down. He met the king by chance when the royal Buick overheated on the way to a hunting trip in Fayoum. This chance meeting was the turning point in the young king's life. No one knew what transpired between them, but this simple mechanic within just a few weeks became one of His Majesty's closest intimates and within a few short years owned huge amounts of land and commercial assets. He was then elevated by the king with the title of "bey." Botticelli left the grease pit forever and became renowned in another profession: that of royal pimp.

In truth, that term here is neither precise nor fair. Botticelli was not vulgar, common or a simple thief like the pimps one might see in brothels and nightclubs. He was to some extent an artist, a connoisseur, a real expert in women, a specialist in the various types of beauty and the arts of the bedchamber. It took him no more than a glance, a piercing look, to identify the right woman for a night with the king. He knew exactly what was wanted. It was his gut feeling, or call it genius, that drove Botticelli to choose a certain woman for the king's bed, picking one out and discarding others who might appear even more beautiful. Botticelli knew that the royal taste in women varied with a woman's age and social position. If they were in their twenties, for example, the king preferred the Parisian gamin look. She had to look like a beardless youth or a girl on the threshold of womanhood, with a flat chest and no behind. With regard to her toilette, clothing, speech and movement, there could be no hint of guile or experience. A woman in her twenties would win the king's heart by dint of her simplicity and naïveté. Before presenting her, Botticelli would warn her not to show off or feign experience. He would whisper in a sly and insinuating tone, "Give yourself to the king. His Majesty knows that you are young and inexperienced, and he will treat you with honor and patience."

In such cases, the king's pleasure derived precisely from corrupting the innocent. The feeling of breaking down coy resistance and defiling untamed flesh delighted him no end.

With women in their thirties or forties, the king's taste swung to the opposite extreme: he liked the fuller-bodied Mediterranean type of beauty, with an ample bosom and a soft, fleshy behind. Before granting her the honor of going to bed with His Majesty, Botticelli would advise this type of woman to flaunt her experience. He would give her a wink, smile and whisper, "What a lucky woman you are! Our great king has chosen to bestow his favor upon you. Women the world over will be envious. You will have a night of pleasure such as you have never known. You'll be astonished at the king's incredible stamina. You'll find that, for all the men you have slept with, you have never known what real lovemaking is."

This was Botticelli's way of insinuating to a woman how she should behave: in the king's arms, she had to show astonishment, telling him that she had never even imagined that such manliness could exist. These words of flattery from an experienced woman to His Majesty, and his happiness at being able to satisfy an experienced lover, gave him the feeling that he was more man than all her previous lovers put together.

There was a third category of seductress that Botticelli excelled at readying for the king: the spicy local woman of the lower classes. These he would choose from among anonymous dancers at the nightclubs. A beautician would spend a whole day with them before they met the king. They had to be immaculately clean and looking their very best, even with their touch of the common. Botticelli would look at his creation and joke, "Our king is a son of his country. From time to time he gets fed up with the schnitzels and smoked salmon, and he yearns for the hearty local fare. But the plate he eats off must be clean."

Occasionally, Botticelli would present the king a wild card, a blindingly beautiful woman who did not fit in his usual categories but was notable for her particularity. Such a woman might be plump or skinny, young or middle-aged, but there had to be something extraordinary about her. In this way, Botticelli was akin to a collector, a connoisseur as well as an impresario and a teacher of seduction.

How did Botticelli convince women to climb into the royal bed? In fact, he did not have to try hard at all. There were always more than enough willing to give themselves over to royal love. Women from the greatest aristocratic families vied for the moniker of royal mistress, and it was not because the king was attractive. In addition to his chronic sexual problem, His Majesty was too lazy for any form of exercise but maintained such a voracious appetite for desserts that he weighed more than one hundred and twenty kilograms. Thus, he was not only unattractive but unfit and unable to satisfy a partner in bed. So why did the woman all compete for him? It was simply because he was the king of Egypt and the Sudan. He held the keys to wealth and happiness. After a stormy night of lovemaking, what could he say if the lady happened to mention that she had always dreamed of owning a piece of fertile land or a farm? Could His Majesty turn down such a request? Even if she was only a young woman he had enjoyed corrupting, a few days later, her father might be the recipient of royal munificence and promoted to the rank of bey or pasha, receiving a plot of land or shares in a large company. The irony is that if word of the king's relationship with a woman got out, it would not sully her reputation but actually help her to find a good husband. Even married women who slept with His Majesty had no inhibitions about bragging that the king could relax only in their arms. The king's relationship with any woman elevated her station, for it was obvious that if the king had picked her out from hundreds of candidates, then she must be something special, and it followed that any man who then took her for his wife would enjoy her exceptional qualities, as well as the honor of possessing a woman who had been favored by His Majesty.

Botticelli was serious and indefatigable. He loved his work, carrying it out with pleasure and good humor. He flitted around high society in search of women and each month would organize an exclusive party in some remote private venue, inviting the royal prospects to come and be presented. At some moment during the party, the king would surprise the guests with his presence, and they would go through the motions of expressing their obeisance to him. The women would soon start to vie with one another to attract the king's glance, displaying their charms with seeming spontaneity, pretending that they were just crossing the room for some other reason as they paraded right in front of him. They knew that a single royal glance could change the course of their family's life forever. The show would go on until His Majesty decided upon one for the night. Botticelli would then bow to the fortunate lady, kiss her hand and treat her with the reverence due to a newly crowned queen. She might then strut around flaunting the fact that she was destined for the king's caresses, gloat as the other women tried to hide their disappointment.

The name Carlo Botticelli on any invitation to a party was an indication of the party's purpose, just as his appearance anywhere could be only for one reason—it meant that a new woman was on her way to the royal bed. That morning a white Chevrolet had drawn up in front of the Automobile Club. Carlo Botticelli stepped out and seemed to know his way as he walked straight to James Wright's office. This was a highly unusual event, which the staff whispered about to one another all day: "Why would Botticelli come to the Automobile Club?"

15

When Abd el-Aziz's fellow workers at the Club learned of his death, they were plunged into deep sorrow. They were also distressed at the way he had died. Had he gone to sleep and not woken up or been struck by a mortal illness or an automobile, they could have accepted it as his inevitable fate. But to die from humiliation! He had simply been unable to cope with having his dignity shattered in front of everyone. He just dropped dead. The staff kept whispering among themselves, "The shame of it! That Hameed, bastard homo, son of a cheap dancer, that he should have raised a hand against Hagg Abd el-Aziz, of the lineage of the Gaafars, landowners from Upper Egypt!"

Time and again they went over the details of Abd el-Aziz's death as if they did not want to forget them, as if they were, in some way, trying to make themselves feel pain. The slaps delivered to Abd el-Aziz had brought them face-to-face with their own reality. Usually, they were so absorbed in their private lives that when something happened, they had to reflect and try to piece together the details. The death of Abd el-Aziz, however, in this sudden and humiliating fashion, had made them only too aware that they were themselves like leaves in the wind, liable to be swept away on a whim. They were servants. They were tools to be used and discarded. Their distress over Abd el-Aziz turned into an ardent desire to see that the right thing was done by his family. They delegated Hagg Yusuf Tarboosh to ask Mr. Wright's permission to attend the funeral.

Mr. Wright answered without a second thought, "You can go wherever you like, provided it is not during work hours."

As the general manager had declined to make an exception, the night staff went to the funeral, and the day staff went off to visit the condolence tent. Many of them went to the apartment of the deceased to check on the children and offer their services. Umm Said thanked them and stated resolutely, "Thank you all so much. We want for nothing, thank God."

Two weeks after the death of Abd el-Aziz, another important event took place. It was four o'clock in the afternoon and the Paradise Café was flooded with Club staff, with the four heads of department, Rikabi the chef, Maître Shakir, Yusuf Tarboosh and Bahr the barman, sitting in the far corner as usual. The café, as always, was abuzz with chatter, the glug-glug of water pipes, raised voices, laughter, the clacking of backgammon pieces and shouts for the waiter. Suddenly, Abdoun, the barman's assistant, stood up and walked slowly to the middle of the café. He was as smartly dressed as ever in his carefully ironed white shirt, black trousers and black patent shoes. Abdoun looked at the Club staff sitting there, clapped his hands a few times to quiet them all down and then stated, "I want to say a few words."

As they looked at him, intrigued, he continued, "What happened to the late Abd el-Aziz could happen to any one of us. Abd el-Aziz was murdered. Alku killed him."

They just stared at Abdoun in disbelief. He took a deep breath as if trying to control his emotions and then loudly and defiantly declared, "That's what happened. Alku killed Abd el-Aziz."

Some of those present sought refuge in silence, while others jumped to their feet to object. They waved their arms around and tsk-tsked in disagreement. They were upset and confused, unable to take in what was going on. What Abdoun was now saying openly had been only intimated previously, surreptitiously, within earshot of trusted colleagues only. First making sure they were not being overheard, they would only then dare whisper some condemnation of Alku's unconscionable behavior. They had never imagined this could be discussed openly. What a calamity for them all! Abdoun was attacking Alku in public! What had the world come to! It seemed somehow unreal, like a dream or a mystery. Fear shot through everyone. They knew that word would spread like lightning, that every utterance, movement or gesture they made now would be passed on in faithful detail to Alku, who would then exact retribution. Upon learning what Abdoun had said, Alku would make an example of them all. Their crime was having allowed Abdoun to speak like that. They had to disown his words publicly and stop him from going any further. It suddenly occurred to them that Abdoun might be in Alku's pay, tasked with carrying out this little performance in order to check on their loyalty. This thought raised their emotions to fever pitch, and their anxiety turned to terror.

Hagg Yusuf Tarboosh clapped his hands together and reproached Abdoun in a voice loud enough for everyone to hear, "Abdoun, my son, you are mistaken and trying to sow discord. Ask God for forgiveness. Our lives are in God's hands, and Abd el-Aziz died at his appointed hour."

"No, Alku is responsible for his death."

At this point, Maître Shakir shouted, "If Alku had Abd el-Aziz beaten, then he must have done something to deserve it."

Upon hearing this, Abdoun appeared to be in the grip of some demonic force. He looked at Maître Shakir and asked firmly, "Then tell me why Alku has us beaten?

Voices rose up in protest at his question, with some people shouting out, "Alku is like our father."

Abdoun paused, then looked around at them before continuing, "Even if Alku is like our father, we don't beat our children once they have grown up. How long will Alku go on having us beaten like animals? You are in your forties and fifties. How can you put up with all that? How would you feel if your wives or children saw you being beaten?"

There was complete silence for a while, broken by Rikabi's hoarse voice, "Abdoun. Just what is it that you want?"

"I want Alku to stop the beatings."

"And who are you to tell Alku what to do?"

"I am a human being, Uncle Rikabi."

"You are an impudent child."

"So clinging to my dignity makes me impudent?"

"Your dignity comes from being lucky enough to earn a living."

Abdoun stared at Rikabi angrily and was about to retort before

Maître Shakir asked him calmly, "So, Abdoun, if someone makes a mistake, is Alku supposed to go easy on him?"

"He should come up with something that does not involve humiliating us. He could treat us like he does the employees in the royal palaces."

"Listen, son, we are not like the palace employees! They are educated people with qualifications."

Abdoun interrupted him sharply, "It doesn't matter that we are not educated. We are flesh and blood and we have our rights."

The staff were aware of the dangerous implications of this sentiment and shook their heads in disagreement, with Karara the waiter shouting, "His Excellency Alku knows better than we do what is good for us."

Abdoun shouted back his retort, "Are you really all just willing to be treated like cattle?"

Yusuf Tarboosh nervously fingered his long string of prayer beads and added, "Alku is our master, and were it not for his graciousness toward us, we'd all long ago have been back in Upper Egypt with our buffalos."

"We wouldn't have ended up looking after buffalos, Hagg Yusuf!" Abdoun replied. "We were all respected in our hometowns. What we earn here is not thanks to anyone's charitable heart. We work our fingers to the bone night and day for those wages. They don't pay us as an act of kindness, and we deserve to be treated like human beings."

Yusuf Tarboosh's face flushed and he muttered some words of prayer. The Club staff, against their better judgment, appeared to be on the verge of agreeing with what Abdoun was saying, when Rikabi the chef called out, "Just shut up. Hold your tongue, you scum, before you utter another word against your master Alku!"

His enormous body was quaking with anger. He strode over to Abdoun and would have hit him had the others not rushed over and stood between them, though it did nothing to calm the emotions and the arguments descending into unintelligible cacophony.

Bahr the barman said not a word, smoking his water pipe calmly and observing what was going on.

Rikabi walked right over and grunted at him, "Why are you sitting here so quietly, Bahr? Why aren't you on our side against your friend Abdoun, or perhaps you agree with him?"

"Leave me alone, Rikabi."

"I'll bet you put him up to this."

Bahr gave him a disdainful look.

"If I wanted to say something, I'd say it myself."

Then he drew a long drag on the pipe, making the water bubble furiously and irritating Rikabi even more.

"All right, Bahr. I'll tell Alku and he'll teach you a lesson."

"As you wish."

"Would you defy our master?"

"You can think what you like," replied Bahr, taking another drag on his water pipe.

Rikabi's face flushed like that of an angry bull. "I'm leaving. I don't have to listen to this rubbish."

Walking out of the café was an exemplary solution. Up to that moment, the staff had been rooted to the spot by the rush of events and their terror at the consequences, but the moment Rikabi walked out, he was followed by Yusuf Tarboosh and Maître Shakir. Then the others dashed out after them into the street as if fleeing a fire, leaving behind the café waiters and a few regulars who did not work at the Club.

Abdoun dragged a chair over and sat next to Bahr the barman, who simply said, "Don't blame them. It's difficult for them."

"Well, Uncle Bahr, I'd just like to understand how Alku can have them beaten and then be thanked for it."

Bahr thought it over a little and said, "Alku is a devil who stops at nothing, but he controls their wages."

Abdoun asked him nervously, "Has Alku ever had you beaten, Uncle Bahr?"

With a wince, he responded, "Of course he has had me beaten, when I was young and had just started at the Club. But as I grew older and became the barman, he stopped having me beaten. Shakir, Tarboosh, Rikabi and I are never touched, because he earns so much from us."

"He gets half of all our tips too."

"Alku says that he uses it to pay for the training school."

"Bahr, you know that's a lie. The palace pays for the school, and Alku keeps the tips for himself."

Bahr smiled and gave him an admiring look, saying, "God keep you, Abdoun. You are clever and brave, but unfortunately, your effort will come to nothing. You will never be able to change the way the staff think because their mentality is tied to the current system. Every word you said will by now have reached Alku's ears. God help you."

SALEHA

It seemed like the angel of death was hovering above our building. I felt a strange sense of foreboding about my mother. I trembled whenever I imagined that I might suddenly lose her like I had lost my father. I would wake up in the middle of the night and go to check on her. I would walk over to her in the dark as she was sleeping, holding my finger just below her nostrils to see that she was still breathing. I only ever left her side when I went to school. I made her sit next to me when I did my homework, and I felt that she needed me as much as I needed her. My mother had plunged headlong into battle to try to get my father's pension. The day Comanus telephoned asking if he could come and see us, my brother Kamel and I were sitting with her. When she put the receiver down, she looked worried and asked us, "Why do you think Comanus wants to come and see us?"

Kamel placed a hand on my mother's shoulder and replied, "It must be good news. Comanus is a good man."

"But he already paid his condolences. What does he want now?"

"Perhaps now he has some news."

My mother gave a sigh, "God help us. We have enough problems."

The following day we all waited for Comanus to arrive, my mother, Kamel, Said, Mahmud and I. He shook hands warmly with us one by one. He was wearing a smart gray suit and a white shirt with a blue tie. From the very first, I felt comfortable with him. He looked like a pleasant, trustworthy man, and I liked the way he smiled and tried to pronounce Arabic consonants. My mother invited him into the sitting room while I went to the kitchen to prepare the Turkish coffee as he'd asked for it, semisweet. I served it with a glass of ice water on the beautiful silver tray my mother saved for guests. As agreed before he arrived, Mahmud and I then withdrew, leaving Comanus with the adults. As usual, my brother Mahmud appeared indifferent to what was going on and went off to his bedroom, but I could not overcome my curiosity. I turned the lights off in the dining room, pushed the door open a little and positioned myself so that I could see and hear without being noticed.

Comanus started off by saying, "I have come to see that you are all well."

"It's very kind of you," said my mother warmly.

Comanus continued, "The late Abd el-Aziz was like a brother to me. Please, Umm Said, if you need anything, just ask me."

"May God keep you, sir."

They fell into silence again. Comanus cleared his throat and said, "I found out what happened when you went to see Mr. Wright. It's very unfortunate."

My mother pricked up her ears. She leaned back against her chair and said firmly, "It just does not make sense that my late husband could work at the Club for five years and that they don't pay a widow's pension. What rules or laws do they operate under?"

"You're right. The rules and bylaws are unjust."

My mother replied with a stronger voice, "The rules and the bylaws mean nothing to me, sir. Please God, the court will make them pay what is due to us."

"But, Umm Said, going to court is a long, drawn-out process."

"I will make them pay."

"The lawyers also charge a fortune!"

"We can afford it, thank God."

"I have come to suggest another solution."

My mother looked at him and said nothing.

Comanus took a sip of coffee and continued: "After much effort, I have managed to persuade Mr. Wright to take two of your boys on at the Club, in the place of their late father. One will work with me in the storeroom and the other doing deliveries. Together they will earn the equivalent of his pension."

My mother remained silent, and Comanus added quietly, "Isn't that a better solution than the headache of going to court?"

"God help us," muttered my mother who seemed to be thinking it over.

Comanus smiled and added apologetically, "Of course, Mr. Wright has agreed to this on condition you do not take the Club to court."

"I understand."

"So, you agree?"

"Please God it will all be for the best. I just need two or three days to think it over and I'll telephone you."

"Splendid!"

"I am so grateful to you, Monsieur Comanus, for having thought about how you can help us. We will never forget this kindness."

Comanus replied with warm sincerity: "It's the very least I can do for the late Abd el-Aziz. But, please, Umm Said, give me your answer soon. It was difficult to win Mr. Wright over, and I'm worried he'll change his mind."

They chatted about nothing in particular for another quarter of an hour, and then Comanus said that he had to leave. They showed him out and returned to the sitting room. My mother sat on the chair next to the window, with Said and Kamel near her on the sofa. As I was on my way to join them, my mother said, "Come in, Saleha. I want to tell you something."

The moment I sat down next to her, she told me excitedly, "The *khawaga,* Comanus, has come up with a new idea."

"I heard it all."

Kamel asked me, "So what do you think?"

"Well, of course, working at the Club is better than having to fight in court."

My mother seemed happy to hear that I agreed. She sighed. "Thank God. God knows our situation."

Silence fell on us again. It felt as if my mother was trying to decide for sure. Then she turned to Kamel and Said and told them with a tense smile, "We haven't got any time to lose. We have to make a decision tonight so I can give Comanus an answer tomorrow."

They both looked at her in silence as she continued to explain, "Mahmud can do deliveries. Which of you will work in the storeroom with Comanus?"

Said replied, "I will not work at the Automobile Club."

"And just why not, Lord Said?" asked my mother sarcastically.

"I'm waiting to see about my diploma, and then I will find a better job."

"And you'll find a job just like that!"

"God will help."

"The country's brimming with qualified people who can't get a job."

"I'd rather be out of work than bunged up in the storeroom."

"And what's wrong with the storeroom?"

"I want to work in my own field. In carpets."

"That's just like you. Can't think about anyone but yourself."

"It's not a sin to think about myself!"

"But it is a sin not to think about us. You should be ashamed to sit there in front of me and turn down the only chance we have of getting through this. Do you never think that your mother and siblings need every piastre we can get? Do you not realize that this job which you are rejecting out of hand is one which your father did for years just to look after us?"

"My father, may God have mercy on him, put up with the misery out of guilt at having squandered his wealth on his relatives."

"How dare you! How dare you speak about your late father like that!" my mother shouted, her eyes wide with anger.

Said looked defiant and said, "Listen. I can read you like a book."

"Speak to your mother with some respect!" Kamel warned him.

Said ignored him and carried on shouting at our mother, "You want to throw me into that storeroom so that your darling Kamel can finish his university studies. He'll be a lawyer and I'll be a menial. No. Things are different now. You've already stopped me from going to university, what more do you want?"

"You are the one who stopped yourself. Did anyone tell you to get such low marks?"

"All right then, I'm a disappointment, a loser. Just let me be. Soon I'll be able to support myself. I'll leave home, and then you won't have to put up with me. Your beloved Mr. Kamel, the lawyer, can get off his backside and do something useful for once in his life."

"Did I raise you to speak like that, Said?" my mother asked, her voice quivering. It had no effect on Said. He stormed out of the room, slamming the door behind him.

Kamel and I sat there in silence. Suddenly my mother burst out in tears. I rushed over to her and started kissing her head and her hands.

Kamel said, "Don't worry, Mama. I'll work in the storeroom."

"But your studies," she replied weakly.

Kamel put his hand on her shoulder and said, "With God's help, I'll do both."

16

James Wright had put aside his usual haughty demeanor and seemed almost to smile at Carlo Botticelli, who was seated in front of him. He offered him a cigar from an ornate mother-of-pearl box, saying warmly, "Mr. Botticelli. How nice to see you."

"Well, may I say the same to you!"

Botticelli's bearing reflected that cold, polite formality used when dealing with the lower orders. For all James Wright's Englishness and his position as general manager of the Automobile Club, the Italian Botticelli was a confidant of the king, and that put him on a higher plane.

With a worried look on his face, Wright spoke, "May I ask as to the health of His Majesty?"

"His Majesty is in good health, but he works far too hard."

Wright affected a look of sympathy and said dolefully, "Egypt is a complicated country with endless problems. I worry what effect all that pressure has on His Majesty."

Botticelli gave him a sarcastic look as if to say, "You bloody hypocrite!" but Wright just carried on speaking, "His Majesty should take some rest."

"I try as hard as I can to convince His Majesty that he should take some time off, even a few days, but he always tells me that he must attend to his country's needs."

"Egyptians are ingrates. They will never appreciate the efforts His Majesty expends on their behalf."

"I agree wholeheartedly. If I were in His Majesty's shoes, I would enjoy life, but his sense of duty is too strong."

They exchanged further platitudes on the subject and then suddenly fell silent, as if they had now covered all the preliminaries and it was time for business. Botticelli took a drag on his cigar, blew out a cloud of smoke and spoke, "Mr. Wright. I think you are aware just how much His Majesty likes to feel connected with the various groups of society."

"Of course."

"His Majesty always loves feeling close to his people."

"That has only increased my esteem for His Majesty."

"If you were offered the chance to make His Majesty happy, would you hesitate?"

"I am at His Majesty's command."

Botticelli smiled and continued, "We're off to a good start."

Mr. Wright looked at him inquisitively. Botticelli, now twiddling with his hat, continued, "It sometimes happens that His Majesty asks me to organize a small party for him where he can get to know young men and women of the better classes in Egypt. Remember, His Majesty is not over the hill like you or me. He is a young man in his thirties."

Mr. Wright nodded and carried on trying to see what Botticelli was driving at.

"Next Monday, I am holding just such a small party. All the guests are young men and women of the better classes. I should very much like to invite your daughter, Miss Mitsy."

"Have you met Mitsy?"

"I saw her in the Gezira Club. She caught my attention, and I thought that I might introduce her to His Majesty."

"What a great honor."

"Please ask her if she would be willing to have the king as a friend."

"She will agree. Of course."

"I'm happy that you understand and are willing to cooperate."

"No, I'm the one who should thank you, Mr. Botticelli. Are there any specific requirements regarding the party? Please do bear in mind that Mitsy is a young woman who has never met a king before."

He spoke that last sentence apologetically, but Botticelli waved the thought away and said, "There's nothing to worry about. His Majesty is not a stickler for etiquette, and he likes his guests to dress however they wish."

Mr. Wright smiled and nodded enthusiastically. Botticelli stood up, put his hat on, as Wright stood to bid him good-bye. Just before Botticelli stepped through the doorway, he turned around and looked him straight in the eyes, "I'll send the invitation to you tomorrow. If fortune smiles, this will be the opportunity of a lifetime for your daughter. You and she will both have a taste of paradise."

Botticelli was always sure to make it perfectly clear at some point what was going to happen. This was his preferred way of dealing with the families of the king's love prospects—he could not allow them to build up false hopes. He called a spade a spade and left them fully cognizant that they were sending their daughters, or their wives, to the king's bed.

That evening, as Wright was having a drink in the Club bar, he went over what Botticelli had told him, welling up with excitement. This was a very serious matter. He would be dealing directly with the king of Egypt and the Sudan. His relations with the king had never gone beyond the official. The king came to play cards at the Club at night, after Wright had left his office. At royal dinners at the Club, Wright had to be present as general manager to greet the king. Over a period of twenty years, that was the extent of his relations with the king and with the king's late father before him. Two or three times a year, Wright would have to smile, bow and say a few words, but this was a different opportunity. As Botticelli had mentioned, this party might be a turning point. Life had taught him that an opportunity arises once, only to disappear unless you are sure to grab it. If the king bestowed his friendship upon Mitsy, Wright's life would change. In a backward country like Egypt, all doors would open for the man whose daughter was the king's belle.

James Wright had heard a lot about wealth amassed simply by dint of royal patronage. He had to make sure that the king fell for Mitsy, for Mitsy's sake, if not for his. He was over sixty. How many years did he have left? Mitsy, as his only daughter, would inherit his wealth. She was the only one who would benefit from her friendship with the king. In his mind, the word "friendship" sounded completely innocent, as he rationalized to himself: the king is a young man looking for friends of his own age. He likes to make friends with young men and women he can trust and in whose company he can relax. People with whom he can forget court etiquette.

Three glasses of Black Label filled him with a feeling of well-being, as he started imagining all sorts of wonderful outcomes. When he'd made his way home, arriving an hour before dinner, his wife, Victoria, was sitting alone beside the heater, reading. Drink loosened his tongue, so he started talking excitedly to her, "Victoria, how are you?"

"Very well, thank you," she replied without lifting her head from the book.

"Where's Mitsy?"

"She has gone to the cinema with some of her friends."

"Could you put the book down for a moment? I have some exciting news."

He quickly recounted what had happened. She listened with an anxious look.

"You do know that Botticelli is a pimp?"

"As far as I know, he is a mechanic in the royal palace."

"He may well be a mechanic, but he is also the king's procurer."

"Oh, my darling, that is just a scurrilous rumor put about by the Wafd Party."

"It's not a rumor. It's a fact. I know women whom Botticelli has sent to the king's bed."

"If a woman has a relationship with the king, she can't claim to have been tricked."

"I am not saying that they have been tricked."

"So what are you objecting to?"

"Don't you agree that being the king's pimp is a despicable job?"

"Your daughter, Mitsy, has been invited to a royal party. Are you upset about that?"

"If that pimp Botticelli has asked to present your daughter to the king, it can mean only one thing!" Victoria shouted at him with anger in her eyes.

Wright went over and sat next to her on the sofa, putting his arm around her and, speaking in a whisper, as if explaining something complicated to a little girl, said, "My darling. Do stay calm and think it over a little. Don't you think that the king is good enough to be friends with Mitsy? He is only a few years older than she. Wouldn't you like your daughter to be friends with a young man of good breeding who just happens to be the king of Egypt and the Sudan?"

Victoria answered drily, "Of course I wouldn't be upset if, of her own accord, she should choose a friend. But for that pimp to present her as a potential conquest, that's a completely different matter."

"Your daughter is old enough to think for herself, so let her decide whom she wants to be friends with. We should encourage her however she decides."

His voice had a hollow ring to it, but he knew how to make her change her mind. He came back to the subject tenaciously, again and again, saying the same thing in different ways. Victoria could never keep up her opposition for very long. Wright went on and on until finally she was worn down.

"James. Please just leave me alone."

"Not until you agree."

"What do you want me to do?"

"I want you to tell Mitsy about the invitation from the king."

"All right."

"Explain to her the potential ramifications of the situation. She must understand that she might live her whole life without ever having an opportunity to view a real king, in his own milieu."

Victoria nodded, pursed her lips vexedly and turned back to her reading.

Wright stood up and asked her, "Can I rely on you?"

This time she did not answer but went on reading. With this, Wright knew that he had won, so he calmed down and left the room. He had charged his wife with informing Mitsy because he avoided trying to deal with her. He no longer spoke to her unless he had to. His relationship with his daughter had reached this low ebb, for reasons he could not quite put his finger on. What had come over Mitsy?

She was standoffish with him and talked back, but he gave as good as he got. They argued so much that he now avoided starting a conversation with her. Everything he did was exactly the wrong thing. She had strange ideas that he did not understand, as if she had gone mad. Whenever she did something stupid, she went on the defensive and provoked him until he raged at her. He would look at her and ask himself how the delicate child he used to cuddle and shower with kisses had become this brash and impertinent girl. What had gone wrong? Even though she was a stupid, vain girl, he never interfered in her life. After he paid for her education and got her accepted by the London School of Economics, she suddenly discovered that she liked acting and decided that she wanted to live in Egypt. This was how, in spite of himself, he wound up now paying her fees at the American University in Cairo, a complete waste of time. Why was she studying drama in Egypt? Did she think that she would get roles in Egyptian films? Wouldn't it be better to study drama in London? What did she like so much about this backward country? He was obliged to be here as he could never command such a large salary or find such a cushy job in London. But Mitsy had decided to live among this riffraff and study drama in a country whose language she could not speak! Good Lord. He could not thing of anything more idiotic. Even if she loved the Orient, even if she loved camels, pyramids, incense, men in gala-biyyas and women in abayas, she could still study in London and visit Egypt during the holidays. Was Mitsy just stupid or out of her mind? When all was said and done, though, it was her life to live. He just wished she didn't treat him so badly, showed a bit of respect. Was that too much to ask? In any case, he had decided to keep giving her a wide berth, only speaking to her when absolutely necessary.

The following day, he sat down to dinner with Mitsy and his wife. He smiled as he asked, "Has Mitsy chosen a dress to wear to the royal party?"

Mitsy said nothing, so Mr. Wright continued in a serious tone of voice, "We have to start preparing now. Mitsy's going to be the king's guest. She should wear the most beautiful thing she has."

"Don't worry," said his wife. "She has lots of lovely gowns."

Wright looked at Mitsy and said, "Buy yourself a new one just for this occasion. I'll pay for it. You don't meet a king every day."

At this, Mitsy threw him a sharp look and asked, "Who said that I am going to meet the king?"

He pursed his lips and, ignoring her provocation, said calmly, "Hasn't your mother mentioned the invitation from the king?"

"She told me."

Wright smiled and said nervously, "You have accepted, haven't you?"

"I haven't made up my mind yet."

"What do you mean?"

"An invitation is something that you can accept or turn down."

"Would you turn down the king's invitation to dinner?"

"I'm entitled to turn it down, if I wish."

"Are you joking?"

"No. I'm perfectly serious."

As Mr. Wright threw his spoon down into his soup bowl with a clatter, he snarled, "If you turn it down, you'll be committing the greatest act of stupidity yet."

"I can do what I want."

"You're a fool."

Victoria, who was following the rising tension, tried to calm things. "Mitsy. Of course you can decide whether you want to go or not. Your father is just giving you some advice. That's all."

"Then I thank him for his advice."

The blood rushed to Mr. Wright's face and he shouted, "We don't need your sarcasm. If you turn down the invitation, you are an idiot, not right in the head. I will not allow you to harm yourself."

"And what are you going to do about it?"

"You'll find out."

There was silence. Mitsy wiped the edges of her mouth with her napkin. Her chair screeched as she pushed it away from the table. She took a few steps toward her father and said, "Fine. I'm not going to the party."

17

When the Club staff returned from the café, they threw themselves into their work as if to disassociate themselves from Abdoun's words and affirm their absolute and unimpaired loyalty to Alku. They took it for granted that Alku would already have heard about what had happened and that he would summon them to ask, "How could you have allowed that lad to speak against me?"

They prepared their answers, rehearsing them in their minds for the eventuality. They would say:

"Your Excellency. That lad is a piece of scum. He is out of his mind."

"We refused to listen to him and told him to behave himself."

"You are our master and our father. We are your children, your servants."

As they expected Alku to bear down on them at any moment, the hours passed slowly with the apprehensive staff muttering prayers to keep evil away. With their nerves at the breaking point, they continued to fret, and when work slowed a little and they were sure that they were not being observed, they went into a side room to discuss the situation anew, as if to make certain that the awful incident had actually happened. They launched into the absent Abdoun, telling each other that he must be mad to have spoken out so insolently, repeating his words in a whisper and feigning incredulity. Bahr the barman and a small number of the staff said nothing. The others tried to outdo one another in spewing curses and heaping scorn upon Abdoun, but even so they were befuddled. Did they really, deep down, disagree with what Abdoun had said? The answer was yes and no. Their expressed anger at Abdoun hid a touch of admiration, but it was coated with such thick layers of fear that they had to condemn him publicly lest they be tarred with the same brush. They too wished that Alku would put an end to the beatings, but they were certain that would never happen. They knew they would never see justice reign. Abdoun had spoken the truth, but of what value was that? When had the truth ever changed anything in their lives? How many times had they lied out of fear or to keep their masters happy? How many times had they accepted the truth of something they knew to be false? How often had they been obliged to feign laughter or sorrow? How many times had they borne false witness out of fear or in hope of a tip? Let Abdoun speak as much as he wants. He could never change a thing at the Automobile Club. Abdoun was either a dreamer or plain stupid, whereas they were wise and practical people with a sense of their own limitations. They consoled themselves:

"People only say things like that in films."

"What does he know about dignity or disgrace?"

"Our dignity comes from being able to earn a living."

Then, with the authority of someone who has a thorough understanding of the matter, Karara the waiter spoke up, "You want the truth? We need to be beaten. If Alku stopped the beatings, the Club would go to rack and ruin. We are insubordinate by nature, like the race of Nimrod. We are driven by fear, not shame. If not for fear of being beaten, we'd do nothing but walk around thumbing our noses at our bosses."

They looked down, some of them nodding in agreement. They wished that Alku would hurry up and punish Abdoun, that he would crush him. They longed to see Abdoun receiving his due and a taste of the stick, screaming and begging Alku to forgive him. That would make them feel safe again. That would confirm for them again that submissiveness to Alku was the best and most rational way to behave. Then they would be able to shake their heads, pucker up their lips in sympathy and say ruefully, "Poor Abdoun. See what happens when you get out of line?"

The whole day passed and nothing happened. The next day, just before noon, the black Cadillac pulled up in front of the Automobile

Club, and Alku climbed out. Everyone who saw him at that moment would confirm that they had never seen him so angry. His black face was ashen, his coarse lips screwed up together, and he had the blood-shot eyes of a drunken man. Marching through the entrance door, Alku looked around impatiently, as if searching for something, as if he had come on urgent business and would brook no delay. Hameed was prancing along behind him, panting like an eager hunting dog. The staff all stepped aside for Alku, no one daring to proffer a greeting. They knew that they were about to witness an event unique in the history of the Club, one that they would be able to tell their grandchildren about. Some felt pity for Abdoun, about to meet his dreadful fate, but most just felt relief that Alku's evident fury was not directed at them. You were asking for it, Abdoun. You'll get the lesson of your life, and you won't stand up to your masters again. Alku will crush anyone who stands up to him and then put him back in his rightful place.

When Alku went into Mr. Wright's office, the servants clustered around in the corridor, pressing their ears to the door. Like children at a circus or a wrestling match, they were on tenterhooks waiting for the action to begin. With a thrill in their voice, they whispered to each other:

"It's the end of Abdoun. Alku will rip him to shreds."

"He may even fire him."

"He'll have him put in prison like he did to Ishaq when he stole a royal pack of cards."

After half an hour, Alku marched out of Mr. Wright's office as resolutely as he had entered it. He stopped in the doorway of the Club and unexpectedly turned around, noticing that the servants had been watching him surreptitiously. He thundered at them, "What are you all standing around for? Get the hell away from here!"

The servants all scattered like chickens, except Maître Shakir and Hagg Yusuf Tarboosh, who walked over to Alku and bowed.

He just stared at them and said, "What do you want?"

"Your great Excellency," Yusuf Tarboosh answered reverentially. "You are our father and we live in gratitude to you."

Maître Shakir took a step closer and continued in the same ingratiating tone, "Please, Your Excellency. Please punish that Abdoun severely."

Yusuf Tarboosh nodded in agreement and added enthusiastically, "Those base things he said cannot be overlooked."

There was no response. Both men looked fixedly at Alku, who, contrary to expectation, curled his lips in disgust, waved them off and shouted, "Get back to work, both of you!"

"But Your Excellency . . . ," Shakir started hesitantly.

"Didn't you hear what I said?" Alku interrupted him angrily. "By God, be off with you."

Perturbed, they both bowed again and hurried away. Alku strode out of the building, trailed by Hameed, and, getting into the car, barked at the driver, "Back to Abdin."

KAMEL

On my first day of work, Comanus took me to the office of Mr. Wright, who looked at me as if we had never met before.

"We are happy to have you working here," he said formally.

I muttered a few words of thanks. We left his office and made our way to see Alku at Abdin Palace. En route, Comanus told me, "Kamel, there is something that you ought to know. Alku is the head of all the staff in both the Automobile Club and the royal palaces. I know you will never forget what he did to your father, may God have mercy upon him. I can understand how you must feel, but I would advise you never to look back. Always remember that you are working here in order to complete your studies and to help out your family. You must think of the past as a closed book. Be careful of saying anything at all untoward about Alku, because he has spies everywhere. His reach is long, and the consequences are highly unpleasant."

I nodded. My meeting with Alku hardly lasted a minute.

"This is the Kamel Gaafar I spoke to you about. He's the son of the late Abd el-Aziz."

Alku took a look at me and with a nod muttered a few indistinct words. Then he turned to Comanus and continued speaking as if I were not there. I felt humiliated and a mad thought sprang to mind— that I could grab Alku and slap him as he had done to my father, then simply bolt out of the palace and never return to the Club. The fantasy was so lifelike in my mind that I started sweating and breathing heavily. I shut my eyes and had just about managed to haul myself back to reality by the time we left Alku's office. On our way back to the Club, Comanus started explaining my job in detail.

I worked as hard as I could from the very first day. I would carry crates up to the restaurant and the bar during the daytime, and then I would sit down and do all the paperwork. How can I describe how I felt working the storeroom? How should you feel stepping right into your father's work clothes after he passes away? When you sit on his favorite chair and use the same cap, prayer beads and prayer rug? You would have mixed feelings. You would miss your father and want to do your duty toward him. Out of pride, you want to keep his memory alive and find some tangible form of his existence in your memories of his voice and smell. You might even start to feel like him. When there was no work to do, I would ask Comanus's permission to read my textbooks or study my lecture notes.

On the first of the month, I handed my salary over to my mother. She cried and hugged me and then nagged me until I agreed to keep part of the salary for my own outgoings. As the days passed, I fell into the rhythm of the storeroom until I almost enjoyed it, except that the vision of my father being slapped by Hameed sometimes returned and left me feeling troubled. I felt guilty for not having avenged myself on those who had humiliated him. I kept having the same fantasy of walking into Alku's office when Hameed was there and thrashing them both. But that would remain only a fantasy. I just needed to work hard enough to keep the job until I graduated. My father had for so long dreamt of seeing me become a lawyer that it was my duty to become one. The other troubling thing was that I was missing the meetings of the Wafd committee. One morning, after asking Comanus for a break, I went to see Hasan Mu'min. We met at the cafeteria.

"I am so sorry, Hasan. I cannot come to the meetings or take on any assignment. At least for the foreseeable future."

Hasan listened attentively as usual, and said calmly, "So you're now an employee of the Automobile Club?"

"Yes."

"Don't worry. You can work with us from there."

"Is there a Wafd committee at the Automobile Club?"

"We're now operating outside the confines of the Wafd Party. We have formed a democratic front including people of all political leanings."

"Where do you hold meetings?"

"You'll know everything in good time. The most important thing is to set up a method of communicating with you in there."

And so it was arranged: he would ring from the grocer Ali Hamama's telephone, and giving his name as "Yegen," he would leave a message for me to call.

When I stood up to take my leave, he embraced me warmly, saying, "Kamel, I admire your patriotism."

Hasan Mu'min was such an inspiration that I would have dropped everything and done whatever he asked. I went over what he had said. How could I do any political agitating from inside the Automobile Club? The members were all either foreigners, members of the Turkish upper crust or large landowners. I doubted any of them would have any interest in Egypt's independence. The exact opposite, in fact. The interests of those social classes were closely bound to the British occupation.

Weeks went by. Work at the Club kept me so busy that I forgot what Hasan Mu'min had said. And then, one morning, when I was alone in the storeroom, sitting at my small desk, old Uncle Suleyman surprised me by rushing in to see me. He looked tense as he came over to me and said, "Listen, Kamel. His Royal Highness Prince Shamel is coming for you."

"Who is he?"

"His Royal Highness Prince Shamel? He is a cousin of the king!"

I had never heard of Prince Shamel, but I jumped to my feet, straightened my clothes and straightened my tie and my tarboosh. Some of the serving staff rushed into the storeroom in excitement and milled around aimlessly. That was their way of showing respect to His Royal Highness, who soon appeared in the doorway preceded by the aroma of his cologne. He was a man of around fifty, very dapper, and handsome with pale skin and combed-back chestnut hair. From the outset, he put one at ease.

I bowed and said, "It is a great honor, Your Royal Highness."

"Is Monsieur Comanus here?" he asked in good Arabic.

"He is on his way, sir."

"What is your name?"

"Kamel."

"Listen, Kamel. I'm holding a party at the Club next week, and I want to see what sort of wine you're going to serve to my guests."

"Yes, sir."

Fortunately, I knew where the wine list was kept and rushed to produce it. As I handed it to the prince, I bowed again. He looked over it quickly and said, "Not bad. All quite good, in fact."

To my astonishment, he kept on talking to me, asking about my family and my studies. I told him that I had taken over my late father's job while also studying law. I was amazed at his knowledge of the subjects I was studying.

"Very impressive, sir," I said enthusiastically.

"I studied law at the Sorbonne," he said with a chuckle. "But that was years and years ago. Talking with you gives me the chance to see how much I remember."

I was transfixed. I could hardly believe what was happening. The king's cousin was standing in front of me and chatting to me like a friend.

He reached forward and examined the books on my desk. He found my anthology of the prince of poets, Ahmed Shawqi, and gave me a knowing look. I said shyly that I was fond of literature, and he asked me, "Do you just read or do you write as well?"

"I have made a few forays into poetry."

The prince laughed and called out, "Good Lord, we've got a poet in the storeroom!"

That made me laugh. He laid his hand on my shoulder, and there was warmth in his voice as he added, "You're a young talented chap. I can see a bright future for you."

He held out a gold pound coin and said, "Here. A small gift."

"That's very kind of you, sir," I said. "But, thank God, I am not in need of help."

"My boy, if I had a son, he would be your age now. Imagine me as your late father and don't stand on ceremony. Please do take it."

He kept his hand held out with the coin, but I held firm. "Thank you so much, sir, for your kindness, but please forgive me."

The prince gave a broad smile, as if he had never been surprised by a refusal. He put the coin back in his pocket and turned to leave but stopped suddenly as if he had remembered something. He smiled again and asked me, "Are you here every day?"

"Except for Wednesday. That's my day off."

"What time do you finish work?"

"At six o'clock."

"Fine. On Thursday at six o'clock, I shall send my chauffeur to pick you up and bring you to the palace. Do you have any objection to paying me a visit?"

"It will be a great honor for me."

As I made a rather deep bow, I said, "At your service, sir," and Uncle Suleyman and I accompanied him out of the Club, walking behind him until he reached his black Buick. We stood there watching until the car disappeared from view. Uncle Suleyman then grabbed hold of my sleeve. "Get inside. I want to speak to you," he barked at me with uncharacteristic abruptness.

I followed him into the storeroom. He was limping along and seemed worked up about something. When we were alone, he turned on me furiously, saying, "Are you out of your mind, Kamel? How could you embarrass His Royal Highness like that!"

"I didn't embarrass him."

"You refused his gift."

"I apologized politely."

"Well, it's a good thing it was Prince Shamel you did that to."

"Why?"

"Because he is one of the kindest princes in the ruling family. Didn't you notice that he himself came to check on the wine? He could have made us all come running to him. But he is a man of humility and tolerance. Had you rejected a gift from any other prince, he would have had you fired on the spot."

"I'm not a beggar, Uncle Suleyman."

"Just listen, son. The prince liked you and wanted to give you something. You must never refuse."

"Well, I just did."

"Who do you think you are, Kamel? If you carry on like that in the Club, you'll bring all sorts of misfortunes down upon yourself. We are all servants of the princes. Can't you understand that?"

I really wanted to tell Uncle Suleyman that I was a law student and not a servant. Even though I had been forced to take a temporary job in the storeroom, that did not make me a servant, but not wishing to offend him, I bit my tongue.

The story spread around the Club. Most of the servants agreed that I was wrong to have refused the prince's gift. I tried to explain my thinking, but, as one, they clung to their own interpretation, some of them simply incredulous. "Listen, son, it's a great mistake to look a gift horse in the mouth. Are you better off than the princes?"

I realized that it was pointless pressing the matter. I feigned agreement and bit my tongue. I heard conflicting opinions about Prince Shamel from the staff. Some thought him a great man, pointing out his outspokenness, humility and sympathy for the poor, while others referred to him as an uncontrollable womanizer, a faithless unbeliever who had married an Italian woman and then divorced her before they'd had children. He then flung himself into endless relationships, changing partners as often as his socks. I also learned from them that Prince Shamel's relations with His Majesty were not good. The king did not care for his self-satisfaction and resented both his liberal way of thinking and his common touch. His Majesty, in fact, considered him a Communist, though he was also jealous of him. Prince Shamel was a gifted artist of international repute whose photography was exhibited in Europe, and as he mentioned, he had received his higher education at the Sorbonne, whereas the king was an unlearned soul, with no university degree, let alone interest in art. The staff recounted two incidents in particular that had caused the chill between the king and Prince Shamel. One time, the king had been sitting with the prince and offered him a cigar, which the prince took and then leaned forward as if waiting for the king to light it for him. It was instinctual and unintended, and he realized his mistake almost immediately, springing to his feet, apologizing, but the king was so angry that he turned his back on the prince, cutting him completely and chatting with the other guests. Finally, the prince made his excuses and left. The other incident occurred when the whole royal family had been invited to a lunch party at Muntaza Palace, and Prince Shamel jumped into the swimming pool before asking the king's permission, a grave breach of protocol. Some courtiers brought this to the prince's attention. When he climbed out of the pool, the courtiers gave him to understand, in the clearest but politest of terms, that he was no longer welcome. He left the palace and never again received a royal invitation.

This tale only increased my respect for the prince. I felt that this man, who had no fear of the king himself, would treat me with kindness and respect, insignificant as I was. Still, I wondered why he was interested in me. It seemed odd that he would invite me to his palace when he hardly knew me. Of course I was looking forward to visiting him, but I hoped that the visit would not end badly and spoil my wonderful impression of him.

On Thursday, at the appointed hour, just before I left the storeroom to go wait outside for the prince's car, Comanus warned me, "Be careful about what you say to the prince. Think twice before you utter a word."

Uncle Suleyman, on the other hand, took me to the car and whispered in my ear, "Listen, Kamel. This is a once in a lifetime opportunity. Don't do anything stupid, like you did the first time you met him."

Prince Shamel's palace was on the banks of the Nile in Garden City. The car made two sharp turns and drew up at the entrance. I wondered how just one man could live in this stately house when thousands of Egyptians lived cramped in tiny spaces. The palace was beautiful and elegant, with impressively high ceilings, enormous halls and marble columns. It all seemed unreal to me, as if I had ended up in a movie. A dark-skinned servant opened the door, and I was received in the hallway by an elegant man in a white suit, white gloves and a blue tie. He bowed to me and said, "Good evening, Mr. Kamel. Please follow me. His Royal Highness is waiting for you in the studio."

I followed him across the hallway. We turned right, and he opened a huge door into an enormous photography studio. The lights were dimmed. I could see scores of photographs on the walls and a number of cameras pointing in all directions. The prince was not dressed as I had expected him to be. He was wearing a blue cotton shirt, a tie and black shoes. He looked tired and was unshaven. He smiled and greeted me warmly, "Welcome, Kamel. I apologize for having been too busy to make myself presentable. We won't shake hands, because I don't want to stain your clothing."

He gave a loud laugh and held his hands out, and I saw that he was wearing rubber gloves with developer all over them. "If you'd like to look at some of my photographs on the wall," he said, "please go ahead."

Everything this man did was infused with elegance. He did not walk back over to his desk until I started looking at the photographs, as that would have been improper. As he took an image out of the developing bath, he worked out where the crop marks should be and then trimmed it down with a paper cutter. I carried on viewing the photographs on the wall. I noticed that most of them were portraits of women, peasants and lower-class people as well as foreigners wearing hats. I was transfixed by their faces. They all showed strong individuality.

As I stood there contemplating a photograph of a lower-class woman in an abaya and a sequined scarf wrapped around her hair, I became aware of the prince laughing. He was standing behind me and asked me affably, "Do you like this woman?"

I turned around and noticed that he had removed his gloves.

"I like the portrait," I answered.

"And why is that?"

"It has authenticity. It has a particular Egyptian seductiveness about it. Does Your Royal Highness know the work of an artist called Mahmud Said?"

"He's a friend of mine. I see him a lot in Alexandria. Where have you seen his work?"

"At an exhibition in the French Cultural Center last summer."

"And what makes you think of the work of Mahmud Said?"

"I think that Your Royal Highness expresses with the camera what he does with the brush."

"What a wonderful thought," he laughed. "I wish all the critics would adopt that! How wonderful that you follow the arts."

The prince's face turned serious and he continued, "I also try to learn by means of photographs, you know. I photograph faces in order to try to understand them. Photography is a wonderful way of recording life. The camera captures a particular moment in time. Our myriad expressions over the course of a single day are all fleeting. They evanesce and we can never bring them back. The camera alone can record them and preserve them for posterity."

"I notice that all the portraits are of women."

"Women are the essence of everything," he said warmly. "They are the starting point. Women are life."

For the first time, I noticed a bottle of whiskey and a glass on the small table next to the desk and realized that his exuberance was aided by alcohol. He gestured for me to wait. "I want to show you something I hope you'll like."

He brought out two photographs, both the same size. I noticed that they were of the same subject—a pretty woman of approximately forty with black hair and wearing a leather jacket. He laid the two photographs side by side on the desk and laughed, saying, "Kamel, you're a poet. I'm sure you'll understand what I'm driving at. I took these two photographs of the same woman, two hours apart. Can you see any difference? Take your time before you answer."

The woman had the same pose and the same smile in both photographs.

"The details are the same in both images," I said.

"I don't mean the details. Concentrate a little. Don't you think that her facial expression is different?"

I carried on examining the photographs. The prince continued in a serious tone of voice, "If we hypothesize that the woman's psychological state is different in the photographs, in which one, would you say, does she appear more contented?"

I pointed to one of the photographs, and he cried out, "Well done! And do you know why she seems happier?"

"I don't know."

"Then come with me," he said with a jovial gesture for me to follow him. We went out onto the balcony. There were plants and flowers everywhere. He went over to a flower pot and said, "This is a thirsty rose. Take a good look at it. Engrave its features in your mind."

I gazed at the rose as the prince darted off and then came back with a watering can. I'll admit that his behavior seemed a little odd to me. Might he have some psychological problem or a slight mental imbalance? I put the thought out of my mind immediately and continued watching him water the rose. He smiled. "I want you to observe the rose now that I have watered it. Don't you see that it is satisfied? The tension has gone. It is at ease."

I nodded in agreement.

"If you go and look at the two photographs now, you'll see the same difference. I photographed the woman before and after love-making. I took a picture of her the moment she arrived at the studio. Then I made love to her and took another photograph."

I felt embarrassed. But he wore a mischievous grin as he said, "I should add that I am quite good at it . . ."

He chuckled at that, and I couldn't help laughing too. I spent two hours with him. As we ate, he drank his way through a bottle of wine, and then we went back onto the balcony. We spoke of everything, art, love and poetry. I told him about my family and my dreams.

Suddenly he blurted out, "Do you know, Kamel, I am not actually Egyptian. My father is Turkish and my mother's Spanish. I was born in Italy in a city called San Remo. I came to Egypt when I was two. Despite that, I feel as Egyptian as you are. I often ask myself what has made me love Egypt so much, and, believe me, I can't come up with a specific answer. Everything in Europe is on a higher level than in Egypt. The streets there are cleaner, and everything is elegant and shiny. But Egypt exerts its ineffable pull. The best thing about Egypt is its soul, and that's something you can't put your finger on."

"The Egypt you love," I said ruefully, "is occupied and humiliated."

"That won't last forever. It will pass. This is a country that has given civilization to the world for thousands of years. Egypt will be victorious, and she will regain her independence."

"But how can we bring down the empire upon which the sun never sets?"

"History teaches that the strongest empires are brought down by the powerless."

"Sometimes I feel that those words are just theoretical."

"No, Kamel. That's the truth. The will of the people cannot be resisted forever. Thanks to what you and your colleagues are doing, the English will soon discover that their occupation of Egypt is costing them more than they can afford, and they will have to leave eventually."

That last sentence shocked me. How did the prince know what I was up to? We sat in silence for a while, and then he added, "I should like you to visit me from time to time."

"That would be a great honor, sir."

That was the signal that our visit had come to an end. I got up and told the prince that I should be going. He shook my hand at the studio door and with a warm smile told me, "Listen, Kamel. From now on, consider me your friend."

"I am honored by that, sir."

As I turned to leave, he suddenly added, "I forgot to tell you. There's an English girl who needs lessons to improve her Arabic. Do you have any time to help her?"

"I have never taught anyone before."

"But you are a poet, and your Arabic is good. She needs only a few hours' help a week."

I said nothing. He put his hand on my shoulder, and still smiling, asked, "Do you agree then?"

"Of course, sir."

"Bravo! Tomorrow at nine a.m. go and see Mr. Wright. The student you'll be teaching is his daughter, Mitsy. I have arranged everything with him."

18

As they carried out the corpse of Abd el-Aziz Gaafar, his wife, Umm Said, and his daughter, Saleha, sobbed. Their neighbor Aisha, Ali Hamama's wife, let out piercing wails that reverberated throughout the building and reached the ears of the people in the street. Then she rushed over and threw herself onto the coffin. When the other mourners pulled her away, she started slapping her cheeks so violently that the women had to restrain her before she hurt herself. It was in this, and in other ways, that Aisha showed her sympathy for the family of the deceased. She had offered her flat to the scores of mourners who had turned up from Cairo and Upper Egypt. Throughout the mourning period, she never once left the family of the deceased even for a day. She cooked for them every day in her flat, sending her daughter, Fayeqa, over with the food, instructing her to give Umm Said any help she needed. In fact, Fayeqa did much of their housework, doing the wash and hanging it out to dry, sweeping and mopping the floor, scouring the water jars, before refilling them, adding a few drops of rosewater and lining them up to cool on the window ledge. She aired the cushions, sheets and bedspreads in the sunshine. And after all that, she even fed the chickens, which Umm Said kept on the roof, cleaning the coop every Friday. But was Aisha's great sympathy for the family of the bereaved devoid of an ulterior motive?

This is a difficult question to answer, because Aisha was well known in the street for her compassion, being the first to help anyone who needed it. On the other hand, the way Aisha stood solidly by Umm Said during her ordeal had another inescapable effect. Fayeqa, spending most of the day cleaning in the house of the deceased, had fallen in completely with the appearance of mourning: yet her unadorned, simple black robe was somehow tight enough to show off her tempting curves and short enough, falling just below knee level, to reveal the gleaming paleness of her calves (particularly when she was sitting). Fayeqa had stopped putting on her regular makeup and made do with a hint of kohl around her eyes, a dab of powder on her cheeks and a touch of red on her luscious lips, though this minimal application somehow made her look more radiant than ever. Instead of painting her nails bright red, she used an almost transparent varnish, so her hands and feet looked far too beautifully manicured to do mundane, menial jobs. In short, Fayeqa's mourning guise in no way detracted from her beauty; on the contrary, it somehow only enhanced her loveliness and allure. Fayeqa looked as if she were performing a scene in which grief was mixed with beauty, sadness with seduction.

It was a moving performance, watched closely by one person— Said Gaafar, who came home from school every afternoon to find Fayeqa walking around with a tray of food or setting the table. As much as he tried, he could not stop watching her quivering bosom, which for so long had afforded him unforgettable pleasure. Said would eat something quickly and then take a nap. When he woke up, he would find Fayeqa in the kitchen washing the dishes, or he would watch her leaning out of the window as she hung the laundry. Then his imagination would run wild with obscenely tantalizing images. At first Said would remember his dead father, feel embarrassed and suffer pangs of conscience. He would make an effort to avert his gaze from Fayeqa's body, but his passion raged on inside him, completely overcoming his misgivings and exciting him until it was painful. The mere presence of Fayeqa aroused him, never mind seeing her walk back and forth around the apartment, causing the blood to drain from his face, turning his vision blurry until it was all he could do not to pounce on her from behind. When she spoke, the playful tone and cadence of her mellifluous voice kept him from understanding her words. Even when she asked God to have mercy on his father, her lips half opened and closed again so sensually that he could think only of kissing her. Said had not touched Fayeqa since she had blown her top and left him on the roof. He had tried time and time again to talk to her after that, but she had stubbornly refused. One day, an opportunity arose when he was alone with her in the kitchen.

"Fayeqa," he whispered, panting with lust and excitement. "I'm going up to the roof. Please come. I need to talk to you."

She gave him a stone-cold look. "Go up on the roof? And do what, Said? What do you take me for? You should be ashamed of yourself."

The rebuke was harsh, but he registered something in her voice that gave him hope. He asked again and received a second refusal but slightly less harsh than the first. He started pleading with her as she continued to refuse, then became angry and confused, finally hesitant and grudgingly agreeing. She followed him up the stairs and stood a little way from him on the roof. When he tried to get closer, she drew away and told him, "Keep your distance."

He did not appear to hear. He seemed to be hypnotized or perhaps possessed as he stepped closer. As she pummeled his chest, her beautiful kohl-lined eyes staring out at him fiercely, she said, "If you touch me, I'll scream till the house comes down."

His face drooped, and in a broken, pitiful voice, he asked her, "Why are you being so hard on me, Fayeqa?"

"I'm doing the right thing."

"I love you."

Fayeqa leaned back a little, bit her lip, raised her left eyebrow and then sighed, "'I love you'? What bank can I deposit that in?"

Her callousness aroused him again, and he whispered hoarsely, "Let me hold you one more time."

"Not a chance."

"Just for my sake."

"Listen, buster! I made a mistake with you and I have repented. If you think I'm going to lower myself again, you have another thing coming."

"Fayeqa."

"A respectable man enters a house through the door."

She uttered the sentence with finality. Then she turned to go back down the stairs, but Said called after her, "Just one minute. I want to talk to you."

Fayeqa shrugged and said, "The time for talking is over, Said."

He watched her walk away. The sight of Fayeqa going down the stairs was, without exaggeration, a living masterpiece, perfectly uniting the elements of sound, sight and rhythm. Her house shoes, clacking against her feet as she walked, sounded like the ostinato of a virtuoso tabla player. With every step she took, her body undulated in three different directions: her heavy thighs rubbed together with a slight swishing sound, her full breasts imprisoned in her robe wobbled and announced their overweening presence, and her large and luscious backside heaved from side to side as evenly as an enormous pendulum. Fayeqa's backside was so undeniably unique in its contours and contents that the particulars could fill up pages. Her backside, so soft and full of vitality, seemed, in its perpetual motion and in the scores of delightful and seductive poses it struck, to possess a life of its own. Fayeqa's body burbled like an active volcano, exuding such strong waves of desire in the direction of Said that he turned to jelly. He spent sleepless nights tossed by swells of such violent passion until he could take no more, and one evening he finally went to talk to his mother. She was sitting on the sofa fingering her green amber prayer beads. Said burst into her bedroom with a hurried greeting before sitting down next to her. "Mother, I want to talk to you about something."

He seemed excited and impatient, desperate to unburden himself.

"What is it, son?" she asked smiling.

"I want to propose to Fayeqa, Ali Hamama's daughter."

"Propose what to Fayeqa?"

"I mean, I want to get engaged to her and marry her."

Umm Said sighed and set her prayer beads down. "Good Lord above. You've gone mad. Your father is not yet cold, and you want to get married?"

Said tried to calm her down, but she became even angrier, shouting, "You should be ashamed of yourself! Is this any way to carry on?"

When they heard her, Kamel and Saleha rushed into the bedroom to see what was going on. Said told Saleha to get back to her own room, but Kamel stayed to hear the story. He looked at his brother. "I can't believe," he said, "that you are thinking about marriage right now. Can't you wait a year?"

"Shut up, Kamel," Said shouted at him. "It's none of your business."

"And how is it none of my business? It's not right for you, and it's not right for Fayeqa's family. How could Ali Hamama agree to your marrying his daughter when we are still in the period of mourning for our father?"

Said, aware of the seriousness of the matter, tried as hard as he could to suppress his anger. "Fayeqa's family," he replied, "don't know anything about this."

At this point, his mother cried out, "Listen, my boy, are you a fool, or do you take us all for idiots?"

Said listened silently as his mother harangued him until she sank back, exhausted, sobbing quietly. Staring at Kamel, Said said, "Mother, I'd like to speak to you alone."

"Your brother is not a stranger," Umm Said mumbled, her face wet with tears. Kamel, however, stood up and said, "I'll leave you two alone, Mother."

After Kamel had shut the door behind him, Said went over to his mother, kissed her head and hands and sat down beside her to lay out his case. He told her that he would rather die than displease his mother. He promised that he would always be her faithful son who sat at her feet waiting for her blessing. But, for the life of him, he could not understand what had made her so angry? He had not committed any sin or broken the civil or religious law. He just wanted to get married. Marriage in itself was not a crime or an offense to the religion, and he was twenty-three. Wasn't that a good age for marriage? Did not the most noble of all beings (here Umm Said mumbled praise on the Prophet) himself say in words that are recorded to this day, "He among you who is capable should marry"? In Islam you are encouraged to marry young, and thank God we are Muslims. Anyway, in a few days' time, he would graduate from the vocational school with a diploma. He had already agreed to take a job in Tanta, please God, and thus he would be able to support his own household and not cost the family a penny. Did his darling mother want him to live alone in a strange town, without a wife to look after him? He explained that it was not as if, God forbid, he was trying to foist a stranger upon the family.

"It's Fayeqa, daughter of Ali Hamama, the neighbors who are almost family to us already. It's Fayeqa," he told his mother, "who has been as distraught over our loss as we children are. It's Fayeqa, who has not left your side for a day, who has served you like a daughter. After everything she has done for us, doesn't she deserve something? After all, Mother, you are an Upper Egyptian, brought up to want things correct and proper. You don't like things to be off-kilter. Is it right for Fayeqa to come in and out of our flat when, according to religious law, Kamel and Mahmud and I should not be in the same room with her? Wouldn't it be more proper if I were to marry her under the law of God and his Prophet before the wagging tongues, which you know there are in our street, start wagging? Is that such a problem, Mother?"

Umm Said was lying on the sofa and had stopped crying. When she gave no response, Said plucked up his courage and continued enthusiastically, "I know what the problem is, Mother. You feel that my marriage before a year has passed is wrong because it is against the conventions of mourning. But marriage in itself, Mother, is not a form of rejoicing. It is at the party after the wedding where the rejoicing takes place, but I can marry Fayeqa without a party. Neither Fayeqa nor I nor her family want to violate the period of mourning for our father. I will marry her quietly, Mother. No party, no ululations, no tambourines and no belly dancer. God forbid, I should have anything like that! All I want is for the *fatiha* to be read now and in a week or two for us to sign the marriage contract so that we can go be together in an apartment I'm going to rent in Tanta."

Said continued this refrain until his mother finally conceded. The following day, at dawn, Aisha was surprised by a visit from Umm Said. After kissing and hugging each other, drinking coffee and exchanging some chitchat, Umm Said gave Aisha a serious look and said, "Tell me, sister. Your daughter, Fayeqa. Has anyone been asking after her in marriage?"

"She's still young, Umm Said."

"Wonderful. I want her for my son Said."

Before Aisha could react to the surprise, Umm Said went on, "But there is one condition. And remember the proverb, 'Without a proviso, no happy ending.'"

"Proviso?" asked Aisha, bemused, looking with cautious curiosity at Umm Said, who was sitting back in her chair.

"If it is Said's fate to have Fayeqa, you need to know our circumstances. Our sorrow over Abd el-Aziz will never end. Not in a hundred years. Our tradition is to stay in mourning for a year, and in Upper Egypt we consider any celebration during the mourning period scandalous and shocking."

Aisha was surprised, and perhaps to give herself a little more time to think, she sighed and said, "God have mercy upon Hagg Abd el-Aziz, the best of all men."

This formula startled Umm Said somewhat. "If it is to happen," she continued, "it will be without any celebrations. No ululations, no guests and no white dress."

Umm Said was certain that Aisha would refuse this condition. Every mother in the world wants to celebrate on her daughter's wedding day, so how could Aisha agree to marry off her only daughter with no fuss or fanfare? Umm Said looked at Aisha expectantly and slightly defiant. "So what do you say?"

Aisha wiped the palms of her hand across her face, a reflex of hers when she was worked up about something. Then she looked back at Umm Said, who was still seated, and uttered the following words, enunciating slowly, "Let us pray for him who intercedes on your behalf, Umm Said."

"Prayers and greetings upon the Prophet Muhammad."

"Listen, Umm Said. I'll tell you something you will never forget."

19

James Wright was sitting in his office going over the Club budget. He was completely immersed in the numbers in the large ledger that lay open in front of him, when he suddenly became aware of the voice of Khalil the office clerk.

"Alku is outside and he wants to come in and see you, sir."

Wright looked at him in disbelief. "Why hasn't he made an appointment?"

"He says that the matter cannot wait."

Wright thought a little and then gestured at Khalil to show him in. In a matter of seconds, there was Alku standing in the middle of the office in all his full height. "I'm so sorry to have come without an appointment, but it's rather pressing."

"Has a new world war broken out?" Wright asked him.

Alku ignored the sarcasm and continued with the same urgency, "Mr. Wright, I am not leaving here until you have taken a decision to restore order."

"You've come to tell me what I have to do?"

Alku bowed. "I'm so sorry," he said submissively, "but something rather serious is going on."

"Good Lord!"

"Abdoun is inciting the staff against the Club management."

"How do you know that?"

"I have eyes everywhere."

Wright cleared his throat and, to give himself some time to think, started cleaning his pipe. He then packed it with tobacco and lit it, and after a long while, he said calmly, "Every day you concoct new problems to get me to fire Abdoun. You have to understand that I will not fire him."

"Mr. Wright," Alku responded in his most ingratiating tone, "Abdoun has said some things that are unacceptable."

"Such as?"

"He claims that we killed Abd el-Aziz Gaafar just because we gave him a slapping and that he died from the humiliation. He said that we treat the staff like dogs and urged them to complain to me about their treatment."

"And has anyone come to see you?"

"None of them would dare."

"So what's the problem?"

Alku looked at him with incredulity. Then he pulled himself together, saying, "Abdoun needs to be punished for what he said."

"I shall not punish anyone for having whispered something to his colleagues."

"I can provide ten witnesses to what he said."

"And Abdoun would produce ten saying the contrary, and then there would be no time for work because we'd be investigating every scurrilous rumor. I don't see the profit of that."

"If we don't punish Abdoun immediately, all the staff will turn against us."

Wright sighed, evidently at the end of his tether. He looked at Alku and said, "Listen. You are the head of the staff. You should be above all these trivial matters. Pay no attention to the chatter that goes on behind your back. If someone says to your face something you don't like, then punish him, but as to all the whispering that goes on among the servants . . . spare yourself."

"What they say today behind my back, they'll say in front of me tomorrow."

"You are blowing it out of proportion."

"Mr. Wright, I have spent my whole life dealing with servants, and I know them very well. They only work diligently if they are afraid. And they are only afraid if they feel that at any moment they can be punished, whether on justifiable grounds or not! If a man of the serving class has confidence in himself and his capabilities, if he thinks he can seek justice, if he feels that he has rights, he will rebel immediately. Justice only corrupts because if you have become accustomed to being treated badly, you cannot understand justice. If you give a servant any respect, he will misbehave. Respect is a difficult concept for a servant because he considers it a form of weakness. No matter how much a servant might complain about the harsh treatment he receives from his master, he can understand the reason for it and he respects it."

"Rest assured," Wright said, having exhaled a cloud of smoke from his pipe. "There is not going to be any rebellion. Keep an eye on the situation and keep me updated."

Alku was on the point of objecting, but Wright went back to reading the ledger. That was a sign that the meeting had ended.

As etiquette dictated, Alku bowed and asked, "Anything else I can do, sir?"

"No."

Alku left Wright gazing at his numbers. He was so distracted that after a few minutes, he could no longer take in what he was reading. He got up and told Khalil that he was not to be disturbed and then locked the door from the inside. Except for a glass of wine with lunch, Wright never drank during office hours. But in his office he kept a bottle of whiskey for guests from which, over the course of a year, only a few glasses had been drunk. Now, however, he felt the pressing need for a drink. The first gulp unleashed all his anxieties. Good Lord, what had let all these genies out of the bottle? He felt cursed. Why was everything conspiring against him? Imagine, his daughter turning down an invitation from the king. How many girls in the world would think of doing that? It was just more of Mitsy's endless objectionable behavior, and as usual her aim was to provoke him. No more, no less. Had he ordered her to turn the invitation down, she would have insisted on going. What could explain her great joy in being contrary? What had he done to make his daughter dislike him so much, and why was he facing one crisis after another? What was going on in the Club? Abdoun was just an ordinary worker, an insignificant insect under ordinary circumstances. He had given him the position as a favor to Odette. And now Abdoun was trying to incite his colleagues to rebellion? Wright smiled at the irony. He went over his conversation with Alku and felt depressed. Alku was right. What

Abdoun had said could only corrupt the serving staff, and under normal circumstances, he would have been fired immediately for much less. Wright took another sip of whiskey.

"Why did I overrule Alku?" he mused. "Why did I say the opposite of what I believe? Am I so afraid of upsetting Odette? How could I have fallen so low? An old dodderer who lies to keep his young lady happy?"

He poured himself another whiskey and sat down, stretched out his legs and took a large gulp, feeling its warmth spread through him. How had Odette managed to make him so subservient? Now he spent his days just waiting to meet her. His normal life, his time in the office and at home, even meetings at the Club, were all passed in anticipation of his meetings with Odette, which now seemed like his real life. Everything else was dull and unreal. The shame of it. Had his desire made him forget his honor? He finished his third whiskey and told himself, "I am an old man and might die at any moment. I have to keep my honor. My relationship with Odette may be sinful, but what I did to Alku is a grave error. Being unfaithful to my wife harms no one except her, but lying and going against my better instincts for the sake of my own desire is a complete and utter abdication of morals."

The alcohol only sharpened his feelings of dissatisfaction. He left the Automobile Club and went for lunch at the Gezira Club. After another glass of whiskey, he could contain himself no longer. He telephoned Odette and asked her if he could come and see her immediately. Her voice was guarded, as if she had been expecting his call. They agreed to meet an hour later at the apartment.

He had another glass, paid the bill and whiled away the hour pacing the streets of Zamalek. At the appointed time, he went up to the apartment, and the moment he had let himself in, she appeared in front of him, and he hugged her. Odette laughed. She stretched her leg out behind her and kicked the door shut. They kissed for a long time, and the heat from her body made the blood flow uncontrollably in his veins. He held her tight, covering her face and neck with kisses, but she pushed him away gently.

"What is it you wanted to see me about so urgently?" she asked affectionately.

"I'll tell you later."

"I want to know now."

He moved away from her and slowly poured two glasses of whiskey as he pondered how to begin. He gave her a glass and sat down on the chair facing the door. "You know how much I love you."

She nodded and smiled.

"You asked me to give Abdoun a job at the Automobile Club," he went on. "And I did it because you asked."

Odette took a sip from her glass and lit a cigarette. "I'm deeply grateful for that."

"Abdoun has been causing some problems."

"What awful thing has he done? Has he killed someone in your great club?"

"He is inciting the staff against us."

"What a heinous crime. Why don't you throw him to the hungry lions as the Roman emperors did to those who annoyed them?"

"Please don't be so sarcastic. I need your help."

"What do you want me to do?"

Wright hesitated a little and then said quietly, "Odette, you have to make Abdoun understand that he can't shoot off his mouth."

"What did he say?"

"He's demanding an end to corporal punishment."

Odette looked at him in shock and shouted, "Corporal punishment? You mean you have your underlings beaten?"

"I don't."

"Then who does?"

"The overall head of the staff. He orders the punishments."

"And you find that acceptable?"

"Oh, please stop it!"

"Even if you don't participate in that crime yourself, you're just as guilty."

"It's not a crime."

"If you beat an underling in Britain, you'd be tried in court and sent to prison."

Wright tut-tutted and said, "We are not in Britain, Odette. Your problem is that you live in cloud-cuckoo-land. You are incapable of seeing reality. I've already told you that Egyptians are different from Westerners."

"So you think that a British worker deserves to be treated decently whereas an Egyptian needs to be beaten?"

Wright sat in silence. He downed his drink in one gulp, and the blood rushed to his face as Odette became more worked up and shouted at him, "Answer me!"

"What can I say?"

"Do you not think that all men have equal rights?"

"Everyone is entitled to the same rights, but their understanding of rights is different."

"Don't play around with words. Go ahead and tell me your honest opinion: Should Egyptians be subjected to more humiliating treatment than British people?"

"Yes. That's what I think!" Wright, now red in the face, barked. He went over to the window, and turning his back to Odette, he shouted, "I've had enough of your lectures. Listen to me and you'll understand once and for all. Egyptians are stupid, lazy liars. If you don't like my opinion, then I'm sorry. I am the general manager of the Automobile Club, and a member of staff I appointed as a favor to you is causing problems with his colleagues. Tell him to keep his trap shut and not to stick his nose into other people's business. Tell him that the Club rules will never change. Any servant found wanting will be dealt with severely."

Wright rattled off this whole speech looking out of the window. When he turned around, Odette had already picked up her handbag and was heading for the door. Wright sprang after her and grabbed her by the arm, but she pulled away.

"Leave me alone."

"Odette, please listen."

"How can I be involved with a racist like you? I don't understand how I agreed to it in the first place. Fire Abdoun or beat him. Do what you want. I don't care. But you'll never see me again."

He tried to hold on to her, but she wriggled out of his grip and slammed the door behind her. Sinking into the chair, Wright felt dizzy. He'd had a lot to drink and felt overwhelmed by the events of the day. And now Odette had stormed out on him just because he objected to Abdoun's behavior. Who was this Abdoun that he could so affect Odette? Why was she so worked up over a menial? A thought he had long been trying to suppress came back to him. What sort of relationship did they have with each other anyway? Was this Negro bedding her and giving her so much satisfaction that she did not need another lover? He was even younger than Odette by several years!

Wright could not completely dispel his anxieties. An affair between Abdoun and Odette seemed improbable, but experience had taught him to not discount the implausible. Abdoun was a handsome young man, and some women are attracted to their social inferiors. They lust for servants, drivers and waiters just as some men run after maids and cooks. He shut his eyes and leaned back in the chair, a bitter taste in his mouth. Why had Odette run out on him? He had longed to go to bed with her, even if just one last time. But his feelings were mixed. He loved her but resented her too. He adored her but hated the weakness she made him show. Sometimes he regretted not having met her when he was younger so that he could have married her and spent his life with her, but other times he wished he had never met her. Thinking back to their last conversation, he wondered, "How could she speak to me so haughtily? Does she think I have no dignity? That she thinks she won't lose me no matter what she says or does. She may have led other lovers by the nose, but I'm a different kettle of fish."

The alcohol was making Wright bolder. "It's time I behaved like a man. If Odette doesn't want me, I won't be begging her. I won't die if she leaves me. To hell with it all."

He had not behaved badly toward her. It was she who had flared up for no reason. If she expected him to run after her, she was delusional. He resolved not to call her again.

He went home feeling better for his resolve. The following day he went to work as usual. He tried to focus on his work, but it was no use. He could not help but think of Odette, seeing and hearing her in a hundred different settings. He could feel the warmth of her body melt him away.

"Naturally, it'll take me a little time to get over her," he told himself.

That evening, as he was sipping a whiskey at the Club bar, he started thinking it over. Had it been worth having that argument with Odette? Hadn't he shown her too much wrath? Even if he was in the right, even if he had decided to break it off with her, wasn't it wrong simply to drop out of her life? Wasn't that a childish way to react?

Why not call her and dump her as she had dumped him, making her see her stubbornness and his rectitude? If he could just have a few words with her, she would regret her actions, and that would be worth the effort. He decided to call her, not because he missed her but simply to apprise her of his decision. It would be a lesson she would never forget. He would dent her illusions in just a few words, giving her to understand her rash stupidity. Then he would simply put the receiver down.

He picked up the telephone and asked for the number, and the moment he heard her voice, he said, "Odette."

"What do you want?"

"I've been thinking about what you said. I think that you're right. We should end it."

"Good."

She said the word calmly and hung up. He was stunned. He had expected her to say more, to get angry and start a quarrel. Then he would have told her how wrong she had been, and she would have told him her side of the argument, but she had not even given him a chance. He was befuddled completely. After another glass of whiskey, he called again, but this time she did not answer. Frantic now, he tried to call her again, holding the receiver to his ear until the ringing tone cut off, then hanging up and trying again. He went back to his seat in the bar and drank another glass, asked for the bill and tried to steady himself. He had drunk too much. He got in his car, and half an hour later he was standing in front of her apartment. He rang the bell a few times. Finally, the door opened. He moved forward, and she stepped back to let him in. She closed the door behind him, and in a voice that seemed to come from someone else, he said, "Odette, I'm so sorry for the way I behaved yesterday. Please forgive me. Don't leave me. I love you."

20

Even if Mahmud Gaafar did have difficulty understanding things and could not express himself clearly, he still had feelings the same as everyone else. The death of his father had been a great shock to him. He had cried like a child all the way to the cemetery. He missed his father's gentle love and his patience with Mahmud's repeated failures at school. He no longer remembered those two times when he had done something so stupid that his father had thrashed him, recalling only his father's disappointed affection. Mahmud felt lost, as if his life's mainstay had gone. His grief over his father was heartfelt, though he still used it as an excuse to skip school. At the start, his mother thought this was a natural response, but after he'd been two weeks at home, she brought him breakfast in bed, then kissed him on the forehead with a doleful look and said, "Death has come upon us, son, but you have got to go back to school and work hard to try to achieve what your late father wanted for you. He wanted to see you finish school."

Mahmud sighed, looked downcast and answered, "How can you think about school, Mother? At a time like this. I couldn't cope with it."

His mother kept at him, and finally, just to end the discussion, he responded, "All right. Let's see how it goes."

After that, two or three times a week at most, he would leave the apartment at the start of the school day, and as was his wont, he would spend the day in the café or playing soccer on the triangle, then grab his school books and go home.

Gradually, his mother stopped badgering him about school. The sudden death of her husband had drained her so that she no longer had the energy to worry about Mahmud, who she knew would give up school completely sooner or later. Perhaps she thought that the money spent on lazy Mahmud's school fees would be better spent for something else. So Umm Said stopped badgering and achieved a sort of peaceful coexistence with her son. When Comanus came to ask for two sons of the deceased to work with him at the Automobile Club, Mahmud was enthusiastic, seeing the job at the Club as putting an end to school for good. No one could reasonably ask him to go to school if he had a decent job. Before taking it, Mahmud had listened carefully to his mother's and his brother Kamel's advice, and his dark face appeared almost happy.

"Mahmud, work is not like going to school," Kamel said. "You can't skip it. If you don't turn up, they'll fire you immediately."

"Son," Umm Said added, "at work you're going to be around people who don't know you. You have to be polite and nice to them all. If someone says something you don't like, take a deep breath. God has given you a strong body, and if you get into a fight, you might kill someone, and what a catastrophe that would be! May God protect you, son."

He had no need of those wise words because he had already decided to work hard. From the very first day, Mahmud felt like he had been born anew. At last he was enjoying the sort of life he had hoped for: he woke up at noon, his mother brought him breakfast in bed and they would chat as he ate. Then he would drink two glasses of tea, one with milk and one with mint, followed by two cups of medium-sweet coffee. After making sure that his mind was clear and his mood settled, he would get out of bed and start his daily routine, which, under whatever circumstances, he had to carry out meticulously before he could leave the apartment and face the world. He would take a shower, washing very carefully every inch of his body. Then he would shave, running the razor over his face a few times until it was silky smooth. Forcing his brush through his wiry hair with the help of Smart's Brilliantine, he would shape it with a broad part on the right. That done, he would put on his sharpest clothes, add a few sprays of Old Spice, and kiss his mother's forehead and hands on his way out the door. When he reached the Automobile Club, he would go straight up to the changing room on the roof, where he would fastidiously hang up his clothes and put on his uniform: narrow black high-waisted trousers, which showed off his strong thighs, with a wide red stripe running down the outside leg seams, a tight-fitting embroidered jacket, which showed off his bulging torso and rippling chest, and an elegant red tarboosh on his head. He would walk out of the Club door and strut down Qasr al-Nil Street to the garage, which was in a narrow alley, just off Ismailiya Square. There Mahmud would sit in his embroidered uniform next to Mustafa, the old driver, and the two of them would wait, chatting and drinking one glass of tea after another until the telephone rang and the telephonist gave them details of a delivery to a Club member. At that point, Mahmud would run the order to Rikabi the chef while Mustafa got the Citroën delivery van from the garage, and when Mahmud returned with the order, they would set off. Mustafa started teaching Mahmud the ropes from the first day.

"Mahmud," he said, "the way you deliver the order is more important than the order itself."

"I don't understand."

"As you hand over the order, you have to smile, lower your voice and bow to the customer, keeping your eyes down."

"What a performance!"

"Listen, son. The most important thing is to make the Club members feel that they are important. Prestige is more important to them than food and drink. Treat them as VIPs, and they'll tip you."

Their deliveries always took them to the homes of Club members in Garden City, Zamalek and Maadi, or sometimes in Heliopolis. People usually ordered hot food or some of Rikabi's wonderful patisseries. Very often they might be having a drinks party and would order a bottle of whiskey along with hot and cold canapés. Day by day, Mahmud slowly learned the routine. At the member's apartment, he'd ring the doorbell and then take two steps backward. The servant or maid might open the door, and Mahmud would ask if he could see the master or the lady of the house. When he or she appeared, Mahmud would spring forward, bow respectfully and say reverentially, "Good evening, sir. Delivery from the Automobile Club."

If it was a foreigner, he would say it in the broken French that he had learned with some difficulty from Mustafa: "Bonsoir, Monsieur. Livraison, Automobile Club."

The servant would take the delivery from him while the member signed the check. In most cases, a banknote would be tendered to Mahmud by the happy-looking master or lady of the house. His handsome, young face, his ebony skin, his pearly teeth, which glistened when he smiled, his giant frame with its bulging muscles, his embroidered uniform, which made him look more like a matador or a cavalryman on parade, his repeated and majestic bows—this all inspired the admiration of the customers, magnifying their sense of importance and with that their generosity. He would split the tips with Mustafa and then divide his share with his mother, which left him with enough spending money for his outings with Fawzy. Mahmud continued working and helping at home in this way, always making sure to ask his mother if she needed anything. He became more sure of himself and offered his opinions confidently on a variety of subjects. He had become a man with family responsibilities, and no matter how late he woke up every day, his mother would bring him breakfast in bed, which he felt he now well deserved.

But Mahmud's job at the Automobile Club also opened his eyes to a different reality: there was a world out there quite different from al-Sadd al-Gawany Street and the triangle, the Rimali Mill and the Ali Abd el-Latif School. It was a wonderful, variegated world, heaving with hitherto unimagined delights. He discovered that there were much greater pleasures than playing football, skipping school or kissing schoolgirls furtively in the cinema. The Club members lived in palatial apartments and wore elegant clothes, just like in the movies. Mahmud started to wonder how it was that some people could be so rich. Where did they get all that money?

"They are rich because they had rich parents, Mahmud. They have no idea of the misery we live in," said Mustafa quietly, half in bitterness and half in scorn. "Their only problem in this world is how to spend their money and have a good time."

As time passed, Mahmud developed a core group of regular customers. There was Sarwat Bey, who was always hosting poker games for his friends, and when his alcohol ran out, he would order a bottle of whiskey and trays of canapés from the Club. Monsieur Papazian, the old Armenian owner of the famous watch store in Ataba Square, who lived by himself in Diwan Street in Garden City and ordered dinner frequently. There was Ahmad Fadaly, the well-known cinema director and lady-killer, who took his girlfriends to his love nest in Shawarby Street; he would generally order dinner for two and a good bottle of French wine. He sent his servants away and would always open the door himself, in nothing but a silk robe, accepting the delivery while his lady friend waited inside the apartment. The nicest of all was Madame Khashab. She was a short, plump Englishwoman, a little over sixty, who dyed her hair black except for a shock of white hair at the front. She was the widow of an Egyptian landowner named Sami Khashab. They had no children, and after his death, she moved to a spacious apartment in Zamalek. Mahmud liked her from the start. He liked her maternal face, her permanent gentle smile and her hesitant Arabic. Whenever he delivered her favorite fruit tart, she would greet him warmly and exchange a few pleasantries with him as he stood at the door. Madame Khashab would ask after his family, and he would give a detailed answer. She would listen attentively, sigh and give him a large tip.

"Well done, Mahmud," she would say. "You're a fine lad. Look after your mother and your brothers and sister."

When he told her that his sister had passed her half-year exams, she congratulated him warmly, and when she held out the tip for him, there was an extra Egyptian pound as a gift for Saleha, who was delighted but also astonished because Madame Khashab had never met her. Mahmud explained that, despite her being English, she obviously loved Egypt and the Egyptians. Not only that, but she herself had the kind and generous character of an Egyptian.

Then one day Mahmud went to deliver the fruit tart to Madame Khashab as usual. She took it from him, they chatted and she gave him his tip and he thanked her as always. But before he could turn and go, she exclaimed as if she had forgotten something, "Just a moment . . ."

She went inside, disappearing for a few minutes, and returned dragging a heavy suitcase.

"Mahmud," she said. "You are like a son to me, aren't you?"

Mahmud nodded.

"These are some very expensive shirts, trousers and jackets," she continued. "They are all your size. Please don't embarrass me by refusing to take them."

The offer came as a complete surprise to Mahmud, who didn't know what to say, but Madame Khashab's maternal look and her kindly smile won him over, so he bowed and picked up the suitcase with one hand, thanking her warmly. Mustafa put the suitcase in the trunk. When Mahmud got home after work, his mother, sitting up waiting for him, was astonished to see him with a suitcase. Mahmud just smiled. "I'm hungry," he said. "I'll tell you about it as I eat."

He devoured an enormous quantity of eggs with sliced dried beef, cleaning the plate with a hunk of bread followed by two large rum babas for dessert. He got up to wash his hands and then sat next to his mother, sipping his tea as he told her how kind Madame Khashab was and how much she liked him. Then he explained about the suitcase. His mother made no comment, so he got up to open the suitcase and lay out the contents. Indeed, the clothes were very smart. Shirts, trousers and three suits all in his size. He held up a blue shirt with a white collar and said, "Look how smart this shirt is!"

Only at this point did Umm Said suddenly let out a stifled wail, "It's between you and God, Mahmud."

He dropped the shirt and rushed over to her, saying, "What's the matter, Mother?"

"She has turned us into beggars."

"What do you mean, beggars? It's a gift from a lovely lady."

"A lovely lady from whom you take old clothes."

"Mother, these are better than new. No one would ever know that they are secondhand."

"Even if no one knows, how can you make yourself a beggar?"

"Mother, I don't understand why you're so angry."

"You'll never understand because you're stupid. The most stupid thing God ever created. An oaf."

The word just slipped out of her. They sat there in silence, Mahmud like a scolded dog beside his mother. Umm Said put out her arms, hugged him and whispered, "I'm sorry, son. Don't be upset."

He shook his head and mumbled, "I'm sorry about it."

His humility only increased her sense of guilt. She kissed him on the forehead.

"My boy," she explained, the way one might to a baby in a cradle, "we are from a great family. Landowners. People with a sense of pride. We used to be well-off, but that's over now and we're poor. We might be miserable and forced to work, but we will never ask for anything from anyone. All we have left is our dignity. Never accept charity, Mahmud."

Feeling encouraged, Mahmud asked innocently, like a child who wanted to know, "Isn't the suitcase just like a tip from a customer?"

"No, my boy. Charity and a tip are different things. A tip is a sign of appreciation for something you have done, but charity is something you give to beggars."

They were silent for a while. Then Umm Said got up and stood facing him. "Do you love me, Mahmud?"

"Of course I do, Mother."

"If you love me, then take this stuff back to the foreign lady."

Mahmud stared at her in incomprehension.

"By the life of your late father, do what I tell you and then I won't be upset."

The following day, after they had made the first delivery, instead of going straight back to the Club, Mahmud asked Mustafa if they could please stop by his home on al-Sadd Street. And with the suitcase in the trunk once more, they set off for Madame Khashab's in Zamalek. Mahmud set the suitcase down in front of the door and rang the bell. A short while later, Madame Khashab appeared in a silk dressing gown. Her face betrayed her astonishment at seeing him, but she quickly smiled and asked, "Is everything all right, Mahmud?"

"Madame Khashab," he answered immediately, "I would like to thank you for the gift, but I cannot accept it."

"For what reason?"

"Because my mother got upset."

"Why would your mother get upset?"

"She says that we are not beggars to take charity from you."

"Oh," she exclaimed and mumbled a few words in English that he did not understand. Then she leaned over, dragged the suitcase back into the apartment and shut the door without saying anything further. Mahmud knew that she was angry and he felt bad. He almost regretted having brought the suitcase back, but when he recalled his mother's sad face, he realized that he had had no option.

The following day, his guilt started weighing on him. He ought to speak to Madame Khashab and explain, apologizing and begging her not to be upset with him. He would tell her that he really liked her and knew that she loved him like a son but that he had been obliged to do as his mother said. Days passed as Mahmud waited for Madame Khashab to order her favorite tart, but after a whole week, she still had not ordered a thing, and Mahmud told Mustafa what had happened. He just shook his head as he held the steering wheel. "Naturally," he said, "Madame Khashab is right to be upset. She did something nice for you, and you threw it back at her."

"So what should I do, Uncle Mustafa?"

"God knows, your mother is also right. You Gaafars are Upper Egyptian landowners, so how can you accept charity?"

"Uncle Mustafa. Now you've confused me. Whose side are you on?"

Mustafa shook his and pondered a while. "Listen, Mahmud," he said. "You want to make things up with Madame Khashab?"

"Of course I do."

"All right. Go buy her a nice bunch of flowers."

Mahmud appeared even more confused. "What are you talking about, flowers, Uncle Mustafa?" he said.

"Just do what I say, Mahmud. Foreign ladies love flowers. The best thing you can give a foreign lady is a bunch of flowers."

Mahmud trusted Mustafa even though he could not fathom this notion. He waited until Tuesday, his day off, and at around three o'clock in the afternoon made his way to Madame Khashab's apartment wearing his best clothes, from the downtown store Chaloun: black trousers, a white shirt and a gray velvet jacket. He was holding a bunch of red and white carnations in his hand. He rang the bell. After two minutes, he rang the bell again, but not a sound was to be heard. Mahmud realized that Madame Khashab either was not in or did not want to open the door. He was walking away when he heard the sound of footsteps. He gripped the flowers with his left hand, fixed a broad smile on his face and resumed his pose in front of the door, a little anxious, but ready come what may.

KAMEL

I could not sleep. Why had the rhythm of my life sped up so much? Why was I lurching from one situation to another? As if against my will, I was being thrust in a certain direction, as if my feet were leading me to a predetermined denouement. It all seemed unfathomable, working at the Club and getting to know the prince. Was it just a coincidence that he had come to the storeroom? Wasn't it odd that he should come and examine the wines himself? Perhaps not. But why would he invite me for lunch in his palace? Why this interest in me? Who am I that the king's cousin should care or approach me to give lessons to the manager's daughter? But the strangest thing is that he knew about my role in the resistance.

"Thanks to what you and your colleagues are doing, the English will evacuate the country." Was it just innocent wishful thinking, or did he know something? Perhaps recent events were all a matter of coincidence, or could they have been carefully planned? I lay in bed, brooding and smoking, and by the time of the morning call to prayer, I was exhausted and finally dozed off for two hours. My meeting with Mr. Wright was at nine o' clock that morning. I polished my shoes to within an inch of their life, ironed a shirt, pressed my suit and gave my tarboosh a good brushing. I arrived a few minutes early.

Khalil the office clerk greeted me. "May God grant you success." He smiled and then whispered, "Mr. Wright is one of the meanest men on earth. He hardly ever smiles. He just sits there with a fixed grimace and looks you up and down."

At nine exactly, I knocked on the door. I heard him call out sharply, "Enter."

"How are you?" he said in English.

"Very well, thank you, sir."

He gestured for me to sit down and then lit his pipe, exhaling a heady cloud of smoke.

"His Royal Highness Prince Shamel has put your name forward as someone who could give my daughter Arabic lessons."

"I'd be happy to, sir."

"My daughter, Mitsy, received her secondary education in London and then decided, for some unknown reason, to come and live in Egypt. She's now studying drama at the American University. She has some basic knowledge of Arabic but needs lessons in speaking and writing."

"Rest assured." I smiled. "She'll speak and write Arabic fluently."

Mr. Wright's glower made me realize I had overstepped the mark.

"I have decided on Tuesdays and Fridays," he informed me, "because Mitsy has no morning classes on those days. You'll start today."

I nodded in agreement. He looked at his watch and exhaled another puff of smoke, which hung in the air between us.

"I've lived in Egypt for twenty years," he went on, "and yet I still find Egyptian behavior odd. For example, I don't understand why the Egyptians cling to a complicated dead language like Classical Arabic."

"Because Arabic," I answered without thinking, "bears our history and is something all the Arab peoples have in common, as well as it being the language of the Quran."

"Delusional."

I said nothing. The conversation was taking a course I had not expected.

Mr. Wright smiled and then shot out another question at me. "Why don't you write in the everyday language you use for speaking?"

"The colloquial is not a written language. It's just a dialect. Lots of cultures have a written language and a dialect that they use for every day. The French and Americans also have various local forms that differ greatly from their written languages."

Mr. Wright shook his head, unconvinced. "The Egyptians will never advance," he added, "if they don't let go of that barren classical language."

"It's not barren," I interjected. "It's one of the richest living languages. Moreover, it is not Arabic that is the cause of Egypt's backwardness. Egypt is backward because it is under occupation."

There was a sudden look of disapproval in his bluish eyes.

"Were it not," he continued, "for what you call 'the occupation,' your country would still be in the Middle Ages."

"We didn't ask for anyone's help. And I don't believe that Britain has occupied Egypt for charitable purposes."

"And do you think," he asked with a look of contempt, "that Egyptians are capable of governing themselves?"

"The Egyptians ruled the civilized world for centuries."

"Yes, of course. You have to look to distant history for your glory because your present is not very inspiring."

"The deterioration in the quality of life in Egypt is due to the occupation that is systematically plundering our resources."

"Before the Egyptians start demanding independence, they need to learn how to think and work properly."

What a nasty, odd man. Just as arrogant as he was when my mother had dealt with him. What makes him talk like that? If he hates Egyptians so much, why does he live in their country? He didn't even shake my hand. He did not utter a word of thanks. Even if he is paying for the lessons, shouldn't he at least thank me for being so obliging? I was really irritated and thought that I should stand up for myself, give him a piece of my mind, and to hell with the Club. But I tried as hard as I could to avoid doing anything I might regret. Then I realized that this was not a spur-of-the-moment argument. He was driving at something. Maybe he was trying to take revenge for my mother's reprimand the first time we met. Perhaps he himself did not want me teaching his daughter and was trying to provoke me into saying something out of line so that he could fire me despite the prince. I decided not to take the bait.

I stood up and asked him calmly, "Mr. Wright, what time should I start the lesson?"

"When Mitsy's ready."

"What time will Mitsy be ready?"

"Wait outside," he snapped. "Khalil will take you there soon."

I waited for about a quarter of an hour outside his office before

Khalil came to collect me. We took the lift to the top floor and made our way to a small room next to the casino. I tried to control my anger and rid myself of the bad taste from our meeting. I swore to myself that if Mitsy exhibited the same vanity and arrogance as her father, I would quit, no matter how much he paid me. Khalil pushed the door, it opened slowly and I walked over to Mitsy, who was sitting at a small round table next to the window.

"Good morning," I said in English.

She stood up and shook my hand warmly.

"Hello," she smiled. "I'm Mitsy Wright. Thank you for having agreed to help me with my Arabic."

21

A week had passed and no punishment had been meted out to Abdoun. Seeing that he carried on chatting and laughing and doing his job as normal, the other staff kept warning each other nervously:

"Just wait. Alku will crush him like a cockroach."

"He'll make an example of him."

But when another week passed and nothing happened to Abdoun, they were disconcerted and confused. They started looking at the matter from different angles: if Abdoun was able to criticize Alku openly and carry on working for two weeks without being punished, then he was not mad or feckless as they had imagined. He knew exactly what he was doing. There was, however, something that still concerned them: Why had Alku not punished someone who had spoken up against him? After all, he had come to the Club and the fury on his face said he knew what Abdoun had been up to, but for all that, he did not make a move against him. What was the world coming to! If anyone had told them such a thing, they would not have believed him. Had Alku been struck by some debilitating illness, or did Abdoun enjoy the patronage of someone mightier than Alku? There was only one explanation that they could settle on: Abdoun had been planted by Alku himself. It was entirely plausible, because Alku was known for playing no end of dirty games, and this could be his latest devilish plot. He had planted among them someone to speak up against him, letting him go unpunished in order to check their loyalty. Karara the waiter took up this notion in the coffee shop.

"Be careful," he told his colleagues. "That lad Abdoun's a spy. Don't let him fool you into saying anything that could land you in the shit."

"You're right," some of those present responded. "Of course we can see that!"

Bahr the barman wagged his finger. As usual he was sitting there smoking a *shisha*. He blew out a heavy puff of smoke and told them, "Listen, all of you. Use your brains. Would Alku need to send Abdoun? He knows everything about us. He already has spies who report every last detail."

"Then you're on Abdoun's side?" Karara asked dejectedly.

"It's not a question of sides."

"How do you mean?"

"The guy is just doing what he thinks is right."

"Impossible!"

"Listen, all of you," Samahy the kitchen boy chimed in. "Abdoun is standing up for what's right. We are all taken aback because we're not used to someone speaking up."

Several of them then retorted:

"Even you, even your brain has gone soft!"

"If you go on like that, you'll go down with him!"

"That Abdoun's a spy. You'll see soon enough."

During the third week, they refrained from discussing the subject of Abdoun. Whenever they got together, they would talk about everything under the sun, tell each other jokes and have a laugh, but something inside them had changed. Except for Bahr and Samahy and a few other sympathizers, the staff now resented Abdoun. He was pushing them toward the unknown. He was upsetting the equilibrium. If he could speak up against Alku and get away with it, then why, for all those long years, had they been so submissive and put up with all his bullying? Their lives had been based on one truth: that Alku was a tyrant about whom they could do nothing. If their faith in that truth was shaken, then nothing was sacred.

As much as their image of Alku as a bully terrified them, it also gave them a sense of security. However harshly he might deal with them, he also looked after them and made them feel safe. At times of crisis, they looked to him the way a child clings to its mother in a crowded room. They derived their strength from him. They knew that he would always put things right. You could say that Alku was a husband, and they were his obedient wives. If they were in a predicament or felt something was going wrong, they would tell each other, "Alku won't like it. He likes everything to go like clockwork. Just wait and see what he does."

But now the ground rules were changing, and it perturbed them. Cause was no longer leading to effect. Something fishy was going on behind the scenes. How was it that Alku could know about Abdoun's outspokenness but not punish him? Moreover, Bahr and Samahy and maybe even others were publicly supporting Abdoun. What would Alku do to them? It would be a mockery if he left them unpunished, but it would not be logical to punish them and not Abdoun. Why would you punish the small fry and not the big fish?

As if the staff's anxieties had been communicated to Alku, he responded with a series of brutal daily inspections of the Club. From out of his black face, his eyes flashed like those of a wild animal about to savage its prey. He was no longer investigating a complaint or checking up on their work. He was searching for the slightest reason to punish them. If someone looked at him wrong or if there was the tiniest delay in carrying out his orders, he would gesture to Hameed, who would seize the victim for a slap and a few good kicks. The staff usually accepted the punishment mutely as if it was their inexorable fate or else cringed before Alku begging forgiveness. Now, a strange phenomenon could be noted. When a worker was being beaten by Hameed, he would make some sign of protest. He might mutter a word or make a gesture with his hand like someone who'd been wronged. These almost imperceptible and trifling objections bore a hidden message, an unspoken grudge: "You're having me beaten for the flimsiest of reasons while Abdoun rails against you in front of us all, and you haven't done anything about that."

Alku understood the message, and he would glower, gnash his teeth, ordering Hameed to beat the man harder.

Rikabi the chef, Maître Shakir and Yusuf Tarboosh in turn each oversaw a state of terror in their respective departments. Their pent-up anger made them snap if one of their subordinates made the slightest error, leading to reprimands and curses and confiscation of tips.

Yusuf Tarboosh slunk around behind his staff in the casino, and if he noticed something not right, he would say quietly to the man, "That's two days' salary gone. You'll learn." Maître Shakir was likewise pronouncing punishments and then walking off, ignoring the poor waiter's pleas. In the kitchens, Rikabi the chef, having meted out punishment to one of his staff, would look at the rest, hold up one finger in an obscene gesture and snarl at them, "By God, I have to put up with you bastards every day. If you think you're Abdoun's boys, you've got another thing coming."

The daily inspections continued, and the random bullying left the staff in a state of dejection. They now all worked in anxious silence, expecting the worst at any moment. The happy atmosphere that had existed as they cleaned the Club each morning was a thing of the past, dispelled by thought of the dark day to come.

In the midst of this misery, Karara the waiter surprised them all by rushing over to Abdoun when he walked through the Club door. "Who sent you," he shouted at him, "to cause such problems and turn us all against each other?"

Karara tried to slap his face but missed and hit his shoulder. Abdoun made no attempt to evade him but grabbed him by his waistcoat, pulling it so violently that he ripped it open at the neck, exposing his chest. Abdoun made the most of the moment of Karara's surprise to direct a punch at his nose.

Looking down at his ripped waistcoat, Karara touched his nose, incredulous that it was bleeding. "I'll rip your fucking clothes to pieces, you bastard!" he roared at Abdoun like a wild animal about to lunge.

But Abdoun anticipated him and jumped backward, landing another punch on Karara's nose, making him scream. Then Abdoun kicked him, and he fell to the ground. It was clear to all that Abdoun would have killed him were it not for three of their colleagues, Suleyman the doorman, Mur'i the lift operator and Labib the telephone operator, who had come out of his cubicle when he heard all the commotion. The three threw themselves between the two men rolling around on the floor, using their every ounce of energy to pry them apart. Karara carried on screaming obscenities, whereas Abdoun turned around calmly and walked up the stairs to the changing room.

The next day, some well-intentioned colleagues tried to get them to make peace with each other.

"We know that Karara slapped you," they told Abdoun. "But you ripped his waistcoat and punched him."

"He started it, so talk to him."

"Don't be like that, Abdoun. Karara is older than you. Come on; let's make it up."

Abdoun allowed himself to be led to the restaurant, where Karara was busy setting the tables.

"Peace be upon you," one of the men said to Karara.

"Peace and God's mercy be upon you," he murmured, realizing straightaway the purpose of their visit. The men started their attempt at reconciliation, saying, "Karara, Abdoun is your younger brother. You're like family to each other."

"It was a moment of madness, Karara. We're back to normal now."

"Both of you are in the wrong."

"For God's sake, Abdoun, shake hands with Karara."

They pushed Abdoun toward Karara, and he held out his hand as the others urged them on. Karara looked at Abdoun and, breathing heavily as if trying to contain himself, firmly shook his hand. A sense of relief descended, and some even cheered. Karara, unconvinced by the reconciliation, forced a half smile. He turned around and went back to laying out the cutlery, signaling that he wanted the parley to be over. The men decided that they had gone far enough and led Abdoun back out of the restaurant, feeling that they had done their good deed for the day. Except that what had transpired between Karara and Abdoun sent a message to everyone: no one should mess with Abdoun. That changed the way they spoke to him. When they disagreed with him, they expressed themselves without sarcasm or derision. The afternoon of the following day, they found him in the café and started firing the usual aggressive questions at him:

"So Abdoun, do you really think that you can fix the world?"

"Are you happy that our tips have been confiscated and we have blows raining down upon us?"

Abdoun looked back at them and answered calmly, "You're in the wrong. Instead of demanding your rights, you're afraid. You don't say anything, and as a result, Alku can do what he likes."

"You're enjoying this, aren't you, Abdoun?" someone asked him.

"By God, just the opposite. I feel bad for you, but if you had just demanded civil treatment from Alku, he couldn't be treating you any worse."

"You want us to go head-to-head with Alku?"

"Aren't we all human beings like he is?"

"You're deluded."

The conversation carried on in this vein until they all fell quiet, drained of the energy or will to keep discussing the matter. They tried to cheer themselves up at the café before going back to the drudgery of work. Their daily routine helped them to forget their predicament. Their submissiveness was a refuge, and they lost themselves in work, having come to the conclusion that with a little patience their ordeal would come to an end, and everything would go back to normal. Alku's rampages, however, only got worse, and bad luck does not come in single doses. As they were all busy doing the cleaning one morning, they were surprised to see Labib the telephone operator rushing toward them, shouting, "Help! Abd el-Malek is in a really bad way!"

22

The party was held in the hunting lodge in Fayoum, where the king stayed when he wanted to hunt waterfowl. It was an elegant, white two-story structure, with nothing else around it but a swimming pool beautifully illuminated at night by an underwater lighting system. Near the pool, two tables had been laid out a little distance apart so that those at one could not overhear what those at the other were saying. At the first table sat the old Princess Mahitab and her consort, Prince Shawkat, with Prince Shakib and his wife, and at the second sat Carlo Botticelli with three women, a white-skinned foreigner in her twenties, a plump olive-skinned woman in her thirties and, between them, Mitsy Wright wearing a low-cut black dress, showing off her cleavage and her beautifully turned shoulders, her long hair falling over them. Botticelli sat chatting with the three women as he looked them over with a hint of worry. He wanted to reassure himself that they were up to scratch. From time to time, Botticelli would get up and ask one of them to come with him. He would take a step backward and look at her as if examining an old master painting and then whisper a remark: "Go easy on the rouge," "You need to freshen your eyeliner" or "Straighten the shoulder of your dress." Then he would return to the table, letting the woman go off to the bathroom to carry out his instructions. He had already examined two of them, and now it was Mitsy's turn. She was surprised to find him pulling her away from the table by the hand.

"I want to speak to you," he said in English.

She got up and went with him. She had worked out what he was doing and was not going to let him give her a beauty critique as he had done with the others. If he mentioned her lipstick or her eyeliner, he would regret it. Perhaps guessing how she might react, he took a different tack. He looked at her and gave her an affectionate smile.

"You are so beautiful."

"Thank you."

"This night might be a turning point in your life. I hope that you appreciate the gravity of the moment."

"How's that?"

"Well, it's not every day that you meet the king."

"What exactly do you want me to do?"

"His Majesty adores beauty," Botticelli said suavely. "And if he asks for something, he always gets it."

Mitsy looked at him with anger in her eyes, but he continued, "You will see that His Majesty is a jolly nice chap and actually quite humble."

Mitsy turned her back on him and returned to her table. Botticelli was not in the least worried by Mitsy's sharp reaction. He knew that she would submit to the king if the time came. Otherwise, she would not have accepted the invitation in the first place. She had turned up, and that's what mattered. Her edginess was just her way of overcoming her shyness in the situation. How strange women are, Botticelli thought to himself as he looked again at the three sitting there in front of him. Were someone to say to any of them that they had come to sell their bodies, she would wipe the floor with him. They had this marvelous power of self-deception. Despite his long experience with women, or perhaps because of it, Botticelli had no great respect for them. Palace rumor had it that in his youth he had been in love with a Greek woman from Alexandria, only to discover that she had been cheating on him with a friend of his, and thereafter he never trusted a woman again. After having convinced scores of women to sell their bodies and finding well-thought-of and respectable women who were ready to go to bed with the king, he no longer believed that any woman could be virtuous. These seductive and delicate creatures all wore a false veneer of innocence but were ready to lie or do anything else for riches. Each had her price. Any woman could be seduced if the time and manner were right. Not surprisingly, Botticelli's opinion of women had led him to avoid marriage, leaving him a bachelor now in his fifties. When drinking with his friends, they would goad him about it, but he would just laugh.

"Why should I get married?" he would ask them. "I always have a mistress. Marriage is a just a chance to be a cuckold."

His friends kept trying to convince him otherwise, but Botticelli would dismiss their efforts with a wave of his hand and declaim, "Gentlemen! You can defend your romantic image of women all you like, but no one knows them better than I do. They are fantastic creatures but with no sense of honor. That's the sad truth, and there's no point denying it. You are like diners waiting for your meal in a restaurant, whereas I work in the kitchen and know how the most tempting dishes are prepared."

Waiting for the king to arrive, Botticelli sat at the table with the three prospective candidates. The table with the princes was superfluous to his plans, and they knew that they were merely extras, there to provide the right backdrop. It would have been unseemly for the king of Egypt and the Sudan to come and pick out a girl for the night surreptitiously, and so Botticelli had invited these members of the royal family to make the whole thing look aboveboard. In their part, the royal extras felt some pride that the king trusted them to observe him in his most private moments. They kept themselves removed from the main course of events, eating and drinking and chatting away in French, the princes spluttering and coughing with merriment as their wives laughed along sweetly and flirtatiously. From time to time they would cast a glance at the king's table in order to check whether they should go on paying no attention to what was happening behind their backs or whether the moment had come for them to make their excuses to the king and depart.

It was after one in the morning, and the king had still not turned up. Mitsy sat silently while the others chatted away with Botticelli, giving forced laughs as they kept glancing at the doorway, worried that the king might not turn up at all but not daring to ask Botticelli. Mitsy sat there among them in her own world. She had a blank smile on her face and an absent look in her eyes. She felt neither timorous nor anxious. She was just astonished. She had been watching everything as if it were a piece of theater. Yet again, she felt that she did not understand herself and that she was behaving out of character, as if driven along by some irresistible force. Why had she come? To present herself to the king or, more precisely, to wait for permission to go to bed with the king. That was the truth of the matter. She had done this to herself and could not claim to be a victim. She could not claim that her father had forced her into this. He could not make her do anything she did not want to.

She had announced to her father that she would not go to the party. She had done this for the pleasure of provoking him, and they had quarreled as usual, but this time he had become so furious that she could sense the heat of his incandescent rage. She avoided him now to the point of not sitting down to dinner with him but instead eating a sandwich or two in her bedroom. Three days before the party, she had knocked at the door of her father's study. The moment he saw her, his expression turned to one of anxiousness. He leaned back in his chair, bracing for any and all surprises.

"Have you told Mr. Botticelli that I'm not going?" she asked calmly.

"That's none of your business," he snapped at her. He was expecting her to answer him back, but she smiled innocently and said, "All right. If you haven't told him that I'm not going, then don't. I've changed my mind. I'll go."

His look of rage turned to one of astonishment and then gradually to one of delight and possibly even gratitude. He smiled and hesitantly, as if fearing that she might renege, he said, "Finally, you've made the right decision. I knew that you were too clever to miss this opportunity."

"I'll go out this evening," she informed him drily, "and buy a new dress as you told me to."

She did not wait for him to respond but turned and left the study, having taken in his astonishment. She seemed to enjoy foisting surprises upon him as much as defying him. Her father could never understand her behavior, but then neither could she.

She always felt the urge to rebel. She hated anything that was taken for granted or prearranged. She liked breaking rules or rushing headlong in the wrong direction. She took delight in pulling the rug from under people who were sure of themselves and their own wise decisions. She had been headstrong like this ever since she started school. If the class was sitting in silence, just at the moment when the teacher thought that he had got all his pupils quietly doing what he wanted, the temptation to make a scene would be too much for her. She would laugh suddenly or shout out to one of her friends and typically ended up being punished. How often had she had to stand in the corner throughout a whole lesson, and how many times had she had to write out the line "I must behave in the classroom"? That did not deter her, however. Her impetuosity stayed with her throughout her youth and even evolved, so that her ongoing challenge to authority also became a search for some hidden truth. As she confronted the status quo, the false smiles and hollow gestures, there was always something that she enjoyed blurting out to everyone's shock and horror. She craved sincerity. That was why she loved Egypt. She preferred to spend time in a small coffee shop in Cairo to going for dinner at the Carlton Club in London. The people here were real, and even if life was difficult, it was authentic, whereas in London things might be refined and elegant, but people were false.

It was this fickle and headstrong nature that helped Mitsy with her acting. When she appeared in a play, she never felt that she was performing. She would lose herself in the character she was playing. Once, during a rehearsal, a director had told her, "Mitsy, you are a very special actress. It's difficult for me to direct you because you are drawing on something inside yourself. I will talk you through your character without giving you any directions. Try to understand the character and then act her out in your own way."

She lived as if she were acting a role on stage. She would look inside herself for specific motivation, and then, having found it, she would give herself over to it. So had she accepted the king's invitation because she thought she might find the experience exciting or because the king's attention would gratify her feminine vanity? These were both plausible reasons, but her strongest motivation generally had to do with her father. Her mother was cold and emotionally inhibited, spending most of the time alone with her books, taciturn and almost totally indifferent to what was going on around her. Mitsy loved her notwithstanding all that, because her mother could not bring herself to tell untruths and always called a spade a spade. Her father was the diametric opposite: he was a liar and a hypocrite. He represented everything she hated. He was condescending and arrogant, always scuttling around after money and trying to cover up his behavior with a façade of moral probity. She resented him because she understood him too well. He had pushed her in the direction of the king's bed for his own benefit while trying to convince her that he just wanted her to be friends with the king. Her father lived in grand style in Egypt, but he never stopped complaining. He whined every day about having to live there even though he knew that in England he could not earn even half of what he made at the Automobile Club. He was paid well because he was English, not because he was the general manager of the Club. Perhaps the time had come to confront him about all his lies. Mitsy wanted to make him look in the mirror and to ask him, "So, you want me to be the king's mistress, and you call that 'innocent friendship'? All right, Mr. Wright. I'll sleep with the king, and in order to show you up, I'll make myself a pushover. I'll part my thighs the moment I see His Majesty. I know that will be of use to you, dear Father."

She told herself that she would go to bed with the king, but how would His Majesty get her there? Would he first kiss her? Would he ask her to strip completely naked in front of him? At this point, she thought back to Thomas, a ginger engineering student in London who never stopped laughing. He was the first man who taught her how to love, and they were happily together for two whole years before it ended abruptly. Did love have its own life span? Did it always burn for a specific amount of time and then splutter out like a candle? Still deep in her thoughts, Mitsy noticed Botticelli laughing away with the other two women, who were pretending to be amused by him. How she hated this slimy pimp. When she had first shaken his hand, she felt so defiled by his touch that she went straight to the bathroom to wash up. Now she felt like doing something to unmask the whole charade. She wanted to tell Botticelli that he was nothing more than a procurer and then to dash the haughtiness of those princes and princesses sitting at the other table by pointing out the true nature of their role as adjunct pimps, with their artificial chatter and forced sickening laughter. It was two a.m., and the king had still not made an appearance. The two other candidates had twice gone to the bathroom to adjust their makeup. Mitsy looked at them and said to herself, "You poor little tarts. So much time have you spent making yourselves beautiful only to see your hopes dashed."

Suddenly the one sitting on her right spoke, "Mr. Botticelli, hasn't His Majesty arrived yet?"

Botticelli gave her a cold stare.

"His Majesty is not a prisoner of punctuality. You can leave if you so wish."

The girl looked worried.

"I'm sorry," she said. "That's not what I meant. Of course I shall wait for His Majesty to appear."

"Whether you go or stay," retorted Botticelli sarcastically, "is of no importance. I don't think that the king will be greatly chagrined if he doesn't find you here tonight."

"Of course, Monsieur Botticelli," she said sycophantically. "I'm just aching to see the king, that's all I meant."

Botticelli averted his gaze from her as if to punish this insolence and started chatting with the other girl. But by half past two, the princes and the pimp were getting a little worried themselves, knowing the king only too well. If His Majesty was in the casino, then time lost all meaning for him. If he was losing at poker, he would sit there all night trying to claw back his losses, ignoring any appointment, no matter how important. When the clock struck three, Botticelli was certain that the king would not appear, but the guests could not go home until they had the king's permission. Botticelli decided to call His Majesty at the Club and request his permission for the guests to leave. Before Botticelli could get up and make the call, however, there was a commotion with the waiters scurrying here, there and everywhere. Then Alku strode out from the lodge and stood bolt upright in his gold-trimmed white uniform near the swimming pool. He looked behind him a few times as if waiting for some signal and then bowed and announced with pomp, "His Majesty the king of Egypt and the Sudan."

The guests all surged over to greet His Majesty the king, who looked at Botticelli and the girls around him and laughed.

"Carlo, *quel joli bouquet de fleurs vous avez mis là*," he said.

This magnanimous royal compliment moved Botticelli deeply.

"I am Your Majesty's humble servant," he said with some emotion, and then he presented the women.

He started with the olive-skinned girl, Inji, the daughter of the aristocrat Hasan Sharkis. Then he introduced the French danseuse, Chantal, who was currently performing at the Auberge des Pyramides nightclub. When it came to Mitsy, Botticelli gave the king a knowing look and smiled with pride as if drawing his attention to the pick of the litter.

"I should like to present to Your Royal Highness Miss Mitsy, daughter of Mr. James Wright, general manager of the Automobile Club."

"Delighted to meet you," the king said with a smile. "I know your father. He's a good man."

Mitsy muttered some words of thanks.

"And what do you do with your time?" the king continued.

"I'm a drama student at the American University."

This appeared to interest the king, and when they sat down at the table, he chatted with her to the complete exclusion of the others, who tried as hard as they could not to appear jealous. It became obvious that the royal choice had been made. The guests from the other table started coming over to request permission to leave, the king seeing them off with a nod.

Botticelli got up with a self-satisfied look and bowed. "I beg Your Majesty's permission to leave," he said. "I should be taking these two beautiful ladies back home."

"That's not what I would call an unpleasant task!"

Everyone had now gone, leaving the king and Mitsy alone in the lodge. The servants were all standing close by in case His Majesty should need them but out of earshot of His Majesty's conversation with his guest. Mitsy was listening to the king with a fixed smile, finding the situation so strange. Her previous impression of the king had been completely off. Was this flabby man sitting in front of her, who looked so ordinary, really His Majesty? The king ordered a bottle of wine and gestured to the waiter to let Mitsy taste it. She took a sip but noticed that he did not fill the king's glass.

"Isn't Your Majesty drinking?" she asked in a disembodied voice.

"Actually, I don't like the taste of wine."

She took another sip, feeling the need of the alcohol.

"Do you know," the king said, "why people taste the wine before drinking it?"

"I don't."

"That custom has a story to it," he said, sounding like some old sage. "The king of France was ill, and his doctor had forbidden him to take any wine. This king gave a party for his nobles and courtiers, and it went on late into the night. Every time someone made a toast, the guests drank, and the king did not. The wine by now had gone sour, but they were obliged to drink it. Not a single one of them dared to mention this to the king. The next day, every last guest fell ill. When the king learned of this, he launched the custom of the host tasting the wine first before serving it to the guests."

"I have learned something new, Your Majesty," Mitsy said with a laugh.

"I read it in a history book," the king answered proudly.

"Does Your Majesty read a lot?"

"At least four hours a day."

She knew he was lying, but she raised her eyebrows and said, "How wonderful."

Why was she kowtowing to the king? Yet again she could not fathom her own behavior. How she hated her own false smile and the sound of her voice. But why was she being so obsequious when she was about to fall into a pit?

"Let's be friends." The king smiled. "From this night on."

"Your friendship would be an honor for me, as it would be for anyone."

The king nodded, and as if thinking about something deeply, he said, "Let me tell you something. I don't judge friendship by time but by my feelings. There are some people I have known for donkey's years, but to me they don't feel like friends at all. On the other hand, I sometimes meet someone for the first time and feel as if I've known him for ages. It's so nice to be able to talk to you. Lately, I have been feeling really lonely."

"Oh, what a sad cliché," Mitsy thought, but she carried on with her part and forced a sad smile. She gave the king a sympathetic look and asked, "How can Your Majesty feel lonely when you are surrounded by people who love you?"

"A man can be surrounded by people," he said with a sigh, "and feel lonely at the same time because no one understands him."

"This dull king is trying to come across as some sort of great thinker," she thought.

He spoke of his hard, austere life and the royal responsibilities, which left him no time for recreation.

"I appreciate Your Majesty's hard work," she told him. "But you must find a way to relax."

"How can I, when I shoulder the responsibility of Egypt, the most important country in the East?"

Even as she kept nodding in agreement, she could not help thinking, "What a hypocrite! He gambles the night away at the Automobile Club and then goes running after women. All this is part of your national duties?"

Suddenly the king fell silent. "Why have you stopped drinking?" he asked her.

"I drink slowly."

"Well keep drinking, because I love to look at the rim of the glass as it touches your lips."

He motioned to a waiter, who rushed over and refilled her glass with a bow.

She took another sip, and the king appeared on the verge of saying something. Suddenly, she felt his enormous hand squeezing hers. Her breath quickened, and she thought she was about to faint. He held her hand up, and as he kissed it, she whispered, "Thank you, Your Majesty."

He took a glass from the table. "Usually," he said, "I don't drink, but I shall tonight in your honor."

She said nothing as he moved so close that she could feel his breath on her face as he whispered lasciviously, "I shall drink from your glass. I shall place my lips where your lips have touched, and that way I shall absorb all your secrets."

Mitsy gave a smile of complete naïveté. "That is one honor," she said, "that I should not like to have."

"What do you mean?" the king said with some irritation.

Mitsy kept smiling and continued gently, "Please do not drink from my glass, Your Majesty."

"And why not?"

"I'm not too well. I have a serious throat infection. My doctor has told me that it is rare but extremely contagious and can be passed on to anyone who comes too close or uses things I have used."

The king stared at her, his smile vanished and his pupils dilated, apparently unable to take this in. Mitsy took a step back and told him apologetically, "My apologies. It's just that I am worried about Your Majesty, with all those responsibilities, catching the infection."

23

Look, Umm Said," said Aisha. "If you want Fayeqa to marry your-son, may the name of the Prophet protect him, I will go and fetch her for him myself."

Umm Said muttered a few words of thanks, but Aisha carried on with gusto, "I know. By God Almighty, were we to search the whole world we would never find better than you. Marrying into your family brings us honor, so you can consider Said and Fayeqa as good as married!"

Umm Said still seemed a little anxious trying to make her point for the last time, "Let me repeat myself, Aisha. Without qualification, no happy ending. No ululations, no guests and no white dress."

Aisha sighed. "Umm Said," she said affectionately, "we'll do whatever makes you happy. With God's blessing."

Umm Said had been trumped. She had not expected Aisha to agree to such austere conditions attached to the marriage. There was nothing to say. Umm Said got up to leave, and Aisha gave her a joyful hug and kiss as she walked with her to the door. Umm Said now felt that it had all been a clever trap laid by that wily Aisha and her coquettish daughter and that her son Said had fallen into it, dragging his mother along with him. Aisha had planned and executed the scheme with such cool calculation. She had stood by her so magnanimously after the death of Abd el-Aziz. Then she had sent over her useless daughter to seduce that fool of a boy, Said, and get her claws into him. And now, after all that, Aisha was agreeing to every last condition for the wedding. What a scheming cow she was.

The next Wednesday, the *fatiha* was read out, and the rings exchanged. The bride's family had been as obliging as possible on the subject of the dowry, saying that financial matters were the furthest from their mind and that they were only interested in their daughter's happiness. Aisha gave Umm Said no opportunity to disagree with her, except for one worrying thing that happened. Aisha was visiting Umm Said and let drop that Said had decided to open a savings account with her to set a little aside once he started his job in Tanta. Umm Said's face turned ashen, but she made no comment.

When she was alone with Said in the apartment, however, she could not control herself and confronted him, "So you intend to start a savings account with Aisha . . ."

Said looked at her as if to say, "What of it?"

"Please God." He nodded. "As soon as I have a job and get my first salary."

His mother stomped over to him, and had he not been taller than her, she would have slapped him.

"You should be ashamed of yourself," she shouted hoarsely. "You know we're short of money. Instead of thinking to help us, you're saving to help them?"

"It's not a big thing," Said said with a smile.

That was his way. He did whatever he wanted and then faced the reactions with complete sangfroid. Once he had decided on a plan of action, there was no reason to get emotional about it. His mother would rant and rave and start crying, but then she would calm down, and that would be the end of the matter.

The preparations for the marriage were going full steam ahead, and two weeks later, on the appointed day, they all went to Friday prayers at the Sayyida Zeinab mosque. As agreed, only the closest relatives were invited. There were no signs of celebration. Umm Said, Aisha and Saleha were still in their mourning clothes. The bride wore a beautiful blue dress with sequins on the sleeves and around the neck. Mahmud, Fawzy, Kamel and the bridegroom, Said, all wore new suits. Ali Hamama, the father of the bride, was beaming in his new brown worsted overcoat, made of English wool, which he wore over a fine beige and brown striped galabiyya, a stark change from his usually unremarkable appearance. In fact, he looked like an actor who was going to take off his glitzy costume the moment the play ended and go back to his shabby everyday clothing. The officiating cleric was a stout man with a compact face so perfectly round that it might have been drawn with a compass.

Ali Hamama reached out and took Said's hand under a white handkerchief, and then he repeated after the cleric, "I give you my daughter, Fayeqa, who is a virgin of sound mind, according to the religion of God and his Prophet and the rite of Imam Abu Hanifa al-Nu'man, and in accordance with the agreed dowry."

Instead of the ululations that usually pierce the air at this moment during Egyptian weddings, there was silence. The guests shyly whispered their congratulations, and Umm Said burst out crying. From the moment she entered the mosque, she had been trying to hold herself together, but just when the marriage contract was signed, she broke down. Who could have imagined that Abd el-Aziz, her cousin and her beloved husband, would die in his fifties and not be present at the wedding of his eldest son? How happy he would have been. Would that have been too much to have asked? Would it have upset the order of the world had Abd el-Aziz lived a few years longer and been able to witness his children's weddings and to know his grandchildren? "May God forgive me," she kept repeating through her tears. Affected by her mother, Saleha started crying too, followed swiftly by tears from Aisha, genuine or not. Saleha took out a white handkerchief and dabbed her eyes as the male guests tried to comfort the women. When the formalities were over, they all went outside, creating the highly unusual sight of two families departing in silence after the signing of a marriage contract. Fayeqa's face had none of the dreaminess that one usually sees on a bride, only the steely look of a victor, or an exultant student, who, having studied hard, had gone up to the dais to receive an award. Indeed, Fayeqa had waged a long and hard campaign for the husband who was now standing beside her. She had used every ruse in the book to hitch Said, letting him see what charms were on offer and then retracting them until he submitted. She really felt for him whenever he stood before her almost weeping with desire, pleading with her to give herself to him. She had felt like a mother who had to be cruel to her child in order to be kind. She had done a lot in order to marry Said, and without a moment's hesitation, she had foregone what all girls dream of: a white wedding dress, a party and the throne that the bride and groom sit on in front of all the guests. She had known both instinctively and from her mother's advice that any delay in the wedding might see the opportunity slip away forever. Her mother's voice rang in her ears: "A girl who knows what she's doing has to bend with the breeze. Obey your mother-in-law. Don't think of crossing her until the contract is signed."

After the marriage, the couple spent a week in the Anglo Hotel on Soliman Pasha Street, courtesy of Uncle Ali Hamama, the bride's father, who deemed this such an unprecedented and historic act of generosity that later he would keep throwing it back in his wife's face whenever they had an argument. After the honeymoon, the couple carried on living separately in their respective families' apartments until Said started his job as a teacher in the vocational school in Tanta, where he rented a two-room apartment in al-Geysh Street. As the train gave off a long whistle and left the station carrying the couple to Tanta, then and only then did Said Gaafar's real life start. He would later feel that his whole life had been no more than a lead-up to his life with Fayeqa. She blossomed in a way that astonished him. From the very first days, she proved her superiority as a lover, a friend, a wife and a lady of the house. He discovered that she was a wonderful cook who never tired of spending long hours in the kitchen. If she tasted a new dish or even heard about one from him, she would not rest until she had found the recipe and mastered it.

She also managed to stretch the modest house budget, which he handed over to her on the first of the month, after first paying a percentage of his salary into the shared savings account. Bit by bit, she acquired everything they needed for the apartment. She bought a Philips radio and a Singer sewing machine on installments. Using the money in the savings account, she bought a beautiful suite for the sitting room and even managed to save a little for a rainy day. She insisted on saving a maid's salary by doing all the dusting, cleaning and washing herself, making sure to keep her hands soft with lemon moisturizing cream. Fayeqa turned the apartment into a perfect little home, so clean that it sparkled.

All the energy expended on her homemaking skills, however, had no effect whatsoever on her sex drive. Marriage freed her from any feelings of guilt, and now Said discovered just how good she was in bed. She had all the right ingredients: she was beautiful and soft, she took care of her body, she was voracious and she gave her husband pleasure any which way he wanted, without a shred of inhibition. Had he not been absolutely certain that he was the first man in her life, he might have thought that she was a woman who had learned the art of love from practice. He remembered something she had let slip one day. She told him her mother had explained to her all about sexual relations because most marital quarrels, according to Aisha, could eventually be sorted out in bed if the wife was sufficiently skilled. Fayeqa allowed her husband free rein and played out all his sordid and dirty fantasies so well that at work and outside the apartment he never looked at other women. But all this delirious pleasure came with a price: Fayeqa learned how to whip him up into a frenzy of desire that she would satisfy only when she had him completely under her control. Said tried to avoid ever upsetting her, as he found her anger hard to bear. The couple's ecstatic physical relationship gradually made them like two footballers scoring goal after goal or a vocal duet whose harmonies take a song to a new level. Fayeqa could now tell her husband's state of mind from a single glance, from the expressions on his face, his tone of voice, his gait or even the way he was sitting.

One day he was grumbling about how difficult the headmaster was at the school where he was working. "Do you know what, Fayeqa?" he said anxiously. "My whole future is in his hands. One word from him can make or ruin my career."

Fayeqa gave him a considered look as she pondered the situation. Then she suggested that he invite the headmaster to dinner and find out what he liked to eat.

Said appeared a little hesitant. "The headmaster is on a different level than me. How can I ask him what he likes to eat?"

Fayeqa smiled sympathetically, like a mother suffering her child's stupidity. She placed her palm on his face, moved closer to him and planted a long, slow kiss on his lips, which made his whole body tingle.

"You can do it, darling," she said.

The following day, when Said came home, he had an astonished smile on his face.

"Imagine that!" he told her breathlessly. "The headmaster has accepted the invitation. He's coming with his wife on Friday."

"Did you ask him what he likes to eat?"

Said could not help laughing. "He told me his favorite is pigeon stuffed with cracked wheat."

It was time to get to work! Fayeqa got the doorman's wife to come and help her clean and rearrange the apartment to look its best. Then she took some money from their savings and spent two whole days peeling and chopping away in the kitchen to produce a truly splendid feast. Fayeqa's pigeon stuffed with crushed wheat was so good that the headmaster not only devoured four whole birds, but, notwithstanding withering looks from his wife, he let out sighs and groans of pleasure that were completely undignified and unbecoming of his position.

Needless to say, the dinner was a rousing success; Fayeqa even managed to strike up a firm friendship with the headmaster's wife. When the headmaster mentioned his daughter's high marks in her final examinations, Said's wife seized the chance and asked him to pass on to her a piece of 21-carat gold jewelry with a Quranic inscription on it by way of congratulations. It was only natural that Said should then receive glowing praise in the headmaster's reports. Fayeqa's virtues, then, gave the lie to all those negative images of a dominant wife. On the contrary, many times a controlling wife manages to keep her family strong and the children's future rosy. There are some husbands who need an energetic wife just as a naughty child needs a strict mother. And there are husbands who would go to the bad without a wife's supervision, and others who, if they enjoyed too much independence, would end up falling into debauchery, causing grief for themselves and their family. Fayeqa controlled her husband for his own good. She could satisfy his baser instincts by providing what was his to take as a husband, all the while running his life like clockwork, keeping house for him and making his boss so happy that he had given him a pay rise and put his name forward for exceptional promotion.

Fayeqa even set very careful limits on his relationship with his family. On their first visit as a married couple to the old apartment, Said asked his mother expansively if she needed any money. "Thank God, no," she replied. "We have enough to keep going." Then she thanked him and showered blessings upon him. She sounded calm and happy, though it was a lie. She was in desperate need but wouldn't dare ask him in front of his wife, and even had Said insisted, she would have given the same answer. So he took her at her word and changed the subject. The matter was left at that, but on the way back to Tanta, Said noticed Fayeqa looking uneasy beside him in the train carriage. She was sighing, giving only curt responses to him and looking out of the window as if she could not bear to look at him.

"What's the matter, Fufu?" he asked apprehensively.

That was the pet name he used for her whenever she was upset and he was trying to soothe her, but Fufu did not reply. She sighed, tears glistening in her eyes as she reached for her handkerchief. At that point, Said's concern turned to anxiety, and he put his hand on her shoulder. She brushed it away.

"Fufu. My darling!" he whispered intently. "By the Prophet, tell me what the matter is?"

When she gave no answer, he repeated the question. Suddenly her face changed and her eyes shot daggers at him. "You!" she said in a voice quivering with anger. "Do you want to spend all your salary on your mother and brothers and sister?"

Said was taken by surprise and answered in a shaky voice, "Of course not. Why would you think that?"

"You offered to give your mother as much money as she needed."

"It's my duty to ask her."

"As the proverb goes, what you need at home you don't give to the mosque. Your mother, thank God, has got two men supporting her, your brothers, Mahmud and Kamel. I have no one apart from you."

"Darling, I only asked her if she needed anything. It was just a question."

"Then I'm glad I'm married to such a paragon of generosity!" she sneered. She turned her back on him and went back to staring out of the window. The gesture expressed anger with a hint of coquettishness. Said tried to calm his wife, cajoling her and making small talk.

But Fayeqa only smiled a little and mumbled a few words in response, the look of disgruntlement frozen on her beautiful face.

That night, when the couple went to bed, Fayeqa came out from her usual nightly hot shower with her rosy flesh and her black hair let down. Her red nightdress was completely open at the top and so short that he could see her thighs. As she stood primping in front of the mirror, the silent desire filling the bedroom was so heavy that Said's vision almost blurred, and he feared his heart would stop. Unable to wait for his wife to finish preening, he got up and embraced her from behind, feeling the smooth flesh of her breasts in his hands. Then he started kissing her all over. Fayeqa gave in to his caresses, moaning and holding him back a little, finally letting herself be led toward the bed. But at the last moment, just as he thought she was about to lie down in front of him, she jumped up as if she had just remembered something and slipped out of his embrace, leaving the overwrought Said panting like a wild bull. Keeping a little distance between their two bodies, Fayeqa leaned toward him and whispered in his ear, "Said, my dearest. I am your darling wife. Every penny you earn should be for us."

In his state of overwhelming desire, Said could not get a word out, and to drive the point home and elicit his agreement, Fayeqa whispered again, "Promise me that you won't spend a single piastre outside our home."

Said nodded in agreement. Then Fayeqa let him do whatever he wanted with her body as she did everything she could to satisfy him, writhing and working him up to the point of supreme ecstasy twice without stopping.

Thereafter Said made no further offers of help to his mother. Not satisfied with this important achievement, Fayeqa instituted a new regime for visits to her in-laws. At the start she made sure that she and Said went to see them every week, but she gradually reduced the number of visits, telephoning them instead, until their visits to Said's family took place only when there was a particular event or reason. After these consecutive victories, Fayeqa started behaving like any brilliant military leader developing new strategies. She would advise Said to tell his mother about their visits a few days in advance, the ostensible reason being, of course, that they should not just impose themselves out of the blue on Umm Said. But the real reason was to make the visits serve some useful purpose, in particular that Fayeqa and her husband could take back with them all the provisions that Umm Said would start preparing the moment she knew they were coming. During their visits, Fayeqa would complain about how hard it was to make ends meet in Tanta, where the cost of living was high and Said's salary meager. She would go on about it so much that Umm Said would end up giving them a box full of ghee, sugar, flour, meat and chicken. Fayeqa, of course, would refuse to take it at first, but Umm Said would insist. Fayeqa would then grudgingly give in and hand the box to her husband while thanking Umm Said in a slightly offhand way so that she would not think her donations were indispensable. Of course Umm Said was not unaware of Fayeqa's maneuvering and scheming. Deep down, she almost admired her wiliness and wondered where the girl had learned all her tricks. As for Said, she knew that he was too selfish to be depended on, but, as with all mothers, she was prepared to overlook her son's shortcomings in order to keep his affection and to be able to see him, if only occasionally.

A few months into their marriage, Said announced his wife's pregnancy. Umm Said was truly thrilled at the thought that Fayeqa was carrying her and the late Abd el-Aziz's first grandchild. Forgetting Fayeqa's mischief, she was overcome by a feeling of tenderness and started telephoning her a few times a week to check on her condition and to advise her against sudden movements or carrying heavy loads because the first pregnancy was always delicate, especially during the first months. She was surprised, then, to hear Said telling her that he would visit her with his wife on Friday. Naturally, she welcomed the visit but added with a hint of worry, "How is it Fayeqa is able to take the train in her condition? It could be risky."

Said, however, assured his mother that the matter was important and could not be put off and that he would like his wife to be present. When the call was over, Umm Said wondered what was behind this visit. Had the doctor not warned Fayeqa against excessive exertions and needless jostling like the bone-shaking train from Tanta to

Cairo? And what was so important that Said could not come alone? Umm Said discussed the matter at great length with Saleha, but neither of them could come up with a convincing explanation.

On the Friday, Said and his wife turned up just before noon, as usual. Said went to say Friday prayers at the Sayyida Zeinab mosque, and when he came back, they all sat around the dining table. They ate duck stuffed with onion prepared by Umm Said, and after lunch, they drank their way through three pots of tea. Then Said did his ablutions and returned to the mosque to say the evening prayers. When he came back again, his mother led him by the hand to the sitting room, shutting the door behind them, and their conversation became louder and louder until it echoed throughout the apartment. Kamel rushed to the sitting room. Fayeqa dragged herself slowly toward the sitting room as if she already knew what was going on.

24

The door opened, and Madame Khashab appeared. The moment she saw Mahmud her face froze.

"Is everything all right? Do you want something?" she asked warily.

Mahmud was bewildered and confused by her tone, but then he pulled himself together and stuttered, "I'm sorry, Madame."

She turned her face away and asked him coldly, "Sorry for what?"

"I'm sorry for upsetting you," he said quickly with some warmth in his voice. "By God Almighty, I'm so angry that my mother made me return your present. Please forgive me."

Madame Khashab was about to say something, but she stopped herself. Mahmud then took a step toward her and held out the flowers.

"I have brought you these," he said imploringly, "to apologize."

There was a moment of silence, and then Mahmud continued, "Please accept the flowers. By the life of the Prophet, don't embarrass me, Madame."

After a little hesitation, Madame Khashab took the bouquet. "Thank you, Mahmud," she said and smiled.

"Are you still angry with me?"

When she did not answer, Mahmud continued. "Madame," he said in a voice full of sincerity, "you told me that you have a good heart and that you like to forgive."

Madame Khashab started examining the flowers, held them up so she could smell them and then said, "The flowers are beautiful. I love carnations."

Mahmud smiled, showing his glistening teeth, as if to say that was the least he could do.

"So have you forgiven me?" he asked again.

She nodded and looked at him affectionately.

"Mahmud," she said. "I consider you my son. I could never be angry with you. When you returned the present, I was upset because I had just been trying to be helpful."

"Thank you, Madame."

Madame Khashab's smile broadened. She pushed the door open wide with her hand and took a step backward.

"Come in, Mahmud."

"Thank you."

"You can't stand there at the door. Come and have something to drink."

Mahmud let himself be invited in as three thoughts occurred to him: first, that Mustafa had been completely right about the effect of flowers on the temperament of foreigners; second, that this was his day off and he could stay there a little; and third, that he had to be careful not to upset Madame Khashab again.

The three thoughts preoccupied Mahmud's brain, making him incapable of resisting when Madame Khashab held out her hand and led him to the sitting room. Then she took the paper off the flowers and arranged them in a vase on the table by the window. She admired the flowers and sat down on the sofa. Mahmud, for the first time, noticed a bottle of whiskey, a glass and an ice bucket on the table and realized that she had been drinking. She reached out for her glass and with a sudden laugh said, "So how are you, Mahmud?"

"Thank God, I'm fine."

He continued watching as she emptied her glass in one go and then leaned over to pour herself another. Mahmud sat there with his hands on his knees, not knowing what to say, when Madame Khashab asked him affectionately, "Should I pour you a glass of whiskey?"

"No, thank you."

"Just one glass."

"Madame, I am a Muslim. We're not allowed alcohol."

Madame Khashab laughed and took a sip of her whiskey.

"Do you pray?" she asked.

"Not regularly, unfortunately. Sometimes I forget and sometimes I don't get around to it."

She seemed to be thinking of something, to be looking for the right words.

"How old are you Mahmud?" she asked him.

"Nineteen."

"All right. And don't you know more now than when you were ten?"

"Of course I do."

"Good. And as a person gets a little older, he understands more about the world, doesn't he?"

"Of course."

"Good. And it is God who created the whole world and everyone in it, so he must understand more than all of us."

"Naturally."

"And if God knows more than all of us, then he must forgive us?"

"Does he forgive us even if we do stupid things?" he asked naively.

"God has to punish us for big sins," she said laughing. "He punishes us if we hurt people. If we lie or steal or murder. But if we drink a glass or two to drown our sorrows, I don't think God would punish us for such a small thing."

That was rather complicated logic for Mahmud, who nodded, a smile frozen on his face.

"So what do you say?" Madame Khashab asked him again. "Shall I pour you a glass?"

"No, thank you."

"All right, as you like. Would you like a glass of chocolate milk?"

He hesitated a little and then answered quietly, "That would be lovely."

"How much sugar?"

"Four teaspoons."

Madame Khashab laughed as she started to understand his character. She nodded, finished off her glass in one gulp and went to the kitchen. Mahmud sat there, looking around. To his left in the sitting room, he could see a large wooden radio set and an aquarium, illuminated from the inside, with colored fish swimming around. In front of him was the dining room with its balcony overlooking the Zamalek corniche. On the wall hung a wedding portrait of Madame Khashab and her handsome husband, Sami Khashab. There was also a large photograph of him some years later, his hair now white, hanging with pride of place in the sitting room, a black ribbon draped down the side. A few moments later, Madame Khashab came back and placed the glass of chocolate milk in front of him and then poured herself another whiskey.

"Do you know what, Mahmud? Your mother was both right and wrong to refuse the gift. She was right because you have to keep your dignity, but she was wrong because I love you like a son."

Mahmud felt uncomfortable, because she had brought the conversation back to the problem which he thought had been solved. The drink was making Madame Khashab maudlin. She sat back in her armchair and stretched out her legs, taking another sip of whiskey.

"I want people to like me," she said softly.

Mahmud said nothing.

She looked at him and continued, "I need people, Mahmud. Do you understand? God did not give me children. I really wanted to have a child. And the only man I loved, the man for whom I left England and came to Egypt, he died and left me alone."

The conversation was progressing at such a speed that it confused Mahmud. He thought Madame Khashab was, to some extent, like those drinkers whom Suleyman would help out to their cars at the end of the night.

"Do you know," she asked him, "what is the worst thing in the world?"

He was incapable of giving an answer. At that moment he was preoccupied with trying to drink the last drops of the chocolate. It was wonderful.

"The worst thing in the world," she continued, "is to be left alone. Look, I've got everything I need, a nice apartment in Zamalek and one in Alexandria near the sea. I'm well off, but I'm alone. Do you understand? Completely alone."

"But don't you have friends, Madame?"

"I do. But I always feel that I need them more than they need me. All my women friends have children and grandchildren. But I'm alone."

Mahmud was moved by her words, but he made no comment.

"Do you know, Mahmud?" she whispered as if speaking to herself,

"I am afraid sometimes that I'll die all alone in the apartment, and no one will know."

"God forbid, Madame!"

"If one day I don't feel well, I have to tell the doorman in case something happens to me during the night, and he needs to call the doctor. Imagine, Mahmud, that you are so alone that the doorman is the only living soul who can help you in an emergency. It's so depressing."

"May God grant you good health," Mahmud said with feeling.

"I'm not very well, Mahmud," Madame Khashab sighed. "I have lots of problems. Drinking relaxes me. After I've had two glasses, I can sleep and not think about everything."

Mahmud finished his glass of chocolate and wiped his mouth with the handkerchief that his mother had carefully put in his right pocket. He took a sip of ice water to rinse the chocolate flavor from his mouth.

"Thank you, Madame," he said. "The chocolate was delicious."

"Shall I make you another one?"

He hesitated a moment and then smiled and replied, "Oh, that would be lovely."

Madame Khashab went back to the kitchen, and a few minutes later Mahmud was savoring a second glass.

"And are you happy," she asked him, "in your job at the Automobile Club?"

"Yes, thank God!"

"Do you earn enough?"

"I hand my salary over to my mother."

"All of it?"

"She gives me a little pocket money from it."

"Congratulations. You're a decent man. If I had had a son, I'd like him to have turned out like you."

As Mahmud was taking the last sip from his second glass of chocolate, Madame Khashab commented, "You really do like chocolate!"

"I love it!"

She got up and went over to the sideboard next to the dining table. She bent over, opened one of the drawers and then went over to Mahmud, holding out her hand.

"Please take it, Mahmud," she said gently. "It's white chocolate from Switzerland."

"White chocolate?"

"Taste it," she laughed. "I'm sure you'll like it."

Mahmud took the chocolate as carefully as a jewel and put it in his pocket. Then he stood up.

"I'll be off now. Thank you so much, Madame Khashab."

"I'd be happy if you would visit me again."

"Please God."

She walked him to the door, and he felt delighted that everything had turned out so well. She was no longer upset with him, and they were friends again. Moreover, he could hardly wait to rip open the white chocolate and taste it.

"Mahmud," she said at the door as he was about to go. "Can I ask you something?"

"Anything!"

"Please stop calling me Madame Khashab."

"Then what should I call you, Madame?"

"And don't say Madame either! My name is Rosa. Call me Rosa."

"Rosa . . . ," he repeated slowly.

"Give my best wishes to your mother," she said with a laugh. "Okay? Tell her that Rosa loves you just as she does."

Mahmud nodded, and Rosa drew near to give him a kiss. She had already kissed him on the cheek two or three times in the past, and just behind the smell of whiskey on her breath, he could recognize her delicate perfume, reminding him of the perfumed soap and the aroma of clean clothes that lingered on his mother. He let Rosa kiss him on the cheeks, but she suddenly put her arms around him. Then he felt her hot breath searing his face.

25

His Majesty looked bewildered. He started at Mitsy and asked her anxiously, "Are you really ill?"

"Three doctors," she told him softly, "have concurred in the diagnosis."

"Isn't there a treatment for it?"

"I'm taking some tablets and slowly getting better. But they have all confirmed that the microbes in my throat will be contagious for quite some time."

The king looked at her with incredulity, as if to say, "Why didn't you tell me about this from the start?"

After a short period of silence, the king stood up, followed by Mitsy. He held out his hand and, as if afraid of catching something, shook Mitsy's hand by the tip of her fingers. Before leaving, he ordered Alku to have her driven home. The moment she reached her bedroom, she got undressed and ran into the bathroom to take a shower. She was a little tipsy from the wine, and as the hot water ran down over her naked body, she closed her eyes and relished the moment. She was pleased with herself. She had created a moment of truth. This was her greatest delight: to uncover lies and show scheming for what it was. She had made a fool of the king of Egypt and the Sudan, treating him as he deserved. She had accepted his invitation and led him on to within a stone's throw of his bed. He had been salivating at the thought of ravishing her, almost snorting like a bull in rut, as she was being cornered. Then, out of the blue, she had this brilliant inspiration and started weaving a skillful lie. When she thought back to how confused the king had looked, she could not help laughing out loud as she stood under the shower.

"Oh, your great Majesty, how I would have loved to have the honor of going to bed with Your Majesty, but I am so afraid that you will catch the bacteria ravaging my throat. What is the matter, Your Majesty? Why do you shudder? Didn't you want me just a moment ago? Were you not just standing there like a ravenous animal? Why have you turned and fled as one possessed?"

Mitsy came out of the bathroom wonderfully relaxed. She slept well, going to university the next morning and getting on with her life. She thought that any question of her involvement with the king was now at an end.

That evening, her father sat silently at the dining table. When she got up and went to her bedroom, she was surprised to find him following her across the hallway. She stopped and turned to face him.

"Mitsy," he asked her. "Come to my study. We need to have a talk."

"Can't it wait until tomorrow?"

"No, now," he said resolutely and stepped aside to let her pass. Mitsy walked ahead of him into his study. The light was on. She sank down into the leather armchair, and Wright sat at his desk, leaning forward on his elbows.

"How did you get on with the king?"

"I think you know."

"I want to hear it from you."

Mitsy sat up straight and answered, "The king wanted to go to bed with me, but I told him that I have a contagious disease."

"Did you have to lie?"

"It was the only way."

"But you went to see the king of your own accord . . ."

"I only went to make you happy."

"Nonsense. Are you stupid or just mad?"

"If you're just going to insult me, I'll go!"

Wright was breathing heavily, as if trying to control his feelings.

"As usual," he said, "you never think of the consequence of your actions. You have put us all in a tricky situation. Botticelli called to ask about your health. The king is not stupid, and if he discovers that you lied, both you and I will pay a heavy price. Don't you realize that the king has stalked women so tenaciously they've had to flee the country with their husbands . . . ?"

"Just because he is the king, it means he can do whatever he likes?"

"Have you never heard of an oriental despot? He is not a constitutional monarch as we have in Britain. He is a potentate in the Turkish mold. He owns the country and everyone in it. He can crush anyone who opposes his will."

"But you are English. The king cannot harm you."

"He can make it impossible for me to stay in Egypt."

His visible anguish only provoked her more.

"Well, how do you suggest we calm the situation down?" she asked him. "Should I sleep with him?"

"Don't be so vulgar."

"Well, if the only way to make the king happy is for me to sleep with him, wouldn't that be the clever thing to do?"

"Shut up!" Wright shouted angrily, taking a large drag on his pipe.

"Mitsy," he continued, "what happened, happened. We have to think calmly and proceed prudently. I suggest that you talk to Botticelli."

"I'm not going to see that pimp again," she retorted.

"I can organize a meeting in my office. I just want you to explain to him all about the infection and reassure him that you are on the mend."

"I don't owe anybody any explanations."

"You're the one who got us into this mess. You will have to do something to get us out of it."

"Oh, stop it. I don't want to talk about it anymore."

She turned and marched toward the door. Wright darted after her and grabbed her by the hand, but she snatched it back.

"If I were in your shoes," she snapped at him, "I'd be ashamed of myself."

He raised his hand and gave her a slap on the face. She screamed. He reached out to try to grab hold of her, but she rushed out of the study, slamming the door behind her.

26

Abd el-Malek the waiter looked the part. He was short and wiry, had an enormous bald pate and a moustache so small it looked like a dark speck under his nose. He looked like an old caricature of a "native Egyptian," and his colleagues never stopped joking about it. There was a lot to joke about, including the fact that he was Christian. They only had to hear his footsteps in the distance before one would shout out, laughing, "Praise the Lord, my son!"

Abd el-Malek would laugh and reply, "Glory be to God on High."

"Pray for us, Saint Abd el-Malek!"

"I pray to God to carry you all off!"

They all chuckled, but Abd el-Malek, turning serious again, replied, "I'll have you know that I am a Muslim."

"How can you be a Muslim, Abd el-Malek?"

"You are all such ignorant children," he said in a learned tone of voice. "Do I, the Copt, have to explain your religion to you? O children, children. Islam means submitting yourself to God, relying upon Him for everything. That's what I do, so I'm a Muslim like you even though I am a Copt."

"God is great," his colleagues shouted.

"What a nice bit of philosophizing!"

The fun continued.

"Abd el-Malek! Why don't you announce that you have accepted Islam so that you can marry a nice girl as a second wife."

"I can't. My wife would kill me!"

"How long have you been married, Abd el-Malek?"

"Twenty years."

"Twenty years with one woman? Aren't you tired of her?"

"Of course I am."

"So what are you going to do about it?"

"I'll just have to put up with her."

This playful banter fostered such a happy and tolerant atmosphere that the men would then repeat to themselves little expressions showing the convergence of their religious outlooks, such as:

"Leave religion to the pious!"

"We are all guided by God."

"Religion is how you treat other people."

The workers all loved Abd el-Malek and were greatly influenced by his enthusiasm, his openness and his devotion to his friends. If he was absent from work, they would walk around saying, "That Abd el-Malek. He's a Copt, isn't he? But by God Almighty, he's a better person than many Muslims."

Had they known that morning that he was so ill, they would have rushed to help him, but he appeared perfectly normal. He chatted with some of them, and, as usual, they joked around. He did not complain of anything. He carried out the tasks given him by Rikabi the chef, then excused himself and went to the toilet. When he returned, he washed his hands in hot water and soap (in accordance with Alku's strict rules) and went back to peeling potatoes. Except that fifteen minutes later, he excused himself again.

"What's going on, you bastard?" shrieked Rikabi the chef. "You just went to the toilet five minutes ago. Just what are you doing in there?"

The other staff laughed, but Abd el-Malek did not. He looked pale and worn out.

"Chef Rikabi, please excuse me," he said meekly. "There's something really wrong with my insides."

"All right. Go. But make it quick," said Rikabi, busy checking a pan on the stove. This time, Abd el-Malek ran to the toilet, and when he returned a few minutes later, his colleagues noticed the sweat running down his pale face. He seemed to be having difficulty walking and was tottering about. The staff clustered around him.

"What's the matter?" they asked him anxiously. "I hope it's nothing serious."

Abd el-Malek looked at them in gratitude and forced a smile. He raised a hand as if to reassure them and was about to say something, but when he opened his mouth, white liquid ran out. His colleagues recoiled, terrified, and one of them shouted, "God help us!"

Abd el-Malek was vomiting in a way that no one had ever seen before. He knelt on the ground with his head forward, his facial muscles contracted amid spasms of vomiting as if some invisible iron hand were squeezing his innards out of him. He knelt there panting, unable to stand up. His colleagues tried to lift him by the arms, but he sank back down to the ground, and his limbs started trembling. Then he had a fit of convulsions and lay groaning weakly. The news was conveyed at lightning speed to Mr. Wright, who did not deem the illness of a member of staff any reason for him to leave his office. He thought it over for a moment and then peremptorily told Khalil, his office assistant, "Tell Mustafa the driver to take him home. Most importantly, clean up after him. I will go and check the kitchen area myself."

Indeed, half an hour later, Wright went to the kitchen to check that it had been cleaned up properly. He ordered one of the staff to give the area a good scrub with some disinfectant from the storeroom. As the smell of disinfectant spread around the kitchen area, the whole affair was over as far as Mr. Wright was concerned. A servant had fallen ill, thrown up and been sent home. An everyday event that did not merit further attention.

When Alku came to hear of it in Abdin Palace, he ordered Hameed to visit Abd el-Malek that evening to check on him. Abd el-Malek had made it home to his apartment in Shubra, dragging his legs and leaning heavily on his colleague Kaylani the waiter, who had accompanied him in the car with Mustafa the driver. The two had helped him up the stairs to his apartment on the third floor and then spent a while calming Abd el-Malek's wife, who had started panicking when she saw how his condition had deteriorated. They sat him down on the first chair in the sitting room. His wife had rushed off to the kitchen to prepare a glass of hot lemon juice, but when she came back a few minutes later, she let out a scream and dropped the glass on the floor. Abd el-Malek's body was heaving up and down, and he was foaming at the mouth. He gave a few groans and then fell back, dead. His wife started wailing, and Kaylani and Mustafa burst out crying like children.

When the news reached the Club, all the staff felt deeply saddened, telling each other dolefully, "Abd el-Malek was such a fine, upstanding man. He never hurt a fly his whole life long."

His colleagues went to his funeral mass. As Muslims, they were a little nervous at finding themselves in a church, and their ignorance of the liturgy meant that they were not quite sure when to stand up or sit down. Notwithstanding, many of them were so overcome that they burst out in tears. They weren't just distressed about their friend Abd el-Malek's death, but were also terrified that death had come upon them, out of the blue, twice, with a second colleague having died suddenly so soon after Abd el-Aziz Gaafar. Not only had Abd el-Malek's sudden death hit them hard, but what happened afterward did not allow them the opportunity to mourn. They needed some time to absorb it. They would have felt better had they been given the chance to shake their heads, bite their lips and recall their fond memories of him with pride and grief, ending with words of consolation, "We are from God and we return to Him. All men are mortal. Men are just shadows on the face of the earth. We are all mortal but care not to think of it."

Fate, however, had ordained otherwise. For, just two days later, before they had recovered from the blow, they were shocked to see Mur'i the lift attendant rushing off to the toilet again and again. A very short while after that, exactly as with Abd el-Malek, they saw him reeling around, throwing up and falling unconscious to the ground. They rushed over, picked him up and laid him on a sofa, shouting for someone to call an ambulance, which arrived within minutes and took him to Qasr el-Ayni Hospital. He was dead upon arrival.

When this news reached the Club, the staff became hysterical. They threw down their cleaning equipment and ran around screaming like terrified mice in a trap. And for good reason. Before they even had time to reckon with Abd el-Malek's death, Uncle Mur'i had now gone and died before their eyes in exactly the same way. What was going on? Was there a curse on the Automobile Club? Had the Grim Reaper, intent on culling their souls one by one, made a den for himself at the Club?

This time, when the news reached Mr. Wright, he took it with the utmost seriousness. He made some telephone calls, and about an hour later, a military vehicle stopped in front of the Automobile Club. Out stepped four British officers, three male and one female, whose uniforms indicated that they were three doctors and a nurse. They had two large cases with them, which the staff rushed out to carry. In the casino, in the presence of Mr. Wright and Alku, who had sped over to the Club, they set up a field clinic. The staff, lined up outside the casino door, stood in silence, their terror at the succession of events having rendered them unable to comment or react. The doctors summoned them in one by one. They examined each staff member carefully, giving him a plastic bag and asking him to bring a stool sample the next day. The atmosphere was heavy and doom-laden. It felt like a curse had fallen upon everyone. Some of the staff wanted to bring the sample back that same day, as if that would put a speedy end to their nightmare. They rushed off to the only toilet they were allowed to use, on the roof. It was a strange sight to see, as they went into the stall, one after another, and came out each clutching a plastic bag full of excrement. If one of them was taking a long time inside, the others started shouting at him to hurry up. The doctors did not exclude anyone from their examination. Having checked all the serving staff and the other employees, they then insisted on examining Alku and Mr. Wright. They left the nurse to accept any samples and write up her notes. Those who had not yet provided a sample were reminded of the urgency of bringing it the following morning.

In the meantime, the head doctor had gone with Mr. Wright to his office. There was no time for small talk. Mr. Wright knitted his eyebrows.

"Dr. Frankham, thank you so much for all your effort."

"No need to thank me. I'm just doing my job."

"Can you give me some understanding of what is happening here?"

Dr. Frankham looked down for a moment. Then he raised his head and said calmly, "Unfortunately, I am not very optimistic."

"About what?"

"There is a high chance that the staff member who died today and perhaps also the one who died two days ago . . . were suffering from cholera. We have sound information that cases have occurred in Cairo and Alexandria."

"How is it I haven't heard about that until now?"

"The Ministry of Health does not wish to publicize cases of cholera in order to avoid an outbreak of panic. We had hoped that they were isolated cases, but unfortunately every day there are new ones. I think that the government is going to make a statement about the outbreak tomorrow."

Wright knitted his brows.

"Cholera outbreak? Can't be! We have meticulous procedures for hygiene here at the Club. I supervise everything myself."

"They cannot prevent cholera, they can only slow down the rate of infection."

Wright lit his pipe, drew on it and blew out a thick cloud of smoke.

"Dr. Frankham," he barked, "are you sure about this?"

"Naturally we have to analyze the samples first, but after thirty years of practicing medicine, I think I know what the results will be."

There was silence between them. Then Wright sighed heavily, "Please understand my position. This will have terribly negative repercussions for the Automobile Club."

"I do understand your concern, but our duty is to deal with a far graver reality. If it is confirmed that your man died from cholera, as unfortunately seems almost certain, then everyone at the Club is in mortal danger, the rate of infection is very quick in such settings."

"And in that case, what must we do?"

The doctor shook his head and looked at Wright.

"There is no alternative. The Club will have to be closed."

KAMEL

I should like to introduce myself," Mitsy said in English with a smile.
"Mr. Wright has told me about you," I replied quickly.

"My father doesn't know me," she said dejectedly. I felt a little embarrassed.

"Then tell me who you are," I said.

"My name is Mitsy, and I am studying drama at the American University. I have studied elementary Arabic with a private teacher here in Cairo, but I didn't like his method. He just taught grammar, but I want to learn Arabic, whether classical or colloquial, in order to be able to get along with people."

"Why are you so interested in learning Arabic?"

"I want to be able to understand Egyptians. I can't understand them if I don't speak their language. Now it's your turn. Tell me about yourself."

"My name is Kamel, and I work here at the Club. I am also studying law at the Fuad I University, and I like writing poetry."

Her blue eyes widened, and she shrieked, "Oh! You're a poet. Fantastic. I'd love to read your poems."

"That would make me very happy, Miss Mitsy."

"Please, let us dispense with titles."

So I started calling her Mitsy. I loved the way she pronounced my name, drawing out the "a" so that it sounded like "Kaaaamel." During the lesson, the way she looked imprinted itself onto my consciousness: she was so elegant and tall, with smooth brown hair pulled into a ponytail. She had smooth skin, bluish eyes, finely shaped lips, beautiful dimples, a broad gleaming forehead and the sort of long, lean fingers you could not take your eyes off, not to mention that adorable area between her upper lip and her nose. She was beautiful, but her spirit was even more attractive. There was something impetuous and instinctive about her. She overflowed with vitality. Everything she did was special, unexpected, even shocking, but also pleasant. She was like a princess who had fled her palace in rebellion and had come to live among the lower orders.

We would meet twice a week. At every lesson, we would read a topic in the newspaper, and then I would explain some new literary text to her, and we would sit and discuss it. Then I would give her homework. I chose some serious pieces of writing for discussion. Together we read articles by al-Hakim and Ibrahim al-Mazini and plays by Tawfiq al-Hakim. As I was teaching her Hafez Ibrahim's poem "Egypt Speaks About Herself," we digressed onto the theme of pride in Arabic poetry and why this was not a subject dealt with by Western poets. I asked her to write her homework in classical Arabic but to speak with me in the colloquial language. If she could not find the right expression in Arabic, I asked her to write down what she would say in English, which I would later translate.

I may or may not be a good teacher, but Mitsy certainly had a sharp mind and remembered new words easily. In the space of just two months, she had shown remarkable progress. She could write in classical Arabic, without too many mistakes, and could speak the colloquial language well enough to be understood, even if with a heavy accent. I looked forward to our lessons. We had long and enjoyable discussions about various topics. Meeting her filled me with feelings of happiness and admiration but also deep concern.

"When I see what the occupation is doing to you Egyptians," she said one time, "I feel ashamed to be English."

"You're not responsible for the policies of the British government."

"In fact I am. You are not responsible for the dictator-king of Egypt because you didn't choose him, but we elect governments whose glory comes from occupying and pillaging other countries. It makes me feel so ashamed."

The gulf between her and her arrogant father was enormous. I could discern the distress on her beautiful face whenever he was mentioned. I could feel that she was skirting around a subject she did not want to talk about. One time, I went to give her a lesson as usual. The Club had just reopened after having been shut for three days because of the cholera. Mitsy had brought some slices of lemon, which she was squeezing into a glass of water.

"I would advise you," she said seriously, "to purify the water. Cholera has broken out. I believe they have disinfected the Automobile Club, but that won't stop the disease from spreading."

I took the lemon from her hand and squeezed the juice into the water.

"We have already lost two of our staff in the Club," I said. "In less than a week."

"Oh, that's terrible."

"Death is not the worst of it! The families of the deceased are left paupers. The Club doesn't pay pensions to Egyptians. Only to foreigners."

"I can't believe that!"

"The Club administration considers Egyptians lesser beings."

I spoke that sentence with eternal bitterness. But as her father was the general manager, I thought I should be more careful.

"Please give the families of the deceased my condolences," she said softly.

"I will pass them on. Thank you."

I started the lesson on Ahmed Shawqi's poem "O Neighbor of the Valley." I taught her poems that had been set to music. She would always write down the name of the poem on a piece of notepaper so that she could buy the record on her way home.

When the lesson was over, Mitsy did not get up to leave as usual. She looked hesitant.

"Kamel," she said. "Thank you so much for all your hard work with me."

Her words made me uneasy. Why was she thanking me now? Had she decided to stop taking lessons? Had I done something wrong or said something to upset her? I was not concerned about the money I was earning for the lessons. I feared losing her friendship. I pulled myself together and steeled myself for the shock. I decided that I would save her the embarrassment of telling me, so I forced myself to smile as I asked her, "Do you think that you have made enough progress with your Arabic?"

"What are you getting at?"

"Perhaps you want to continue studying without my help?"

"Of course I still need your help."

I tried to hide my relief.

"Then what is it?" I asked her.

"I want to get closer to Egyptians."

"It'll take a little longer until you can speak Arabic well enough."

"The language is an important means of getting to know people, but it's not everything."

Mitsy smiled with the naughty expression of a child about to do something provocative and dangerous.

"I want to visit the native areas of Cairo," she said slowly, "so that I can get to know real Egyptians."

"How will you be able to talk to people you don't know?"

She looked at me almost reproachfully, as if she had not been expecting that challenge.

"I just need to know exactly what you want," I added quickly, "so that I can help you."

She pursed her lips and seemed to be thinking.

"I'm looking for the truth, Kamel," she said haltingly, as if searching for the right words. "I don't want to observe from the outside. I don't want to be just an English girl who lives in Zamalek and has fun in the sun. I don't want to spend my time in the Zamalek Club and write letters to my friends in London telling them how lovely the weather is. That's all so shallow. That's not why I came to Egypt. I want to live a real life with real people. That's why I thought I would go and see the areas where real Egyptians live. Do you understand?"

"I do."

"Will you take me there?"

"Of course."

"Kamel. You are a student at the College of Law, and at the same time, you also work in the Automobile Club, not to mention the time that you spend giving me lessons. You won't have enough time."

"I can always find time to accompany you."

I was lying. Going out with her would be a pleasure, but I did not know how I would fit it in. I was already struggling, trying to do my studies until late and sometimes studying right through the night. Then in the morning I would take a shower and go to work, not having slept a wink. Even now I have no idea how my body coped. I applied myself to my job at the Club and kind Monsieur Comanus let me study in the storeroom and gave me some free time before my examinations.

I agreed to take Mitsy on an outing the following Wednesday, my day off. Our first trip was to the area around the Sayyidna il-Hussein Mosque. We met in the square in front of it following afternoon prayers, and then we wandered around the square and the neighboring streets.

"Now," I said, "I'm going to show you al-Muezz's gates of Cairo."

"Did they close these gates," she asked me as she looked at them with childish awe, "every night after the inhabitants of Cairo had gone to sleep?"

"Yes."

"Then what would a Cairene have done if he arrived after the gates had been closed?"

"I don't know. I suppose it would have been up to the guards to let him in or not."

"Fantastic!" she clapped her hands like a little girl. "I've always dreamed of living in a town whose gates were closed at night. Just imagine me turning up at the closed gates and having to wait there all night until the guards opened them, and then I would pad through the gateway like a cat!"

Mitsy suddenly stopped walking and let out a meow, and we both laughed heartily. I was always being surprised by her eccentric behavior. After walking around a little, we sat down in the Fishawi coffee shop. I ordered a glass of green tea for her. As she sipped it, she raised the glass to her nose, closed her eyes and savored the aroma. She was wearing a very smart blue outfit with a white collar. She was leaning back in the old wooden sofa and looking at me.

"Can we go on an outing like this every week?"

"Certainly."

"How would you feel," she looked at me mischievously, "if next time I were to put on a headscarf and wear a galabiyya with a wrap around it with Egyptian slippers?"

"Then," I said without a second thought, "you'd be the most beautiful local girl in Egypt."

She smiled and made no comment. I felt a little embarrassed at having been so forward.

"I'm sorry," I said.

"Sorry for what?"

"For what I said just now."

"Oh, you innocent poet!" she said in English, laughing out loud. "You seem to know a lot more about poetry than you do about women. There isn't one on the planet who would be angry at being complimented by a man."

We had entered a completely new realm. The girl sitting opposite me now, with her eyes shut, savoring the aroma of the tea, was different from the one I had seen previously. I was having a sense of déjà vu, as if she were someone I had known in the distant past, someone who belonged to me or was somehow connected with me. Mitsy looked at me as if she could guess what I was thinking.

"I like talking with you," she said in English.

"Why are you using English with me?"

"Can you just forget that you are a teacher!"

"But I am a teacher."

She gave me a "don't be stupid" look, and we spent over two hours in the Husseini district and then took a taxi back. I planned to drop her off in Zamalek first and then take the taxi on to Sayyida Zeinab.

"Why are you protecting me like some Eastern woman?" she asked.

"Does it annoy you?"

"On the contrary," she enthused. "I dream of being the slave girl of some oriental potentate and living with three hundred other slave girls. And we all dance for the sultan, each hoping to be the one he spends his night with."

She waved her arms around as if dancing. I looked at the driver's astonished face in the rearview mirror.

"You really are a great actress," I said.

"Why do you say that?"

"Because at the drop of a hat you can take on any character you want."

Before she got out of the taxi, she leaned in so close that I could feel her breath on my face.

"I'll tell you a secret. My idea to go and explore parts of Cairo was not just so that I could mingle with Egyptians but also because I wanted to spend some time with you."

I was a little confused. For a moment I thought the natural thing to do would be to hold my arms out and hug her. We shook hands as she got out, and I asked the driver to take me to al-Sadd Street. I tried to do some studying, but I couldn't stop thinking about Mitsy. I went over what had happened between us. I felt like I had walked through a minefield, because I had managed to keep control of myself and made sure to keep a certain physical distance between us. Although we had chatted away and laughed, I had kept myself on the straight and narrow. Even though I forgot myself from time to time, I had managed to keep our relations proper and formal.

If you spend time in the dark and then suddenly come out into the sunlight, it takes a while to adjust. That is how I felt about Mitsy. She was too dazzling for me to cope with. Finding her so wildly attractive, I knew I had to keep away. Had she been less pretty, I might have dared to try to woo her, but what hope could an oaf have to get the attention of a princess? Even if the guards made way for him, the gap between them was something that he would never be able to bridge.

After our trip to the Husseini district, I found myself slipping into a danger zone without a middle course: our friendship could flourish or flounder, we could have a romantic relationship or I could lose her forever. Was I ready for an adventure like that? I kept asking myself that question, but deep down inside me, I knew that all my calculations were useless, mere mental exercises. It was Mitsy's choice to drag me into the deep end, whether I wanted to or not, and it would be she alone who would determine the tempo, depth and course of things.

At our next lesson, I made a point of being rather formal, imagining her easy familiarity the time before might have been an exception and wanting to allow her the chance to pull back a little.

"Oh, just stop that, Kamel!" she cried out with a look of childish disbelief.

"What do you mean?"

"Aren't we friends now?"

"Of course."

"Then why are you wearing an artificial smile again, and why are you using that monotonous tone of voice?"

She came so close beside me that her arm touched mine. I slid away a little, and she laughed, "Are you afraid of me?"

I was in a quandary, but she took pity on me and carried on talking in her usual way. We decided that our next Wednesday outing would be to Sayyida Zeinab.

"You live there," she said with a smile. "Are you going to invite me home for a cup of tea? Then I could see your mother and complain about you!"

When she laughed, the dimples in her cheeks drove me mad. But I knew that trouble was waiting for me at home, and sure enough when I told my mother that Mitsy wanted to come and visit, her face turned ashen.

"The daughter of that Englishman Wright?"

"Yes, but she is completely different from her father."

"What does she want from us?"

"I invited her to come and meet you."

"I don't want to meet her."

"Oh, Mother, Mitsy is a lovely girl, and she adores Egypt."

My eagerness only seemed to worry my mother more.

"Listen, Kamel," she retorted. "We've got enough troubles of our own. We don't need the daughter of that Englishman Wright along with all her nonsense."

I tried a different tack. I leaned over and kissed my mother on the head, and then, with feeling in my voice, I told her, "Mother! You brought us up to be honorable people. You've always behaved properly with guests, and you've never shown me up. Mitsy is my guest, and I have invited her to our home."

My mother said nothing but heaved an enormous sigh.

"All right, let's drop the matter," I said theatrically. "I won't go on about it. Let's forget the subject."

"What do you mean?"

"All's well that ends well. Mitsy wanted to come and meet you, but you would rather not. I'll just tell her that you had to go somewhere and I'll find some way to apologize."

I stood there looking sad and resigned. After a few moments, as expected, my mother half-apologetically asked me, "When does she want to come and visit?"

"Wednesday morning."

"All right. She can come, please God. Since you already promised her, it would be wrong to go back on your word."

Then my mother started firing practical questions at me. Did Mitsy speak Arabic? Should we invite her for lunch or just tea with some snacks?

I hugged my mother and kissed her hands. I always knew how to exploit her good nature. Sometimes my conscience would prick me, but I still have to laugh when I think of the tricks I used to get around her.

At ten o'clock on the Wednesday morning, as we had agreed, I waited for Mitsy in front of the Sayyida Zeinab mosque and then took her on a walk around the district, including the Rimali Mill and Tram Street. Watching the street vendors, she asked me to explain their snatches of song as they hawked their wares. Then I took her to our apartment. She was quite a spectacle walking up the stairs. Her Royal Highness, the princess from the empire upon which the sun never sets, was coming from al-Sadd Street to visit her subjects, the wooden stairs creaking with her every step. I was about to reveal my vision to her, but I thought she might not approve. As planned, my mother was at home alone, looking her best, wearing a beautiful black dress with a new veil. Saleha had gone to school, and Mahmud was still asleep.

"Welcome. Please come in. It's an honor for us," my mother said as she shook Mitsy's hand and then gave her a big hug before leading her to the sitting room. They needed no help to get along. Almost at once, they were sitting there chatting and soon laughing away. My mother offered her a whole range of beverages and snacks and then invited her to stay for lunch, but Mitsy made her apologies.

"Your mother's so lovely," she said the moment we were outside in the street.

"Thank you."

"She has a gorgeous face, very noble features, and she is so nice and kind."

"I have a biased opinion, being her son, but I agree."

We reached the square, and I looked around for a taxi, but she smiled and suddenly told me, "I don't want to go home now. Can we go and sit somewhere?"

"Of course."

I invited her to Café l'Auberge. At that time of day, it was empty. We sat at a corner table at the back. A waiter rushed over to us and seemed happy at Mitsy's being there. He proudly repeated the few words he knew in English, and Mitsy told him, "I can speak Arabic quite well!"

"God be praised," the waiter said, astonished. We ordered mint tea.

I watched the way she put her lips to the glass to sip the hot tea. I did not know what to say.

Without looking at me, as if talking to herself, she said, "You have done so much for me, and I'm such an odd person."

"You're different, I'll admit, but in a positive way. But how do you manage it without alienating the people around you?"

"The truth is I don't fit in."

"Don't you have friends?"

"I do, but they don't understand me."

"Then maybe you need new friends."

Mitsy sighed, and her blue eyes became blurry. It was as if she could not look me straight in the face.

"My relations with my father are very tense."

"That doesn't surprise me. You and your father are chalk and cheese. I have often wondered how someone like Mr. Wright could produce such a lovely girl like you."

Having uttered that last sentence without thinking, I immediately felt embarrassed.

"I'm sorry," I said.

"You're right," she said softly. Then she fell silent, as if trying to gather her thoughts.

"I'm living a nightmare," she said.

After some coaxing, she told me in detail what had happened with the king. I listened without saying a word. Finally, she asked anxiously, "What do you think?"

Overcome with emotion, I replied, "I need a little time to take it all in. I'm perturbed by the king of Egypt's behavior."

"Well," she smiled sadly, "I'm perturbed by my father's behavior."

"We have to accept our families for what they are . . ."

"I'm not trying to change my father, but, put quite simply, he has ruined my life."

"Well, my brother Said is also unbearable, but I try to find a way of getting along with him."

"Perhaps I would get on better with my father if I got away from him. The problem is that I don't have a job, and he pays all my expenses, so I have to live in the same house."

"Have you looked for a job?"

"I have, and I couldn't find anything. But I'm going to start looking again."

"How can I help?"

Mitsy smiled and looked at me gratefully.

"If you want to help me," she said sweetly, "then stay near."

She reached out and laid her hand on mine. I had an overwhelming desire to hug her, but I controlled myself. I gently withdrew my hand and asked her, "Would you like to go somewhere else?"

Suddenly she became jolly again.

"Oh, what a polite man you are!" she said.

"Why do you say that?"

"Because you really need to go. Just look how delicately you put it by asking me if I want to go somewhere else . . ."

I laughed because she was right. I had some studying to catch up on. I took her home by taxi, and then I continued on to Sayyida Zeinab. I took a hot shower and put on my pajamas, and then sat down at my desk with my textbook, but I could not help thinking of Mitsy. I went over what she said, and my imagination started to run wild. I could see myself battling viciously with her rotten father in order to get her out from under his thumb. James Wright was just a lowdown pimp, but I could not say that to Mitsy. What he had done was unjustifiable. English morals were different from our Eastern customs. English families allowed their daughters to have romances before marriage. So be it, but what Wright had done went beyond that. He had tried to push his daughter into bed with the king for his own benefit. He could not have had any other motivation. If his daughter became the king's mistress, he would enjoy many privileges and make a fortune. In face of this sordid behavior, his daughter had shown bravery and real nobility of character.

Whenever I thought of what she had done with the king, I had to laugh. What a talented actress. She had turned the drama into a farce. I tried to concentrate on my studies until around three in the morning, when exhaustion overcame me, and I fell into a deep sleep.

In the morning I went to the Club and did my regular day's work. At around six in the evening, Monsieur Comanus had already gone home, and I was getting ready to lock up when the telephone rang.

"Kamel," Labib the telephone operator said excitedly. "His Royal Highness Prince Shamel is asking for you. I'll connect you now."

The prince greeted me quickly, and before I could respond, he continued, "Listen, Kamel. I need you to do something for me. I hope you'll be able to do it without further ado."

"At your command!"

"Tomorrow morning at seven I will be waiting for you at the palace."

"Seven in the morning?"

"Yes. Seven o'clock on the dot. Don't be late. I shall be waiting by the side door on Aisha al-Taymouriya Street."

"Might I be told the purpose of our appointment?"

"I'll explain everything when I see you," the prince said and hung up.

I locked up the storeroom and went out onto the street and decided to walk home. I needed to think. First the odd story of Mitsy and the king, and now the prince was calling me out of the blue. Despite his charm, I was now closer than ever to thinking that he might be a little deranged. What could he want from me at seven in the morning? And why the side door? The only explanation was that he did not want anybody to see me going into the palace, I decided that the purpose of this visit had to be unnatural: the prince might be homosexual. There was nothing about the way he held himself or moved that pointed in that direction, but I had heard that some homosexuals look completely normal. The odd thing was that he had a reputation as a lady-killer. Maybe he was insatiable or swung both ways. My concern was starting to turn to terror. I felt put upon from all sides. It seemed most plausible that he was a homosexual. Hence the early morning at the back door. Did he mean to take me off to some side room and try to ravish me? My mind filled with all sorts of upsetting visions. I could see myself trying to wriggle out of his grasp. I could not get the image out of my mind. Even so, I could not wriggle out of the appointment. I had promised the prince, and he had helped me so much. I owed my job with Mitsy to him.

So I woke up at six o'clock the next day and told my mother I had an early lecture before work. I took a taxi from the square, and when we reached Garden City, I got out on the Corniche to prevent the driver from knowing my destination. I continued on foot to the prince's palace but got lost in the winding streets of Garden City, which all looked alike. I walked past a uniformed guard on the street and was about to ask him where the palace was, when I remembered that the prince was intent on keeping the visit a secret. So I asked him, "Excuse me. Do you know Aisha al-Taymouriya Street?"

He eyed me suspiciously but then gave me directions. Finally, I saw the palace, and when I rushed over, I found the prince standing outside. He shook my hand as I panted and, since it was quarter past seven, gave me an accusatory look.

"I'm sorry for being late," I spluttered. "But I got a bit lost."

He laughed and answered, *"Ce n'est pas un début encourageant. Viens."*

He made a gesture, and I followed him. After walking along the outside wall, we entered through a small iron gate into the garden, down a few steps, where he produced a key to open another door. To my astonishment, he locked the door behind us. It was a small underground apartment, which must have been for a chauffeur or some servants. I followed the prince further inside, crossing the small living room and down a long, dark, narrow corridor. Finally, we came out into a large, bright room, and what I saw was stranger than anything I could have expected.

SALEHA

For as long as I have been aware of the world, I cannot remember my brother Said ever being nice to me. I have no memory of him playing with me as a child, buying me a toy or taking me out to play. He was always a source of worry and aggravation. I did love him, but I have to be honest and say that I resented his presence at home and tried to avoid him. I would go to my bedroom and lock the door. So I felt relieved when he married Fayeqa and moved to Tanta, since we no longer had to deal with his problems and, for the first time, could enjoy a placid family life.

During his first visit home as a married man, Said had offered to help my mother out with some money, but she turned down the offer. The next day, as we were sipping our tea, I asked her, "Why did you refuse the money from Said?"

She thought awhile about how to answer. "Your brother is now responsible for his own family," she told me, avoiding my gaze. "May God provide him support."

"Said only has his wife to support. He ought to give you something as Kamel and Mahmud do."

"Well, he offered to, and I refused."

"Had he really wanted to help, he wouldn't have asked."

"Oh, you shouldn't think the worse of him."

"You yourself said that Said is selfish. So why are you defending him now?"

"When you are married and have children," she smiled and said dolefully, "you'll understand. A mother loves her children unconditionally. However they wrong her, she'll carry on loving them."

There was something in her tone that made me fall silent. She sipped her tea and said quietly, "May God guide and help him."

Said's wife, Fayeqa, was just as irritating as he was. Her mere presence in our home riled me. I did not like her and knew that she had no use for me or my mother. Fayeqa loved no one except herself. All her altruism after the death of my father had been devised to snare a husband, no more and no less. The moment she achieved her aim and married Said, her true nature emerged, and she started to treat my mother and me as rivals for her husband's love. Each time before Said and Fayeqa came to visit, my mother and I would work our fingers to the bone preparing a spread for Fayeqa to sneer at with her usual condescension. She was obviously trying to show her husband that she was the better cook or else she meant to provoke an argument and cast herself as the victim. My mother would listen to Fayeqa's comments and give an embarrassed smile, but I could hardly contain my anger.

One time, when Fayeqa mentioned that the okra needed a bit more salt, I responded, "If you think so little of our cooking, you might come and help us in the kitchen with your superior knowledge."

Fayeqa was taken aback. She beat her hand on her chest and sobbed. "Oh good Lord. I didn't mean to offend. I'd rather cut out my own tongue than say anything to upset you or my mother-in-law."

But even as she was apologizing, she put on that dreadful cloying voice and flounced around. Just like her mother, she had no sense of decency. She would play the temptress with her husband in front of everyone, as if we weren't there, as if to show my mother that "the son you devoted your life to raising is no longer yours but now belongs to me alone, and with the ring on my finger, I can control him."

Another time, my mother and I were sitting with Fayeqa on the balcony, when she suddenly started up petulantly, "Mother-in-law, I want to complain to you about something."

"I hope it's nothing awful."

Fayeqa ran her hands through her hair, sighed and continued, "Your son Said won't leave me alone. I'd like to be able to do my hair, you know. I have to take a shower twice a day. Each time I tell him, 'Just let me have a break, Said,' and he implores me. Really, I'm getting exhausted, but what choice do I have?"

Fayeqa let out a cackle. And after an embarrassed silence, my mother quickly replied, "Listen, my girl, those are matters for you and your husband. You shouldn't be talking about them to anyone, not even your relatives. Saleha, please go and make us some tea."

My mother was trying to spare me. I went to the kitchen furious with Fayeqa. All this talk about her sex life made her sound like a slut. It was hardly surprising considering that she was Aisha's daughter, but I felt she was sending me a message. She was a year older than I was, but we were different. Whereas her mother had brought her up to get married, my father had encouraged me to get an education. I felt that she was jealous of my success at school and wanted me to see a husband was much more important than an education.

Fayeqa and Said's visits were always marked by these little provocations and irritations. Their visit that day had been suspicious, with Said calling my mother to tell her that he was coming with his wife. We had been surprised that Fayeqa would make the trip in the first months of her pregnancy. After eating the *mulukhiya* with rabbit, which they had requested, Said went off to the sitting room with my mother, and I heard my mother's raised voice, with Kamel soon joining in and shouting too. Fayeqa was sitting outside the room, her head down, listening. I was used to these arguments, and as I had an examination the next day, I shut myself in my bedroom and studied until I could do no more. Then I made my ablutions, said my evening prayers and climbed into bed.

In the morning, my mother looked exhausted and tense. I did not ask her what had happened because I wanted to keep my mind clear for the examination. When I got back from school, I was able to report that I had got top marks. My mother gave me a kiss and then sat me down beside her. I could tell that she was still on edge.

"Said, your brother," she said with a smile, "has found a husband for you."

"A husband?"

The word sounded so strange.

"Who is it?" I asked mechanically.

"He's a camel merchant called Abd el-Barr from Kom Ombo. He's forty. Very well off. He has already been married, but his wife was barren so he divorced her."

I did not know what to say. The surprise was too much for me to take in. My mother sighed and asked me quietly, "What do you think?"

"What does Kamel think?"

"Kamel insists that you finish your studies."

"Then we should do as he says."

"We need to think on it very carefully, Saleha. The worst thing is to rush into a decision on a matter like this."

That night I lay in bed and shut my eyes, but sleep did not come. I thought about what my mother had said. I knew that I was pretty. I always felt proud when I looked at my naked body in the bathroom. I considered myself well proportioned and attractive, not to mention the smooth black hair and the green eyes that I inherited from my grandmother. Enamored as I was with my own looks, I had not thought about marriage at all. It just had not occurred to me. Marriage was for me a faint notion, something that happened to other people. Of course, like all other girls I did hope one day to have a home and a husband and children, but I always dreamed of other things before marriage. I had always imagined my life to be a series of hurdles that I would overcome one by one until I finally became a university instructor, my father's dream for me. I could still hear his words: "Saleha, God gave you and Kamel to us to make up for the useless Mahmud and Said. Be strong. I want you to be first always."

Now I found myself pushed in another direction. The word "bride" kept echoing in my head. "Saleha, the bride." For the first time, I felt myself a seriously, and respectably, desired woman. It was different from what I felt when men gave me lascivious looks. In spite of dressing modestly, it sometimes seemed that they could see right through my clothes, and I felt cheapened by that. Now I was happy at the thought of being a bride, quite apart from the idea of marriage itself. That a man should ask for my hand meant that he had chosen me above all other girls and was willing to spend hundreds of pounds to make me his wife and the mother of his children. That thought alone made me happy and stirred my imagination. I took out a pile of magazines I had borrowed from Kamel, *The Illustrated, The Studio*

and *The World of Art.* I spread them out on the bed and looked at
the photographs of the actresses, imagining that I was as beautiful
as they were, that I was wearing a short-sleeved summer dress or a
white silk outfit and an elegant black hat with a veil over my face. I
could see myself wearing all those fashions, with a handsome young
man who looked like the actor Anwar Wagdi or the singer Farid al-
Atrash drawing close to me, bending over to kiss my hand and ask
for a dance. Everyone would stop to watch us and the other dancers
making way and forming a circle around us. At the end of the night,
the young man would ask me to spend my life with him in a small
house with a garden on top of a small hill, undisturbed by anyone.
As I gave myself over to such daydreams, I knew that even if I were
to turn down the offer from Abd el-Barr I would always be grateful
for his expression of such admiration and respect in asking for me
to be his wife and bear his children according to our religion and
customs.

The morning call to prayer sounded as I lay in bed. I heard my
mother going to the bathroom, making her ablutions and whispering
her prayers. After a little while, she came into my bedroom. She gave
me an anxious look and asked, "Are you awake?"

"I couldn't sleep."

She sat down on the bed and looked at me. Then with a sigh she
asked, "Have you thought about Abd el-Barr? Said is nagging me, and
I just don't know what to do."

"Mother," I answered in a state, "we have to listen to what Kamel
says because he has our best interests at heart. Said is only out for
himself."

My mother seemed about to object but she did not.

"All right," she said as she got off the bed. "Try to get forty winks
before you have to get up for school."

After she left the room, I had a worrying thought. Why was Said
bringing his pregnant wife from Tanta specifically to plead on behalf
of a suitor? Why was he pressuring my mother for a speedy decision?
Had he suddenly become so interested in my future? Perhaps it was
merely that he could not bear it that his younger sister was going to
university when he had not even got his school certificate.

When I saw Kamel, he looked at me and said solemnly, "Saleha, the worst thing you could do would be to give up school to get married. You have to finish your studies."

I nodded. He smiled and continued, "I am certain that you will make the right decision."

The next Friday, Said and Fayeqa arrived for their visit. This time Said was taciturn and brooding as if spoiling for a fight. Fayeqa, on the other hand, was as sweet as could be, which only increased my suspicions. After lunch Said went out to do an errand, leaving Fayeqa at home with my mother. They sat together on the balcony for around an hour, during which time they could not stop whispering.

In the evening Said and his wife went back to Tanta, and my mother came into my bedroom and sat down next to me, hugged me and asked me, "Do you want to hear some good news?"

"Of course!"

"Your intended, Abd el-Barr, is going into business with Said, a textile factory. Abd el-Barr will provide the funding, and Said will manage it in return for half of the profits."

"So Said wants me to marry him for that reason. I knew he was only out for himself."

"If Said didn't believe that Abd el-Barr was a decent man, he wouldn't go into partnership with him."

"A man with money can find scores of people like Said, but it would be difficult for Said to find someone to fund a factory for him."

"You speak about your brother as if you really dislike him."

"I resent his behavior."

"Anyway, have you thought about the marriage proposal?"

"I have decided to finish my studies."

"Oh, Saleha, you're a girl. However much you study, your fate is to get married, and Abd el-Barr is a respectable man who can offer you a comfortable life."

"It seems that Fayeqa has managed to win you over."

My mother seemed troubled, and her voice shook as she spoke.

"I wish she had won me over. I'm tired of all this thinking. I'm afraid of giving my agreement and wronging you, but I'm also afraid of turning him down and then having regrets."

"I won't have any."

My mother said nothing for a while, as if not wanting to quarrel with me.

"In any case, I agreed with Said that we will invite Abd el-Barr for lunch next Friday. Let's at least see what he's like before we make a decision."

27

When Mahmud got home, he seemed a little out of sorts. He greeted his mother and kissed her hand.

"Should I get your dinner?" she asked him.

"Thanks, but I've already eaten with some friends. Good night."

As he walked down the hallway, he had the same feeling he had as a child when his father took him to the cinema for the first time. A feeling of sheer astonishment at a dazzling world full of animation and color that he had never even imagined. In the heavy silence of his bedroom, he undressed, put his pajamas on and threw himself on his bed, where he lay looking at the ceiling and thinking about how baffling it had all been. That was the last thing he would have expected. Good Lord. Had it really happened?

Madame Khashab, whom he now called Rosa, had been going about her business quite normally, in a motherly way. She had kissed him good-bye on his cheeks, as she had often done before, but suddenly she pressed herself against him and kissed him on the mouth. Mahmud was not completely devoid of experience, having kissed a fair number of girls in the gloom of Cinema al-Sharq, but the way Rosa kissed was different. She pressed her lips and tongue against his and lingered, sliding around in his arms and letting him feel the heat of her body. Then she shut the front door of the apartment with one hand as she pushed him inside. He tried to resist, but she started groping him, getting him more excited than he had ever been in his life. She had not given him the chance to say no. She pulled him into the bedroom, gently pushed him down onto the bed and started kissing him ravenously, stroking his arms and shoulders and massaging the thick thatch of hair on his chest.

"You're so beautiful, Mahmud," was all she could whisper, her breathing become shallow. "So beautiful."

At some point, Mahmud's vision had become blurry, and he could no longer make anything out. Rosa had led him along the tender paths of delight, swimming in deep waters familiar to her but which he was entering for the first time. She whispered instructions into his ear and apparently climaxed three times before he did. The two of them lay there naked, subsumed in the deep silence, that existential, visceral and postcoital mystery. Mahmud was like a man bewitched, unable to decide if it had all really happened. How had Madame Khashab gone from the decent lady whom he treated like his mother into a naked woman who could excite him as much as the women in the blue magazines he used to swap secretly with his school friends? He was also perplexed by the intensity of the sexual experience, which had been so searing and explosive, nothing at all like the frenetic orgasms he had while fumbling with girls in the gloom of the cinema. Rosa lay there next to him, and after a while she opened her blue eyes and seemed to be looking at him with pure gratitude. Her face was blushed as she whispered, "Can I hold you?"

"Yes."

She slid her arms around him and laid her head on his chest. Mahmud looked down at her naked body and saw how raddled it was. Her neck was deeply lined, her heavy breasts sagged pendulously to the side and there were liver spots all over her flabby skin.

"Do you think I'm beautiful?" she asked as if reading his mind and wanting reassurance.

"Of course."

Rosa planted a kiss on his neck, smiled sadly and looked up at the ceiling.

"No, Mahmud. I used to be beautiful. I'm old now. You're young, and you must know many prettier women."

Mahmud said nothing but felt a little uneasy. He really wanted to leave, but suddenly Rosa became jolly again. She got out of bed, took his hand and said playfully, "Come on, let's take a shower."

"You go first."

"No," she said with a giggle. "Come with me. Let's have a shower together."

She pulled him into the bathroom, laughing, turned on the shower and started soaping him up, patting his muscles.

"My fantastic stud!"

Then she handed him a big pink sponge. "Mahmud, will you scrub my back?"

He had hardly started doing so before she whirled around, threw her arms around him and started insatiably kissing his stomach, working her way up to his chest and finally to his mouth, while her hand slithered around between his thighs. They fell onto the bed again, still dripping wet. This time Rosa went slowly. The first time she had gone at it hammer and tongs, but with her initial thirst quenched, she could now allow herself to luxuriate in total pleasure, as the two of them gave themselves over to a veritable tidal wave of lovemaking that left them both spent. Mahmud asked if he might take another shower before he got dressed. As he said good-bye at the door of her apartment, he felt that everything between them had changed. The way he felt when he embraced her, the timbre of her voice, even the perfume that earlier had seemed maternal—all of them now drove him mad with desire.

Mahmud lay on his bed thinking over what had happened with Rosa until he fell asleep. The following day, he went to the Club and worked as usual but could not banish the questions: Might he discover that what happened with Rosa had been a dream? Perhaps a hallucination?

If not, had Rosa fancied him from the start, or was she suddenly overcome with lust? She was over sixty, but at what age did a woman lose her libido? Was it only foreign women or did all women, whatever their age, desire men with such ardor? Did his mother have such feelings? Did her sedate and dignified appearance belie an incandescent desire for sex? He felt awkward to imagine his mother feeling passion, but then he told himself, "Of course my mother and father did what I did with Rosa; otherwise, how would my siblings and I have come into the world?"

Mahmud plunged headlong into this new reality. Rosa did her

best to satisfy him in bed, teaching him so much about the technique of lovemaking that after a few weeks he became quite expert at it. They met so often that they developed their own rituals, which he loved. Rosa would start off by feeding him up. She served him various delicious meals, such as kebab and kufta from Abu Shaqra, chicken and brain sandwiches from the New Kursaal and *fatta* with calf's foot from Hati el-Geysh. When he expressed his astonishment at how much she knew about Egyptian food, Rosa shook her head and laughed. Just like any good mother, she told him, "Mahmud, I've lived in Egypt longer than I lived in England."

She taught him to drink wine. It tasted a little acrid at first, but then he felt the soothing sensation work its way into his brain. Time after time, his visits to Rosa followed the same routine: Mahmud would eat heartily, drink a whole bottle of wine and then go to the bathroom to brush his teeth and take a shower. He would come out wearing only the cashmere dressing gown Rosa had bought him. Then he would sit down next to her saying nothing, his legs crossed, as if he were waiting for the train. Rosa would sit there squirming a little, getting herself worked up and chatting away about nothing in particular. She would ask him about his family or grumble about how lazy and what a liar her doorman was, as if her relationship with Mahmud was nothing unusual or as if they were a married couple or a pair of lovers whose relationship was not simply sexual but extended into everyday life. Mahmud would sit there giving terse answers without looking at her. Suddenly, she would move closer to him, and he would feel her hot breath, or she might start stroking his curly hair or running her fingers along his broad lips. Mahmud would take his cue from that, and then the performance would start. He would enfold her in his strong arms, giving her no chance to resist. Then, like a toy he had played with long enough, he would carry her off to the bed. After kissing her for a long time and caressing her slowly, he would then run his hands all over her body until she relaxed and opened up to him, at which point he would make violent and merciless love to her. He seemed to be trying to hurt or punish her. Mahmud would pump away at Rosa like a machine, devoid of any false emotion or fake sentiment. He went at her with ever-increasing roughness, like a street brawler with Rosa his adversary. He would find her weak spots and then set at them as if there were no tomorrow, until she could do no more than lie there like a rag doll. Mahmud's lovemaking, so rough and crude, drove Rosa wild. He seemed to have uncovered in her a land mine that had lain hidden for years under her polite and refined veneer. He took her back to a distant past, a primordial time when men and women did not disguise their animal lust but simply acted on it without shame or guilt, the way they might eat when they felt hungry. There was another reason why Mahmud was so good in bed: being slow-witted, he went about it slowly. He could lie there caressing Rosa for an age, forgetting time and space. Then, with the careless rhythm of a piston, he would make Rosa scream with wide-eyed delight as wave after wave of uncontrollable pleasure flowed through her. Rosa always had a few orgasms before Mahmud ejaculated. At that point, she would behave like a celebrant performing the rituals of a festival. With a happy and grateful look, she would kiss him on the face, neck, chest and hands as if he were a cat in his owner's arms. Mahmud was such a fantastic lover that when Rosa thought back to all her previous lovers (including her late husband), she realized that she had never before experienced sexual pleasure such as Mahmud gave her.

His tumultuous nights with Rosa became such a fixture of his life that he could no longer imagine going without them. He lived for them the way a drug addict waits for his next fix. If a few days passed without a visit to Rosa, the absence of sexual relief beset him like a muscle cramp. She released all his pent-up sexual frustration, so he now slept soundly at night and no longer dreamt of sex. She gave him a life of ease: delicious food, fine wine and a soft bed. He felt some pride at bedding Rosa, for here he was, a dark-skinned Egyptian, expressing his manhood for the first time with an English lady who had become attached to him. His feelings toward her were strong and contradictory. One time when she was not feeling well, he visited her as she lay in bed every day for a week to check on her. There was no doubting that he loved her, although not in the usual sense of "love" between a man and a woman. By dint of their sexual exertions, he had managed to uncover the real Rosa, and he felt for her the sort of affection that one might feel for a work colleague, and when they were not having sex, he treated her with all due respect and enjoyed

her company. Sometimes it even seemed to him that he was doing a
sort of favor for a close friend, the way he might help someone tidy
up or move some heavy furniture around. He did, so to speak, a bit of
heavy lifting around the place to keep her happy and, once finished,
would go and sit in his comfy chair. Occasionally, after they had finished lovemaking, he would feel a storm welling up inside him and
an urge to get away. In those moments, Rosa was nothing more to
him than a haggard old woman, pretending to be younger than her
age, and he, young enough to be her son, was no more than a lad who
had been seduced into fornication. With that, he felt a sudden resentment and wished he had never met her. Such sudden bouts of aver-
sion might make him snap at her, but he would soon come back to
himself and apologize, refusing to leave until he was certain that she
had forgiven him. The waves of repulsion stemmed from his feelings
of guilt. Mahmud had always been too lackadaisical and lazy to follow the strictures of his religion in an organized manner, except for
going to say his Friday prayers, but sometimes his conscience would
prick him.

"How will I be able to stand before God when I have been so
sinful?"

One time when he was particularly encumbered with such feelings and wanted to get things off his chest, he went to see to his best
friend, Fawzy (the only one to whom he ever told his innermost
secrets). Aisha told him that Fawzy was up on the roof, and there
Mahmud found him sitting in the dark, in a white galabiyya, rolling
hashish cigarettes at a small table, of which Fawzy handed him one as
he gestured at him to take a seat. Mahmud tried to refuse, but Fawzy
pressed the cigarette on him. He lit it for him, and as it glowed, it
started to give off the telltale aroma.

"Listen, mate," he said, "hashish is a panacea. May God never let
it dry up!"

Fawzy took a drag on the fat spliff and held it in, allowing it to
have a strong effect. Then he coughed and looked at Mahmud with
bloodshot eyes.

"What's up, chump?"

They were sitting by the wall of the roof terrace with the hustle
and bustle of Tram Street stretching out in front of them. Mahmud

opened his mouth to say something, but his dark face suddenly grimaced.

"Fawzy!" he said, his voice quivering as if he were on the verge of tears. "I'm fornicating with Rosa. It's a cardinal sin, and I'm afraid of God's punishment."

"You," said Fawzy, pursing his lips and shaking his head, "are a complete idiot."

"Why's that?"

Fazwi placed his hand on Mahmud's shoulder and then, as if explaining something to a child, said, "Why look a gift horse in the mouth? Rosa is an English lady who likes you and looks after you. Or would you rather run after those putrid girls and have to fork out a fortune on them?"

"It's wrong, what I'm doing with Rosa."

"So you've turned into a shaykh? And didn't you kiss those girls too?"

"The sin of kissing is different from the sin of fornication. Uncle Darawi, the shaykh at the mosque, said in his sermon on Friday that fornication is one of the cardinal sins."

Fawzy thought it over for a moment.

"All right, then," he said. "Go and marry Rosa."

"Marry someone my mother's age?"

"Do a traditional oral marriage."

Mahmud did not seem to understand. Fawzy heaved a sigh and explained gently, "In the old days, Mahmud, do you think they had officials and documents? No way. In the old days, people got married just by saying they were in front of two witnesses. No need for papers. So get married like they used to do way back then. I'll go with you, and we'll find as a third guy someone from the triangle. You just tell her, 'I take you as my wife,' and she tells you, 'I take you as my husband,' and we say, 'We have witnessed the marriage.' That way everything will be perfectly aboveboard."

Mahmud shook his head. "I can't do that," he said decisively.

"So you don't like the idea of fornicating, but you don't like the idea of getting married either?"

"I've never heard of a marriage without papers or a contract. That would be a total sham."

Fawzy took a deep drag on his spliff and, after another fit of coughing, continued, "All right. Forget it. Do you want to hear another idea?"

"Go on."

"Listen up. Years ago, when the Muslims fought against Europe, didn't the victorious army take the women of the defeated as concubines? After every war there would be concubines left on both sides, Muslim concubines for the Franks and Frankish concubines for the Muslims. We learned that in history at school, don't you remember?"

"I was never any good at history."

"Think, Mahmud. Had you lived in those days and been in a war and taken a woman from the enemy army, you would have been entitled to use her as a concubine and sleep with her without having to get married, and it would have been perfectly permissible according to our religion."

"So what's that got to do with me?"

"Just imagine that you lived five or six centuries ago and that you have waged war against the Franks, defeated them and taken Rosa as your concubine. It would be well within your rights to sleep with her."

"First, I am alive today and not five hundred years ago. Second, I haven't fought the Franks. And third, I don't want any concubines, and even if I did, I would never take one who is sixty years old. What's all this shit about concubines and Franks? You're just stoned and spouting garbage."

"Actually, I am stoned," replied Fawzy calmly, rolling another spliff. "But I am speaking sense. Listen, Mahmud. However tormented you might feel, don't leave Rosa. She has taken the bait, and now you have to reel her in and find the fortune."

"You're speaking in riddles."

"It's your brain that isn't working."

"Just leave me alone."

Fawzy moved over to him. "I know what will make you happy again," he told him as if imparting a dangerous secret. "And I'll tell you, on condition that you do exactly what I say without further discussion."

SALEHA

On Friday morning, Abd el-Barr sent some of his staff over with enough presents for an army—meat, vegetables and cakes. Said went with him to say Friday prayers in the Sayyida Zeinab mosque and then brought him to the apartment. I was in my bedroom having Aisha put the finishing touches to my face. I had taken in my new blue dress a little to accentuate my curves and had put polish on my fingernails and toenails. I had put makeup on and done my hair in ringlets with a kiss curl on my forehead. In the mirror I thought I looked quite good.

"May the name of the Prophet protect you," Aisha said, laughing. "By the Prophet, you look stunning!"

We made our way to the sitting room, Aisha and my mother and me walking between them. Mahmud had been waiting in the hallway to join us.

Aisha raised a finger to her mouth, threw back her head and let out a resounding ululation, but a withering look from my mother silenced her. I felt breathless with excitement and almost lost my balance a few times as I tried to walk in my high heels.

I will never forget the moment I entered the sitting room. It was a very bright day, and the sun was flooding in. Abd el-Barr, who was seated between Kamel and Said, jumped up to greet us. At that moment I felt terror turn into astonishment. I had a fixed image of Abd el-Barr in my mind as a fat camel merchant in a galabiyya and a turban, speaking volubly as he spat on the ground, a great big wallet stuffed with banknotes sticking out of his pocket. That was how I had imagined him, but instead I saw a decent-looking, polite man in a smart blue suit, a white shirt and red necktie. He was olive-skinned and handsome. Abd el-Barr ate lunch with us and stayed until just before dinner. We sat and chatted. He made such a good impression on us all that even Kamel, the one most against the marriage, could not say a word against him. Had Abd el-Barr looked or behaved badly, it would have been much easier to refuse him, but his successful visit just made the situation more complicated, and the discussions about him raged on. After he left, Aisha, Fayeqa and Said pressed me hard, with my mother remaining neutral and Kamel trying to make me turn him down.

"Our late father," he kept telling everyone, "dreamed of seeing Saleha as a university teacher."

"If he were still alive," Said retorted, "and saw Abd el-Barr, he'd be the first to commend him."

"How do you know?"

"Can you deny that Abd el-Barr is a really fine guy?"

"I have nothing against him, but I'm against Saleha getting married at this time. She is working so hard and doing so well. It would be criminal for her to give up school and become a housewife."

"Listen, brother, she can finish her studies after she gets married. Lots of brides complete their baccalaureate at home."

"If Saleha gets married, she won't have time to study."

"If that's the case, then she's stupid and not cut out for studying," Said said.

I looked at him and made no comment. I wanted to point out that he was the one who could not get into university.

"Saleha," Kamel said, "it feels uncomfortable talking about your future with you sitting there saying nothing."

"I need to think it over," I said.

"There you are, getting all hoity-toity. Who do you think you are?" barked Said.

"As a daughter of the Gaafar clan," interjected my mother, "she can be as hoity-toity as she wants!"

"Well, Abd el-Barr could marry a hundred girls better than Saleha."

"By God, if he were to search the whole world, he wouldn't find anyone as good."

"Shit. It's the blind leading the blind here!"

"Watch your language, Said!"

I thought that Said was going to launch into another argument, but he got up, and as he left the room, he shouted, "Throw away the opportunity of a lifetime if you want. I'll give you two days before I go and apologize to Abd el-Barr. For all I care, little Mademoiselle Saleha can go to hell." He slammed the door behind him, leaving his words lingering in the air.

The next day I couldn't concentrate at school. When I came home, I sat down to lunch with my mother. Kamel and Mahmud no longer ate lunch with us since they started working at the Automobile Club. Suddenly I blurted out, "Mother, I'll marry Abd el-Barr."

She sat saying nothing, as if trying to absorb the shock. Then she advised me to think it over very carefully, because marriage is not a game. I repeated my decision, and she looked at me and then got up and hugged me. I could feel tears on her face as I clung to her and kissed her forehead. That evening, Kamel came into my bedroom, and with the barest trace of a smile, he muttered, "Congratulations, Saleha."

"I know you're against it, Kamel."

"I pray God it turns out for the best."

"I know you want the best for me. But I promise you, I'll finish my studies after I get married."

"I wish you every success, please God."

He then scuttled off, not wanting to talk about it anymore, having lost the battle. The next day, Said went and announced our official agreement to the marriage. Why had I agreed? No one pushed me into it. I was not sacrificing myself for the sake of our family's future, as happens in the movies. Had I turned him down, no one would have forced me. Perhaps I felt that it was my mother's wish that I marry him, even if she had not said so explicitly. Perhaps I was sure that I would be able to finish my studies. Perhaps because Abd el-Barr was actually quite attractive. Or perhaps because I wanted to be a bride, or perhaps it was for all those reasons. Abd el-Barr was so happy at the news that he showered us all with expensive gifts. Even Kamel, who was clearly opposed, received a beautiful Swiss watch. Abd el-Barr spent money like water, and I was dazzled by his generosity.

We set a date after the first anniversary of my father's death. Abd el-Barr rented a large apartment in Sayyida Zeinab Square so that I could be close to my family and would not let us spend a piastre furnishing it, installing a splendid kitchen and buying beautiful furniture for the entrance hall, as well as elegant sets of furniture for the living rooms and the bedroom. The days passed quickly, and soon the moment was upon us. I cried copiously as I look leave of my school friends and teachers. My emotions were mixed and contradictory—the notion of being married made me downcast and happy at once. Sometimes, the thought of leaving the family home plunged me into heart-thumping anxiety, and at other times, I felt excited and optimistic at the thought of starting a new life with a home of my own; I would have children and give them the best upbringing and education possible. What more could any girl want?

I tried to imagine what would happen on the wedding night. All I knew about marital relations was what I had gleaned from the whispers of girls at school. What did a man do with his wife? Would it be painful? Did a woman need it as much as a man did? I had no answers until Aisha explained it all to me. To this day I laugh when I remember how it happened. Aisha was preparing my body for the wedding. She came into the bathroom with me every day for a week in order to carry out her program, step by step. My mother watched with a mixture of curiosity and embarrassment as Aisha worked her hands over my naked body. Whenever Aisha started using coarse expressions, my mother would shudder and find some pretext to leave the bathroom. Two days before the wedding, as I was taking my clothes off, Aisha suddenly put her hand between my thighs, and I recoiled, pushing her hand away.

"Listen, girl!" she laughed. "No need to be embarrassed, although you're as coy as your mother! I've left the best bit for last."

She sat me down and, humming a vulgar ditty, started removing my pubic hair. My mother came back in and observed the process with a serious look on her face. She tried not to look at me but asked Aisha, as if requesting to be told her duties, "Do you need anything, Aisha?"

"Your daughter," she said, giving a crude laugh, "will soon be all smooth and peachy down there! What a lucky fellow he's going to be!"

My mother made no comment. She sat there with dignity, trying to remain oblivious and not show her embarrassment.

"Oh, Umm Said," Aisha blabbed on, "I think we need to explain a few things to your daughter before the wedding night."

"Explain a few things?"

"Good Lord!" Aisha said, beating her hand on her chest. "You can't let the girl go into it blind! Shouldn't she know what to do with a husband on the wedding night?"

My mother nodded as if taking the point. Then she came over to me and mumbled, "Listen, Saleha. You need to know what happens between a husband and wife. Well . . . nowhere is off-limits."

My skin was stinging where Aisha had waxed me. Like my mother, I was pretending not to be interested in order to hide my embarrassment. My mother continued, avoiding eye contact, "It is a fact of life that God created woman to be a receptacle for man. Relations between a man and woman are based on affection and compassion."

"Oh, Umm Said." Aisha laughed out loud. "For goodness sake! You sound like you're giving a sermon in the mosque! Listen, Saleha, my dear. Don't listen to your mother! I'll tell you exactly what you have to do with your husband."

My mother seemed happy to have been relieved of this onerous task. She left us alone in the bathroom. Aisha had finished depilating me and was rubbing her hand over my body to check whether she'd missed a spot. Then she took on a serious expression.

"Do you know," she asked me, "why the wedding night is called 'the night of the entrance'"?

I said nothing.

"People call it 'the night of the entrance' because the man enters into the woman."

Even now I laugh to recall Aisha's explanation. She was a woman who could not be embarrassed. When she had given me her detailed explanation, she said, "Remember it, Saleha. Don't ever forget it! Never be ashamed in front of your husband. Wear a skimpy nightdress for him. Dance for him. Behave like a tart in bed. As high and mighty as a man might be, he'll turn to jelly at the thought of sex. If you can carry it off, Abd el-Barr will be putty in your hands."

That is when I realized that Fayeqa's ability to control Said was no coincidence. The strange thing is that though I was mortified, I was not offended by Aisha. She was just explaining facts of life, of which I knew nothing because they always took place behind closed doors. That was how men behaved with women, even my late father, may he rest in peace.

As the wedding day approached, I was beset by a mixture of both terror and curiosity, like a little girl on a scary fairground ride. The party took place on the roof terrace, with guests both from our street in Cairo and from Upper Egypt. I looked at the scene with a sense of detachment, as if through a murky glass. There was a crowd, food, women ululating, tambourines, shrieks and kisses. All the sounds seemed to be coming from afar, as if I were drugged or dreaming. Abd el-Barr decided that we would spend our honeymoon in Alexandria because I had once told him that I had liked the city ever since first visiting it as a child with my father. We reached Alexandria before dawn and stayed in a hotel fronting the sea in Mahattat al-Raml. I was still wearing my white wedding dress, and the staff welcomed me warmly in spite of the tiredness in their eyes. I greeted them in return, although I was almost fainting with embarrassment. I could not bear the thought that they knew what Abd el-Barr and I were about to do the moment we shut the door. For all their sweet and polite words of welcome, I could see a lascivious look in their eyes as they mentally undressed me.

We had a large room with a balcony overlooking the sea. As Aisha had instructed, I would shower and put on my short low-cut black nightdress. I did what she had said, but despite my best efforts to overcome my shyness, I found myself incapable of standing like that in front of Abd el-Barr, so I put on a full-length silk dressing gown. Sitting at the desk, Abd el-Barr smiled.

"Brava, my bride!"

"Thank you." I managed to mouth the words as I sat on the edge of the bed. My breathing was shallow. My limbs turned to jelly, and everything Aisha had told me vanished from my mind. Abd el-Barr stood up and started walking toward me. I think I might have aroused his pity, as he suddenly asked me, "Are you feeling embarrassed?"

I did not answer. He laughed and said, "All right. I'm going to take a shower, but I won't be a moment!"

I nodded and smiled. I noticed that he seemed to be holding something in his left hand, but I could not see what. I sat there in a state of total confusion until I heard the bathroom door open, and he called out with a laugh, "I'm ready, my little bride!"

I said nothing. I heard him come up behind me, but I was frozen to the spot and unable to turn around. I could almost hear my heart pounding. Then I was aware of Abd el-Barr putting his arms around me.

28

The blood test showed that Mur'i had died from cholera. The samples from the other staff came back negative, except for three who turned out to be carriers: the sous-chef and two of the waiters. They were rushed off to hospital for treatment and their families placed in quarantine. The Automobile Club shut its door for three days during which the whole building was disinfected by the medical corps of the British army. When the Club reopened, unprecedented precautions were instituted. Antiseptic soap was distributed to all the staff, and their caftans were changed daily, returning freshly ironed from Abdin Palace. The tablecloths and napkins and anything that could carry the infection were sterilized in an autoclave installed on the roof terrace. All water was boiled before being used for cooking, and if it was for drinking, lemon juice was added to it. Cold shellfish dishes were taken off the menu in the restaurant. All vegetables were soaked in a dilution of permanganate for a whole hour and then washed in boiled water, and they had to be served piping hot to the members. Even the ice cubes for the whiskey were now being made from boiled water. The staff followed the new precautionary measures to the letter, unable to get out of their minds the memory of Abd el-Malek and Mur'i lying there dying. Dispirited and frightened, they continued to feel that death was stalking them in every nook and cranny of the Club, ready to take them at any moment. Who would be the next victim? How was it possible that a life could just be snuffed out like that? Whoops, and you were gone. All your good times, and your bad ones too. Your voice and breathing just stop, and you turn into a cold corpse honored by a speedy burial. Had Abd el-Malek not been joking with them just a day before he died? Had Mur'i not just celebrated the marriage of his daughter a couple of weeks ago? Had he not seemed to be in good health that night? After the wedding, they had all ganged up to bring him back with them to the men's apartment, where they sat up all night smoking hashish together. Had any one of them imagined that Uncle Mur'i, such an amusing chatterbox that night, would disappear from the face of the earth a few days later? They were all living on tenterhooks now. Any of them might be next. After all, as Kamel Gaafar had translated the words of the English doctor, "The new precautionary measures must be followed to the letter. Notwithstanding, the cholera microbe remains an ever-present danger. If any of you feels unusual in any way, you must inform us immediately so that we might treat and save you."

Needless to say, dealing with the imminence of death had not been part of their daily routine. Many now started saying their prayers regularly, beseeching God at length for mercy and forgiveness. Some tried to cope otherwise with alcohol and hashish. After the night shift, instead of going to the Paradise Café, they would go to the men's apartment to get drunk or light up a water pipe with hashish and brood. But despite persistent effort, there was no forgetting their ordeal. Their attempts at laughter sounded hollow, and they would slowly sink back into grief and hopelessness. It was no use. The fates were ranged against them. They were living like shadows. Before they had been merely abused and fleeced by Alku and flogged by Hameed, as they tried to put aside a few meager piastres for their families. They bore this misery with a vague and lingering hope, which they hardly dared even verbalize, that their lives might suddenly improve, that some unexpected event might release them in one fell swoop and lead them to a happier life, that God in His mercy would have a change of mind and lift their cloud of wretchedness. How could anyone resist what God had in store for him? Take Yusuf Tarboosh. He had been just as desperate, but by God's blessing, the king found his presence at the gambling table lucky and showered him with money. Does God Almighty not bring things into existence with a single word? Does He not provide sustenance to whomsoever he wishes?

That vague hope was one of the reasons for their opposition to Abdoun's rebelliousness. They believed that wisdom dictated that they should bend with the wind, bear all the humiliations and live with injustice while they dreamed of salvation. That was better than starting up all sorts of hopeless arguments with Alku, who in any case would end up on top. Reason dictated that they should just be patient until God provided salvation.

As time passed, they believed less that Abdoun might be Alku's stooge and started considering him no more than a stupid waste of space. Although a few were still prepared to speak up for Abdoun, most remained opposed. If he got worked up about dignity and rights, they would refute him or just ignore him or stare at him with the sort of sympathetic smile you might give a child imitating an adult. In any case, the daily discussions with Abdoun had now been overtaken by the recent succession of sorry events: the deaths of two colleagues, the discovery of cholera, the shutting of the Club and the new sanitary measures.

Every day brought them a worrisome new development. Even with the Club disinfected and operated with new precautions, its reopening was a flop. The king, who was meticulous about his own health, stopped coming. His example was followed by the princes, pashas and most of the members. For the first time, the Club shut its doors at one a.m. The paucity of customers meant that the staff's real source of income, tips, dried up. Their salaries were low, and without gratuities, their children would surely starve. The Club was in the doldrums, but Mr. Wright came up with a solution to the crisis. He asked Dr. Frankham, the senior medical officer in the British army, to stamp, sign and issue a certificate stating that the Automobile Club had received the all clear and was free of the cholera microbe. Dr. Frankham hesitated, explaining that on the practical level, it was impossible to confirm that any locale was completely microbe free. But after a long conversation, they reached a compromise. Dr. Frankham would issue a certificate stating that the Club had been disinfected to the highest possible standard. Mr. Wright had scores of copies made and ordered them to be posted to every member.

Soon, they started gradually coming back. Whenever a member turned up, Maître Shakir, following Mr. Wright's instructions, would explain in great detail how the Club had been disinfected. He would take him to the kitchen to see the precautions for himself and then take him up in the lift to see the giant autoclave on the roof. To seal the deal, Maître Shakir would then sit him down at a table and, with a reassuring smile, tell him, "The Club has been disinfected under the supervision of the British army medical corps, and as Sir must already know, English doctors are the best in the world."

Within a month of the issuance of the medical certificate, most of the members had returned, and finally, His Majesty honored the Automobile Club with his first visit since its closure. That night, the staff were all in a festive mood. The king seemed to be in tip-top form, his companions joking with him and each trying to outdo the next to keep him in good cheer. The moment he saw Yusuf Tarboosh, the king told him, "Joe, *reste à côté de moi. J'ai besoin de chance ce soir.*"

Yusuf gave a deep bow and mumbled, "At your service, Your Majesty."

Thus life at the Club returned to normal. The tips started to flow again, and there was an atmosphere of cautious optimism. But would the staff's lives go back to normal or was there still more tragedy in store? One morning, the late Abd el-Malek's widow came with her two little angelic boys, Michel and Raymonde. It was very moving to see them with their mother. The men clustered around them, welcoming them with a sorrowful warmth. She had brought along the little ones to ask for financial assistance from Mr. Wright, who peremptorily refused to meet with them, leaving a very blunt message for them with Khalil the office clerk, "There is nothing to discuss. You have already received the end-of-service payment."

Abd el-Malek's widow asked him, "Did you ask him about a pension, Uncle Khalil?"

Khalil cast his gaze downward and mumbled, "I did ask him, Umm Michel, but he told me that there are no pensions for Egyptians."

"But, Khalil, the end-of-service payment will only keep us going a month or two. After that, how will I be able to feed my children? Please go and talk to the Englishman again, or let me go and talk to him."

Her pleading tone so aroused Khalil's sympathy that he flung caution to the wind. He went off again to Mr. Wright's office. Wright said nothing but picked up his newspaper and carried on reading while gesturing to Khalil to get out. Downcast, he returned to Umm Michel, who realized from his expression that his efforts had failed and she started crying. The staff then took up a collection and handed the cash to Suleyman, the doorman and oldest member of staff, who then pressed the sum into the widow's hand.

"The late Abd el-Malek was our brother and dear friend," he told her. "The same goes for his family and children. Please, Umm Michel, if you need anything, call us and we'll bring it over to you."

The widow's feelings of gratitude exacerbated her grief, and she burst out sobbing as she muttered some words of thanks and then left, taking her children with her. Two days later, the scene was repeated with the widow of Mur'i the lift attendant, who tried her luck with Alku. She went to his office in Abdin Palace to request assistance, but Alku reaffirmed that the Club bylaws did not allow the payment of pensions. Mur'i's widow neither broke down nor begged but became angry and started shouting, "What do you mean, no pensions? How are we going to eat? If someone dies, are his family supposed to starve to death?"

She was a hard-nosed Upper Egyptian woman who had married Mur'i late in life, after the death of his first wife. They had produced three children, who were still of school age. Her sense of injustice only inflamed her anger. She was completely unaware that shouting at Alku was considered completely taboo.

His eyes bulged in disbelief as he gestured at her and barked, "Get out!"

Mur'i's widow held her ground, shouting back at him, "So you would send me away like some beggar! I just want what my children are entitled to!"

At this, Alku gave a look to Hameed, who got the hint and grabbed Mur'i's widow by the arms, dragging her out of the office. Two palace guards were called to help him, and she did not stop screaming as they frog-marched her out, "Shame on you, you heathens! Do you want me to go begging in the streets?"

She put up a struggle, trying to slip out of their grip, but Hameed thumped her on the back and shouted breathlessly, "Listen, woman!

We're treating you nicely out of respect for the late Mur'i. If you don't leave, I'll have the guards arrest you and throw you into prison."

She now became aware of the danger of the situation, and her shouting turned into tearful imploring. Hameed realized that her will had now been broken and stepped back a little, gesturing to the guards to eject her. Then he turned around and walked slowly back to Alku's office.

News of this incident spread among the staff, and they felt a sense of consternation. How could you throw the widow of your colleague out onto the street? How could Hameed give her a thump and threaten her with prison for simply requesting a pension so that she could feed her children? It was the same as had happened with the family of the late Abd el-Malek. The children of the late Abd el-Aziz also would have been reduced to begging had Comanus not have been kindhearted enough to take on Kamel and his brother Mahmud at the Club. The staff were well aware that what had happened with the families of their late colleagues could happen to their own families at any time. Should they die, fall ill or be incapacitated, their own children might end up having to beg in the streets, and if they came to the Club to request assistance, Mr. Wright would also refuse to meet them, and Hameed might thump them and have them thrown out.

The staff now started exchanging angry whispers:

"How much would it cost the Automobile Club to pay pensions to the families of the deceased?"

"Nothing! Peanuts compared to the Club budget."

"They have losses of hundreds of pounds every night in the casino, but there's nothing when it comes to the families of the deceased!"

"It's just plain wrong!"

Their resentments increased to the point where they could no longer remain silent. They decided to do something about it, and to speak to one of the department heads. After thinking it over and discussing it among themselves, they went off to see Maître Shakir, who, vile as he might be, did have a shred of decency, unlike Rikabi the chef. They felt they could talk to Shakir, and they knew that, moreover, he was on good terms with both the management and the membership. After the usual formalities and questions about one another's health, they came straight to the point, "Surely you can't be happy about what has happened with the children of the late Abd el-Malek and Mur'i."

Maître Shakir said nothing, eyeing them cautiously.

"We have to have a pension, Shakir," they said variously. "How can we work for years in the Club and then when we die our children are left to rot?"

Shakir let them fire out their questions. Then he asked them calmly, "How can I help you?"

"Go and see Mr. Wright and tell him."

"He'll just tell me that the bylaws don't allow it."

"Then tell them to change the bylaws. They're not written in stone!"

Shakir thought it over a little and then told them, "My advice is to forget the whole thing. Mr. Wright will never change the bylaws."

"It's an injustice. A sin. They'll have to answer to God."

"You'll have to live with it. If Alku gets wind of what you've been saying, it'll be a catastrophe for you all."

They tried to continue the conversation, but Maître Shakir cut them off and left them standing there. After a little further discussion, they decided to go see Hagg Yusuf Tarboosh. He had just finished saying his afternoon prayers. He shook hands with them one by one, his hand still wet from his ablutions. They repeated what they had told Maître Shakir. He bit his lip and shook his head, and as if fearful of being overheard, he spoke quietly, "By God, if it was up to me, I would have given you all pensions, but my hands are tied."

They stood there looking so crestfallen that Hagg Yusuf added in a conciliatory tone, "Why don't you put a little aside every month?"

"And how are we supposed to do that?" they countered. "Where do we get the money from, Uncle Yusuf? It's not like we're rolling in it."

Tarboosh gave them a look of irritation and retorted, "You seem to have forgotten yourselves. You don't know how lucky you are. Praise God and avoid the devil!"

They did not stay and argue with Yusuf but went back to inform their colleagues on the results of their efforts. Their bitterness was turning more and more to indignation, until Suleyman the doorman surprised them with his idea. Suleyman was in his seventies, the oldest member of the staff, and all his teeth were gone. He could hardly drag himself along due to the pains in his joints. For all that, he came up with something completely unprecedented in the history of the Automobile Club.

Alku had come for an afternoon inspection tour. He had climbed out of his car as usual and made his way to the entrance with Hameed scurrying along behind him. Suleyman had walked over to him and bowed, but just as Alku walked past him, he suddenly grabbed the sleeve of his embroidered jacket. Alku jerked his hand away and looked at Suleyman in disbelief, but the latter just called out in a tremulous voice, "Master Alku! The families of Abd el-Malek and Mur'i are begging you!"

"Begging me for what?" Alku roared.

"For a pension from the Club."

"We don't have pensions."

"How are they supposed to live, Master Alku?"

"What's it got to do with you, Suleyman? Mind your own business."

"How is it not my business?" Suleyman was starting to get angry. "We are all one big family."

This was more than Alku could stand. He made a gesture to Hameed and shouted to some of the servants standing in the entrance hall, "Grab hold of him!"

Such a call usually ended up with the offender being immediately restrained, but this time the servants stood their ground. They made no movement, seemingly refusing to carry out the order. Suleyman was their senior and held an elevated status in their eyes. Moreover, he was not a well man and could hardly walk. Hameed could not possibly beat him as he had the others. One of the servants walked over to Hameed, with an ingratiating smile on his face. He was about to ask Hameed to overlook the matter, but before he could utter a word, Hameed's flabby body started quaking with anger, and he roared thunderously, "I said grab hold of him! Are you deaf!"

There was nothing they could do. Two of the servants went over to Suleyman and grabbed him by the arms. Hameed's eyes bulged as he walked over to him and started slapping him. Suleyman put up no resistance and looked confused. The blows rained down on the old man's face as the servants tried to hide their dismay, averting their gaze and trying to hold their breath lest some sound betray their feelings of disapproval or sympathy. They waited until the punishment was over and Alku, with Hameed following him, had gone into the Club, before rushing over to Suleyman, who stood rooted to the spot with a sad smile on his face. They kissed him on the head and tried to comfort him.

"Never mind, Uncle Suleyman."

"Alku will get his punishment from God."

"He'll answer for this one day."

Uncle Suleyman dragged himself over to the bench. He listened to their words of consolation with a grateful yet absent look. He did not seem able to take in what had happened. It seemed incredible that he could be set upon like that at his age, and his look of startled bewilderment remained until he finished his shift and went home. The following day, after evening prayers, when Abdoun went to the café, he noticed Suleyman at the table by the window. Some of the staff had brought him there to take his mind off things before his next shift. Abdoun went over to him and shouted angrily, "How dare anyone lift up his hand against you!"

Suleyman looked down and muttered a few words of thanks to Abdoun, who then looked at the men sitting with him and asked, "So who's going to be next?"

They became flustered and retorted:

"Shut up, Abdoun. You're all we need now."

"Yes. Here's another misfortune for you to crow over!"

"Alku had Abd el-Aziz beaten up," Abdoun responded. "And he just lay down and died. Abd el-Malek's and Mur'i's children have nothing to eat. And now, to round it off, Uncle Suleyman, the oldest among us, has been smacked about like a child. All that and you sit there doing nothing. What are you afraid of? What worse could happen?"

No one said anything, so Abdoun continued, "As long as you stay terrified of Alku, you'll live like dogs."

"Abdoun, we're not sitting here doing nothing. We went to see Maître Shakir and Yusuf Tarboosh to ask them to go and speak to Alku about the pensions. But they won't."

"Of course they won't," Abdoun smiled. "Shakir, Tarboosh and

Rikabi—they're all in on it with Alku. They won't take our side against him. You seem to have forgotten how it works here in the Club—the big guys share the bonus with Alku. He lets them fleece us, and they pay him off."

The other staff knew deep down that Abdoun was speaking the truth. They were about to ask him what they should do, but then they remembered that his way of thinking was fraught with danger. So they sat there saying nothing. Abdoun sat there downcast too for a while. Then he looked up at them and said, "Listen. We need to get what we deserve. I'm going to go and see Alku."

"Go and see him?"

"Yes. I'll go and see him and demand that he put an end to the beatings. I'll tell him that we are not animals or children to be beaten."

They looked at him incredulously, and one of them said, "You're certifiable."

"If Alku had Uncle Suleyman beaten over just a word he uttered," another added, "then what do you think he'll do to you?"

"We'll see," Abdoun smiled. "I've made my decision. Alku has gone to Upper Egypt, but he'll be back in two days' time. The moment he gets back, I'm going to go and see him."

There was some agitated muttering, and someone asked, "Is anyone going with you?"

"If anyone wants to come along with me," Abdoun announced, "then he is most welcome. If no one wants to, then I'll go and see Alku on my own."

KAMEL

The air in the small room was thick with cigarette smoke and lit by a weak lightbulb dangling from a wire in the ceiling. Around the paper-strewn tabletop sat some people, among whom I was surprised to see Hasan Mu'min. I stood there like a rabbit in the headlights and said nothing. He stood up and embraced me.

"I'm aware that Hasan Mu'min is an acquaintance of yours," Prince Shamel said. "Let me introduce you to the others."

They all stood up as they shook hands with me. The prince introduced me first to a pretty, petite woman with short hair, called Odette, then to Abdoun, the barman I already knew from the Club, though we had never spoken. Then there was a bald man in his fifties with a paunch, whom the prince proudly presented to me, "Mr. Atiya Abd el-Aziz, the greatest trade union leader in Egypt."

I shook his hand respectfully, noting that his grip was strong for someone of his advanced age. The prince added, "It's Atiya who organized the last textile workers' strike in Mahalla."

Atiya seemed to be chuffed at the prince's words and whispered something I did not catch. There was also a skinny man with completely white hair who looked like a retired civil servant. The prince introduced him to me, "Mr. Awni," the prince said before gesturing for everyone to be seated. I sat in the only empty seat.

"First of all," the prince said, "I must explain who we are and what we are doing."

I looked at him, and he stopped for a moment, appearing to be searching for the right words.

"We are a joint working party of Wafdists and Communists.

Odette, Abdoun and Atiya are from the Egyptian Communist Party. Mr. Awni and Hasan Mu'min are from the Wafd. I am an independent and their colleague in the working party."

Odette gave me a look and then added cheerfully, "His Royal Highness is being far too modest. In actuality, he is the working party coordinator."

The prince smiled and continued, "The Wafd is the Egyptian nationalist party, but in recent years it has been hijacked by feudal landowners controlled by the palace and the English, and they have ignored the rights of the masses in order to cling to their class privileges. That's why the Wafdist Vanguard has been established, to represent the true heart of the party against the occupation and against feudalism. After much thought and discussion, the Wafdist Vanguard decided to form a joint cell with the Communists, and we are united around one demand, which is the evacuation of Egypt by the British and the independence of Egypt. After we gain our independence, there will of course be different views as to the state we wish to build. But for now, we are working toward two aims: first, to denounce the king's corruption and treachery, and second, to make the occupation so costly for the British that they will leave."

After a short pause, the prince went on, "Do you agree to join us, Kamel? To be brutally frank, I should let you know that participating in this organization is a crime under Egyptian law that can lead to life imprisonment."

"I'd be honored to join you, sir," I said with some emotion. The prince gave me a searching look.

"Kamel," interjected Hasan Mu'min, "is one of the bravest men I know. He distributed our pamphlet under the eyes of the police. He is a true nationalist with nerves of steel."

"I know," said the prince. "I've had a full report on him."

"I hope all the details were correct," I joked.

"Before admitting a new member, we carry out a thorough check to make sure that he is not a stooge of the security services. In your case, there was no problem because Hasan Mu'min seconded your candidacy. But I insisted on getting to know you myself so that I could sound out your character. I am happy to say it is sound indeed."

"Thank you, sir," I said quickly.

"We should all like to thank His Royal Highness," added Hasan Mu'min, "for his efforts in the service of the nationalist cause."

The prince smiled and tried to shrug off the praise. Then Atiya continued, "When we bear in mind that the other members of the royal family have thrown their lot in with the occupation as servants of the English, Prince Shamel's example is even more praiseworthy."

"All right!" The prince laughed. "We can't spend the whole meeting patting each other on the back! We have a lot to get through."

The prince put on his spectacles, arranged the papers in front of him and started reading. At that moment I felt I was seeing his true self, which, until then, had been masked by his eccentric jolliness. This was the real Prince Shamel, a serious man with an alert and resolute expression. In a semiofficial tone of voice, the prince expounded on the jobs already completed. He spoke of pamphlets and strikes and the statement that would need to be issued on the cabinet reshuffle. I was having difficulty keeping up, still in a state of shock. My mind wandered away from the current discussion, and I started wondering how this group had come into existence and how Hasan Mu'min had come to know Prince Shamel.

Then, I recalled what Hasan had said at our last meeting, "We are now working with a broad coalition." I also remembered the prince telling me that my participation in the resistance was no mere coincidence. He had known everything all along. Returning to the proceedings, I heard Odette's gravelly voice. "Comrade Abdoun. Please update us on the situation at the Automobile Club."

Abdoun's face turned somber as he leaned forward and started speaking as if delivering a report, "The king spends his evenings in the Club. He never misses a night. He is addicted to gambling. This week, he won a fortune from Fuad Pasha Hindawi. Rumor has it that Fuad Pasha lost so as to win a seat in the cabinet in the upcoming reshuffle."

"Have you heard anything about the reshuffle?" Odette asked.

"The staff in the casino heard the king telling Fuad Pasha to get his levée suit pressed."

The prince seemed intrigued by this and added, "This means that he'll appoint him. Just as I expected, this government's days are numbered."

"We'll need to mention this," Atiya said, "in the statement we're drafting."

"The new government will be just like the old one," Odette said. "It'll be a minority government made up of stooges of the English. Our struggle is not with the government but with the corrupt king who is subservient to the occupation and acts against the people."

"That's correct," the prince added. "Our statement needs to point out that a cabinet reshuffle will not solve the crisis."

"I'll finish editing it and show it to you next time."

The prince nodded and looked down at his papers, when Abdoun spoke up, "If I may, there is something that I should like to bring to our attention."

"Please be brief," the prince said. "We have a lot to get through on the agenda."

"I am going to see Alku," Abdoun said, "to demand that he put an end to corporal punishment."

"And do you think," asked Odette, "that Alku will agree?"

"I don't expect so."

"Then why are you going to see him?"

"Mainly to break down the barrier of fear and show my colleagues that it is possible to stand up to him."

"Indeed," added Atiya, "the most important thing is to break down the barrier of fear."

"Alku will get the greatest shock of his life," the prince laughed. "He has never imagined that one of his subordinates might stand up to him."

"Your late father," Abdoun said, looking at me, "was the first man who showed some guts in dealing with Alku."

I felt embarrassed at his having mentioned my father. I nodded and smiled as if thanking him. Abdoun then turned back to the prince.

"I'm going to go see Alku tomorrow at midnight."

"Call me afterward, so I will know that you are all right."

"Excuse me," interrupted Odette, "but I object."

There was silence as everyone looked expectantly at Odette. She adjusted her spectacles and took a drag on her cigarette.

"We need to define the purpose of every step we take. Let me remind you of what our purpose has been from the start. We are in agreement that the king's love of gambling has turned the Automobile Club into the seat of Egypt's government. We are in agreement that we should expose the king's sordid dealings and his subservience to the English. We have all stated that a revolution is needed to destroy the old order completely so that we can build the Egypt that we want. Abdoun managed to infiltrate the Automobile Club so as to provide us intelligence. You are all aware that we are planning an important operation inside the Club. Thus, we should not be distracted or draw unnecessary attention to ourselves."

"So you're against what Abdoun is planning?" the prince asked.

"Yes," replied Odette.

"I've become the most outspoken of the staff," said Abdoun, "when it comes to demanding their rights. What's wrong with that?"

"What we need from the staff," Odette smiled patronizingly, "is for them to serve as a conduit for intelligence on the king, the court and the government."

Abdoun looked at her incredulously. "The staff of the Club," he said with feeling, "need to understand that they are respectable people with rights and not just servants of His Majesty."

"You're correct in principle, of course, but that is not our immediate objective."

"I see no contradiction between our plan and raising the consciousness of my colleagues. Very soon I'll have most of them on our side."

"As I've already said, that is not our immediate objective."

"Comrade Odette, I don't understand you. You are in favor of recruiting the cadres in the factories but oppose the recruitment of anyone from the Automobile Club."

"Yes, because," she said without a moment's hesitation, "those in the factories are workers and not servants. There is a difference. If a worker can be correctly politicized, he becomes a real asset, but a servant's way of thinking is generally so mangled that he is resistant to any change."

"What you've said doesn't apply to any of my colleagues at the Club."

"Even if they were recruitable, the time is not right. You have to carry out our plan for the New Year's Eve party. That's only two weeks away and the plan will only work if the Club staff are in their accustomed mode of behavior. It'd be a mistake to push them into a confrontation with Alku."

"A confrontation with Alku is inevitable."

At this point Odette became agitated. "Now is not the time," she retorted. "Going off to see Alku will only result in collective punishment. What you are intending would jeopardize the operation we have been planning for weeks. I've already had to intervene with James Wright to stop you getting fired from the Club. I can't do that again."

"Then don't."

"Why are you being so difficult?" Odette shouted in irritation. "I have made myself clear. Your task at the Club is to gather intelligence. Nothing more. Nothing less. Your proposed scheme will put your colleagues under unbearable pressure, and we will all be exposed."

"What do you think, sir?" Abdoun asked the prince.

"Odette is right. An escalation in tension could have a deleterious effect on our plan." The prince said nothing for a few moments and then turned to Odette.

"On the other hand, if Abdoun backs down from having his meeting with Alku, he might lose his colleagues' confidence forever."

"So what's to be done?" she said.

No one said anything as the prince weighed all the various considerations.

"We don't have any choice," he said. "Abdoun, go and see Alku, but in my capacity as this working party's coordinator I would ask you not to take such initiatives again without consulting us."

Then the prince turned to me and chortled, "The first meeting you attend and you have to sit and watch a quarrel! What will you have to say about us now!"

"Only good things!" I said with a smile.

The prince picked up the thread again, "Differences in opinion are natural and usually help us reach the right decision."

The prince seemed to be the one who always had the final word, followed by Odette, who had a strong personality and wielded some influence over the others. After approximately an hour, the prince said to me, "Before we bring this meeting to an end, I would like to ask that, at our next meeting, you provide us with a two- or three-page analysis of the political situation. The analysis should reflect your opinion of what is happening and your expectations for the new cabinet. You will read it out to us and we'll discuss it."

I nodded my agreement, stood up and shook hands with everyone there. They started leaving.

"Wait a moment," Hasan Mu'min told me. "I'll go with you."

It was around nine o'clock, and although the sun was shining, there was a cold edge to the breeze.

"So what do you think of the working party?" Hasan asked.

"I'm glad to be part of it."

"In a few days' time," he said, "we're going to undertake an operation that will be the talk of all Egypt."

"Can you tell me anything about it?"

"Our organizational rules prevent me from giving you any information, unfortunately."

"I'm a member of the organization, like you are."

"But you haven't been involved in the planning of this operation, and thus you are not entitled to know the details."

My disappointment must have been apparent.

"The prince likes and trusts you," he said, as if trying to console me. "I'm sure he'll involve you in one of our upcoming operations."

We reached the tram stop where we would go our separate ways. Hasan gave me a warm hug and said, "Stay strong, young hero! See you at the next meeting."

I hailed a taxi and sped off to the Automobile Club. I was about half an hour late for my lesson with Mitsy. I rushed up to the top floor, but she was nowhere to be found. I was sure that she must have gotten angry and left. I felt downcast. It had not been my fault that I was late. Could Mitsy not have waited?

I went off to look for Khalil, the office clerk, and accosted him, "Uncle Khalil. Something came up and I arrived a little late for my lesson, but Mitsy has disappeared."

"In fact, she never came."

"I hope nothing has happened to her."

Khalil said nothing, and then the bell rang, and he scuttled off to Mr. Wright's office. I sat down and lit a cigarette. It was unlike Mitsy not to turn up for her lesson. I could not be the reason. I had never done anything to offend her. After a while, the door opened, and Khalil reappeared. His voice sounded anxious.

"Mr. Wright wishes to see you."

"What for?"

"I don't know. He just told me that he wanted to see you straightaway."

I followed two steps behind Khalil. Before he knocked on the office door, he leaned over to me and whispered, "He has been in a bad mood all morning. Be careful, Kamel."

29

When Mahmud came down from the roof, he felt much better. Fawzy could always dispel his worries and get him to see things differently. As much as he might disagree with Fawzy, he always came round to his opinion. For Mahmud believed that Fawzy knew much more than he did and that he was rarely wrong. So the next day, Mahmud started to carry out Fawzy's plan to the letter. He went off to visit Rosa and spent a few hours with her, during which he was so rough in bed with her that her shrieks echoed from the bedroom walls. He left her lying there while he took a hot shower. Then he got dressed and sat in the sitting room.

Rosa, having put on her silk dressing gown, came over and joined him there, putting her arms around him and planting little kisses on his forehead, as she asked him in an anxious whisper, "Can you stay the night with me?"

"Sorry, Rosa. I've got something I have to finish."

She hugged him as if trying to squeeze the last few moments of satisfaction from his body before he left.

Mahmud did not respond. He was concentrating on carrying out the plan. Rosa was about to give him a long, deep kiss, but he pushed her away gently, moving away a little and lighting a cigarette. He had a worried look on his face.

"What's the matter, Mahmud?" Rosa asked him anxiously.

"I've got a problem."

"What is it?"

"As if you need my problems."

"Please, let me see if I can help you." Her voice was trembling with a mixture of sympathy and desire.

"You know," Mahmud said, without looking at her or letting her see from his eyes that he was repeating the words Fawzy had taught him, "that I work and give my salary to my family and that I need every piastre. On top of working at the Club, I had a bookkeeping job for a grocer, which gave me a little extra income. Unfortunately, the grocer died two days ago, and his family are going to close down the shop."

"Is that why you've been looking so downcast?" Rosa smiled.

Mahmud looked down and said nothing, so Rosa put her hand on his cheek and whispered softly, "How much did you earn at the grocer's?"

"A pound a week."

She got up and went off to her bedroom. When she came back, she slipped a banknote into the breast pocket of his shirt and whispered, "I'll give you a pound a week. So don't worry about it."

According to the plan, Mahmud had been supposed to hesitate and decline the money, but Rosa's speedy response to his request, his joy at having the pound in his pocket and his feelings of gratitude, all made him throw his arms around her.

"So," she whispered in his ear, "are you going to spend the night with me?"

At this point he remembered Fawzy's instructions, and as Mahmud gently pushed her away, he told her, "I can't tonight."

Rosa sighed and went with him to the door. Just as he was leaving, she held his face in her hands and said, "Please, if you ever need anything, just tell me."

"Thank you, Rosa."

She gave him a peck on the mouth.

"I love you, Mahmud. I wonder if you love me as much."

He smiled and nodded. Then he gently eased himself out of her embrace and left. Rosa now gave him a pound every Thursday. On the first of the month, when his mother tried to give him some pocket money from his salary, Mahmud resolutely refused to take it.

"Mother," he told her, "thank God that I'm now starting to earn some decent tips. You can keep my whole salary."

His mother poured her blessings down on him. The four pounds he was earning from Rosa every month was more than enough to cover the cost of his and Fawzy's nocturnal excursions. His relationship with Rosa had settled into a fixed routine. Day by day, she became more attached to him and started calling him at the Automobile Club to check that he was all right and to hear his voice. He enjoyed Rosa's company. After having sex with her, he would tell her all about his life, and she would listen intently, giving him some bits of advice. Mahmud used to tell himself, "Rosa has a lot of life experience. She loves me and wants the best for me. I should learn from her." Mahmud considered Rosa a kindly and devoted lady friend. He loved her in his own way but not in the way she loved him, and he found it uncomfortable when she tried to get him to say things he did not feel. She kept on telling him that she loved him in the hope that he might reciprocate. He tried and tried to avoid saying it, but her persistence won out, and he sounded like a little child trying to pronounce a difficult word for the first time. He had often thought of being frank with her and telling her that, in spite of their relationship, they were friends and not lovers. He had been on the point of saying it a few times, but at the last moment he always felt sorry for her and kept it to himself.

"I've got a problem," Mahmud told his friend Fawzy during one of their regular sessions on the roof. "Rosa is in love with me and wants me to be in love with her."

"So be in love with her, chump," retorted Fawzy taking a drag on his fat spliff.

"I can't go on with her this way," Mahmud sighed. "I do like her. She's a nice, kind lady, but I can't love her the way she wants me to. Do you see?"

"By the Prophet, you're useless. What's all this talk of love, you idiot! Women only want one thing. Just go and see her one time without doing anything with her. Then you'll see what happens!"

Fawzy's method of making light of Mahmud's anxieties always left Mahmud with a feeling of relief. Their chats were akin to a psychoanalysis session, during which Mahmud could get everything off his chest and then face the world again.

His relationship with Rosa had been going on for three months now, and he spent the whole twelve pounds he had earned on his evenings out with Fawzy. Mahmud's life had fallen into perfect shape now that he was finished forever with the nightmare of school. He was having regular sex and had become a man of means.

One night, Mahmud told Rosa what was going on with Abdoun and Alku at the Automobile Club. She turned serious on him and told him, "Listen, Mahmud. You have got a family and responsibilities. Don't get involved."

"But it's also wrong for Alku to beat us like kids. All right, he's never beaten me. But if he ever beat me in front of other people, I honestly wouldn't be able to cope with it."

"He only does it if someone puts a foot out of place. I mean, as long as you work properly, he'll never beat you."

Mahmud appeared perturbed, but Rosa smiled and told him, "Promise me that you won't get involved."

"I won't."

"Promise?"

"I promise."

Rosa was a woman whose motherly instincts were as sincere and gushing as her sexual appetite was visceral and raw. This schizophrenic behavior confused Mahmud to the point where he thought of her as two different women behind the same face. She was lover and mother. The former was only interested in getting satisfied sexually, and the other treated him with sincere kindness in a way that moved him. One night, he went to deliver a dinner order to a German Club member called Madame Dagmar. Mahmud thought her name sounded strange, and Mustafa told him that she had come to Egypt thirty years ago with her German husband and that they had opened the famous Librairie Max in Soliman Pasha Street. Her husband had died two years earlier, and his son and daughter decided to go and live in Germany, leaving Dagmar running the bookshop and living alone in her apartment in Garden City. Mahmud rang the bell and stood waiting at the door with the delivery. The door opened quickly, and there appeared Madame Dagmar. Her smooth and completely white hair was cut in a boyish bob, which, along with her skinny body, gave her a military air. Her metal-framed round spectacles gave her the appearance of a grandmother or a headmistress.

Mahmud took two steps forward, bowed and uttered his usual greeting, "Bonsoir, Madame. Automobile Club."

She looked him up and down. "Can you take it into the kitchen?" she said in a monotone.

She stepped back and opened the door. Mahmud came in, looking at his feet and stood in the hall.

"The kitchen is through here," Madame Dagmar said. "Follow me."

He followed her through the sitting room to the kitchen, and after putting the food parcel on the marble table, he pulled the bill out of his jacket pocket. She paid the bill, leaving him a tip of fifty piastres. He put the banknotes in his pocket and thanked her in a low voice. He suddenly felt confused. The situation was rather strange. Here he was with this German lady, and they were both standing alone together in the kitchen. Why had she asked him to come inside the apartment when the package was so light that she could have managed it herself?

Mahmud smiled, nodded good-bye and turned to leave the kitchen, when Madame Dagmar called out, "Just a moment."

Mahmud stopped, and Madame Dagmar walked up to him. Then, smiling, she held out a whole pound. "Have it."

"Oh no, Madame!" he retorted. "It's too much. You have already given me a tip."

She reached over and pushed the pound into his breast pocket. He thanked her profusely, but she suddenly came right up to him, and in a lascivious whisper, she said, "I want you."

The situation had become tricky. Mahmud barely managed to stutter in response, "At your service, Madame."

She reached out and started feeling up his broad shoulders, then her face froze, and in a serious tone of voice that did not seem quite appropriate for the situation, she told him, "I want you to come and visit me the way you go and visit Rosa Khashab."

Mahmud blinked. He was speechless. He gave her a worried look, and all he could think about was how she could possibly have known about his relationship with Rosa. Dagmar was still smiling when she asked him nervously, "So what do you say?"

He had a whole pound in his pocket, which he could use for going out and having fun, but at the same time, the woman was the furthest thing he could imagine from sexually attractive. She had the body of an old soldier. Lank and dried out. No juicy backside or anything up front. Had he not feared her wrath, he might have turned her down, but he was just a delivery boy at the Automobile Club, and she was a rich, foreign lady who could cause him a lot of trouble.

"At your service, Madame," he said weakly.

"Come and sit down," she told him affectionately. "We can have dinner together . . ."

"I'm sorry, I can't. I have to get back to work."

She gave him a peeved, almost angry, look. "Then finish work and come back."

"I finish quite late."

"I'll wait for you."

"Could we do it tomorrow?"

"Okay. Tomorrow, finish work and come to me."

The moment Mahmud got out of her apartment, he heaved a sigh of relief. He needed to think over this bizarre development. He carried on working absentmindedly, and when he got home, he tried to think some more, but it was all too much for him, and he fell into a deep sleep.

The following day, before going to work, he dropped in on Fawzy. It was Aisha who opened the front door, telling him, "You've come just at the right time! It's one o'clock, and your friend doesn't want to wake up."

Mahmud went in and had to smile when he saw Fawzy in his pajamas, snoring away. He woke him and waited while he took a shower. Fawzy came back from the bathroom, towel around his neck, his hair dripping. They drank tea, and as Mahmud told him what had gone on with Dagmar, Fawzy worked his way through a number of bean and egg sandwiches with pickled cucumbers. When he had finished, he lit a cigarette.

"That needs some thinking over, Mr. Mahmud! Of course, you'll have to go and see her."

"But she's a dried-out old lady, not even remotely attractive."

"It's work, sunshine! Everything has a price. But this time, my boy, we'll make a pretty penny."

The following day, after Mahmud had finished his shift, at two in the morning, he changed out of his work clothes and telephoned his mother from the Club to tell her that he would be staying that night with one of his chums. He went out onto the street, greeted Suleyman and then hailed a taxi to Madame Dagmar's. He entered the lobby, but the moment he pushed the call button for the lift, the doorman appeared, rubbing his sleepy eyes. He looked at Mahmud with disbelief and asked him officiously, "Going to see whom?"

"Going to see Madame Dagmar on the third floor."

"And what is the purpose?"

"She asked me to come and visit her when I finished work."

The doorman's expression changed into one of suspicion mixed with contempt. He opened the lift door and said to Mahmud, "Come with me."

They rode up to the third floor in silence except for the loud whirring of the lift. As the doorman knocked on the apartment door, his expression turned to one of respect. Dagmar peered through the small grille in the door, and the doorman greeted her.

"Sorry for the trouble, Madame. This young fellow says he has an appointment with you."

Her face relaxed and she said, "Yes. Please let Mahmud come in."

Mahmud gave the doorman a sour look as he bowed and walked off. Dagmar was wearing a red robe and heavy makeup, which made her look like a rag doll. The moment Mahmud stepped inside, she bolted the door and threw her arms around him. She kissed him on the neck and chest, then rubbed her face against his chest, panting, hot to trot. Not knowing what to do with himself, he gently disentangled himself and asked her, "Might I have something to eat? I'm starving."

30

Abdoun is going to see Alku," the staff told one another excitedly. It beggared belief. Abdoun, the assistant barman, was going to stand before Alku and demand an end to the beatings. Alku would never back down. He'd been having them beaten ever since they started at the Club and not for a day had any of them ever thought to protest. They simply trembled when Alku walked by and thanked God when he ignored them and just carried on. How could one of them now be going to confront him with a demand to stop the beatings? What would be Abdoun's fate? Alku's reaction would be ferocious. Whatever Alku's reasons might have been for ignoring Abdoun's rebellious talk until now, this time he would grind him into dust. On their breaks, they milled around Abdoun. "Are you still planning to go and see Alku?" they'd ask.

Abdoun ignored their mocking tone and insinuation and said, "Yes. I'm going to tell him to stop beating us."

Then all the comments would rain down on him:

"So you think that you're the nation's leader?"

"We'd better say good-bye then, because you ain't coming back!"

"Abdoun! Rushing in where angels fear to tread even though God tells us not to throw ourselves headlong into our own doom!"

"God tells us to stand up for what is right and against injustice," Abdoun would answer.

The exchange would rage on, but Abdoun did not waver, and the staff eventually left him alone. If Alku were to wring his neck, it would be no more than he deserved. What they feared more than anything, though, was Alku's anger spreading and falling upon them.

Should that happen, they would have to disassociate themselves from Abdoun, and they all went over the things they might say:

"Your Excellency, we have had nothing to do with the lad, Abdoun. He's a lowlife. Utterly mad. Please don't blame us for him."

"You are our father, and we're your children and servants."

The following night, Alku returned from Upper Egypt. The staff were waiting expectantly, but there was a surprise in store for them. "Abdoun isn't going to meet Alku on his own. Bahr the barman and Samahy the kitchen boy are going with him."

"We used to have just one mad guy," someone jeered. "Now we've got three!"

The staff were all aware of the danger. They always knew that Abdoun's plan was outright insubordination and that it might spread like a contagion. Sure enough, he had recruited supporters. Today it was Bahr and Samahy who had decided to go with him, but who might join tomorrow? The bar was empty except for a man and woman drinking beer at a far table. Karara shook Bahr's hand and then got straight to the point.

"Bahr, you're a grown man. And you've got sense. How can you go along with Abdoun? As his manager, you should talk sense into him."

His colleagues echoed the sentiments. Bahr listened, squinting with one eye as he checked the clean glasses and lined them up on the shelf over the bar. Finally, he told them calmly, "I'm going with Abdoun. I can't let him face Alku alone."

"Have you taken leave of your senses?" asked Karara, raising his voice. "You want to go head-to-head with your master, Alku?"

"What's it to you, Karara?"

"What's it not to me! You and that lad Abdoun are going to cause nothing but trouble for us. If you stand up to Alku, he'll take it out on all of us."

"All right then, Karara," scoffed Bahr. "Go and kiss Alku's hand."

They stared at each other, muttering insults. Karara put his hand on Bahr's shoulder and was about to say something, but Bahr removed the hand and announced, "Gents! Thanks for the advice. Now excuse me. I've got work to do."

He went back behind the bar. His colleagues despaired of talking him out of it, so they went off to try their luck with Samahy. They apologized to Rikabi for disturbing him, gestured to Samahy and walked him out of the kitchen. His eyes were watering from chopping onions, and as he wiped them with his sleeve, he asked, "Everything all right, guys?"

They hesitated for a few moments, and then Karara launched into him, "Listen, Samahy. We've come to warn you. Don't let Abdoun talk you into standing up to your master, Alku. It'll be worse for you. You're just a kitchen assistant, and married, with two kids, at that."

It was the truth, and it gave him a jolt. Samahy looked pained and worried as he muttered, "May God preserve us."

They looked at him, unsure of what he was thinking. Samahy, avoiding their gaze, spoke up, "I mean, do you think it's right for old Suleyman to get beaten at his age?"

"He brought it on himself."

"He just asked for a pension for the widows and orphans. Is that a crime?"

"Then go along with Abdoun. It'll be the end of you."

"Abdoun is just demanding our rights. He should be thanked."

"Thanked for what? May God destroy his home."

It was clear their discussion was getting them nowhere. Samahy sighed and told them, "I've given Abdoun my word."

"May God take you, lad!" Karara could not hold back his irritation. "Listen, Samahy. When you go and see Alku, you're speaking for yourself. Don't drag us into it."

Samahy nodded, smiled weakly and went quietly back to the kitchen. The staff remained on tenterhooks all day long. At midnight, while His Majesty the king was playing poker, as usual, with some of the pashas, Samahy and Abdoun got changed, and the three men took a taxi to Abdin Palace. They traveled in silence. They were aware of the risk involved and felt that if they spoke to each other their resolve might crumble. At Abdin Palace, they greeted the guards and went in to go to Alku's office. His ubiquitous spies had kept him up to the moment on the subject of their visit.

Hameed looked at them calmly, as if they were expected, giving them no supercilious look nor the usual dressing down for turning up without an appointment. He simply asked, "Everything all right?"

Abdoun cleared his throat.

"We have come to see Alku on an important matter."

Hameed smiled and went into Alku's office. A few minutes later, he came back out, and in an almost friendly monotone, he said, "Alku will see you now."

It was a surreal situation, like a dream, they were proceeding as if down some enchanted passageway with no idea where it would lead. Now there was no turning back. They saw Alku sitting there at his desk, looking high and mighty, which unnerved them, and they said nothing until Alku barked at them, "Hameed said you wanted to see me."

None of them replied, so Alku shouted ominously, "All right. Speak up!"

Abdoun managed to control his fear and started off in a tremulous voice, "Your Excellency. We have just come to ask you for what we are entitled to and certain that you will reject this out of hand." He spoke as if to his equal and a spark of interest lit up Alku's face.

"So what do you want?" he said.

"We have come to ask you to stop the beatings."

"I only order beatings," he said with a smile, "when one of you steps out of line."

"Your Excellency, it is of course your prerogative to punish those who make mistakes. We can accept any punishment other than a beating."

Alku suddenly smiled, which they found strange and worrying. Then he looked at Bahr and asked him, "Do you agree with what he said, Bahr?"

Bahr nodded. "Being beaten is an offense to our sense of dignity, Your Excellency."

"Your Excellency," Abdoun added, "all the staff hope that you will forgo corporal punishments."

Alku looked down in silence for a few moments and appeared to be thinking. Then he got up and lumbered over to them. When he was right next to them, he said, "All right. Agreed."

The lightning speed of his acquiescence stunned them into silence. Alku nodded and smiled.

"From today on, no one will be beaten. If fault is found in someone, his pay will be docked, or he will be subjected to an administrative sanction. You will be treated like the staff in the palace."

"Thank you kindly, Your Excellency," Bahr smiled.

Samahy muttered some unintelligible words, but Abdoun took a step toward Alku to thank him.

"Your Excellency, I promise that you have taken the right decision. You will not regret it."

Such overfamiliarity despite good intentions would under normal circumstances have itself been considered a punishable act of insolence, but in keeping with his surprising and unfathomable response, Alku simply looked at them meekly and said, "All I want is for you to feel good about yourselves at work."

The three of them started thanking him volubly. Alku was smiling broadly, showing his glistening teeth. As he showed them to the door, he added jovially, "All right. You can get back to work now."

KAMEL

From the look on Mr. Wright's face, I could see trouble was looming. He answered my greeting with a cold stare and said nothing. But I decided not to let him humiliate me this time.

Without being invited, I just sat myself down in the seat in front of his desk, paying no heed to his look of incredulity.

"Khalil told me that you wanted to see me."

"I want to ask you about Mitsy," he said, stuffing tobacco into the bowl of his pipe.

"She is progressing in leaps and bounds with her Arabic."

"I've heard," he said, blowing out a thick cloud of smoke, "that you have been going out with her."

"That's correct."

"Why are you going out with my daughter?"

"Because it will help her to improve her Arabic."

"Mitsy is an actress," he smiled nervously. "A talented one. And like most artistic people, she goes through fads and phases. She throws herself into something only to discover that it's not for her, and then she moves on."

"What are you insinuating?"

"Your job is to teach Mitsy Arabic, not to take her on outings."

"I treat Mitsy like an adult."

"You need to understand," he said, raising his voice, "that you are just Mitsy's teacher. You give her a lesson, and you get paid."

"That's what it was like at the start, but Mitsy and I have become good friends," I said, now trying to provoke him.

"Oh. Really?" he said with a sarcastic smile on his face.

He put his elbows on the desk and leaned forward as if about to lunge.

"You're Nubian, aren't you Kamel?" he asked with ardent disdain.

"I'm Upper Egyptian."

"What's the difference?"

"The Upper Egyptians descend from the tribes who came to Egypt with the Islamic conquest. The Nubians are a different ethnic group with their own language."

He made a hand gesture to show his complete indifference and retorted, "I shall consider you Nubian, whatever the case may be. Have you heard of the German explorer Carl Hagenbeck?"

"No."

"Carl Hagenbeck was a great wild animal trader in Europe in the nineteenth century. He used to send hunters into forests all over the world to trap animals, which he would then sell to zoos."

I made no comment. He chuckled and continued, "The topic of Hagenbeck might not mean anything to you, but I'm sure that you will be most interested when you hear the rest of the story."

I sat there in silence and he went on, "At some point, Carl Hagenbeck wanted to upgrade his inventory. Along with animals, he started hunting natives, whom he displayed in cages. The idea caught on like wildfire in zoos all over the world. Can you imagine that hundreds of thousands of Western visitors, men, women and children, used to go and gawk at the caged Africans?"

"That's really vile," I retorted. "Inhuman."

"That might be how you see it, but millions of Westerners would not have agreed with you."

"Does your civilization have ethics that allow you to hunt humans and put them in cages?"

"Your question presupposes that all mankind has reached the same stage of development."

"I would have thought it goes without saying."

"Well, not exactly. Do you think you could convince me that Shakespeare and Alexander Graham Bell have the same mental capabilities as some primitive Indian or African?"

I stood up and walked over to him. "Mr. Wright," I said, trying to control myself, "I need to go and unlock the storeroom. Will you allow me to go?"

"No. You can't go until I've explained what connects you and Mr. Hagenbeck."

"I told you, I've never heard of him before."

He was not listening. He opened his desk drawer and took out an old photograph, which he passed across the desk to me.

"Among Hagenbeck's human acquisitions was a Nubian family. Doesn't that arouse your curiosity? Hagenbeck sent his hunters to Nubia, and they managed to capture an entire Nubian family, three generations. They put them all in a cage, and the Berlin zoo acquired the rights to show them. Then the cage made the rounds of all European zoos. That's the family in the photograph. If you look closely, you can see the grandfather in the cage, next to the son and his wife, who is holding an infant. Unfortunately, it would appear that the grandmother died during capture."

I averted my gaze.

"I'm not interested in the photograph," I growled.

"Oh," he scoffed, still holding out the picture, "and here I was thinking that you might like to see some of your Nubian forebears."

"Mr. Wright. Are you trying to humiliate me?"

"I can't see what I have said that might humiliate you."

"You are saying that my forebears were like animals."

"You can interpret my words any way you like. I have not made anything up. That is a historical truth. Nubians were hunted, put in cages and exhibited in most of the zoos in Europe."

"I don't wish to listen to this."

I did not wait for him to respond but got up and marched out of the office. When I turned around to close the door, I could see him looking at the papers on his desk with a self-satisfied smile. It was more than I could bear, and I made my way to the storeroom, where I sat and waited for Monsieur Comanus. When he turned up, I told him that my mother was ill, and I needed to be with her. He gave me the day off and made me promise to call him in the evening and tell him if my mother was feeling better.

I wandered aimlessly around the streets downtown, so blinded by rage that I kept bumping into people. The humiliation was torturing me. I had to do something. I wanted to go back and give that racist idiot a thrashing in front of everyone, damn the consequences. That pimp who crowed that my ancestors were animals is the same man serving up his daughter for the king's pleasure. Is that what you understand by the word "honor," Mr. Western Civilization? Even if we were animals, at least we would not pimp our daughters. I stopped walking. I could not take it anymore, and I went back to the Club, heading straight for Wright's office. My appearance seems to have shocked Khalil, because he sprang out of his chair.

"Are you all right, Kamel?" he asked me anxiously.

"I want to see Mr. Wright."

"Didn't you just see him?"

"Mr. Wright and I have some unfinished business." My voice was loud enough for the general manager to hear.

Uncle Khalil grabbed my hand.

"Come with me," he whispered. "Please."

Uncle Khalil dragged me out onto the street and away from the Club.

"The last thing you need to do," he said, "is to go making problems with Mr. Wright."

"He treated me like a piece of dirt."

"That's nothing new with him. He despises all Egyptians, but God gave us brains, and we can think for ourselves. You're a hardworking lad. Don't ruin everything that you've worked for. If you went in now and had it out with Mr. Wright, you might feel a little better, but both you and your brother would be fired."

His comment reminded me that my mother depended on our salaries, and I recalled the sight of her stricken face when my father passed away and how relieved she looked when I handed over my pay.

"Just do as I do, Kamel," Khalil continued. "In one ear and out the other. No matter how humiliating, the pain will fade. What matters is being able to earn a living."

I was not convinced by his logic, but I smiled and clasped his hand.

"Thank you, Khalil."

He gave me a quizzical look, as if to be sure he had reached me.

Feigning joviality, I told him, "Don't worry! I won't do anything stupid."

I went home and sat at my desk. My stomach was churning over the insult to me and to my family.

The following day, I went to a meeting of the organization. There was a long agenda and a discussion of recent events, including the stance of the nationalist workers and the war against the independent trade unions being waged by the palace, the English, the minority capitalist parties and the Muslim Brotherhood, who were well known for their opportunism. Finally, the prince spoke, "Before I declare this meeting over, I want to inform you that I have decided to assign a mission to Abdoun and Kamel. I briefed Abdoun yesterday. I need to sit down with you today, Kamel."

Once the others had left, I, now sitting alone with the prince, suddenly blurted out, "Sir, there was an incident with James Wright yesterday. I think you should know about it."

The prince looked apprehensive as I told him in detail what had happened the day before. I felt humiliated all over again, repeating what Wright had said about the Nubians that he considered my forebears. The prince listened and at last he spoke, "James Wright thinks you're responsible for his problem."

"And what's his problem?"

"His problem is that Mitsy refused the king, and he thinks that you are the reason."

"He's wrong. Mitsy has her own mind."

"I believe you, but he won't."

"Even if I were the reason, what right does that give him?"

"None, but don't forget that James Wright thinks that his daughter's friendship with an African is an offense to him and his family. A racist is just an ignorant man afraid of people who are different from him. However sickening you may have found his story, he didn't insult you directly, and he'd defend himself by saying that he was only remarking on a well-known episode from history and that you took it the wrong way."

"To insinuate that my ancestors were put in cages like animals—how else could I take it?"

Visibly moved, the prince smiled at me. "I'll have a word with him tomorrow. At the very least, he won't be repeating it."

I thanked the prince, then suddenly felt as if I could burst out in tears, and it must have been obvious that I was trying to stop myself. Noticing this, the prince withdrew and played a bit with his photographic equipment. After a while, he came back to see whether I had pulled myself together again.

"You need to learn," he said affectionately, "how to direct your anger to the larger purpose. Who gave the Englishman the right to insult you? The British occupation makes him feel he has the unquestioned authority to demean Egyptians. His offensive behavior is a direct result."

"But I can't just sit saying nothing," I exclaimed, "until the British evacuate the country."

The prince raised his hand as if to silence me.

"Kamel," he said wistfully. "Please. You'll take us back to square one. I told you that I'll have words with him. Now, I want to brief you on the mission. I want you to think about it as the appropriate way to respond to Wright's insults."

"I'm ready," I answered at once, "to carry out any orders you give me."

"Bravo," the prince smiled.

He got up and went over to a wooden chest at the far end of the room. He came back with a blue package, sat down next to me and opened it, taking out a small glass orb and handing it to me. I rolled it around in my hand, examining it, as he said, "I'll now tell you exactly what you have to do."

SALEHA

He started pulling at my nightdress, and I understood what he wanted. I took it off and almost died of shame. He pushed me down on my back and then lay on top of me. I was breathing heavily and could feel my own heart racing. He put his arms around me and slipped his tongue into my mouth. I could smell the tobacco on his breath and thought I was going to faint. Almost immediately, he got off me and sat up on the bed. He smiled at me and said, "Congratulations, now you're a woman."

He took a quick shower and, after a few minutes, came back and lay down beside me, kissing me on the cheek and whispering, "Good night." I lay there staring into the darkness until I heard his breathing become regular. I took a shower and returned to bed.

I was bewildered by what had happened. Abd el-Barr on top of me, the way he lay there sleeping with the smell of tobacco still on his breath, those things made me feel incredulity and shame. It was the same routine every night we were in Alexandria. The day after we returned to Cairo, my mother and Aisha came to see me. The moment I opened the door and saw them, I flung myself into my mother's arms. She burst out crying and said, "I can't believe that I'm coming to visit you in your home, Saleha. May God have mercy upon you, Abd el-Aziz. If only you had lived to see your daughter married."

I hugged and kissed her and tried to calm her down. My mother and Aisha had brought enough food to last a week. Duck stuffed with onion, pigeon stuffed with cracked wheat, three roast chickens as well as a pan of savory rice with clotted cream. After a while, Abd el-Barr came out of the bedroom, welcoming my mother and Aisha and joining us in the sitting room. He was polite and friendly as usual. I got up to make some tea, and my mother and Aisha followed me into the kitchen. My mother was flustered, but Aisha was laughing.

"We've come to see if you're all right! Is everything fine?"

"Thank God, yes," I said, putting the kettle on.

Aisha sidled over to me and asked in a low voice, "You mean the thing's been done?"

I said nothing, dying of embarrassment.

My mother took pity on me and grabbed Aisha away by the hand, saying, "That's enough, missus! The girl's shy."

Aisha, a few steps away, looked me up and down. "So," she asked, "are you . . . satisfied?"

"Yes."

"Fantastic!"

She made me laugh in spite of myself and put her arms around me, whispering gently, "Do you want help with anything?"

At that moment, I felt I loved Aisha. For all her faults, she, unlike her daughter, Fayeqa, was a wonderful, sincere person. Day by day, I started getting used to my new life. The feeling of being a housewife made me happy. My home was my kingdom to organize the way I wanted. I would wake up at first light and take a shower, get myself ready and go and make my husband's breakfast. Abd el-Barr needed a few hours' more sleep than I did. He never woke up before noon. I would make him a hot breakfast of mashed fava beans, falafel and an omelet. Then he would take a shower and go to work, and I would not see him again until after midnight. When he came home, he would find me dressed up and waiting with what should have been his dinner. It was taking me a little time to get used to the shift in my daily routine. I was an early sleeper, and I ended up having to drink a big mug of coffee in order not to doze off before my husband came home. Marriage did not change Abd el-Barr's character. He was still as generous and kind as he had been during our engagement, and in the first days I felt almost happy. But there was something that caused a ripple in the halcyon calm, something I felt too ashamed to even think about. I tried to ignore it, but it kept me awake at night, preying on my thoughts.

Nights with Abd el-Barr continued along the same lines: he would sit on the edge of the bed, completely naked, and then ask me to take off my nightdress in front of him. At the beginning, when I protested, he just stared at me and said, "You should do what your husband asks. Get undressed."

I did as he ordered, trying not to look at him. He gazed at my naked body, filling me with shame. Then he would start kissing me and get me to lie down on my back, at which point he would wrap himself around me and wriggle a little on top of me until I felt a little wet spot on my body. Then he would jump up and go to the bathroom. When he returned, he would plant a little kiss on my cheek, before lying down with his back to me and sinking into a deep sleep. I always waited for him to drop off before going to the bathroom. Standing under the hot shower, I would go over it and feel strangely sullied. I felt like I had been accosted and would sob quietly so that Abd el-Barr would not hear me. I had no idea why I was crying. Was it because he forced me to get undressed? Or because he just plumped himself on top of me without saying anything? Shouldn't he say "I love you" or whisper some sweet nothings? I felt sure that what we were doing in bed was not normal. None of the things Aisha had explained to me took place. I noticed that Abd el-Barr was waking up a little tense in the morning. He would not look at me and hardly said anything. As we ate breakfast together, he would gradually come back to himself. As time passed, it became clear to me: it was I who was suffering from some defect and most certainly incapable of satisfying my husband in bed. It was obvious that he could hardly bear me and was just making do. Overwhelmed by guilt, I tried to ingratiate myself with him. I made him ever more delicious dishes to eat, pranced around and tried to get him to laugh. All of this to try to make up for the defect he had discovered in me. I could manage to put it out of my mind during the day, but each night brought the same ordeal.

After a few weeks, I could not bear it anymore. I had to do something. I told Abd el-Barr that I wanted to go and visit my mother. As I was walking up the stairs, I felt very emotional, realizing just how much I missed our home, and the wonderful memories flooded through my mind. Rather than going straight in, I knocked on Aisha's door. She saw the state I was in.

"What's the matter, my little darling?" she asked me.

Feeling sorry for myself and unable to withstand her kindness, I started crying. Aisha put her arms around me and started soothing me. Then she went and made me a glass of lemonade. This time when she asked what was wrong, I answered weakly, "I've got a problem with Abd el-Barr."

"Nothing serious, God forbid."

I told her what happened between us. She looked concerned and asked me for precise details. Looking down at the floor, since I could not look her in the eye, I told her.

When I had finished, Aisha sighed. "My darling little one!"

"What am I doing wrong, Aisha?"

"He's a bit weak down there."

"Weak down there?"

"Of course. There are some men who feel so intimidated on their wedding night that they can't hold themselves back, but within a day or two, they can perform normally. But Abd el-Barr has been like this for more than two months. He can't seem to help it."

"Could I be the cause of that?"

"Nonsense!" she said beating her breast and sighing. "You're as pretty as the moon, Saleha, like a white horse in a fairy tale, but the steed doesn't know how to mount you."

The comparison made me uneasy, but I was at least happy to hear that I was not doing anything wrong. At least there was nothing wrong with me as a woman. Aisha again went over the proper way to have marital relations.

"All in all," she sighed, "we have to give him a chance. He might improve. And you can help him along."

"How?"

Aisha cackled and her eyes twinkled. She leaned in and started giving me all sorts of obscene advice. The surprising thing is that I listened to her. Perhaps I no longer felt embarrassed, having got used to her way of speaking, or perhaps I had decided that I wanted to do all I could to help Abd el-Barr overcome this impediment. I got Aisha to agree not to mention this matter to my mother. It would only upset her.

I left Aisha's apartment and went to my mother's, where I tried to behave as if everything was fine, and then I went home in a different frame of mind. I felt spurred on. Knowing what I had to do, I was getting into the spirit, like someone taking a test she had studied for. I was all set to help my husband the way Aisha had told me, to get over my shyness and do everything to rescue our marital relations. As Aisha was always saying, "When a married couple are in bed, shame and sin go out of the window."

The first two nights, Abd el-Barr simply went to sleep. On the third night, as usual, he asked me to get naked. I took off my nightdress in front of him. He put his arms around me and had me lie down on the bed, then lay on top of me, kissing me. I had to act quickly, before he could climax. So I wriggled a little and pushed him gently aside. Then I started caressing his body. I kept my eyes shut, concentrating on Aisha's instructions and letting my hand carry them out. Suddenly, Abd el-Barr shoved me so hard that I almost fell on the floor.

"What are you doing?"

"I'm trying to help you," I answered without a second thought.

He jumped off the bed and looked me right in the eyes, his face grimacing as if in pain. I had never seen him as angry. He paced up and down, naked, and then came back and sat in front of me on the edge of the bed, as if trying to catch his breath.

"I just don't believe it."

I said nothing, and he screamed at my face, "Saleha! How can you do those filthy things? Is that what you were brought up to do?

I had covered my naked body with a sheet, saying nothing. I was afraid. My life seemed to be getting only more complicated. I felt really bad about what I had done. How could I have told Aisha, and why did I just do what she told me without thinking?

"I want to know," Abd el-Barr said quietly, "how you learned to do that."

"Aisha told me."

"What has Aisha got to do with it?"

"I consulted her."

"Why would you consult her?"

"I felt that something wasn't right between us. Aisha has a lot of experience. She told me what I could do to help you."

Abd el-Barr sprang up again, threw on a galabiyya and sat down in the chair near the window. I got dressed and sat down on the bed again. Until that moment, I thought we would be able to sort it out. I would apologize. I would tell him that I knew I had been wrong and would not do it again.

In a subdued voice, I said, "I'm sorry, Abd el-Barr. I didn't mean to."

He said nothing. He was sitting back in the chair, and I could not make out his expression. I saw him lean over the table. He was doing something with his hands. I called his name. He did not turn around. I got up and edged my way over to him and, looking over his shoulder, it took me quite a time to absorb what I was seeing. It was very strange. I could see a razor blade broken into two halves and lines of smooth white powder. Abd el-Barr was leaning forward and snorting like a bull. I was alarmed.

"What are you doing?" I shouted.

He did not respond. He was not listening. He inhaled all the powder in two snorts and leaned back in the chair, saying nothing, his eyes closed, his breathing heavy. Then he slowly stood up and turned toward me. His eyes were glaring and his face thunderous. I could hear him panting and see the beads of sweat on his brow. Suddenly, he grabbed me by the hair with a jerk. I screamed out in pain and he shouted at me, "How could you go telling Aisha about our private life?"

"I'm sorry!"

He carried on shouting and yanking my head. "Are you trying to embarrass me, you bitch?"

"Forgive me, Abdu. I won't do it again."

My hair was hurting me, but I was more upset than anything. I was ready to kiss his hand to make him forgive me. I pleaded, "Stop, Abdu. By God Almighty, I won't do it again."

"Shut your mouth."

He punched me in the face. I went dizzy. My vision was blurry and I thought I was going to faint. I had to escape. He hit me again and kicked me in the stomach. It was excruciating, but I did not scream. He pushed me, and I fell onto the bed. He threw himself on top of me and reached down, trying to push my legs apart. In spite of my shock and terror, I managed to clench my thighs tightly together.

"Open them!" he panted.

He kept trying to force my thighs apart, and as I realized that he was trying to get his fingers inside me, I decided to put up a struggle. I was focusing all my strength into my thighs, but Abd el-Barr was strong. My muscles were almost in a cramp from clenching, and I knew I could not hold it much longer and that he was going to win. Everything went dark, and I felt my body going limp. Suddenly, I had an idea. I bit him on his upper arm. I can hardly believe what I did. I sank my teeth into his arm and could feel them piercing his flesh. He screamed, pushed me away and jumped off the bed. I felt a heavy blow to my back as I tried to move away. Stumbling out of the bedroom, I pushed over the armchair and pulled the door shut behind me. This slowed down Abd el-Barr just long enough for me to reach the front door. I ran down the stairs as quickly as I could and got out onto the street. It was two o'clock in the morning. The few people out and about threw me a curious glance. I realized that Abd el-Barr was not coming after me, but all the same, out of sheer terror, I half ran all the way home. Then I remembered that I did not have the key. I kept pushing the buzzer until my mother opened the door. She looked worried, and I threw myself into her arms.

"For God's sake, Saleha, I hope nothing awful's happened!"

31

Mahmud drank a whole bottle of red wine and wolfed down half a roast chicken. When he finished, Dagmar smiled and asked, "Do you want anything else?"

Mahmud shook his head to say no. Dagmar got up and brought him the other half of the chicken, which he devoured in a matter of minutes. Dagmar said nothing, but Mahmud realized that he had now eaten all the food on offer. He got up and walked across the hall to the bathroom, which he noted was nice and large and all done out in a soft shade of turquoise. He washed his hands and face and went back to the sitting room. Dagmar was wearing a baby-doll nightdress, which showed her scraggy body with its sagging liver-spotted skin. Her breasts were no more than two sad memories. She tried to snuggle up to him on the sofa, but he held up his hand to stop her.

"Do you have any whiskey, please?" he asked.

Looking a little cross, she asked him, "Shall I pour you a glass?"

"Just bring the bottle."

She was about to refuse, but something crossed her mind, and she got up and fetched a bottle of Red Label and a bowl of ice cubes.

"Do you know, Mahmud"—she cleared her throat—"it's not good to drink too much whiskey."

Mahmud nodded in agreement as he poured himself a large glass and slugged it down neat. He closed his eyes as he felt the burning sensation in his throat.

"I'm sorry, Madame," he said with a smile. "Please give me a little more time."

Dagmar made no response. She kept her gaze fixed on him, her heavy makeup giving her the look of a worn-out old actress in a touring troupe. Mahmud poured himself another large whiskey and drank it the same way. Then he sat back and breathed deeply. She made an attempt to cozy up to him, but he held out his hand to stop her from going any further. Dagmar muttered some words in German that he could not understand, and then she looked away sullenly. Mahmud just sat there with his legs stretched out on the sofa. A few minutes passed in silence. He could feel the whiskey taking effect and gave a sigh of relief as he realized that he was now up to the job in hand. He turned to Dagmar, holding his arms out, and she threw herself into them. Under normal circumstances, he could not have found her attractive, but the alcohol had taken him into the stratosphere. He held Dagmar in his strong arms and then started to kiss her long and slow as he had learned from Rosa, and as he ran his coarse lips up and down her body, his mind was empty. He went on kissing her slowly, moving from spot to spot, until he became aware of her body writhing at his touch. Dagmar was moaning loudly. Then Mahmud stood up, still holding her. She weighed nothing as he carried her over his shoulder into the bedroom, and she groaned as he laid her down on the bed. Mahmud helped her out of her nightdress, and then, when she was stark naked, he threw himself on top of her.

His lovemaking with Dagmar was completely mechanical and consisted of a succession of movements, like the steps of a dance or calisthenics. There was no intimacy or affection, such as he felt with Rosa. What possible sort of relationship could he have with this miserable, raddled old German woman? A straightforward working relationship, according to Fawzy. Mahmud treated Dagmar's body like a machine, but one that he knew how to operate efficiently. As Mahmud pounded away at Dagmar, she screamed and shouted in German, and her face took on varying expressions of utter joy and astonishment, wide-eyed disbelief and helplessness. Sex for the first time in years was driving her mad. Madame Dagmar arrived in seventh heaven quite a few times, then she lay back and closed her eyes, savoring the postcoital bliss. Mahmud got up and went to the bathroom. He stood under the hot water, scrubbing himself as if trying to wash off any trace of what had just happened. He got dressed and found Dagmar in the sitting room waiting for him in her blue silk robe. She looked calm and relaxed and gave him a hug.

"Mahmud," she whispered, "you've got to keep visiting me."

"I'd like my money."

He uttered the words with an ease that astounded him. That was what Fawzy had told him to do, but he had spent the day hesitating over it. Now he had just blurted it out, and he felt ashamed. Dagmar smiled at him gratefully, as if to say, "After everything you've done, you deserve it." She went into the bedroom and came back with a pound, which Mahmud put into his pocket, thanking her quietly. She went with him to the front door, planted a kiss on his cheek, asking him matter-of-factly, "When can you come again?"

"Saturday."

That was the day that Rosa met her friends at the Turf Club.

He carried on visiting Dagmar. He could not bring himself to touch her until he was so drunk that everything became a blur. When he was done, he would ask himself how he could go to bed with such a scraggly old woman, but time after time he managed to give her a good servicing. Following Fawzy's advice, he only sold love four days a week. Two nights with Dagmar and two with Rosa, and the remaining days he would get off work and either go home to eat and have a long sleep if he felt tired or sit up late smoking hashish with Fawzy on the roof.

With Dagmar, he never developed the friendly feelings he had toward Rosa; he was just selling a commodity. Pleasure for money. And Dagmar treated him like a masseur or a tennis instructor. She told him what she wanted without a hint of shame. During sex, she would whisper an order to him to do this or that. When it was over and he went into the bathroom, she would often call out to him in an emotionless voice, "Take a shower and come back. I want you to do it again."

Her direct way of going about things freed him from having to pretend. At the same time, he felt a little demeaned by it. Not only that, but when he was not having sex with her, he found her off-putting. He could kiss Dagmar, stroke her all over, carry her in his arms, lay her down on the bed and drill her without mercy, but the moment the sex was over and he had taken a shower and got dressed, she became no more than an old woman with whom he did not feel comfortable. He kept wondering why he felt comfortable with Rosa, whereas whenever he asked Dagmar for anything, he was hesitant and apologetic. When asking her for dinner, for example, he would say, "Excuse me, Madame Dagmar. Sorry to trouble you, but I'm hungry."

Dagmar would give the knowing nod of someone who understands the terms of commerce. She would go into the kitchen and come back with a tray of food. The quantities were much smaller than at Rosa's, where a broad spread was always on offer. Dagmar's dinners were carefully rationed: half a chicken with a small plate of rice or a small portion of macaroni cheese, which in Mahmud's terms was about two mouthfuls. Dagmar was stingy. She was mean with her food, and if Mahmud wanted more, he had to ask for it. She never refused, but she never looked happy about it. Mahmud came to learn that after sex she became gentler and more obliging. He put up with her frowning and her muttering in German during the act, and then, when she lay there in contentment afterward, he would make his requests. Mahmud followed his sex schedule almost religiously. He was now giving his whole salary from the Club to his mother and sharing what he earned from Rosa and Dagmar with Fawzy. The latter amount he considered ill-gotten money, which could sully his mother and sister if he gave it to them. He explained his concerns to Fawzy.

"All right," said Fawzy. "If that money is what you call 'ill-gotten,' we'll have to spend it on hashish and women. Illicit things are what you spend illicit money on!"

This exegesis seemed to calm Mahmud. If he forgot his religious worries, his life seemed quite acceptable, stable and even happy. But his sexual adventures had changed his opinion of women. He was no longer awed by their beauty. They had lost their mysterious seductiveness. He felt as if he had dissected a rose and could no longer see its beauty but only the constituent parts. He now looked at women the way a driver might check over a car for its good and bad parts, knowing that, whatever the model or make, he would be able to drive it. The paintwork and accessories were no longer of interest;

he just wanted to know how the engine would purr. No matter how beautiful, elegant, refined, haughty or vain a woman might appear, Mahmud could not help wondering what she would be like in bed. He would think of himself stroking her to make her open like a flower and let the honey flow. In spite of his apparent good manners, Mahmud now treated all women, except for his mother, his sister and Rosa, with a sort of latent disdain. He talked to them condescendingly, with a look one might give to a child spouting nonsense. He had an inner dialogue: "Stop pretending to be preoccupied with this or that. All this glamorous flirting doesn't fool me, because I know that at some point you will drop the pretense and beg to be pleasured, like all other women."

The previous day was his break from lovemaking. Mahmud had finished work at two in the morning and had gone to visit Fawzy, who was sitting up late on the roof. They drank some delicious mint tea as Fawzy busied himself rolling spliffs. He gave one to Mahmud and lit the other. As he smoked, Mahmud leaned against the wall of the roof terrace and started thinking aloud.

"I'm starting to feel sorry for women."

"What are you going on about?"

"Well, it seems to me that women are just like men. If they don't get sex, they start getting all ratty."

Fawzy nodded. "Of course, my boy," he said as if an expert. "If they aren't satisfied, they can cause no end of problems. If they've never had it, they can control themselves. But once they've tried it, they can't stop thinking about it."

"Rosa and Dagmar should put up a statue of me."

Fawzy chuckled, and handing Mahmud another spliff, he said, "God is great! You've finally started getting some sense into that head of yours."

Mahmud smoked the second spliff, and the hashish made him taciturn.

"You know," Fawzy said looking at Mahmud. "Next week is the Eid al-Kebir. I hope you're going to make the most of it?"

"What do you mean?"

"It's the big feast! Rosa and Dagmar should each be giving you a present."

"I can't go asking for presents."

"Oh, Mahmud, my friend!" said Fawzy in exasperation. "No one is saying you should ask for presents. You drop a hint or two, and they'll get the point."

"And what if they don't?"

"Then give them a stronger hint. For example, tell them that you are thinking of buying a leather jacket before the feast."

"I can't say something like that!"

"What a child!"

Fawzy went on making fun of Mahmud, and they flung friendly curses at each other before changing the subject.

Mahmud went home just before the dawn call to prayer, and as usual, the next day he found himself acting out Fawzy's directions. Rosa fell for it immediately. She kissed him on the cheek, went into her bedroom and returned with two pounds.

"Here's some money for the feast, Mahmud," she said.

Dagmar, on the other hand, just gave him a suspicious look. "Are you asking for something?" she said.

His resolve completely crumbled, and, embarrassed, he muttered, "No," and then left her apartment.

On the following visit, Dagmar had the same serious look on her face, but she gave him a new white shirt as a present. When Fawzy examined it later, he could not help thinking that it was a bit cheap of Dagmar.

The boys were now rolling in money, and they started acquiring the appurtenances of luxury: smart new suits, Lucky Strike cigarettes, Ronson lighters and Persol sunglasses. They did not worry about how much they spent when they went out together, and they no longer loitered around the girls' school trying to persuade this or that one to go and sit with them in the back row of the cinema. They had moved on from schoolboy distractions. They started frequenting a brothel that Fawzy had discovered in the Ataba district. He negotiated with the madame a price of twenty-five piastres for a girl. Fawzy would sit there chatting away with the corpulent madame before giving her the fifty piastres, and then the two men would go into the inner room to choose a girl. Fawzy would always choose a different one, unlike Mahmud, who was enamored of one called Nawal from Alexandria.

She was pretty and thin with sad, dark eyes and shoulder-length hair. When Mahmud went off with her to a bedroom, she would take off her red robe and lie there naked. He would look at her for a little and then move over to her, whispering, "How are you, Nawal? I've missed you."

Each time he had sex with her, which was always forceful and passionate, it felt different, in contrast to how it was with the two older women. When he was done, he would keep his arms around her and feel her hot breath on his face. She would stroke his back and broad shoulders, kissing him gently on the neck.

One time, he asked her, "You're a nice girl, Nawal. How did you end up here?"

"It's my fate," she whispered curtly, and he realized that she did not really want to discuss the matter.

After Mahmud had been with Nawal a few times, Fawzy felt it was his duty to intervene, and as the two friends were sitting on the roof one evening, he said, "You seem to have become quite attached to that Nawal."

"She's a nice girl."

"Nice or not, you're paying to have a good time. You've got to try out another girl, and then when we've been through them all, we'll go to another establishment."

Mahmud looked as if he had been found out.

"Listen, Mahmud," Fawzy told him in a fatherly voice, "don't go getting soft on that girl Nawal. It would be a disaster. She's just a tart who'll sleep with any scumbag."

Mahmud winced at the description, but the following week Fawzy took him off to a different brothel in Abbasiya. Mahmud was hesitant, but Fawzy told him decisively, "Listen, Mahmud. The only way to get you to stop thinking about her is for you to find an even prettier one."

No matter what happened to the two boys and whatever adventures they went through, Mahmud was always grateful to Fawzy for looking out for him. As they were now flush with money, Fawzy suggested they start putting aside a bit every month for a Lambretta scooter.

"What are we going to do with a Lambretta?" Mahmud asked innocently.

"We'll go places."

"Which one of us will drive it?"

"You can use it to get around town, and when you're done, I can use it. When we go out together, one of us will drive and the other will ride pillion."

"We can both go on it at the same time?"

Fawzy sighed and assured Mahmud, "Of course we can. Listen, Mahmud, as you sit riding the Lambretta, you'll see a whole different world."

The two friends started saving, and within two months, they had enough for a deposit. They went to the scooter dealer in Fuad Street, and Fawzy talked Mahmud into signing a hire purchase agreement for a year at fifty piastres a week. Then they registered the Lambretta in Fawzy's name. The boys left the motor vehicle registry with the Lambretta, now bearing a white license plate. Mahmud was quite content to sit behind Fawzy, but his greatest pleasure was driving himself and feeling the breeze against his face and body. Then he felt himself on a higher plane, a life of hitherto unimagined fine living. He was on top of the world, but events soon hurled him in an unexpected direction.

One night, Mahmud went off to see Rosa on schedule, but the moment he got there he felt something was wrong. Rosa's face did not light up to see him; neither did she hug or kiss him but kept her distance, with a strange smile on her face.

"Sit down," she said seriously. "I want to talk to you about something."

Mahmud was nonplussed and sat down on the sofa.

"You do love me, don't you?" Rosa asked him.

This question usually made him uneasy, and he would typically lie, but this time he nodded affirmatively.

Suddenly, Rosa screwed up her face and screamed at him, "You're a liar, Mahmud!"

He was shocked into silence, but Rosa continued shouting.

"How can you love me and be seeing someone else?"

"I'm not," Mahmud retorted. Then he bit his lips and knitted his brows like an accused child trying to prove his innocence. Rosa got up and took a few steps toward him.

"You're seeing Dagmar," she said. "I know everything."

As she uttered the name "Dagmar," she lost control and grabbed Mahmud by the shirt, screaming at him, "If you love her, why do you come and see me? Tell me!"

It took Mahmud a few moments to take in what was happening, but then his anger got the better of him, and he brushed Rosa's hand from his shirt with such force that she groaned. He got up and checked his shirt to see if she had torn it. At that moment, only one thought was going through his mind: he was the great Mahmud Gaafar, a bodybuilding champion, renowned throughout the Sayyida Zeinab for his courage and manliness. How dare this woman scream and lay a hand on him?

Rosa was about to say something else, but Mahmud barked at her, "That's enough, Rosa. Don't keep on at me or grab me by my shirt. Understand?"

"You're seeing someone else, Mahmud," she said softly, trying to be affectionate again, but Mahmud was unmoved.

"I can do what I like."

She looked at him and started crying silently.

Mahmud got up and went over to the front door, but as he grabbed the handle, he heard Rosa pleading, "Mahmud. Please don't go."

He did not turn around. He just walked out, slamming the door behind him.

32

News of the meeting spread quickly among the staff, who whispered in tones of disbelief and confusion, unwilling to celebrate until they received confirmation from the triumvirate of Abdoun, Samahy and Bahr.

"Has Alku really ordered the beatings to stop?" they asked.

"Alku has promised us," they answered, "that henceforth no one will be beaten. If anyone falls out of line, his pay will be docked instead."

The staff stood there as their bafflement turned into a stream of questions: "How come Alku agreed so easily? What exactly did you say to Alku, and what did he say to you?"

Abdoun and his two colleagues could give no clearer answer than to say that they were just as astonished at Alku's easy assent. Their meeting had lasted only a few minutes. At first they had panicked and could hardly get their words out, but then they had asked him to stop the beatings and, to their surprise, he agreed. There was not a great deal more that they could tell their colleagues, who kept prodding them for additional details, until some of the staff came up with apocryphal details, which they repeated enthusiastically to one another: "Alku told Abdoun, 'You are all my children, and if the beatings are upsetting you, I'll stop them.'"

The image of a kindly Alku, by which some tried to explain what had happened, gave them a sense of security and self-worth. For the first time, they no longer felt like tools to be used and then discarded willy-nilly but like respected employees of the Club. They had duties and they had rights. No one could beat or humiliate them. If they did something wrong, there would be an investigation and administrative sanctions.

Most of the staff did not see things that way, nor did they believe in the new and kindly Alku. Happy as they might have been about the end of the beatings, they were still apprehensive, and their joy was not unalloyed. Five or six had sympathized with Abdoun and his two colleagues from the outset, and when the delegation achieved its aim, they felt bold enough to declare their support for them. In the café, however, the arguments raged on between those who had supported them and those who were dubious.

Someone said, "I can't believe that Alku would suddenly turn over a new leaf."

"Well, aren't we flesh and blood and entitled to our dignity?" another asked.

"So Alku just discovered our dignity yesterday?"

"It was our mistake. We stayed silent and accepted all the humiliation. The moment we demanded our rights, he had to comply."

"So now Alku's afraid of us?"

"He needs us just as we need him. If we stay united, he can't get the better of us."

"That's just Abdoun's delusion. Alku can do what he wants with us and with our families."

"You're a coward. You've just got used to being made of jelly."

"By God, you've all suddenly turned into heroes! Abdoun has brainwashed you."

"Abdoun got us our rights."

"Did he perform a miracle? Any one of us could have gone and complained to Alku."

"Then why didn't you? Why did you put up with the beatings for years without opening your mouths?"

"That Abdoun's got too big for his boots. It's all going to end badly. You'll see."

The workers carried on exchanging sharp words and accusations, and had calmer heads not prevailed, it might have ended in a fistfight. The latent aggression turned into bickering, which everyone knew served no useful purpose. The department managers were gravely

1[349]

concerned, and when Samahy gave him the news, Rikabi the chef let out a long groan.

"Alku has put a stop to the beatings? How lovely. You must be stoned, Samahy, my lad."

"I'm not stoned, Uncle Rikabi," Samahy retorted. "Don't believe me if you don't want to."

Talking back to Rikabi would usually have merited some punishment, but the chef managed to contain himself and walked over to the sink to wash his face with hot water before giving instructions to his kitchen staff and then rushing off to the still empty restaurant. There he found Maître Shakir sipping a glass of tea. He greeted him quickly, sat down next to him and told him what had happened. At first Shakir could not believe it, but when Rikabi assured him it was true, they both went off to see Yusuf Tarboosh, who, upon being informed, asked God for forgiveness, shook his head and then wondered aloud, "How is it that Alku would listen to a lad like Abdoun? It's some sort of farce."

The three managers waited until midnight and then headed off to Alku's office. Hameed met them with a frown, but he treated them politely, and without saying anything, he gave them to understand that he knew why they were there and that he was with them. They found Alku in his office smoking a cigarette. Shakir was the first to speak.

"Your Excellency Alku. You know just how much we love you and are devoted to you."

"Get on with it," Alku said nervously. "I don't have much time."

They were not sure how to continue, but Yusuf Tarboosh spoke up. "We have heard a strange piece of news, and we have come to ask Your Excellency if it is true."

"You heard right. I have abolished the punishment of beating," he said, looking at them provocatively.

"If Your Excellency has done away with beatings," Rikabi said brusquely, "there'll be repercussions for the standard of work."

"The staff will only work properly," seconded Shakir, "if they live in fear of beatings."

Yusuf Tarboosh said nothing for a few moments, and then, fingering his prayer beads, he spoke up, "Your Excellency Alku, with all due respect. Administrative sanctions are meaningless to the staff. If there are no beatings, they'll run amok, and we won't be able to control them."

"Your Excellency Alku," Rikabi suddenly piped up, "the staff will neglect their work, and Your Excellency will hold us responsible."

The three of them stopped speaking, as if realizing that they had gone too far. Alku inhaled and then blew out a thick puff of smoke.

"All right. Our little meeting is over. Get back to work."

They fidgeted a little, but Alku shot them a look that brooked no defiance, and they headed back to the Automobile Club. Their frustration quickly turned into a sense of resentment toward Alku. They felt let down. He had stripped them of their power. Now how would they manage their subordinates? There was no longer any deterrent. Their staff would now become more obstreperous, neglecting their work, talking back. As it became clear that Alku would not change his mind, they had to change their modus operandi. Maître Shakir stopped upbraiding the waiters, Rikabi stopped swearing so much at his assistants and Yusuf Tarboosh no longer exchanged small talk with his staff in the casino. The three managers now barked out their instructions in a gruff way that left no room for discussion or comment. They avoided doing anything that could cause friction among the staff, knowing that they no longer had the high card. If their staff answered them back, they had no practical recourse. At the same time, the managers watched over them more closely than ever, just waiting for the right moment. They expected, and deep down they hoped, that the staff, in their breezy new attitude, would commit some serious mistakes that would upset the smooth operation of the Club. At that point, they would go off to see Alku again, saying, "Didn't we tell you, Your Excellency Alku, that without the beatings everything would go to pot? Now you can see for yourself."

Except that, contrary to all expectations, everyone worked so hard that they had nothing to complain of. The staff were punctual and carried out the most exacting instructions to the letter. Their performance improved so much that on three inspection visits, Alku too could not find the slightest fault. The Club was cleaner than ever, the men all immaculately turned out with ironed caftans, smoothly shaved faces and neatly trimmed fingernails. Everything was functioning so well that many Club members noticed the difference, some even making positive comments. Hassan Pasha Kamel, for example, gave Maître Shakir a generous tip, telling him, "Thank you, Shakir. Service at the Club has improved by leaps and bounds."

Maître Shakir accepted the tip and the praise with a scowl, muttering a few words of thanks. The three managers were unnerved at being undermined in their belief that only the threat of a beating motivated the men. But it was undeniable that something fundamental had changed. The staff were more efficient and more obedient than ever. They bowed politely and carried out orders superbly, even having thrown off their abject submissiveness. The servile, ingratiating smiles disappeared, and instead they wore polite and friendly smiles exuding confidence, a sense of responsibility and pride. Even when receiving a tip, instead of being humbly grateful, they now thanked the members in a clear and forthright tone of voice, as if to say, "Your generosity is not charity but recognition of the value of our work, and we thank you for that."

This new regime lasted for a month, a month that the staff would remember for its uniqueness, but it ended as suddenly as it had started. Perhaps it had been too good to last.

One morning, after they had finished cleaning the Club and had washed up and put on their caftans and were going to their stations, Maître Shakir suddenly appeared, out of breath. He had not used the lift but had dashed up the stairs like a man possessed. He ran from the restaurant to the bar and the casino, shouting ominously, "Come down to the first floor now!"

"Is everything all right?" they asked apprehensively. "Has something happened, God forbid?"

"Am I not making myself clear?" he growled. "I've told you, get to the first floor. Now!"

SALEHA

My mother put her arms around me and shut the door gently. As we crossed the hallway, she whispered, "Calm down, Saleha, please."

I felt safe again the moment I went into my mother's bedroom. I had missed that place so much and the smell of the perfume that filled it. I stopped crying, and my mother sat down next to me. She kissed me and started examining my wounds. I had a cut on my leg, and there were deep scratches all over my thigh. My face had swollen up around my mouth and forehead. My mother disappeared for a few minutes and came back carrying a tray with a bottle of antiseptic, cotton wool and a bowl of ice cubes. She cleaned the wounds and put cold compresses on my face and then made me a glass of tea. Unable to look her in the eye, I told her all about my problem with Abd el-Barr, Aisha's advice, Abd el-Barr's violence, the white powder and his attempt to break my hymen with his hand. I told her every last detail. My mother listened with a sad look on her face. Then she put both hands on her head.

"Oh God, that's all we need. Haven't we been through enough? God help us."

She went out of the bedroom and left me alone. I was completely exhausted, and going over what had happened, I felt as if it was someone else's experience. I do not know how long I sat there before my mother came back with Kamel following her, wiping the sleep from his eyes. I realized that she had told him. He muttered a greeting and then sat down, searching for the right words to say. He lit a cigarette.

"I had a feeling," he said quietly, "that there was something not quite right about Abd el-Barr."

We sat in silence again.

"Listen, daughter," my mother said hoarsely. "A good wife has to stand by her husband in times of crisis. If it's just a question of behaving badly, that can be fixed. But drugs are a different kettle of fish. You never know where you stand with a drug user. The husband of your cousin Asma was a cocaine user, and your own father did everything he could to make him divorce her."

Kamel added, "A cocaine user is capable of anything and will end up either going crazy or to prison."

"Oh, it's just too dreadful," my mother muttered. "God help us all."

After a few more comments in the same vein, they both fell quiet, trying, it seemed, to work out what to do next.

Kamel got to his feet with a sad half smile. He leaned over and kissed me on the forehead.

"Try to get some sleep. Don't worry. There's a solution to every problem, God willing."

He left the room, and my mother put her arms around me.

"Go and take a shower," she said. "I'll fetch you something to eat."

After taking a hot shower and giving in to my mother's nagging to eat something, I started to feel well again. After all the tension, the fear and pain, I was back home again. I could sleep in my own bed with a sense of complete security. My mother was in the next room, and Kamel and Mahmud were there. I slept well, and the next day I had a long talk with my mother as we sat drinking tea. I busied myself in the kitchen as if nothing had happened. I asked my mother all sorts of little things about the apartment, as if just spending a normal day at home as I had before. It was as if I had just woken up from a nightmare but forgotten the details. I was relishing the feeling, but I knew deep down that I could not just run away from everything. What had happened with Abd el-Barr would stick to me. I would be a woman who had failed in her marriage and come back to her father's home. Kamel managed to get away from work and came home to eat lunch with us. He tried to put on a happy face and told me little stories that made me laugh. After lunch, I suddenly felt tired. I knew it would take me some days to get over my horrendous experience. I went to my bedroom and slept soundly and woke to the sound of Said's voice. My mother must have telephoned him, and he had come from Tanta. After a while, I went to the sitting room and found him with my mother and Kamel. He looked uneasy and gave me a curt greeting.

"Saleha, what you have done?"

"What should she have done?" my mother said.

Said ignored her, and in the tone of one imparting words of wisdom, he said, "You should have stayed at home and sorted it out."

"Do you have any idea what Abd el-Barr did?" I asked him calmly. He gave no answer.

"Said," my mother said, "Abd el-Barr has been snorting cocaine."

"How do you know?" he answered sharply.

"Saleha saw him with her own eyes."

"And what does your daughter know about drugs?"

"There is no God but God! Do you think we would just make this up? We are telling you that Abd el-Barr has not consummated the marriage, he does cocaine and he beats your sister. What else do you want?"

"It doesn't matter. He's still her husband."

My mother could not contain herself any longer. Waving her hands around, she shouted furiously at him, "So you're trying to say that your sister is in the wrong?"

"I'm saying it's a mistake to encourage her to do what she is doing."

Said looked at me and smiled nervously. "Come on, Saleha. Go and get dressed and I'll take you home."

"I can't go back there," I said imploringly.

"You will go back," he raged, "whether you want to or not."

"You can't force her," Kamel shouted, "to go and live with Abd el-Barr."

"Abd el-Barr is a decent man."

"A decent man who is a drug addict and a wife beater!"

"By law, he is allowed to teach his wife manners."

"I will not allow any human being to beat my sister, and I will not let her live with a drug addict."

"It's a load of rubbish!"

"And you're only interested in yourself," Kamel answered, looking defiant.

Said said nothing for a few moments and then took a different tack.

"Kamel, Saleha is my sister, and I love her as much as you do. I don't want any harm to come to her, but please consider my situation. Abd el-Barr is my partner in the factory, and we are supposed to sign the contract in six months' time. If I lose Abd el-Barr, it will be difficult for me to find another business partner. I'm just on a salary now, but the factory is my big chance, and we'll all benefit from it."

"So what do you expect from Saleha?" Kamel asked.

"Just to put up with Abd el-Barr until we've signed the contract, and then we can do what we think is right."

"You want our sister to go and live with a drug addict until things work out for you? You really are vile."

"Shut your mouth," screamed Said as he gave Kamel a shove. He was thrown off-balance but then grabbed him by the sleeve. I threw myself between them as my mother screamed, "Enough! Shame on you both!"

KAMEL

We are all responsible for what happened to Saleha. Said presented her with Abd el-Barr and nagged her until she married him. My mother and I failed in our duty to protect her. Saleha trusts our opinion, and had I stuck to my objection to the marriage, that would have been the end of the matter. Why did she suddenly agree to it? Maybe her acquiescence irritated me so much that I simply gave up. Maybe my job, studies and work for the organization had used up all my energy. It now fell to me to get her a divorce. I could hardly believe Said's selfishness, handing his sister over to an impotent drug addict just to get his contract signed. I had made up my mind to go and see Abd el-Barr that Wednesday, my day off, but in the end I could not wait that long. So the following day, when I finished my shift in the storeroom, I made my way to his office in Tawfiqiya Square. He was taken aback to see me but gave me a warm welcome. He looked at me as if he knew what was on my mind.

"What can I get you to drink?" he asked in a friendly manner.

"Nothing, thanks."

He made a gesture to his office boy to fetch some tea. I did not object. I did not want to waste my anger on trifles.

"Was it difficult to find my office?" he said, smiling.

"No. Everyone knows this street."

"I have been renting this office for the last ten years. It has the advantage of being large and quite comfortable. The other tenants in the building are decent, and it is downtown. Very easy to find."

I made no comment.

"I would never be to able to find anything like it for such a low rent," he carried on. "Guess how much I pay per month!"

"Abd el-Barr. Let us not ignore the reason for this visit."

"What do you mean?"

"I think you know."

"If you're talking about the matter with Saleha," he smiled, "let's not talk here. I have a few things to do, but if you can wait half an hour, I'll invite you to lunch, and we can speak more freely."

Realizing he was trying to avoid a scene, I raised my voice, "We need to talk now."

The office boy put a glass of tea down in front of me and went out. Abd el-Barr came over and sat in the armchair opposite me.

"And just what do you want, Kamel?" he asked in an aggressive whisper.

"I want you to divorce Saleha."

"You do know that she ran away from our home?"

"She ran away because you were beating her."

"I hit her because she was behaving outrageously."

"If anyone raises a hand against my sister, he has me to answer to."

His eyes almost popped out of his head. He looked like he was about to say something but just sat there looking at the ground, and then he lit a cigarette, and I noticed his hand shaking.

"Listen, Abd el-Barr," I said quietly. "Just as we entered into all of this in a decent way, let's end it decently."

"It was your brother who arranged this, not you."

"It's Saleha who is asking for a divorce."

"So in your family, it's women, not men, who make the decisions?"

"We all speak up for ourselves."

"And what if I don't want a divorce?"

"You'd be happy living with a woman who doesn't want to be with you?"

"If we were to listen to every hysterical woman, there'd be no families left in all of Egypt. Women don't make good decisions. They're fickle."

"My sister, Saleha, is better educated than you."

I said that just to provoke him. He was breathing heavily and trying to control himself.

"That's enough, Kamel," he said quietly. "Let's not talk any more now. Wait until you have calmed down."

I got up and walked over to him.

"You have to divorce Saleha immediately," I shouted.

"Lower your voice."

"I'll speak however I like."

"Seems you lack manners, just like your sister."

"If anyone needs to learn manners, it's you."

He jumped to his feet, let out a shout and threw a punch, but I ducked it, grabbing his arm and twisting it behind his back, and yelled, "I'll rip off the arm you used to hit my sister!"

At this point, the office staff rushed in to separate us.

"I'll ruin your name!" I bellowed. "You low-down drug addict!"

He responded with a stream of invective, but he seemed shaken.

Seeing my accusations had hit a nerve, I started shouting at him again, "You should have got over your drug habit before marrying a woman from a decent family!"

The staff started trying to counter my accusation, but their protests were not terribly convincing. It seemed they knew the truth. As they hustled me out of the office, they took their time, as if to give me a chance to carry on insulting him.

"I'll give you one week," I shouted. "If you don't divorce Saleha, I'm going to report you to the police for using drugs."

I stumbled out onto the street. I was overwrought, but at the same time I felt happy about having shown up Abd el-Barr in front of his employees. I had managed to get back at him for humiliating my sister. I reached Soliman Pasha Street and walked down the Estoril passage to get to the Automobile Club. I started my shift in the storeroom with my mind completely distracted. Comanus noticed, but when he asked me what the matter was, I told him I was exhausted from my studies.

I finished my shift in the evening, and when I arrived home, I saw Saleha. The bruises on her face had turned blue. She put her arms around me and clung to me as she used to do when she was a child.

"Come to my bedroom," I told her. "I have a few things to tell you."

"Stay here and talk," my mother said, getting up. "I'll be in the kitchen."

I sat next to Saleha.

"I want you to look on all of this," I told her, "as just a bad experience that you'll forget."

"What if Abd el-Barr won't divorce me?"

"He'll divorce you, whether he wants to or not."

"Have you seen him?"

I nodded, and she asked me anxiously, "What did he say to you?"

"Don't worry yourself about it. We got you into this mess, and we'll get you out of it. As far as I'm concerned, the most important thing is for you to go back to school."

"I can't. I can't face my school friends now that I have failed in my marriage."

"You didn't do anything wrong. It happens to lots of girls."

Saleha looked straight ahead as if mulling it over, and then she burst into tears. I kissed her head and tried to soothe her. A little while later, the three of us sat down to dinner. I tried to distract Saleha with a few funny anecdotes. That night when I went to my bedroom, I tried to study but could not. I lay down fully clothed and smoked a cigarette. I thought of my father and how much I missed him. How much he had put up with for our sake. Now that I was shouldering the burden, it seemed like catastrophes were occurring in swift succession. "May God have mercy upon your soul, Father!" I thought. "You kept all your troubles from us. You never complained." Then I got up, did my ablutions, said the *fatiha* for my father's soul and prostrated myself on the ground for longer than necessary. I prayed to God to have mercy upon him and to let him enter paradise. When I went to bed, I felt better. Prayer afforded me a real sense of calm. It made me wish that I prayed more regularly, but I was always getting distracted or giving in to laziness. I felt guilty at my religious laxity, even though I thought that it was not God who needed our prayers, but we were the ones who needed to pray in order to become better people. I believed in God's justice and mercy. I believed that he would forgive us our religious shortcomings. I was going to try hard to be useful and to work in order to support my family, as well as study and do my duty for my country.

Once I made these resolutions, I felt better and found the will to get out of bed and continue studying. I had been asked to translate an article about Egypt from *The Times* and give it to Hasan Mu'min the next day. It took me about two hours. The author had written at great length about the king's depraved behavior and his nocturnal antics. I made myself a glass of mint tea and sat down; it was three in the morning before I went to bed. I was so preoccupied with Saleha's misfortunes that I almost forgot about the mission that the prince had tasked me with.

The next morning, I arrived at the Club before ten o'clock. I had hidden the glass orb in my briefcase, which usually carried my textbooks. The staff were at that moment cleaning the building from top to bottom. I looked behind me to make sure that no one could see me. Instead of making my way to the storeroom, I went up the stairs into the casino and locked the door behind me. I knew that I had only a few minutes. The room was gloomy and reeked of smoke from the night before. I found the wooden stepladder leaning against the wall just as the prince had described. I picked it up and was dismayed to find it so heavy, as I could not just drag it along the floor in case it made a noise. With great difficulty, I carried it to the middle of the room and positioned it gently underneath the chandelier. I gingerly climbed up a few steps until my shoulders were level with the crystals. There was a small metal rung in the chandelier into which the glass orb fitted perfectly. I checked to see that it was firmly fixed in place before climbing back down. Suddenly, I heard shouting outside. It was part of the plan for Abdoun to pick a fight with one of the staff on the roof in order to divert their attention. I put the stepladder back where I found it, opened the door cautiously and slipped out undetected, tiptoeing down the stairs. By the time I reached the entrance hall, I was certain that my mission had been successful. Suddenly, I saw Labib the telephone operator standing in front of me.

"All hell's broken loose on the roof," I spluttered, trying to act natural. "I want to go up and see what's happening, but if I do, Monsieur Comanus might turn up and find the storeroom still locked."

"Don't worry," Labib said. "Go and open up. I'll go and see what it's all about."

"Let me know that they're all all right, Uncle Labib. I don't want to sit downstairs worrying."

I opened the storeroom door and turned on the light. Then I lit a cigarette. After the first drag, I told myself, "You've done it, lad!" I found the danger strangely exciting. I was still proud of myself for having distributed the pamphlets in Sayyida Zeinab and fooling the English soldiers. This time, I had carried out my mission even with so much on my mind, lacking sleep and distraught over Saleha. Thank God, I hadn't slipped up and given myself away. I made a pot of Turkish coffee and smoked another cigarette. Then Comanus turned up, and I greeted him, asking him what he wanted me to do. I thought it best to behave naturally because at some point they could question Comanus if they discovered the orb. I lugged a few things to the restaurant and then asked permission to sit and study.

After a while, Comanus came and sat down next to me. He had a warm smile on his face. "How are you getting on with your studies, Kamel?" he asked.

"Thank God, I'm doing fine. And how are you, sir?"

Comanus took off his spectacles and wiped them with his handkerchief as he always did when feeling pensive. Then he put them back on and said, "By God, I have to say, Kamel, that things at the Club have been a little odd lately."

"What is it?"

"I'm worried about the staff. They've been to see Alku, and they asked him to end the beatings he gives them."

"They're right."

"I know that it's a sensitive subject for you because of your father, Hagg Abd el-Aziz, may God have mercy on him."

"Not just because he was my father; it's inhuman to have someone beaten."

"But it surprises me. The staff have put up with it for twenty years. What suddenly made them object?"

"Everyone has his limits."

"But the strangest thing is that Alku has agreed."

"Well, that sounds all right to me."

Comanus said nothing for a few moments. Then he gave me a worried look and said, "You don't know Alku. He's evil and unpredictable. There's no way that he has suddenly turned into a kind person. God help us. I think that the Automobile Club has got some dark days ahead of it."

33

Mahmud did not know what to think. In his heart of hearts, he knew that Rosa loved him, and he felt bad that she had been so upset by his relationship with Dagmar, but at the same time he was angry that she had humiliated him by pulling on his shirt. Mahmud recounted all of this to Fawzy, who smoked a whole spliff as he listened to his friend, appearing to weigh the matter over carefully. Stubbing out the spliff on the roof terrace wall, he said with a cough, "Rosa has got no right to be angry. If you back down, she'll be no end of trouble in the future."

Mahmud nodded. "I'm never going to see Rosa again," he said.

"Don't get ahead of yourself," Fawzy said.

"After what she did?"

"Give it a little time, Mahmud," Fawzy said with a wink. "Some good may come out of it. Your difficulties with Rosa might yet work in your favor."

"How's that?"

Fawzy laid out the plan, and Mahmud executed it perfectly. He refrained from going to see Rosa for two whole weeks. He primed Labib the telephone operator to tell her that he had not been to work and that no one knew why. Mahmud disappeared completely from sight. When Rosa telephoned to order food from the Club, Mahmud would hand the package to Mustafa the driver.

"Please," he said to Mustafa. "Take the package up, and I'll wait here. If Madame Khashab asks after me, tell her I've left the job."

Mustafa would smile gently and take the package up to her. The last time, Mahmud was waiting as usual in the car while Mustafa went up with the fruit tart that Rosa had ordered. After a while, he came back, sat behind the wheel and clapped his hands with a belly laugh.

"Mahmud," he said as he started the engine, "what have you done to Madame Khashab? She's crazy about you. When I told her that you're still not back at work, she went mad!"

Mahmud said nothing as Mustafa drove along, chuckling. He had long since guessed that Mahmud was seeing Rosa but had not wanted to mention it. By nature, he was good-hearted and did not like to embarrass anyone or interfere, no matter how close the acquaintance involved. That day, as they sat in the garage drinking tea, the older man seemed on the verge of saying something, but he held back. They had chatted a little about this and that, when at last Mustafa placed his hand on Mahmud's shoulder.

"Mahmud, you know how fond of you I am," he said. "Your father, may God have mercy upon him, was like a brother to me. I can appreciate that you are young, and young people have their own rules."

Mahmud gave him an inquiring look, but Mustafa kept looking at the ground as if trying to find the right words.

"I will give you one piece of advice, and I won't say it again. What would you think, Mahmud, if the car had no brakes. What would happen to it?"

"There'd be an accident."

"Good. Now a human being is like a car. He has to have brakes. If a young man goes around sleeping with this woman and that woman, eventually it'll end in tears. May God forgive you and show you the right way."

Mahmud sat there in silence. He loved and respected Mustafa, and he had expected him to say such thing.

"Listen to what I have to say," Mustafa continued. "If you want to get married, get married, but don't live in sin. Sin is sweet at first, but it leaves a bitter aftertaste. As God told us, 'Do not draw near to fornication, for it is an indecency, and its way is evil.'"

Mahmud nodded and muttered agreement with an embarrassed smile on his face. That was all Mustafa had to say on the matter, and he changed the subject. That night, on the roof, Mahmud repeated old Mustafa's words to Fawzy, who at that moment was licking the edge of a cigarette paper.

"Mustafa is old enough to be our father," he said disdainfully. "He has to think like that. If he were our age and had the chance to be with a woman like Rosa, I bet he would."

"But I am living a life of sin."

"What's the matter with you, Mahmud? All it takes is a word from someone and you change your mind!" Fawzy bellowed as Mahmud sat there sulking silently. Fawzy felt sure he had him back under control and smiled.

"You do trust me, don't you, Mahmud?"

"Of course."

"Then just keep on doing what I told you."

The plan necessitated Mahmud staying away from Rosa for a third week, at the end of which Mahmud told Labib the telephone operator that he could put her calls through.

Not long after that, Mahmud heard Rosa's anxious voice asking, "Mahmud, is everything all right?"

"Yes, thank God."

"I need to see you."

"I've got work to do."

"All right. Come over when you finish work."

"All right."

Mahmud spoke that last word in a voice that seemed not his own. At the end of the shift, Mustafa drove him to his apartment in al-Sadd Street. Mahmud went in the main door and waited until he heard the car drive off. Then he went back out and took a taxi from Tram Street to Rosa's building. He wanted to avoid having to listen to another sermon by Mustafa on sin. It was after three in the morning when Mahmud went up to the fourth floor and rang the bell.

Rosa opened the door so quickly that she must have been waiting behind it. The moment she saw him, she whispered, "Mahmud! Where have you been?"

She pulled him inside and flung her arms around him. He stepped away from her and stood in the middle of the sitting room. She stepped toward him and, in a trembling voice, told him, "Shame on you, Mahmud, for leaving me all alone so long."

"But, Rosa," he said angrily, "you insulted me and you grabbed me by the shirt."

"I'm so sorry, Mahmud. I'm sorry."

She hugged him again and covered him with kisses as he stood there impassive. But he was starting to get excited, so he put his arms around her and walked her into the bedroom. That night, he pounded away at her as if to inflict punishment and pain, as if trying to ascertain whether she had learned her lesson and understood that she should never deal with him that way again. She did not fail to play her part, shrieking like a naughty child, though with pleasure, screaming and shouting and begging for mercy, promising to be good. Rosa had orgasm after orgasm, during which she writhed and shuddered into contortions he had never seen before. Mahmud had already planned to stay the night, having telephoned his mother from the Club to say that he was going to stay with a friend. He slept in Rosa's embrace. As they ate breakfast in the morning, he saw that she looked relaxed and happy. They chatted away, and when it was time for him to leave, she hugged him and nuzzled her face against his chest. As he pushed her gently away, he noticed tears on her face.

"Rosa, what's the matter?" he asked, holding her hand.

"I'm afraid you're going to leave me," she whispered. Then, after a pause, she continued, "Mahmud, I can't live all alone again. Before I met you, I was so miserable. I would just drink and wait to die. You have no idea what you have done for me. You've put some meaning back into my life. Please, Mahmud, don't leave me."

They carried on seeing each other, and Rosa never again uttered a word about his relationship with Dagmar. Fawzy's plan had succeeded, for Rosa had now realized that the choice was straightforward: either he could go on seeing other women too, or he would dump her.

Mahmud's life went back to its old rhythm. Two nights with Rosa, two nights with Dagmar and three nights without them. He and Fawzy were having the time of their lives. Girls, excursions, sex in brothels, the best quality hashish, smart clothes and riding around on the red Lambretta.

One night, as they were sitting on the roof, Mahmud suddenly piped up, "There's a new woman who wants me to sleep with her."

Fawzy clapped and yelled, "You're the top! How did you get to know her?"

"I was making a delivery on Thursday, and she grabbed me."

"Maybe Rosa or Dagmar told her about you."

Mahmud ignored Fawzy's teasing tone.

"I don't know what to do."

"You've got another one in the bag."

"I can't."

"Is she Egyptian or English?"

"Egyptian."

"Well-off?"

"Very. She's a Sarsawy."

"The Sarsawys with the gold shop?"

Mahmud nodded.

"She's our fatted calf. Don't let this one slip through your fingers!"

Mahmud swatted the suggestion away.

"What's this 'calf' shit! She's ancient."

"All right, but you're already doing it with two other old ladies."

"She's older than they are. She must be at least seventy. I'm astonished that someone of her age is still interested in sex."

"You've hit the jackpot! The older they are, the more they pay."

"She can go to hell with her money."

Fawzy looked Mahmud straight in the eye and asked him, "Are you going to turn down more money?"

"I'm telling you, I can't sleep with her."

"All right, big guy. If you don't mind, then, I'll have a go."

34

When James Wright wanted to see Alku, he would usually send a message through Khalil the office boy. This time he called him himself.

"Get here right now," he told him curtly, not waiting for a response before hanging up. Alku knew that the matter must be serious, so he left immediately for the Automobile Club, and when he arrived, he found a group of men, official looking but plainclothes, in the entrance hall. Suleyman the doorman told him under his breath that they were secret agents. Alku dashed across the entrance hall with Hameed scuttling along behind him. The staff rushed over to Alku, but he ignored them. They watched him with a mixture of fear and anticipation, as if waiting for him to explain what was going on. In Mr. Wright's office, he found Muhammad Alawi Pasha, the king's private secretary, and Anwar Bey Makki, the head of state security. Alku knew them both well. These two positions were among the most important in the country, not just by dint of their portfolios but because of their proximity to the king. Anwar Bey Makki oversaw, in the full sense of the word, the king's movements and was in charge of all the security measures carried out by the royal guard. He had the authority to approve or cancel any and all royal visits based on his judgment of the security considerations. He only needed to croak out, "Your Majesty's safety cannot be assured during this visit," for the event to be canceled, no matter how important it was.

Alku bowed and greeted those present in French. They responded as if they were distracted, and Alku realized that something serious had happened. He stood there with an officious smile. Wright picked up a photograph on his desk and handed it to Alku.

"Look at this and tell me what you think."

Alku looked at the picture, and an expression of horror appeared on his face. The photograph showed His Majesty in a tall pointed red hat with multicolored pom-poms, sitting at the poker table beside the French danseuse Charlotte. Underneath the photograph was the caption, "Down with the decadent and corrupt king."

Alku took his time looking at the photograph, passing it from one hand to the other. He needed a moment to absorb this shock.

"This picture of His Majesty was taken here in the Automobile Club," said Wright, "when he was honoring our New Year's Eve party with his presence. Thousands of copies are being handed out on the streets of Cairo."

Alku gnashed his teeth and grimaced. Then he looked at Wright and asked him gruffly, "Do you know who is distributing this photograph?"

Wright gestured dismissively at Alku and barked at him, "Never mind who is handing them out. How was it even taken? You are responsible for this. No one could take such a photograph of His Majesty like this without the help of your staff."

"Mr. Wright, you might remember my having told you," Alku said, "that something had changed in the staff's manner and that I asked you to take measures to reinstitute discipline, which request you refused."

Wright had not been expecting to be shown up in front of the two high officials. He banged his fist on the desk and shouted at Alku, "When a man has been negligent in his duties, the easiest thing for him is to try to pass on the blame."

Alku fell silent and looked at the photograph again. Everything about it indicated that it had been taken in the Club. Moreover, the photographer had taken it at just the right angle to show all the details.

"I'm not shirking my responsibility," Alku said quietly. "I shall investigate the matter, and when I find the culprit, I shall show him no mercy. All that I ask is that you back me up in any punishment I decide to mete out."

Wright made no response. He was doing all he could to hold back a flood of invective because of the two august visitors. He gripped his pipe in his teeth and exhaled a thick cloud of smoke. He looked up at the ceiling for a moment and then gestured at Alku.

"You can go now."

Alku muttered his good-byes, turned and left.

"The situation is very grave indeed," Anwar Bey Makki said. "What has happened constitutes two crimes: an invasion of His Majesty's privacy and an underhanded attempt to malign him. You cannot have forgotten, Pasha, that we live in a Muslim country. The thought of the king gambling and keeping company with a woman of easy virtue can do great harm."

Alawi Pasha had no answer but, in his position as the king's private secretary, felt that he ought to say something.

"What do those vile saboteurs want for Egypt?" he yelled. "His Majesty works day and night to lift his people out of their ignorance and poverty. Do they consider it improper for him to distract himself a little? Is he not a man who needs some relief?"

"Rest assured," Anwar Bey Makki replied, "they will pay dearly for this."

Alawi Pasha waved his hand and said, *"Ils sont vraiment des salops."*

Anway Bey Makki leaned his head forward and continued, "Mr. Wright. We have a few questions that need answering, such as who photographed His Majesty and how did he get the camera into the Club? How is it that none of the members or the casino staff saw him? It could well be that the photographer has an accomplice among the Club staff."

"How can I be of help?" Mr. Wright said.

"To begin, we'll need a list of all the names of the staff and the members of the Automobile Club," said Anwar Bey in a firm yet polite tone of voice.

Mr. Wright nodded. "I will have a list drawn up and sent over to you today."

Anwar Bey looked at Alawi Pasha as if to say, "Shall we?" and the two of them stood up to go.

As they were leaving, Wright shook their hands, and with a tense smile, he said, "Alawi Pasha. Please convey my most abject apologies to His Majesty."

"His Majesty," retorted Alawi Pasha sharply, "used to consider the Automobile Club a safe haven where he could relax, but unfortunately it now appears that your club has been infiltrated by saboteurs and Communists."

"I give you my word that this will not happen again."

"I fear," said Alawi Pasha, smiling acerbically, "that you will not have an opportunity to fulfill your promise. His Majesty is not likely to return to the Automobile Club. His numerous palaces and royal retreats afford him complete privacy."

"I hope that His Majesty will give us one more chance."

Wright's voice had an imploring tone to it, but Alawi Pasha just puffed on his cigar and said, "I'll be frank with you. Once you have lost the king's confidence, it is exceedingly difficult to gain it again."

Alawi Pasha left for Abdin Palace, but Anwar Bey Makki took a few minutes to give instructions to his officers before his driver took him back to his office. The night shift staff were immediately summoned from their homes, joining the rest of the staff assembled on the first floor. They were kept waiting in the corridor that led to the administrative offices. Scores of them were standing there, quaking, exchanging whispers as two tough-looking security agents stood at the door, sending the staff one by one into the office, where two officers were carrying out the interrogation. There was a third, and more junior, officer in charge of another team of secret agents, who were checking the building from top to bottom. This officer went into every room, with the agents leading the way like a pack of hunting dogs, turning everything upside down, until he indicated that they should follow him elsewhere. They did the same with the rooms on the roof, the restaurant and the bar, but they uncovered nothing. In the casino, the agents examined everything even more carefully as the officer cast an eagle eye into every nook and cranny. Again, they came up with nothing and stood awaiting further orders from the officer, who suddenly pointed overhead, "Look up there!"

The agent raised his head. The officer continued, "Get a ladder."

In a few minutes, two of the staff were carrying a tall wooden stepladder, which they positioned underneath the chandelier. The officer clambered up quickly and examined the various components of the chandelier. Then he came back down and left with his policemen. An hour later, two English army engineers turned up with a machine that looked like a vacuum cleaner, with which they checked out the whole Club, noting the readings it was giving, until finally, they came across the camera in the casino and detached it from the chandelier.

That night, Anwar Bey Makki convened a meeting with his senior officers, with the glass orb placed in front of him on his desk. Having briefed them on the situation, he said, "What happened can only be interpreted one way. First, this camera is a new model and beyond the means of ordinary Egyptians. Second, its placement in the chandelier means that someone installed it there and then needed to remove the film and have it developed. All of this indicates an organized conspiracy." He fell silent for a moment and then continued, "The most important thing now is for us to ascertain that there are no other cameras installed. We will have to make a careful search of all the palaces and the royal retreats."

The meeting lasted a whole hour, during which they studied the situation from all angles. A detailed plan was laid out to uncover the saboteurs and to foil their schemes. By the end of the meeting, each of the officers had been charged with his respective duties.

That same day, Wright wrote a notice in English and affixed it to the door, apologizing that the Club would unfortunately not be open due to a short circuit, which was being repaired. Labib the telephone operator gave the same excuse to all the members who called to reserve a table. The Automobile Club was closed for the whole day. The staff interviews finished at one in the morning, and the officers left, but the staff had to stay in the Club. Alku had forbidden them to go home after the questioning and ordered them all up to the roof. It was an unprecedented scene, with the staff from both shifts lined up on one side of the roof and Alku standing on the other. It was also odd to see half of the staff wearing their work caftans and the other half their street clothes, all of them anxious and huddling together as if for protection. The photograph of His Majesty gambling, in the silly hat, sitting beside his mistress, had been taken in the Club without anyone noticing, and then it had been printed and handed out in the streets. A catastrophe had fallen upon their heads from a completely unforeseen direction. Now Alku was going to inflict some punishment on them all. In spite of their terror, they were resigned. Not one dared to speak up, plead ignorance or even make a comment. It was as if they were being driven inexorably toward a fate they had to confront. No words of protest or pleas of ignorance would change things a whit. Even though they had committed no crime, deep down they had accepted the inevitability of being punished. Given the crime was of such a shocking magnitude, whatever they were about to suffer was justified, at least to a certain degree.

Alku looked them over, his face ashen as he ground his teeth. He put his hands behind his back and paced the length of the roof twice. Finally, he stopped and, looking daggers at them, he roared, "Which of you bastards installed the camera?"

A general muttering arose as all tried to disavow any knowledge of the photograph. Alku raised his hand and shouted, "Enough, you pack of dogs. We brought you here from Upper Egypt. We cleaned you up, helped you to get apartments and treated you like human beings, and in return you betray His Majesty the king!"

This time their mutterings were intelligible, "We have been framed, Your Excellency! By God, we haven't done anything!"

By now Alku was panting with anger. He said nothing for a while, trying to control his breathing, and then thundered at them, "Wailing like a bunch of women! By God, I shall show you no mercy. I don't accept that the camera could have been installed without your knowing. You bunch of turncoats. You all deserve a good thrashing, and you would get it, by God, if I had not given my word."

Alku fell silent, and suddenly an ugly, nervous smile appeared on his face. Then he spoke again, spitting out his syllables like darts. "Henceforth, you will not get a piastre in tips. You will subsist on your salaries alone."

It took a few moments for the shock to sink in. By the time some had started imploring Alku for a more merciful punishment, he had turned on his heel and, as if hearing nothing, had marched off down the stairs, heading for his car with Hameed prancing along behind him.

SALEHA

Said quarreled with Kamel so loudly that it might have come to blows had my mother not intervened. Afterward, Said went back to Tanta, and calm returned to the apartment.

The next morning, Aisha came to visit us. When my mother started to speak, Aisha interrupted her, "Fayeqa told me everything."

My mother sighed.

"So, what do you think?"

Aisha wiped her brow with the palm of her hand and answered, "Look, Saleha. I know that Said and Fayeqa want you to stay with Abd el-Barr until they sign the contract for the factory."

No one said a word. Aisha wiped her face again and continued, "God knows, Saleha, that I love you as my own daughter. I want the same for you as I would for Fayeqa. Of course you have to get a divorce."

My mother's face showed great relief.

"God preserve you, Aisha," she said quietly, "for speaking so honestly."

"Fayeqa didn't like it when I told her," continued Aisha. "She gave me hell on the telephone. Naturally, she is looking out for her husband's interests. But I speak the truth, and Saleha cannot stay with that man for a day longer."

"Kamel is trying to make Abd el-Barr divorce her," said my mother. "I hope God will provide someone better next time."

Aisha went back to being her usual, jovial self. She bit her lips, raised her eyebrows and added, "Of course she'll find someone better next time. Saleha is a living doll. And she is still intact. Virgin as the day she was born. Any man would want her."

In spite of my anxiety, I could not help laughing. Aisha seemed unable to hold a conversation without talking about sex. My mother gave her a big hug at the front door as she left. I was touched that she was on our side. If Said went into business with Abd el-Barr, it would be to Fayeqa's benefit, but even so, Aisha believed that I should have a divorce. For all her racy talk, she was good in all senses of the word. How many men would stand up for the right thing if it went against their own interest? After hearing what Aisha had said, I felt a sense of relief. Why should I not go and study mathematics, which I loved so much? I was immensely cheered as I reviewed my theorems with music blaring out of my radio. I got off to a creaky start solving the problems but slowly got back into the flow. Numbers fired my imagination. I always imagined them like stars scattered across an imaginary sky as I performed operations on them in my head. I was so absorbed in my books that I did not notice the bedroom door opening. Suddenly, I was aware of a movement. I turned around and found Kamel standing there.

"I'm so happy to see you studying again," he smiled.

"I'm not exactly studying. I'm just going over a few problems for fun."

"All the Gaafars are talented. By the way, I have been making inquiries about you doing the baccalaureate from home."

"I don't understand."

"The Ministry of Education has instituted a system whereby you can sit for the baccalaureate from home. We can bring tutors for you, and then you can sit the examination."

"But I'm afraid I'll fail," I said without thinking.

Kamel sat down next to me and put his arms around me.

"You will pass, God willing. I'll bring the form you have to fill in on Saturday."

I was overcome with a sense of gratitude. Kamel leaned over and kissed me on the forehead before leaving the room, shutting the door gently behind him.

I thought about what he had said. I could not go back to the Sun-

niya School. I would not be able to bear the looks of pity or schadenfreude from the girls and the teachers. But nor could I bear the
nightmare of being a new student in a different school. There was
also the possibility that a state school would not admit me at all.
I had heard that the Ministry of Education had tried to ban married or divorced girls from going to school. The only option was
what Kamel had suggested. I would have to cover the whole syllabus at home, but the thought made me feel suddenly invigorated.
I threw myself back into the problems until the dawn call to prayer
sounded.

The next day, I woke up at noon. I took a shower and rushed to the
kitchen to help my mother, but she insisted that I have breakfast first.
She made me a plate of fava beans mashed with olive oil and lemon
juice, which I took to the dining room and ate hungrily. I heard the
doorbell, and after a little while, my mother appeared, looking worried. She walked over to me and whispered uneasily, "Saleha, Abd
el-Barr is here."

I looked at her and said nothing.

"Abd el-Barr," she repeated, "is in the sitting room and wants to
see you."

"I don't want to see his face."

"Saleha, the man has come all the way over here."

"Have you changed your mind, Mother?"

"Oh, Saleha, I haven't changed anything, but the man is in our
home. Courtesy dictates that you see him. You will have to deal with
him before it's all over. If you refuse to see him, he could start making
things difficult."

I realized that by law I was still the wife of Abd el-Barr. It was in
my best interests not to upset him further until he had agreed to a
divorce. I asked my mother to make some tea and wait with him until
I got dressed. I put on the white dress and combed my hair, leaving two locks dangling over my forehead. I put on some red lipstick
and a bit of powder. I was astonished at what I was doing. If I could
not stand Abd el-Barr, why was I making myself look nice for him?
Maybe it was to let him understand what he was losing or perhaps to
let him see that his absence was having no effect on me.

When I went into the sitting room, I found my mother sitting across from Abd el-Barr, who was wearing a gray suit and a white open-necked shirt. He jumped up and smiled as he greeted me. "How nice to see you, Saleha."

I mumbled a few words under my breath and looked away. My mother stood up.

"Excuse me. I've got things to do in the kitchen."

I sat in the chair near the door, as if to show that I could leave at any moment. Abd el-Barr cleared his throat.

"Saleha, I want to tell you that I'm not a drug addict."

"Whatever you say."

"The first time in my life was the day you saw me doing it. A friend of mine gave me the powder and told me that if I was down in the dumps or stressed, I should take it. It was the first and last time."

He continued talking quickly, as if delivering a prepared speech.

"Please forgive me for getting upset with you, Saleha."

"Upset" seemed an understatement given his punches. I said nothing. I could hardly contain my fury.

Abd el-Barr continued in a subdued voice, "Kamel came to my office to throw accusations at me, and I let him for your sake."

"It's only natural that Kamel should be angry."

"I've come all the way to your home," Abd el-Barr said with a smile, "and I have apologized."

"Even if I were to accept your apology," I shouted, "we cannot live together!"

"But things like this happen all the time in marriages!"

"Our life together is finished."

Abd el-Barr suddenly got up and came over to me. I stood up and took a few steps away from him.

"Saleha," he said, "let's not destroy our marriage."

"It's fate."

"All right. Take a little time to think things over," he said hoarsely.

I almost felt sorry for him, but I answered him quickly in order to put an end to the matter, "I have decided that I want a divorce."

His expression changed suddenly, and he started shouting, "Who do you think you are?"

"Please don't be rude," I shouted back.

"My mistake," he shouted even louder, "was in coming to see you. You don't deserve to be treated with respect."

"Watch your words!"

The last sentence was spoken by my mother. She had been listening to the conversation through the door and was now standing between us with a look of anger on her face.

"As long as your daughter behaves like that," he snapped, "there will be no divorce."

"You'll divorce her whether you want to or not."

"I'll go to court and get a ruling that she has to return to her husband."

My mother indicated the door and said, "I will not respond to you since you are in my home. Please be so kind as to leave."

My mother's tone was so resolute that he got up and left, muttering angrily. I heard his footsteps recede into the distance, then the front door opening and closing. By the time my mother came back, I was beside myself.

"Abd el-Barr just wants to demean me," I shouted like someone crying for help.

"There is not a man alive who can demean you," she said as she put her arms around me. "God is great, and he will help you through this."

KAMEL

When I was called in for questioning, my mind kept running over scenes from movies. Scenes in which investigators could catch an inconsistency in your story, by your nervous look, by a slip of paper you dropped or by a thread on your clothing from the crime scene. I was terrified because I was not a good liar. I went into the room trying to quash my terror. The investigating officer was in his forties and wearing a smart white suit. There was something false and cloying about the way he moved. He treated me condescendingly as he sat slumped in the armchair looking me over.

"Name and position at the Automobile Club?" he asked.

"My name is Kamel Gaafar," I answered quickly. "I am a law student at the Fuad I University, and I work as a storeroom assistant under Monsieur George Comanus."

I wanted to make it clear to him that I was not one of the serving staff but had clerical duties and was a university student. I think that the message hit home because he sat up a little and smiled.

"So sorry to disturb you over this, Kamel. But as a law student, you will understand. My instructions are to investigate all those who work in the Club. I will even be questioning Monsieur Comanus."

He asked me about the hours and nature of my work. He asked whether I had seen anything unusual recently. In spite of his formal smile and the superficial politeness, he fixed me with a searching and suspicious eye as I answered all his questions. I attempted to appear calm and natural.

He lit a cigarette and gave me a friendly smile, saying, "You know,

I did the same syllabus at the police academy as you're doing at the College of Law. What year are you in?"

"Second year."

"What subjects are you studying?"

I reeled them off.

He listened and then suddenly asked, "How do you suppose someone could take a photograph of His Majesty without anyone noticing?"

"I have no idea."

"Perhaps you can help with the power of your imagination. We have already found the camera, but the question remains who brought it into the Club and how."

"I have no idea."

"Come on, try to come up with a scenario for how someone might have brought the camera in."

"Neither the staff nor the Club members are subjected to any form of search when they enter the Club. Anyone could bring in a camera."

"Correct. But how was it set up in the casino?"

"Perhaps he waited until all the staff had gone home and then fixed it to the chandelier."

"How do you know that it was fixed to the chandelier?" he retorted while looking at me with an almost hostile stare.

I was taken aback but managed to control myself as I answered him, "All the staff know that the camera was discovered fixed to the chandelier."

He smiled and nodded. I looked at him defiantly. Did he think that he could incriminate me with games like this?

"Once more," he said in a friendly manner, "please forgive me, but I am just carrying out my orders. Can I ask you to do something for me?"

"Of course."

He wrote something on a small piece of paper, and as he handed it to me, he said, "Here's my telephone number. If you come across any information that might help our investigation, would you call me immediately?"

I took the piece of paper and said, "I spend the whole day in the storeroom and don't really know what happens in the Club. But if I learn anything useful, I will let you know straightaway."

"Thank you, Kamel. You may go."

"I notice," I said as I stood up, "that you were not taking notes. But I would like eventually to sign the written transcript."

As he held out his hand, he smiled and told me, "This has not been an official interview, only a chat between friends. Don't worry."

I was confirmed in my bad impression of him. Why at the end did he tell me not to worry? Did he suspect me of having fixed up the camera? It must have gone through his mind. An investigator needs to leave all possibilities open. I tried to assure myself that I was in a strong position and that he would not be able to lay anything at my feet. Going to the casino and attaching the camera had taken less than fifteen minutes. Not a soul had seen me going upstairs to the casino or leaving it. Labib the telephone operator had seen me standing in the entrance hall, but he would have been convinced that I had just arrived at the Club since I had asked what the hubbub on the roof was all about. Abdoun had managed to get the film out of the camera and was sure that no one had seen him. There was not a shred of evidence against me, but I was still plagued by fear. What I feared most was that one of my colleagues would be accused. If that were to happen, I would face a real dilemma. My conscience would not allow an innocent to suffer on my behalf, but on the other hand, were I to own up to it, I would bring down the whole organization with me. I had to hold myself together. I could not change what had happened.

I went out into the street. It was four o'clock. I had a whole hour until I had to meet the others. Hasan Mu'min had summoned me to an emergency meeting and warned me that I might be under surveillance. I decided to walk to the prince's palace, to calm my nerves and have a chance to reflect. I took a circuitous route down small side streets, stopping every now and then. I would light a cigarette and look around me. I arrived a quarter of an hour early. I did not want to meet the prince on my own. I was exhausted and had neither the inclination nor the energy for small talk. So I kept my distance from the palace and continued walking until I reached the bank of the Nile, where I sat down on a marble bench. I could see myself attaching the camera, sitting with Mitsy, arguing with Abd el-Barr.

I tried to find some explanation for this rush of events. It felt like I was in a movie, drawing near to its denouement. Was this all normal, or did I have a problem? Were the lives of the people strolling by full of similar problems? Why had I fallen into this vortex only after the death of my father? A few minutes before five, I walked around the palace, entering through the open garden gate and descending into the apartment where we held our meetings. I knocked on the door, and the prince opened it.

"Please come in, Kamel," he whispered with a nod.

The others were already there. I greeted them and sat down at the far side of the room next to the window. The prince put on his gold-rimmed glasses and leafed through the papers in front of him on the table.

"First of all, I should like to congratulate you upon the success of the operation. Thousands of copies of the photograph have been distributed in Cairo. Next week we will print a large number of copies for distribution in the provinces. They may have discovered the camera, but we got what we needed. Everywhere, people are going on about the scandalous photograph of the king."

The feeling of excitement was palpable in the room. Atiya added enthusiastically, "We have struck the corrupt tyrant a painful blow."

Odette continued in a serious tone, "This goes beyond the king's personal corruption. We have exposed the reactionary capitalist regime that is subservient to the occupation."

Everyone muttered in enthusiastic agreement.

"Have you followed the reactions in the press?" the prince asked.

"There has been a total silence about the scandal," Hasan Mu'min said quietly as he nodded affirmatively.

"I thought the press would be braver," the prince said with a smile.

"There are some newspapers," Hasan added, "that are tools of the palace and receive secret monthly subsidies, but there are also some independent newspapers which believe that publishing the photograph would be an act of lèse-majesté.

"We don't need them," Atiya said. "All we have to do is distribute the photograph ourselves."

"I have to thank Abdoun and Kamel," the prince said looking at me affectionately. "They carried out the operation to the letter."

Abdoun mumbled a few words of gratitude, and I added feebly, "I did my duty. Nothing more."

"The regime's reaction will be violent," the prince said. "As far as the head of the secret police is concerned, it's a matter of life and death. If he doesn't find the culprit, he'll lose his position."

"They will intensify their efforts," said Odette. "We have to proceed with the utmost caution. I would ask that we all review our security procedures before adjourning today."

"We must avoid any unnecessary telephone calls," added the prince. "We don't know who may be under surveillance. The security services may be eavesdropping. We shall continue meeting every Friday at seven in the morning. You'll be informed in the case of any change."

The prince then turned to Abdoun and asked, "How are things at the Automobile Club?"

Abdoun took a little time, as if gathering his thoughts.

"Alku has punished the entire staff. He has suspended gratuities. The staff salary barely covers a family's needs for a couple of days. With this, they'll be going hungry very soon."

"Will they protest?" interjected Atiya.

"We are weighing up the options," said Abdoun, "but it's a tricky situation. Alku has carte blanche from the general manager to punish the staff however he chooses. He has never been more powerful."

"That's not a punishment, my lad," Atiya retorted. "It's a crime. How can people be obliged to work for next to nothing?"

"The tips are not part of our salary, officially," replied Abdoun. "And what's more, none of us has an employment contract."

The prince took a sip of coffee and asked, "Let's all think about this. When we distribute the photograph in the provinces, will it exacerbate conditions for the staff at the Club?"

There was silence for a few moments, and then Odette spoke up, "On the contrary, distributing the photograph in the provinces will confirm that the staff had no part in what has happened."

"They will still be held responsible," said Abdoun, "because the photograph was taken in the Club."

"Yes, I know," replied Odette. "But if the photograph is distributed in the provinces, it will mean that the conspiracy is bigger than the staff of the Club."

"What I fear," said the prince in a serious tone, "is that the staff will buckle under the pressure."

"Even if they do," responded Abdoun, "they don't have any information to give. No one saw Comrade Kamel attaching the camera, and no one saw me taking out the film."

The prince nodded, and shuffling his papers, he said, "We now need to go over our plans in exact detail. Any error now could bring us all down."

This last sentence aroused the fear of those around the table, and they listened carefully.

"The photograph has to be distributed at exactly the same time in all the provinces. If any of our comrades, in any of the provinces, are late, they will be exposing themselves to arrest."

"I have made this clear to all the comrades," Hasan Mu'min assured him.

"Please go over the instructions with them again."

"When will it take place?" I asked the prince.

He thought a moment and answered, "In practical terms, we have a number of tasks: we have to print a large number of copies of the photograph, and we have to make sure the printers are secure and decide on the distribution point in each province. All that will take time. We will not be able to do it for a least two weeks."

The meeting went on for two hours, and at the end, Odette reviewed the security precautions with us. I rushed home to al-Sadd Street, which was thronged with people as usual. I climbed the stairs to our apartment and rang the bell rather than using my key because I knew that my mother would still be awake, and I wanted to see her opening the door. Just seeing her and giving her a hug would make me feel better. It was the same feeling I used to have when I came back from school to find her standing at the door as if she had been waiting there ever since saying good-bye in the morning. My mother implored me to eat a meal, but I refused, so she made some sandwiches and put them on my desk. I took a shower and made my ablutions, then said the evening prayers and sat down to study.

I was so absorbed in my books that I did not notice the passage of time. Suddenly, I thought I heard a voice coming from the street. It was after two in the morning. I tried to ignore it and concentrate on my reading. After a few moments, I heard the voice again but more clearly. Someone was calling my name. I got up and went over to the open window and looked. There was Mitsy standing in the street in a blue coat with her curls falling over her face.

"Mitsy? What's happened?"

She made a gesture with her hand and shouted in a voice that reverberated strangely in the quiet of the night, "Kamel, can you come down? I need to speak to you urgently."

35

Fawzy primped for the evening. He combed his hair meticulously and plastered it with hair cream. He dabbed half a bottle of eau de cologne all over his body and squeezed the bulging muscles of his chest and arms into a tight T-shirt that made him look like a pale-skinned giant walking alongside the black giant who was Mahmud Gaafar. They took the Lambretta, Fawzy in front and Mahmud riding pillion, all the way to the sugar factory in Garden City. It was seven in the evening, and the street was quiet and almost empty. Fawzy seemed as self-assured as if he'd done this quite often, but Mahmud was typically uneasy and distracted. He had been of more than two minds about coming along, but Fawzy had nagged him to come. Now, he was afraid. This was different from his times with Rosa and Dagmar. Madame Tafida al-Sarsawy had asked him bluntly to sleep with her.

"I'll pay you what Dagmar does," she had said.

He could not understand how these women knew about his activities. They must get together somewhere and exchange secrets. When he telephoned Tafida to tell her that he was coming over, she was overjoyed. He'd also told her that he would be bringing Fawzy along. At that, she fell silent for a moment and then said, "He's most welcome. He can come with you, but then he must make his excuses and leave us."

Mahmud, feeling embarrassed, said, "Fawzy is a friend of mine, and he would like to spend time with you, madame."

"Well, he's most welcome," she answered quickly. "What matters is that you and I do what we talked about."

Mahmud was again taken aback by her forthrightness. What a dreadful woman! The closer they came to her building, the greater his anxiety. There was no telling how she'd react to Fawzy. Whenever he tried to imagine the situation, he just became more unnerved. Before they went into the building, Mahmud suddenly stopped and implored Fawzy, "For my sake, let's skip this. I've got a bad feeling."

Fawzy snorted in disbelief.

"It's child's play," he said. "Get a grip on yourself, man!"

Mahmud knitted his brow and held his hands up.

"How am I going to tell her that you'll be filling in for me?"

Fawzy grabbed Mahmud by his enormous arm and dragged him forward, telling him, "Don't worry. I'll handle it."

"Fawzy! The woman's old and looks terrible, like a bad dream!"

"Listen, I told you I can do it. What's your problem?"

Mahmud gave in. As the two of them went into the entrance, the doorman stopped them. This shook Mahmud, but Fawzy took the matter in hand. He cleared his throat and said, "We are here to see Madame Tafida al-Sarsawy."

Fawzy discerned the suspicion in the doorman's eyes, and he said brazenly, "Well, why are you just standing there? I said we have an appointment with Madame Tafida."

The doorman looked at them for a moment and then stepped back to clear the way.

"Madame Tafida," he said, "is apartment seventeen on the fourth floor."

Mahmud almost told him that he knew which apartment she lived in but chose to remain silent. They got in the lift, but at the door of the apartment, Mahmud was still hesitant. Fawzy reached out and pressed the doorbell. A few moments later, the door opened. It is difficult to give a faithful description of Madame Tafida. She was scrawny and wrinkled, and her skin was covered in liver spots. Her wide eyes were rimmed with eyeliner, and she had drawn on thin eyebrows. She had angular features and thin, red-painted lips, which gave the impression of a febrile personality. Although her face seemed to be fixed in a frown, from time to time it would break into a supercilious smile with a hint of bitterness. Tafida observed everything suspiciously as if looking for the hidden lie or plot behind it all. All who knew her found her to be disconcerting, an arrogant, argumentative cynic who never stopped causing problems. On top of all that, she had a certain bygone-days quality to her, as if she had just stepped out of a time machine or a black-and-white movie, the sort of look you find in a photograph from an old album.

"Good evening, Madame," Mahmud said.

"Nice to see you, Mahmud," Madame Tafida said and then gestured at Fawzy and asked brusquely, "Who's that guy?"

"Have you forgotten, Madame?" Mahmud answered quickly. "He's my friend Fawzy. The one I told you about."

She nodded and fixed a suspicious look on him. She still had not invited them in. Mahmud just stood there while Fawzy boldly took a step toward her.

"Good evening, Madame Tafida," he said. "I asked Mahmud to bring me along. When I heard what a lovely person you are, I wanted to meet you. I already had a picture of you in my mind, but now that I have seen you, you are lovelier than I imagined."

The words sounded odd, and Fawzy looked at Tafida with complete insolence. Tafida's face turned the colors of the rainbow. Her facial expressions changed. She looked a little anxious, but then she gave a startled blink as if she had just had a thought, and she took two steps backward, "Please come in."

The two boys went into the high-ceilinged and spacious sitting room. Madame Tafida lived alone in a twenties-era six-bedroom apartment with two bathrooms. She sat down on the sofa and looked at them as they sat on armchairs next to each other. The whole situation was weird, and Mahmud kept wondering how she could receive them in her apartment without having uttered a single word of welcome.

Someone had to make the first move, so Mahmud mumbled, "How are you, Madame Tafida? Please God you are well."

Tafida did not answer. She looked carefully at him, as if she could see through his words. Then she looked at Fawzy, and now for the first time, in the light of the lamp, she could see his svelte body and his brawny muscles. Fawzy picked up on this and smiled.

"My name is Fawzy, and I'm at your service, Madame. Anything you want from Mahmud . . . I can do it for you."

Tafida seemed frozen. She stared at them as if unable to take in the strange turn of events, but then her gaze lost its harshness, and she said, "Would you like something to drink?"

"Red wine," Fawzy called out.

She got up and went toward the kitchen, but Fawzy called after her, "Of course, we can't drink on an empty stomach."

As Tafida turned to look at him, he added, "Get us something nice to eat. We have to eat properly if we are going to have some energy."

Mahmud was embarrassed by Fawzy's cheek and looked at the ground saying nothing. He sat there with his hands on his thighs like someone at a funeral. Tafida stood there as if confused about what she should do, but then she turned, went out into the hall and disappeared somewhere in the apartment. Mahmud glanced across the hall, and having assured himself that she had gone off to the kitchen, he looked daggers at his friend.

"What the hell!" he said. "You're going to get us both into deep shit."

"Don't worry," Fawzy said disdainfully, laughing. "You've got to treat these rancid old birds harshly from the word go."

"You're overdoing it."

"Listen, sunshine, didn't she ask you to sleep with her?"

"She wanted to sleep with me, not with you," he spat out. "And even if she did ask for sex, you have to treat her with some respect. She's an old lady from a good family, and you're treating her like some tart."

"But she is a tart."

"Just be careful, because if Madame Tafida gets upset with us she could cause us loads of trouble."

Fawzy gave him a look of exasperation.

"Shut up, Mahmud. Stop spouting garbage. I know what I'm doing."

They had to break off their conversation because Tafida appeared slowly wheeling a trolley upon which she had arranged a bottle of red wine, already opened with the cork resting on the side, three wine-glasses and a number of small plates of snacks: white cheese, olives, pickled cucumbers and a roast chicken cut into four pieces. There were also three silver forks and a wicker breadbasket covered with a white napkin.

Mahmud's nerves had taken away his appetite, so he just had a glass of wine and a piece of chicken, but Fawzy ate with gusto, downing a few glasses of wine as he chatted away about nothing with Tafida like an old friend, and then he suddenly asked her, "Do you own the Sarsawy gold shop in the jewelry district?"

"The shop belonged to my father, may God have mercy upon his soul. My sister and I inherited it."

"How many brothers and sisters do you have?"

Tafida appeared to resent this question, and she hesitated a little before conceding an answer, "I have one brother and one sister."

She was about to say "younger than me" but stopped herself. Fawzy finished eating, heaved himself out of his chair and went to the bathroom. When he came back, he headed straight for Tafida and sat down next to her on the sofa. He put his hand on her shoulder and whispered into her ear, "Do you know how lovely you are?"

It was a strange word to use for Tafida's tired, wrinkled and over-made-up face. For the first time, she used a formal tone of voice, "Thank you for the compliment."

Fawzy suddenly felt he was being toyed with. "Don't get all coy and innocent with me," he said to himself. The wine had emboldened him, and he leaned over and pressed his nose against Tafida's neck and stroked her lower back with his hand.

"I'm not giving you a compliment," he said in a shaky voice. "You really are lovely. You are all woman."

Tafida squirmed, but Fawzy moved even closer to her.

"Please," she tried to object. "Don't do that."

Since Fawzy was sure he was going about things in the right way, he took her display of coyness as a sign of acquiescence. She neither stood up nor moved away, and despite her apparent reticence, her face betrayed a different emotion. Fawzy snuggled up to her even more, putting his arms around her and kissing her neck as he whispered, "You're so lovely."

Tafida tried to push him away coquettishly.

"Stop it, Fawzy. You've gone mad!"

"I can't. You're as lovely as the full moon."

Mahmud observed the scene, stunned into silence. Why was Fawzy behaving like that with her, and why was she giving in to him? He could not fathom it. He had not gone in for all this malarkey with the two old ladies he had befriended. In fact, the opposite had happened. It was the women who had done the sweet-talking. Even Tafida, the first time he saw her, had been the one who initiated it. It was not his style, all those sweet nothings. He had to admit that Fawzy was much more forward than he was. As Mahmud sat immersed in his thoughts, the scene was moving on quickly. The old lady had given in and was moaning and giggling softly as she sat there with her legs open, looking like a circus animal responding to its trainer. Fawzy was kissing her passionately on the mouth as she uttered stifled whimpers. Then he nibbled her ear as his hand strayed over her flat chest. Mahmud could not take it anymore and jumped to his feet.

"I'll be going, Fawzy. Good-bye, Madame."

The formality of the phrases sounded odd under the circumstances. Fawzy pushed Tafida aside and tried to gather his thoughts. Then he got up and dragged Mahmud aside, whispering sharply, "Don't you dare go."

"What should I do, just sit there?"

"We came together and we're leaving together."

"Look, you're getting on with it, and there's no point in me sitting here. Besides, it's not a pretty sight."

"I've told you, you're not going."

Fawzy's tone was resolute, and Mahmud gave in. Fawzy went back to Tafida and grabbed her by the hand. She sprang to her feet as if she had been anticipating this sign from him. He put his arms around her, and the two of them made their way across the hall into the bedroom.

36

We have lost His Majesty's confidence. This is the greatest loss the Club has faced since it was founded. The king's privacy has been breached, and Club members will now stop coming for fear they will be photographed too."

Wright's face was flushed from the effort of trying to control his anger.

"I assure you," replied Alku, "that I shall find the traitor who installed the camera."

"Leave that to state security. I want you on another matter."

Alku looked at Wright who filled his pipe bowl and then puffed.

"I want you," Wright continued, "to convince His Majesty to start spending his evenings at the Club again."

"That's a tall order," Alku said ruefully.

"But it is possible. I know how close you are to the king."

"His Majesty is still shaken by what happened."

"We just want him to give us another chance."

"I shall try."

"Listen," Wright said resolutely. "If you manage to persuade the king to come back to the Club, I'll make it worth your while."

That night, Alku thought it over at length and resolved to do everything he could. Naturally, he was salivating over the financial reward on offer, but he also needed to be rehabilitated. Somehow, the scandal had dented his pride and his standing. After twenty years of wielding complete control over the staff in the royal palaces, he had allowed the reins to be loosened, and now someone, with the help of Alku's own staff, had managed to infiltrate the Club and take that photograph of the king in his pointed hat, then distributed the photograph throughout Egypt. This scandal would leave an indelible stain on his name if he didn't do something soon. Whenever he thought about it, he became enraged at Wright. Alku had warned him from the moment Abdoun started inciting the staff against the management, but Wright had ignored the warning, obviously so as to stay on good terms with Odette. If only Wright had listened to Alku and fired Abdoun, none of this would have happened. And what exactly were the state security officials doing? All their investigating and poking around seemed to yield nothing, not even a suspect. Alku had been to see Anwar Bey Makki, head of state security, to tell him that Abdoun was the one who had been inciting insubordination among the staff. But Anwar Bey Makki, while lending him the sympathetic ear of a man listening to a precocious child, said only, "Thank you for your help in this matter. I can assure that we are aware of this and are studying the matter carefully."

Alku drew up a plan to make good on his promise to Wright. He could always read the king's mood. With one glance, he knew whether His Majesty was angry or cheerful or sullen. And so Alku bided his time until the moment was right. The king had just finished bathing and had sat down to enjoy a hearty breakfast. Alku approached, placing the French newspapers on the table, then sighed and knitted his brow.

"Your Majesty, I feel so bad for Mr. Wright."

"What does he want from us?" the king asked disapprovingly.

"Since the unfortunate incident in the Automobile Club, he has been calling me every day to express his regret."

"And what good does that do us?"

Alku looked at the ground and shook his head.

"Your Majesty is right to be angry about what happened, but as a servant of Your Majesty, I have never seen an Englishman so devoted to the throne as Mr. Wright."

The very words pleased the king no end. Contradictory emotions seemed to cross the king's face as he nibbled on a sausage.

"Whatever Wright might say," the king said, wiping his mouth with his napkin, "what happened is treason. I have been photographed, and my privacy has been breached."

"If I find out who did this," Alku muttered, grimacing, "I'll wring his neck with my bare hands."

"Don't worry. State security will arrest the culprit soon enough," the king replied with apparent disdain. Then he leaned forward and took a big slurp of his favorite compote. Making the most of the king's gustatory satisfaction, which was apparent on His Majesty's face, Alku added, "Mr. Wright has certainly made an error. He himself does not deny that. However, Your Majesty, haven't state security officers and the royal guard also failed in their duty? Is it not their job to assure Your Majesty's security at all times . . ."

"They have all been lax."

"Mr. Wright has admitted to his own shortcomings, but he has also pointed out that state security and the royal guard are security professionals, whereas, at the end of the day, he is only a civilian manager who has nothing to do with security and surveillance procedures."

The king seemed to be thinking the matter over as he took another spoonful of compote.

"Your Majesty," Alku continued in a whisper, "the ubiquitous distribution of this vile photograph indicates the existence of a greater plot against the throne. We must be sure that the saboteurs have not installed cameras in the royal palace. I hope that state security will do their duty before they start blaming the general manager of the Automobile Club."

The king nodded in agreement. Having made it this far, Alku changed the subject and did not raise it again until a few days later, when the king was sitting alone in his bedroom. Alku bowed, and in the voice of one imparting a secret, he said, "My duty to the throne dictates that I must tell Your Majesty of an incident that happened yesterday."

The king looked at him with a mixture of curiosity and astonishment. Alku said nothing for a moment and then continued, "Your Majesty, it pains me to have to speak of a prince of the family of Muhammad Ali when I am but a servant of them all."

The king looked concerned and asked, "What's happened?"

Alku mumbled as if unwilling to go on.

"His Highness Prince Shamel, Your Majesty."

"What of him? Speak!"

"I should like to apologize in advance for what I have to say, but I have promised Your Majesty to speak truthfully. His Highness Prince Shamel has embarked on a campaign of lies which are detrimental to the throne."

"What has he said?"

"Your Majesty, I really do not like to repeat the scurrilous things he has said, but God is our judge. Yesterday Prince Shamel was dining at the Automobile Club, and he told his companions that he considers the Wafd Party the sole legal representative of the Egyptian nation."

Overcome with emotion, Alku fell silent and then forced himself to continue, "His Highness Prince Shamel went so far as to tell his guests that Nahas Pasha, the leader of the Wafd Party, is more popular than Your Majesty the king of Egypt and the Sudan."

The king looked at him in disbelief.

"Are you sure?" he asked.

"Mr. Wright called me personally this morning and briefed me on this. He is furious."

"How did Wright know?"

"His Highness Prince Shamel had had a bit to drink and spoke loudly enough for the servants to hear, and they reported it to Mr. Wright."

The king's face turned ashen, and he said nothing.

"How can His Highness Prince Shamel," Alku continued, "talk like this in the Automobile Club of which Your Majesty is the patron?"

The king furrowed his brow and then made a gesture with his hand.

"I'm not interested in Shamel's prattling. Everyone knows that he is a Communist and quite mad."

"Your Majesty is perfectly correct. The throne has to be above all this tittle-tattle. Mr. Wright, as the general manager of the Club, is so furious that he is requesting Your Majesty's permission to take the necessary steps against Prince Shamel."

"What does he want to do?"

"As lèse majesté is a crime under Egyptian law, Mr. Wright will not allow Prince Shamel to do it again. If His Highness says another word against the throne, Mr. Wright will issue him with a warning and will then terminate his membership of the Club."

The king's expression turned from one of concern to satisfaction.

"Tell James Wright," he said, "that it is within his remit to take whatever steps he deems appropriate to assure the smooth running of the Club."

There were a few moments of silence, and then Alku cleared his throat, adding sotto voce, "Would Your Majesty allow his obedient servant to give his opinion?"

"Speak."

"His Highness Prince Shamel's enmity toward the throne is well known, but he was only able to be so bold in the Automobile Club because Your Majesty does not go and spend time there anymore. If Your Majesty were to start going there again, Prince Shamel would not dare to turn up."

Alku said no more, letting the thought percolate slowly in the king's head. One afternoon a week later, the king was sitting on a balcony in the palace eating ice cream as Alku bowed and said softly, "Your Majesty, may I address a request to you?"

The king gave him an inquiring look.

"Mr. James Wright asks whether Your Majesty might deign to grant him a short interview. He is just asking for ten minutes of Your Majesty's time."

The king agreed to see Wright, and Alku dashed off to deliver the news. Wright seemed relieved and muttered, "Thank you."

It was highly unusual for Wright to thank the head chamberlain openly.

"At your service," Alku bowed.

At exactly four o'clock in the afternoon the following day, Wright presented himself to His Majesty, who smiled and said in English, "Good afternoon, Mr. Wright. How are you?"

The king gestured to Wright, who took a seat and launched directly into the matter at hand. "I hope Your Majesty will give due consideration to what I am about to say."

The king nodded and looked at him.

"Your Majesty, I would ask Your Majesty to forgive us and to honor us with your presence at the Automobile Club."

"I will not go to that place. It is riddled with Communists."

"I can give Your Majesty my word that what happened will never happen again."

The king said nothing while he appeared to mull it over. Wright plucked up the courage to continue, "Your Majesty, I don't want the saboteurs to feel that their crime has brought about the result they hoped for. Your Majesty is too great a personage to have his life changed by those riffraff."

Wright pronounced the word "riffraff" with such contempt that it had an effect on the king. Wright picked up his argument again. "The person who founded the Club was Your Majesty's late great father, and Your Majesty is the present patron. The Automobile Club is nothing without Your Majesty's patronage. I would request Your Majesty to give us the opportunity to make amends."

"Fine," smiled the king. "I shall think it over. Mr. Wright, it has been a pleasure to see you."

This was a royal indication that the meeting was over. Wright stood up and nodded with a grateful smile as he left. Was the king really intent on going back to the Automobile Club? The answer was a definite yes. As far as the king was concerned, the Club was a wonderfully diverting place which held happy memories for him. Going to the Club allowed him to break away from rigid court protocol. He was always childishly happy when sitting with his friends in the Club, freed from royal conventions, meeting beautiful women, playing poker and eating to his heart's delight. The king did not dine in the restaurant but had a never-ending succession of dishes sent over to his table in the casino—sandwiches expertly made by Rikabi, roast beef, cocktail sausages, schnitzel and pastries stuffed with minced meat, chicken and cheese. When the cards were going his way, His Majesty would sit there happily, a sandwich in one hand, his cards in the other hand. He'd joke with his fellow gamblers, "We should all stand for a minute in memory of the Earl of Sandwich. That fellow bestowed a great invention on mankind. Do you know who the Earl of Sandwich was?"

The gamblers would profess their ignorance of the name to give the king a chance to display his cultural knowledge. He would continue with childish pride, "The Earl of Sandwich was an Englishman born in 1718, and he invented the sandwich."

This was a sign for the gamblers to heap their praise on the king and his refined sense of culture and various other talents. Then dessert would arrive, an assortment of the king's favorites: *basbousa* with buffalo cream, crème caramel and compote. He would graze his way through them as he played successive hands. The king missed all these diversions and had been longing to be able to spend evenings at the Club again, but he needed a justification for his decision to go back there, and this was precisely what Alku had provided him with. To anyone who might ask him, the king could say, "The mass distribution of the photograph is proof that the plot against the throne is widespread and was the result of careful planning. The issue is not localized or specific to the Automobile Club."

Or he might say, "Mr. Wright, the general manager of the Club, has implored me to go back to the Club. I was very moved by him. This Englishman is more devoted to the throne than many Egyptians." Then His Majesty might add with some emotion, "The Automobile Club belongs to the throne. I shall never allow it to fall into the hands of saboteurs and Communists."

These, in fact, were the reasons behind his decision. His Majesty's return to the Automobile Club was a fittingly impressive sight. All the staff came down and assembled in the entrance hall, headed by Alku and James Wright, who was dressed in a natty navy-blue suit, set off by a gleaming white shirt and a red tie. They had been waiting in the entrance hall for approximately half an hour before the king's red Buick appeared. It drew to a halt in front of the door, the guards and valets running in all directions as His Majesty stepped out.

Wright rushed toward him, bowed deeply and declared, "Your Majesty, we thank you from the bottom of our hearts."

The king nodded but made no comment. He gave a haughty smile and strode toward the lift. The staff were confused, expecting the formalities of receiving the king to take much longer. But His Majesty was dying to get back to the gambling table which he had missed so much, and words of gratitude, much as they might have gratified him, would have only served to remind him of the painful incident of the photograph. Everything went back to normal. The king took his place at the head of the green felt table with his friends, who were chatting away, drinking and playing cards. The staff felt their gloom lifting and hoped that the king's return would mean an end to the bad times. Alku could not go on punishing them when His Majesty himself had forgiven them. That night, the staff did all they could to provide perfect service. Over the next days, they were so expectant that Alku would summon them and announce the restoration of their tips that they had even prepared small speeches of gratitude. When a week had passed and nothing changed, they started wondering, "What does Alku want? Why doesn't he lift the punishment? How long are we going to have to work for nothing?" With every passing day, they were becoming more and more hard up, and their frustration started to affect their work. They would go around fulfilling members' requests, but their minds were elsewhere. They realized that the situation was more dire than a simple storm they had to weather. Alku seemed intent on ruining them. He seemed to be taking a devilish delight in causing them grief. They could not cover their essential household expenses, much less the rent and their children's school fees.

What had happened to the Automobile Club? It now seemed cursed, with catastrophe after catastrophe. Every day, a new disaster. At least they had had some protection and security. They had had stability. Rules. Unjust perhaps, but better than this chaos. Abdoun and his friends had opened the flood gates of hell. What had they gained in standing up to Alku? In the past, they could avoid a beating by doing their work properly, but now they were working even harder and for nothing. They used to put all the tips into the green velvet padlocked box in the casino. Every Friday, Maître Shakir would unlock it, separate the folded banknotes and lay out the coins on the table. Then he would total it all up in front of them, setting half aside for Alku and doling out the other half according to seniority. They used to stand like excited children waiting for a treat in front of Maître Shakir as he counted the tips. Friday evenings had been the high point of their week, the moment when, after a week of hard work, the customers' appreciation would reach them. That was all over now.

They dropped their tips into the velvet box in the knowledge that they would see none of it, not a piastre.

The staff could not hide their consternation and anger. Some of them would mutter with exasperation, "Isn't it wrong, Maître Shakir, to deprive us of the means of supporting our children?"

"Does it please God," another asked, "that we're all working for nothing?"

Maître Shakir would ignore their comments and just carry on sorting out the coins. If the grumbling continued, he would yell at them, "Stop this bloody whining. I'm just the messenger. If you want something, go and talk to Alku."

The mention of Alku was enough to make them fall silent. Despite their resentment, they were still unwilling to stand up to him, and they lived in the hope that he would lift the punishment. They had to try to get back on his good side rather than do anything that might anger him more. Any unconsidered action or word out of place might make the problem intractable. Wisdom dictated that they should just grit their teeth and get on with things, for if Alku saw how much they were suffering, his heart would surely soften. They bore their suffering for two whole months. They waited it out, falling deeper into debt and putting off paying their household bills, clinging on to their hope that at some point Alku would forgive them. This hope was all they had. Most of them were married and had children of school age, and even the bachelors among them used to send postal orders on the first of each month to their families in Upper Egypt.

By the ninth week, they could take it no longer. One afternoon they all met in the café. The night shift staff came before their shift had begun, and the day shift staff came before their shift had ended. They formed a great throng. The department heads were absent. Maître Shakir was sitting there smoking a water pipe, but when he saw them all arriving, he guessed the purpose of their meeting, ordered the bill and left. Bahr the barman was the only department head who turned up. He sat smoking a water pipe silently in one corner of the café. Everyone was seated, except for Karara the waiter and a few others who could find no seats or perhaps simply wanted to be seen and heard.

"So what do we do now?" Karara cried out as if kicking off the show. "What are we to do about this catastrophe?"

"We've got wives and kids to support!" someone grumbled out loud.

"How are we going to keep our families going? Are we going to have to steal or beg?" asked another.

"Uncle Suleyman," someone called out, "I'm going to have to give up this job."

"You can't," said Suleyman, smiling sadly.

They fell silent, overcome with sudden fear. Suleyman shook his head and continued, "If any of you quit your job without Alku's blessing, it'll be the end of you. You think it's as easy as that? Twenty years ago, when the Club first opened, there was a waiter called Anbar from Luxor. He did something wrong, and Alku beat him. In those days, Alku used to beat us with his own hands. Anbar had a difficult time with that. He sat up all night, and the following morning, he walked out of the Club. He disappeared. You know what Alku did? He told the police that Anbar had stolen some money. They arrested him and put him on trial, and he got three years in prison."

They shuddered as they imagined Alku getting them sent to prison too. After all their hard work, to be kicked in the teeth like that!

"Listen, everyone," said Karara. "We have to find a way out of this."

"But what can we do?" whined Samahy.

"We have to find out who installed the camera."

"If the bloody police can't find out, how can we?"

Abdoun was sitting in the corner. He got up and walked to the center of the café, where they could all see him, and said, "Listen, everyone. You need to understand that the ban on tips has got nothing to do with any camera being found."

"Beat it, Abdoun," Karara shouted with a look of disgust.

Abdoun paid no attention and continued calmly, "Alku was going to ban tips whatever the circumstances. If it hadn't been that scandalous photograph, he would have found another reason."

"What do you mean?"

"I mean that when he agreed to stop the beatings, he must have decided then to take his revenge on all of us."

"That's enough poisonous talk," shouted Karara. "There has been

a scandal involving the king, and it's natural that Alku would punish us. Instead of trying to stand up to Alku, we should apologize
to him."

"Apologize for what?" asked Abdoun. "What have we got to do
with it? State security officials are the ones responsible for the king.
What's more, the king himself has come back to the Club and treats
us as if nothing happened. That means that Alku is more upset about
the dent to the king's reputation than the king himself."

The staff mumbled among themselves and exchanged confused
whispers.

"Listen, everyone," Abdoun continued, "we are in a dispute with
Alku, and we are in the right. Alku wants us to continue being subject
to his whims, and we are demanding to be treated with respect. We
do our work and get paid, and if we do something wrong, we should
be disciplined without humiliation."

The staff were all at their wit's end, and their dismay was visible.

"So, Abdoun," asked old Suleyman, "what should we do?"

"Hold on to our dignity," answered Abdoun.

That set the cat among the pigeons. "What bloody dignity!" they
called back at him.

As their shouts mingled, it became clear that not all of them
agreed. Most were furious with Abdoun, but Samahy, Bahr and some
others put up a valiant defense of Abdoun, who said nothing as the
controversy raged around him.

"Abdoun is right."

"Was he wrong to stand up for our rights?"

"Who told him he could speak for us?"

"You say that now, but didn't you thank him when he got Alku to
stop the beatings?"

"We thanked him out of politeness, nothing more. And now we're
all living a catastrophe."

"Listen, Abdoun," said Karara. "What do you say to us going to
apologize to Alku?"

There were shouts of approval.

"Good idea!"

"Absolutely. If Abdoun apologizes to Alku, he'll forgive us."

"I have nothing to apologize for," declared Abdoun.

"You have to apologize!" shouted Karara, and other voices seconded his call.

"I will not apologize," said Abdoun, staring them down. "And I will not let anyone beat me. Not Alku or Hameed or anyone. Instead of demeaning yourselves even more and letting Alku have you beaten like cattle, be men and demand your rights with your heads held high."

Suddenly, Karara rushed over to him and screamed, "Where the hell did you come from? You've made our lives a living hell, and I hope God does the same to you."

Some of those standing around rushed forward to keep the two men from coming to blows. The staff were now in a state of deep gloom as they realized that the problem was insoluble.

Suleyman strode slowly to the middle of the café and gestured toward them, saying, "Listen, guys. We need to sort this out."

"Sort it out? That's what we're trying to do!" someone called back at him.

"Abdoun is too proud to go and apologize to Alku," he said, trying to make his weak voice audible. "So we will go instead and ask him for forgiveness."

Some people called out in support of this idea, but Abdoun shouted above them, "Apologizing to Alku will achieve nothing. The more you demean yourselves, the more he will demean you."

"You're an odd bird, Abdoun," Suleyman shouted in a rage. "Who put you in charge of us? We are free to do what we want. If you don't like what we say, you're free to leave."

Abdoun gave a sad smile, but Suleyman repeated his remark.

"Good-bye, Abdoun, you can leave us. I want to tell the men something that you won't like to hear."

Having been told to go, Abdoun just looked at Suleyman in disbelief, before turning on his heel toward the exit.

"Wait, Abdoun. I'm coming with you."

That request was uttered by Bahr, who put down the mouthpiece of his water pipe and followed Abdoun out. He was followed in turn by Samahy and a few others. Those who supported Abdoun numbered ten out of a total of forty-four. Once Abdoun and his friends had left, the others felt easier and clustered around Suleyman, who expounded his idea to them. He would go and tender a new apology to Alku. Those left gave their enthusiastic support to the plan.

"Take me with you, Suleyman," Karara called out.

Thus the delegation was made up of the two men. Suleyman, the longest-serving member of staff, and Karara the waiter, the one most devoted to Alku and most hostile to Abdoun and his supporters. Just before midnight, Karara asked permission to leave from Maître Shakir, and Suleyman got one of the waiters to stand in for him at the door. Mustafa took them to Abdin Palace and then drove quickly back to the Club. When they got to Alku's office, Hameed eyed them suspiciously as Suleyman politely stated, "Mr. Hameed, I have come with Karara to see His Excellency Alku."

"Regarding . . . ?"

"We have come to beg our master Alku to put an end to the unsettled state of affairs prevailing in the Club."

Hameed stood up slowly and went into Alku's office. About half an hour later, they were ushered in. As usual, he looked majestic and fearsome in his embroidered chamberlain's uniform and gold spectacles and smoking a fat cigar. He looked at the two men, and Suleyman addressed him, "Your Excellency Alku. We are your servants. We owe you everything. Abdoun and his gang are completely wrong. We have come to you to disassociate ourselves from him."

Alku threw a cold, uncomprehending glance at Suleyman. Karara took a couple of steps forward, and with an ingratiating smile and a shaky voice, he added, "By the Prophet, please do not send us away empty-handed. Please don't be angry with us anymore and let us have our tips. Our families are going hungry, and surely Your Excellency is not happy about that."

Alku shrugged his shoulders and blew out a cloud of smoke which obscured his face.

"If you have nothing to do with that guy Abdoun," he asked calmly, "why have you remained silent until now?"

"Your Excellency," answered Suleyman, "none of us will even speak to him anymore."

"If that Abdoun were to say a word against Your Excellency," added Karara, "we'd murder him."

"Most certainly!" Suleyman nodded. "We have ostracized Abdoun and his gang. None of us would even exchange a word with them."

Alku said nothing. He made no comment. He held the cigar in his fingers as he checked the carefully manicured nails of his left hand. He looked like the cat who got the cream. Karara and Suleyman took Alku's taciturnity as a good omen, and encouraged by this, Karara took another step forward and said, "Your Excellency. We are at your disposal. If you want to beat us, beat us, but by the Prophet, please allow us to earn a living."

KAMEL

P lease come down."

I just about managed to control myself, and I gestured to her to wait. I flung my clothes on and flew down the stairs. I was out of breath by the time I reached her. "Mitsy. What's happened?" I asked.

"Can we go and sit somewhere?"

Fortunately, it was the first of the month, and I had a reasonable amount of money in my pocket. I took her by the hand, and we walked toward Sayyida Zeinab Square. After a few moments, a taxi appeared on the other side of the road, and I flagged it down. We got in, and I told the driver, "Semiramis Hotel, please."

I knew that the café there was open all night. We did not exchange a word the whole way. It would have been pointless to sit there chatting when I did not know what had happened. We went into the hotel lobby and chose a table which looked out onto the Nile. When a waiter appeared, I ordered coffee and Mitsy ordered a lemonade. I looked at her face in the light. She had circles under her eyes, a look of exhaustion and the pallor of someone who had not slept for days. She lit a cigarette and looked at me.

"I have left home."

"Couldn't you have waited until daylight?"

"I can't stand it anymore."

"All because you didn't go with the king?"

"The matter of the king is just one of the reasons. My troubles with my father go back a long way. If there ever was someone with whom I differ on absolutely everything, it's my father."

She shook her head and sipped her lemonade.

"It saddens me to say," she continued, "that I have no respect for my father."

She looked down for a moment, and then raised her head to say something, but suddenly she burst out crying. I reached over to stroke her hand.

"Mitsy," I said, "please calm down."

"I'm tired of it all. My father orders me around because he pays for my keep. He's always trying to belittle me. I feel humiliated."

"Don't worry. We'll wait until daylight, and then you are coming home with me."

"You don't need more problems. You have enough to do with your work and studies and your sister's problems with her husband. I will not let myself be a further burden."

At that moment, I wanted to take her in my arms.

"You will never be a burden on me," I whispered.

"Thank you!" she said with some emotion.

"I'll work out how you can thank me later!"

Mitsy smiled for the first time. How beautiful she looked at that moment. Her smile changed her pale, exhausted face and her tired, sad eyes into something surreally beautiful and magical. We asked for two coffees. I tried to distract her, and we talked until five in the morning. When I had paid the bill and we went out onto the street, I felt, in spite of everything, supremely happy at having her walking beside me.

We took a taxi home. I held her hand as we walked up the stairs. Suddenly, everything was strange and dreamlike. Here I was taking Mitsy to live in our apartment. I opened the door with my key and asked her to sit on the sofa in the sitting room. I walked down the corridor to my mother's bedroom. I found her sitting on her prayer rug and reading the Quran, having finished her morning prayers. I greeted her and kissed her on the head, but she gave me a concerned look and asked, "Where've you been?"

I sat down next to her and explained the situation, about Mitsy's having left home and how as a foreigner she did not know anyone in Egypt and had no money for a hotel. I will always be in awe of my mother's capacity to cope with bad situations. She was by turns surprised, then astonished, before thinking it over and finally looking at me sternly, "Since she has come to take refuge with us, she can stay with us as a respected and honored guest until she is reconciled with her family."

"I don't think she'll ever make up with Mr. Wright."

"The girl cannot just cast off her father."

"Mother, I know some details that I can't share with you. Her father does not have her best interest at heart."

"Good God!"

"I think we should let her stay with us for a few days until she has found a job and an apartment."

"Then she is welcome. But there's something I have to say to you."

My mother was silent for a moment, searching for the right words.

"I have noticed, Kamel, that you seem to be fond of her. That's up to you, but you must understand that our house must remain as unsullied as a mosque. Mitsy will share Saleha's room, and you are to keep your distance from her as long as she is in our home."

"Yes, Mother."

"Do you promise?"

"I promise."

She sighed as if my compliance with her demand had dispelled her anxieties. Then she stood up and went into the sitting room with me. My mother gave Mitsy a big, warm welcome, putting her arms around her and then leading her off by the hand. When I tried to follow them, my mother stopped and smiled. "Leave Mitsy to me. You can go off and busy yourself elsewhere."

I left the two of them and went to my bedroom. I did not even try to sleep, knowing I would not be able to. I lay on the bed, smoking and staring at the ceiling. My exhaustion was playing havoc with my feelings. I suddenly felt a surge of violent hatred toward James Wright. That man was a total bastard. Could I ever have imagined that he would behave in such a vile manner? Could I ever have predicted his actions from my few interactions with him? This question led me to think about the relationship between a man and his character. What was the first impression that someone like Wright or Abd el-Barr made? From the first, I had not felt comfortable with either of them. When we first see someone, we have a fleeting impression which fades as we get to know him. If we were able to interpret that first impression carefully, it might well give us a detailed insight into his character.

That was the last thought I had before falling into a deep sleep from which I woke up late. I ran into the bathroom, flung my clothes on and took a taxi from al-Sadd Street to the Club, where I found Monsieur Comanus waiting for me in his office. He greeted me reproachfully, "And what time do you call this?"

"I'm so sorry for being late."

"You cannot be late! Work is work. Go and fetch the empty beer crates from the bar."

I carried the crates back to the storeroom. Then I did a few chores and sat down to go over the inventory. I was so tired that I had to do the simple arithmetic over and over again. I became aware of a hand touching my shoulder and saw Monsieur Comanus standing there, smiling.

"Monsieur Comanus," I said quietly, "I apologize again for being late. I stayed up late studying and couldn't wake up."

He looked at me sympathetically and said, "Don't be late again!"

"No, sir!"

I quickly started reading the lists again in order to avoid further conversation. I did not want to talk to Comanus about Mitsy, even though I was fond of him and trusted him. At that moment, I somehow considered him a foreigner and expected him to be angry if he knew about the presence of Mitsy in my home since she was a foreigner like him. I then felt ashamed at that stupid and racist assumption. Comanus had been a devoted friend to my father and had helped us out by giving Mahmud and me a chance to work in the Club. When it was time to go home, I shook his hand and told him, "I want to thank you for everything that you have done for me and my family."

Monsieur Comanus gave an embarrassed smile and replied, "I haven't done anything. Your father was like a brother to me."

I felt better for having thanked him. After all he had done for me, he did not deserve to be treated like a stranger. I was about to go back and tell him about Mitsy, but then I realized that would be stupid. I was exhausted and could not think straight. I went for a walk down Soliman Pasha Street and then suddenly had an idea. I called the prince from the telephone in the tobacco shop.

The moment I heard his voice, I blurted out, "Your Royal Highness! I would like to come and see you now."

"Is everything all right?" he asked worriedly.

"I can't discuss it over the telephone."

He hesitated a moment and then said, "All right. Come over."

Half an hour later, the head footman was leading me to the studio. The prince was in his work clothes, seated at a table cropping some photographs, just like the first time I'd come to see him.

He gave me a warm welcome and invited me to sit.

"You've got me worried, man!" he said. "What's going on?"

That was all the prompting I needed. I told the prince about Saleha and Abd el-Barr, as well as about Mitsy staying with us. I did not keep anything from him. The prince listened calmly, occasionally asking questions. When I finished, I felt as if I had freed myself from some heavy burden. The prince got up and poured himself a whiskey, adding a few ice cubes, and as he sipped it, a mischievous smile appeared on his face.

"Are you in love with Mitsy?"

I said nothing, and the prince gave an enormous chuckle.

"Looks like you are!"

"Mitsy is a very lovely person," I mumbled.

"Have you ever been in love before?" His eyes twinkled with glee.

I shook my head, and the prince called out, "Ah, *le premier amour, cher poète!* You must set down your feelings for Mitsy in poetry!"

There was silence again, and then the prince became serious and said, "With regard to the other matter, if you want my opinion, your sister must get a divorce. She can't live with a man like that."

"He's refusing to grant her one."

The prince said nothing, thinking it over. Then he handed me a sheet of paper.

"Write down for me," he said, "the name and full address of the gentleman in question."

I did as requested. He glanced at it, then placed it on his desk. Shortly afterward, as I was taking my leave, he grasped my hand and said, "I can't promise anything, Kamel, but I shall do all I can to help you."

37

It was after midnight when the two friends left Tafida al-Sarsawy's apartment on the Lambretta. They disappeared at top speed, saying nothing, as if stunned into silence by what had just happened. After a while, Fawzy started humming a song by Abd el-Wahab, and Mahmud noticed that he was not heading home to the Sayyida Zeinab district.

"Where are you going?" he shouted.

"Somewhere nice," Fawzy shouted back, laughing the laugh of someone in a good mood. Fawzy headed to the citadel district, then turned right into a narrow alley and parked the Lambretta. The friends went into an ancient building and climbed a narrow, winding staircase to the roof. Mahmud had never been to this smoking den before. The customers were seated on wooden benches against the wall. In the middle of the roof terrace, there was a large metal drum with lumps of glowing charcoal, and the serving boys were rushing to and fro carrying water pipes and small braziers. The customers seemed to know Fawzy, as did the proprietor, who got up and greeted him with a big hug. In the brash voice he used when trying to seem important, Fawzy asked the proprietor, "How are you, boss? It's been ages!"

The two friends took a seat in a corner, and one of the serving boys scurried over with a water pipe and some glowing pieces of charcoal. Fawzy took a lump of hashish out of his pocket and bit off small pieces from it, placing a small lump on each of the prepared tobacco bowls. He lit the first one and took a deep drag, making the water gurgle in the pipe. Then he handed the mouthpiece to the serving boy, who drew in deeply and exhaled a cloud of smoke from his mouth and nostrils. Then Fawzy turned to Mahmud.

"We have to distract ourselves after what happened with that Tafida woman."

Mahmud preferred the delightful rush he got from wine to the heavy-headedness and dullness he got from hashish, but he took a few short drags on the water pipe anyway. Handing it back to the boy, who finished off what was left and then started fitting another bowl of tobacco and hashish to the pipe, Mahmud sat back on the bench and asked Fawzy, "And just what were you doing with Madame Tafida? I was sitting there embarrassed as hell."

Fawzy guffawed and said, "Listen to me. You've got to be rough with women like that."

Mahmud nodded but remained unconvinced. Fawzy reached into his shirt pocket and unfolded two pound notes.

"My high and mighty attitude got us double what you get with all your politeness!"

Mahmud sat there with a vacant smile, saying nothing. Yet again, Fawzy had managed to outdo him. Yet again, he had shown him that he knew more about life and people. Mahmud had been expecting Tafida to blow her top at any second and tell them to leave, but to his amazement, while Fawzy's vulgar moves upset her at first, in the end, she gave in to him. After Fawzy had been to bed with her, she came out looking less wrinkled and much more relaxed. Fawzy had taken her in his arms one last time and nibbled her ear, at which she let out a girly shriek most unbecoming in someone of her age. Fawzy told her, "Tafida, I'll be back on Wednesday."

She nodded, looking at him dreamily as he placed his hand behind her neck and pulled her toward him, as if to head-butt her.

"I'll make sure you're satisfied like tonight."

That was how Fawzy instigated a new type of relationship with women. Mahmud might have frenetic sex with his two lady friends, but he still treated them with some respect. He thought of Rosa as a good friend, and even with Dagmar, for all her sharpness and sever-ity, he was gentle and tried not to hurt her feelings. When she told him that her daughter had given birth to a baby girl in Germany, he congratulated her and asked her to write the baby's name down on a piece of paper so that he could learn how to pronounce it. Mahmud, it could not be denied, was selling sexual favors, but he did so with polite gentility. Fawzy's coarse behavior with his mistress was naked machismo, but perhaps he needed to be that way. He had acted outrageously with Tafida; it was as if he did not want her to forget that she was paying for sex. Unlike Mahmud, Fawzy was offering sex-with-humiliation. He had made Tafida look at herself. He had shattered any illusions she might have had. While caressing her body, he gave her gentle goading slaps whose subtext was, "You can't fool me into thinking you are anything but a cheap frustrated old hag who'll pay anyone to go to bed with her. That's how it is. If there is any pretending or lying, I'll be the one doing it."

Fawzy felt nothing but contempt for Tafida and did everything he could to show it. When he was servicing her, his face took on an aggressive and vengeful look. Oddly though, Tafida rather liked this treatment and his roughness, but the way she simply let Fawzy toss her around like a rag doll was mystifying, as she was neither a sophisticated woman nor a battered wife. Her sharp features and hostile expressions made her look like a shrew, but Fawzy managed to tame her, and each harsh word or coarse gesture made her only more submissive. But why did Tafida, otherwise so dignified and standoffish, not reject Fawzy's humiliating treatment and instead became only fonder of Fawzy? Was it that being over seventy, she would seek out pleasure at any price? Or did the humiliation absolve her somehow in her mind from guilt? Tafida, after all, was an Egyptian, not a foreigner like Mahmud's two mistresses. As such, she was the product of an Eastern culture which condemned extramarital relations. Much as she might yearn to give herself over to sexual pleasure, deep down she must have felt a measure of shame. And so, perhaps Fawzy's humiliations were the punishment she inflicted upon herself, a way to scourge her of sin. Whatever the reason, Fawzy's relationship with Tafida was so crude that Mahmud could neither understand nor approve of it, even if Fawzy insisted on dragging him along to Tafida's apartment. His presence encouraged Fawzy's braggadocio, turning his actions into a theatrical event performed for an audience of one. Tafida, wearing a silk dressing gown over her nightdress, would open the door for the two boys. She would first shake hands with Mahmud, then give Fawzy a hug, and attempting to make her voice sound gentle and seductive, she would ask him, "How are you, my darling?"

At which point, Fawzy would retort coldly, "What are you doing still up? It's bad for you to stay up so late."

She would ignore his impudence and sit next to him, snuggling up and whispering, "I've missed you."

The sight of Tafida prancing about like a teenager, with her thinning dyed hair and makeup plastered over her crumbling face, her forced coquettishness and her abortive attempts at being soft and gentle, all of this simply provoked Fawzy. He would move to caress her, for example, but then instead grab her by the nape of her neck and pull her dyed hair until she screamed. Then he would guffaw and say, "Get up and get to work. Mahmud and I are hungry."

"I've got kebab and kufta for you," Tafida would say as she scuttled off to the kitchen, with Fawzy shouting after her, "Don't forget the wine!"

Tafida would come back with a tray of kebabs and a bottle of French wine, and Mahmud would jump up to help her set the table while Fawzy just sat there smoking.

Fawzy never thanked her or complimented her on anything she did. He never made a comment unless it was to criticize. He would inspect the table laid with heaps of food and then look cross. "You've forgotten the tahina."

Or he might test the baguette with his fingers and then throw it down on the table with disgust, complaining, "This bread's stale."

Tafida would rush to fix the mistake. Fawzy would eat with gusto and drink glass after glass of wine. Then he would get up and go to the bathroom, where Tafida had laid out towels and perfumed soap for him, as well as a brush and comb so he could groom his curly hair. He would take a bath and reappear wearing a dressing gown over his naked body. Tafida would be sitting there waiting, her face flushed, her breathing quick with excitement. Fawzy would sit down and put his arm around her without uttering a word. Then he would lean forward over the table, smoking a spliff as he drank more wine. During that lust-laden silence, Mahmud could not bring himself to say anything. He would just look straight ahead with a fixed smile, embarrassed at being there. Fawzy would carry on as if he were on his own, disregarding Mahmud. He would take a big drag on the spliff, hold the smoke in for maximum effect, then cough, take a glug of wine, wipe his hands across his broad hairy chest, belch loudly—a sign of manliness—and turn to Tafida, who was sitting there on tenterhooks. He would make no show of friendliness nor smile or whisper sweet nothings, instead simply dragging her by the hand into the bedroom when it was time.

The little show that Fawzy put on for Tafida made Mahmud cringe, and he could neither talk nor eat with any appetite. He would have to wait at least an hour for Fawzy to reemerge from the bedroom. He disliked sitting there with nothing to do, but he knew he could not get up and leave. Sometimes, Tafida's lovemaking screams would reach his ears and make him angry for some reason he could not understand. He would go out onto the balcony to look at the cars and pedestrians down below. The time would pass slowly, but finally, Fawzy would appear again, showered and with his clothes back on.

"Come on, Mahmud. We'll be off now!" he would announce proudly.

Fawzy got his two pounds. Then he started choosing items he wanted from her apartment. If he liked something, instead of stealing it, he would place it on the table in the sitting room. After getting his two pounds and carefully putting the banknotes away in his wallet, just as his father did with his earnings from the grocery, Fawzy would pick up the item he had chosen and state casually, "Tafida, I'm taking this."

She did not dare to say a word. She would nod and smile and then cast a long glance at the item, as if to say farewell. Fawzy's plunder included: a perfume bottle, an electric razor, a pocket torch and a bottle of whiskey. Fawzy was earning eight pounds a month from Tafida, not to mention his booty, but he kept all the money for himself rather than sharing it with Mahmud.

"Fawzy! Where's the money you get from Tafida?" Mahmud would ask angrily.

"In a safe place."

"Whatever I get from Rosa and Dagmar, I share it with you immediately, but you stash away your take. You're just selfish, Fawzy."

"Mr. Mahmud! What a thing to say!" Fawzy said quietly as he looked at his friend. "I'm like your brother, and what's mine is yours. I've put the money in a post office account. You never know what might happen. If we need something, we've always got a reserve."

Mahmud was not convinced and felt hurt, but he said nothing more about it and changed the subject. He was not capable of arguing with Fawzy long enough to resolve any matter. Fawzy was his teacher, one who guided and protected him. A soldier could not reproach his commanding officer! The most you could do was offer a comment, but if the officer disagreed, that would be the end of the matter. Mahmud needed Fawzy, and besides, he enjoyed his company. The two of them were living large. Nights out, money, girls. Every pleasure you could think of. The only thing that ruined Mahmud's happiness was having to go to Tafida's apartment with Fawzy. Every week, Fawzy would nag him until he gave in and went along.

The previous time, Mahmud had refused and tried to put his foot down, saying, "Fawzy, I'm not going."

"Why not?"

"Because you're just going there to sleep with her, so why do I have to go?"

"Listen. I want you there. What do you have to lose? You eat and drink for free. What's the problem?"

"I don't need it."

"So, when your friend needs you, you give up on him. Is that what you call being a man?"

"I'd never give up on you, but I'm not going to Tafida's."

Fawzy tried to get him to change his mind, but whenever Mahmud recalled his embarrassment at sitting in the sitting room while Fawzy was banging away at Tafida, he just became angrier. After much haranguing, Fawzy was still having no luck, so he threw his last card down on the table. "All right, Mahmud. You don't need to come to Tafida's ever again. But please, just come tonight, for the last time. Tafida's got a surprise for us."

"What surprise?"

"If I told you, it wouldn't be a surprise!"

Mahmud still appeared hesitant, but Fawzy promised him that it would be worth his while. Tafida had gone to great lengths to try to prepare them a nice surprise, and it would be wrong for Mahmud to cancel. So he should go this time. When the two friends went to Tafida's apartment that evening, the visit proceeded along the usual lines. Tafida offered them a bottle of wine, stuffed vegetables and vine leaves and two roast chickens, one of which Fawzy ate all by himself. Then Fawzy went off to the bathroom and came back wearing the dressing gown over his naked body.

"How are you?" he asked Tafida playfully.

"I'm ready."

"Then get on with it."

Tafida jumped up from her armchair and went into another room as Fawzy smiled mysteriously at Mahmud. After a while, Tafida appeared again in the middle of the hallway.

"Ready?" she called out mischievously.

"You can come in now!" Fawzy replied theatrically.

Mahmud started to feel worried that something strange was about to happen. He turned to ask Fawzy what was going on, but the lights suddenly went off, and they were plunged into total darkness.

SALEHA

I woke up late and took a hot shower, emerging refreshed. I brushed my hair, put on my housedress and went to the kitchen, but my mother was not there. As I looked for her, I noticed that the sitting room door was open, which was unusual. Walking over to it, I beheld a strange sight: my mother was sitting there with a foreign girl. The moment my mother saw me, she rushed over and pulled me by the hand back into the hallway.

"The daughter of a foreigner, the general manager of the Automobile Club, is staying with us," she said softly.

"What does she want?"

"She's had an argument with her father and left home."

"What's it got to do with us?"

"Kamel brought her here. He wants her to stay with us until she can find her own place," my mother said, smiling meaningfully. The mere mention of Kamel's name was enough to make me accept anything.

"If that's what Kamel wants, it's all right with me."

"She'll be sleeping in your bedroom. I'll make up a bed next to yours."

I was immediately taken with what seemed like an exciting adventure.

"What's her name?" I asked.

"Mitsy. Come along. I'll introduce you."

Mitsy jumped up and smiled.

"Are you Saleha? Lovely to meet you. Kamel has told me so much about you."

"And you speak Arabic!"

"Your brother has been teaching me."

The way she pronounced the consonants was childish and sweet. We had some tea and ate breakfast. Mitsy insisted on helping my mother and me in the kitchen. I lent her one of my galabiyyas, and she looked so funny wearing an Egyptian housedress, holding the ladle and listening as I explained how to stir the okra stew. When Kamel appeared, the four of us sat down to eat. We all chatted during the meal, but I felt a sort of silent understanding between Kamel and Mitsy. After lunch, my mother went with Kamel and Mitsy into the sitting room. I tried to call her away so that they could be alone, but she insisted on staying until Kamel went off to study in his bedroom. By the end of the day, I felt completely delighted with what had happened. I told myself that God had sent Mitsy to bring me out of my misery. I sat with her and my mother, who was explaining our circumstances. Mitsy spoke of her love for theater and how much Kamel's lessons had helped her. She spoke of Kamel with enthusiasm and admiration. At the end of our chat, my mother kissed her and said, "I want you to feel at home here, among your family."

She looked at us, my mother and me, and said with some emotion, "Thank you! I shall never forget what you are doing for me."

"It's nothing," my mother answered quickly. "We are really happy to have you with us."

Just before midnight, my mother called Kamel from his bedroom and took him to the roof. After a while, Kamel came down carrying the parts of a fold-up metal bed on his shoulder and spent the better part of an hour putting it together. He then brought down a mattress and pillows, which my mother covered with a sheet and two clean pillowcases. Finally, Kamel threw himself onto the bed to check its stability and gave a satisfied smile. Mitsy laughed.

"If it collapses while I'm sleeping," she said, "you're the one responsible!"

"I'm also responsible for you," he replied.

No one said anything, but I felt that she was moved by his response and that, had I not been there, she would have thrown her arms around him. I felt some sympathy for her feelings, which I could now discern clearly. I was always entranced by love stories, and because

I loved Kamel, I loved anyone he loved. As the days passed, I grew closer to Mitsy. Every night, we would sit up in my bedroom talking until we heard the dawn call to prayer. After a few days, she told me of her problem with her father. I felt for her but was careful not to express a strong opinion about her father's behavior. As angry as she was with him, she might still be upset to hear someone else criticize him.

"Now I'm looking for work," Mitsy said.

"I'm sure you'll find something. You speak Arabic and English, and you're pretty and clever."

She thanked me but looked a little embarrassed. I was astonished to hear myself telling her all my life without feeling embarrassed. I felt that she understood me completely. When I had finished, she stretched out on the bed looking at the ceiling. Then she smiled and said, "Saleha, you have also made a brave and honest decision. You must never go back on it."

"Abd el-Barr is refusing to divorce me."

"Forget about finalizing a divorce. The most important thing is for you to start studying again."

"I feel like a failure."

"How can you be a failure when you haven't started your life yet? You haven't done anything wrong. It's your family who made a mistake."

"They didn't pressure me."

"How could you have married a man you didn't know?"

"I told myself that I'd get to know him after marriage."

"Marriage isn't a means of getting to know someone. You have to know the man and be in love with him, and then, at a certain moment, you both decide to spend the rest of your lives together. Then marriage makes sense."

"Lots of girls get married before getting to know their husbands."

"Marriage without love is a contract for the sale of a woman's body, whatever religious or legal face we put on it. If you get married without love, then you're just a piece of merchandise."

I had never thought of it that way. If that was the crux of marriage, then all that merriment and celebration was just to prettify a commercial transaction.

"I disagree. I can't deny that I agreed too hastily to marry Abd al-Barr, but I have never been a piece of merchandise."

She jumped up from the bed and came over to me.

"I'm so sorry, Saleha," she said. "I always get carried away with my opinions. I'm always upsetting my friends without meaning to."

I gave her a kiss on the cheek. Her hair smelled lovely. I got up, went to do my ablutions and said my prayers as Mitsy watched. When I finished, I took off my headscarf, and Mitsy said, "You look so beautiful when you're praying."

That night, we did not end up going to bed until after the dawn prayer. When I woke up at noon, I looked over and noticed that her bed was empty. After a while, I heard a light knocking on the door. Mitsy came in smiling and said, "I waited until you woke up . . ."

I noticed that she was carrying a heavy linen bag. She threw it down onto the bed and took out a pile of books.

"These are the books for the baccalaureate," she said excitedly. "Kamel brought them while you were sleeping."

38

The staff had waited eagerly for Suleyman and Karara to come back from their meeting with Alku. They all found a moment from their work to go down to the entrance door or to go up to the restaurant to ask about the outcome.

"What happened with Alku?" they all asked.

Suleyman and Karara seemed to have agreed to give the same answer: "Come to the café tomorrow at five o'clock, and we'll talk."

The staff's anxieties ran wild. Some of them thought that this answer meant that Karara and Suleyman had failed in their mission, while others thought that they merely wanted to save themselves the kerfuffle of having to repeat themselves over and over again. The following day, most of the staff went to the café, filling the whole right side. Abdoun and his friends sat on the left. Suleyman waited until everyone had settled down and then made his way with Karara to the center of the café. There was silence as Suleyman stated slowly, "Alku refuses to let us have our tips again."

Shouts of objection went up, but Suleyman waited until they calmed down again before continuing, "Alku wants to be sure first that we have understood the error of our ways before he lets us have our tips."

"Alku has to give us our tips! It's our right!" said Abdoun.

Suleyman gave him a look of rage and shouted, "Hey, son! What job do you do?"

"I'm an assistant barman."

"You're a servant, then!"

"No, Suleyman. I'm not a servant. I do my job and I get paid."

"And we," said Suleyman angrily, "have been servants our whole lives long and accepted our situation and were happy until you put a wrench in the works."

"God forgive you!"

"You, Abdoun, and Bahr and Samahy and the rest of your lot— you have your way of thinking, and we have ours. You want to go head-to-head with Alku! You're the cause of our woes."

Abdoun smiled sadly and replied, "Suleyman, we objected to Alku's beatings."

Avoiding his glance, Suleyman responded, "Well, thanks a million, Abdoun. We don't need more problems. We were happy and contented until you turned up and started agitating. And now, the whole Club is in chaos. All the arguments and squabbles have left us unable to earn a living."

Some voices seconded Suleyman's opinion.

"Abdoun," Suleyman shouted, getting himself worked up, "you knew what the Club was from the start. You must have been told, before you came to work here, that Alku is strict and hard-hearted. So why did you come?"

"It's our right to work, and it's our right to be treated with respect."

Suleyman blew his top at this, screaming at Abdoun, "You can speak for yourself but not for us!"

There were shouts of support for Suleyman, but Abdoun looked at him and said, "Alku will never reinstate the tips just because you beg him and kiss his hand. We have to take a united stance and demand our rights."

"You can take your united stance and stick it," replied Suleyman. "We have a different plan. We will keep begging him to forgive us until he reinstates the tips."

Abdoun looked at his colleagues with a mixture of sorrow and disgust.

"We," he told them, "will neither beg for forgiveness nor kiss any hands. We will defend our rights and make him reinstate the tips. You'll see for yourselves."

Abdoun turned to leave the café amid a clamor of sarcastic jeers:

"We'll see about that, idiot!"

"You're not as clever as you think!"

"You're deluded!"

Abdoun walked straight on without turning back, followed by Samahy and Bahr and some others. Suleyman then continued solemnly, "Brothers! We have nothing to do with them. Karara and I are going to beg Alku again tonight, and please God, he will listen to us."

KAMEL

It was our second meeting in one week. The comrades had managed to complete the mission ahead of schedule. We had distributed thousands of photographs in most of the provinces. I decided to show up ahead of the meeting in the hope that the prince might bring up the personal matter that he had offered to help with, but he did not mention it. It was as if the conversation had never happened and as if he had not promised to help me. I resented being ignored and told myself that while Prince Shamel was a good man, a fighter and an artist, he did not have time for my problems.

Now I regretted having sought him out for help and felt dismayed and frustrated. My only consolation was Mitsy's presence in our apartment. She was curious about everything, and it was delightful to see her standing in the kitchen with my mother. She was enjoying real Egyptian life. Once, she asked me to go up to the roof with her to watch Saleha hanging out the wash.

"I have seen clothes being hung out since I was a child," I told her.

"Come up to the roof with me," she said, smiling, "and I'll show you just how beautiful it is.

Saleha blushed and said softly, "I don't think it's worth watching what I do."

Paying no attention to Saleha's comment, Mitsy grabbed one side of the washtub while Saleha grabbed the other. I opened the front door for them, and our procession went up the stairs. I was taken by the oddity of the scene. An Egyptian girl and an English girl carrying the wash. Mitsy Wright, born and raised in London, carrying a tub of damp clothes on al-Sadd al-Gawany Street. They put the tub underneath the line on the roof. Mitsy pulled me back a few steps by the hand and told me, "Stand here so that you can see properly. Now, Saleha, please start hanging out the wash, and imagine that we are not watching you. Try to pretend that you are alone."

Saleha seemed a little confused but leaned over and took out an article of clothing and started hanging it out.

"The hanging of the wash," Mitsy said in the tones of a teacher addressing a class of children, "is one of the most beautiful expressions of Egyptian femininity. When an Egyptian woman reaches out to arrange an item on the line, her body achieves its highest humanity, realizing the height of her attractiveness and powers of seduction."

Saleha stopped and looked at us with an embarrassed smile.

"Please don't be embarrassed," Mitsy said. "I'm not talking about you personally. I'm an actor, and I have studied body language. I just want to explain how beautiful the sight is to Kamel."

Saleha bent down and pulled out another item to put on the line.

"Just look how the form exudes femininity," Mitsy carried on enthusiastically. "As an Egyptian woman hangs out the wash, she is as alluring as a belly dancer in whose dance the seduction is frank and direct, a sort of invitation to sex. When a woman is hanging out the wash, her appeal is subdued and coy. The woman moves as if unaware of the excitement she arouses in any man watching her. Look. When the woman puts the clothes peg in her mouth and then takes it in her two fingers to peg the wash on the line, the use of the peg is loaded with strong, sensual overtones."

That was more than Saleha could bear. She dropped the wet shirt into the tub.

"Mitsy!" she said with apparent anger. "I can't concentrate on what I'm doing. Either leave me alone or I'll go downstairs and come back in the afternoon."

"Okay," Mitsy said with a laugh. "I'm sorry."

We left Saleha hanging out the wash. Mitsy brought as much happiness into our family as a young child discovering things for the first time, making silly comments which made everyone laugh and enjoy repeating them.

That night, I studied past two in the morning. I went to take a shower, wearing just my trousers and a shirt. Since Mitsy had come to stay with us, I never went out of my room in just my pajamas. I was walking down the corridor, but before I reached the bathroom door, I heard a whisper behind me, "Kamel . . ."

I turned around, and there was Mitsy standing in the dull glow of the night-light.

"What's wrong?" I asked.

"I want to talk to you."

Confused, I replied, "Mitsy, if my mother finds us standing here together, she'll be angry."

"Why would your mother be angry?"

"Because I promised not to be alone with you in our apartment."

Mitsy ignored what I had said and whispered, "Kamel, I'm in love with you."

I stood there saying nothing, hardly able to breathe. Mitsy came so close that I could smell her delicate perfume, and she gave me a peck on the lips. Then she smiled, turned and retreated back to Saleha's bedroom, shutting the door behind her. I was rooted to the spot. It felt like I was dreaming, but my astonishment gave way to joy. Mitsy had freed me of my deepest worries and anxieties. She had made me confront a reality I had long been trying to avoid: that I was in love with her too. I loved her voice, her laugh, her smile, her face and her hands. I even found the mistakes in Arabic entrancing. I went back to my bedroom and slept blissfully, waking up refreshed. After I showered and got dressed, I found Mitsy having breakfast with my mother and Saleha. She gave me a knowing smile.

"I'm late for work," I said.

"Wait a moment," Mitsy told me excitedly.

She quickly made me a sandwich, and as she gave it to me, she said, "You like white cheese. Take this and eat it on the way."

Saleha smiled, and my mother then added in a half-serious tone of voice, "Take it! Don't embarrass the girl!"

I took a taxi to save time. En route, I thought of Mitsy. Her kindness this morning had a new flavor. I thought of her delicate fingers as she gave me the sandwich. Where did all that beauty come from?

I finished all my chores at work, and then, having asked permission from Monsieur Comanus, I sat down to study. By the time the clock struck five, Comanus had already left, and I was alone in the storeroom. Suddenly, Khalil appeared and told me excitedly, "Kamel! Come quickly. Prince Shamel has sent his car. It's waiting for you in front of the Club."

I turned off the lights and locked the storeroom door, trying to guess why he was asking for me. Was he going to give me a new mission? A servant led me to the prince's office, where I found a surprise waiting for me. Abd el-Barr was sitting there in front of the prince. I did all I could to remain calm.

"Welcome, Kamel," the prince said with a smile. "Please, take a seat."

I shook the prince's hand and sat down on the sofa. I noted that Abd el-Barr was avoiding my eye.

"You charged me with finding a solution to your sister Saleha's problem," the prince said. "I have spoken with Abd el-Barr about the question of a divorce, and he seems willing to come to some understanding."

"Basically," interrupted Abd el-Barr, "I don't want her. It was a mistake to marry into this family."

"Watch what you are saying!" I shouted at him.

Abd el-Barr shot a furious look at me and retorted, "I am watching what I'm saying, in spite of you."

I jumped to my feet in anger, but the prince shouted at me, "Kamel! Please stay seated. We are not here to argue."

There was silence for a few moments; then Abd el-Barr cleared his throat and continued, "Your Royal Highness, I have spent a lot of money on this abortive marriage. I just want my money back."

"What money?" I shouted. "You scoundrel."

"Be quiet, Kamel!" the prince shouted. Then he turned to Abd el-Barr and said calmly, "Mr. Abd el-Barr, tomorrow my secretary will contact you to finalize the divorce. With regard to your expenses, we shall pay them for you."

I was about to object, but I said nothing out of respect for the prince, who continued, "So have we come to an agreement? You are a clever man and surely don't wish to create problems. Thus, I expect you'll fulfill your part, remembering that while I prefer an amicable solution, I have other means at my disposal."

Abd el-Barr nodded but made no comment. The prince shifted his attention to some documents on the desk before him. That was a signal for Abd el-Barr to leave. He stood up and shook hands with the prince, and then he passed near me as he was leaving and mumbled, "Good-bye."

I did not answer. The moment he was gone, I blurted out, "Sir, that man is making a fool of us."

The prince smiled, leaned back in his chair and said, "Kamel, I'm old enough to be your father and am much more experienced than you. Abd el-Barr's honor has been wounded because you all know that he is an impotent drug addict. It's natural that he should try to take his revenge on you. You were not here for my whole meeting with him. Had I not threatened him, he would not have agreed to a divorce. My secretary will give him a reasonable sum of money, and if he still refuses, then I will resort to other methods."

"Might I know how much money you're going to offer him?"

"By God, that's none of your business!" the prince said with a laugh.

"Thank you, sir," I said.

The prince got up from behind his desk and walked over to me. I jumped to my feet. He put his hand on my shoulder and said, "I have also taken care of the other matter. A small, furnished apartment in Garden City has been rented for your friend Mitsy. The rent is paid for a year, and this week I shall find her some work."

"Sir, I cannot find the words to thank you."

"There's no need for gratitude among friends," he interrupted. "I decided on an apartment in Garden City so that you can have complete privacy. It will be a fantastic love nest."

He winked and let out one of his guffaws. I was dazzled by his nobility of spirit and felt guilty at having thought that he'd forgotten about me. In an effort to relieve me of my feeling of indebtedness, he said in a serious tone, "Soon, we will be assigning new tasks to you for the organization. Come with me. I want to give you something."

I followed him across the spacious hall to the studio. He turned on the light and then took out from a cupboard something that looked like a cigarette-rolling machine, the same size as the radio in the sitting room of our apartment. He set it down in front of me on the desk and said, "This is a paper shredder. Take it. All your colleagues have one. It's very easy to use. Put the paper in this side and turn the knob like this. Before you go to sleep tonight, you must destroy all the organization documents you have."

39

It happened during the busiest time of day, when the king was there and the Club was crowded. The bar was teeming with customers when Bahr shot a look at his assistant, Abdoun, and the two of them left the bar together. There was something resolute about their gait, as if they were leaving, never to return. In the kitchen, Samahy suddenly got up and walked out without requesting permission from Rikabi, who started calling after him, but he disappeared quickly without looking back.

"By your mother's life," Rikabi roared, "you'll pay for this."

The same thing took place in the restaurant. The waiters, Nouri, Banan and Fidali, to the customers' astonishment, set down the plates they had been carrying on the nearest table and walked out of the restaurant. In the casino, Jaber and Bashir also walked out. They all stopped work at the exact same moment and, as if according to plan, all started walking away. They went down the stairs and assembled in the Club's entrance. No explanation was forthcoming until Bahr went to Maître Shakir and told him that he and his colleagues were waiting for him in front of the telephone cabin. Bahr did not give Shakir a chance to reply or ask anything. He got to the end of his sentence, then turned and went back to join the others. What happened that night will forever remain unique in the annals of the Automobile Club: eight members of the staff stopped work without permission and assembled in protest in the Club's entrance hall. Maître Shakir rushed over to them and said in hushed, but angry, tones, "What's got into you? Have you taken leave of your senses?"

Abdoun answered immediately, "We are not working, and we want to see Alku."

Maître Shakir looked at him with incredulity and said, "You want to see Alku? Go to his office!"

"We are staying here," said Bahr, "until Alku comes to see us."

As if knowing that there was no point in discussing the matter, Shakir turned and said, "All right. You don't want to work? Don't work! But standing here will get you nowhere. His Majesty is upstairs, and the Club members will see you as they come and leave."

No one answered. They stood their ground. Maître Shakir, in growing confusion, thought it over for a few moments and then said, "Go into one of the offices until Alku arrives."

The offer was unexpected, and the men looked at each other hesitantly, but Bahr decided the matter by saying, "We are not moving until we see Alku."

The group muttered support, and Maître Shakir did not argue further. He disappeared inside the telephone cabin for a few minutes, then came out and, without acknowledging the men still standing there, went directly up the stairs and rushed back to the restaurant. Club members coming in through the front door on their way to the lift looked with astonishment at the strikers standing there, immobile and silent, as if they themselves could not believe what they were doing. Were they really refusing to work and waiting to confront Alku? It seemed like a strange dream. They knew that Alku would arrive at any moment, and yet they felt no fear. They were holding their ground to a degree that astonished even them. Where did they get their courage? It was as if, the moment they got over their initial fear, it disappeared completely. At that moment, they felt different. They were not servants, and Alku was not their master. They were staff at the Club demanding their rights, and if they felt so inclined, they could refrain from working. Their self-assuredness manifested itself in a new attitude and tone of voice.

"Listen, men!" Samahy called out. "When Alku gets here, let me talk with him."

They looked at him and smiled. There was a certain disparity between his skinny build and the audacity he was showing.

"I'll be doing the talking," Bahr said. "I know Alku better than you."

Samahy looked resentful, but Bahr laughed and added, "Don't get angry, Samahy. I'll let you talk, but when I've finished."

Samahy nodded, and after a short while, Alku appeared, striding across the threshold, followed by Hameed and Suleyman the doorman. The strikers stood where they were. They did not rush over to greet him as usual.

"Why have you left your posts?" he asked with a breathless scowl.

"Your Excellency," said Bahr firmly, "we have been working for nothing for three months."

"It's the same for your colleagues."

"We've got nothing to do with them," replied Bahr. "We're the ones standing here in front of you, and we won't go back to work until we get what we're owed."

Alku looked them over as if unable to believe what was happening, and then in a strange, hoarse voice, he said, "Get back to work."

"We will only go back to work," said Bahr, "when you have returned our tips to us, because that's what we're owed."

"Yes!" added Samahy, who could hold himself back no longer. "If you want us to go to work, pay us what we're owed."

That did it. Puny little Samahy, to whom Alku usually never addressed a word and whose name he could not bring himself to utter, was standing up to his master! Alku glowered and ground his teeth.

"For the last time," he announced, "don't be stupid and go back to work."

His voice boomed terrifyingly, and then there was silence. He stared at the men, but they just stood there, immovable and unshakable.

"We have made it clear," said Abdoun. "No pay, no work."

"What's come over you, you sons of dogs!" shrieked Hameed, shaking with rage. "Is that any way to speak to your master?"

"Let them be," Alku said, turning to Hameed. "They can do what they want."

He spoke that last sentence as if it had some hidden meaning, then turned slowly and walked out of the Club. After a few steps outside, he stopped with his back toward them and addressed someone out of sight. Suddenly, a whistle sounded, and soldiers ran into the Club. There was no way for the strikers to put up any resistance. The soldiers arrested them and violently dragged them out. The strikers shouted out in protest, but the soldiers kept slapping and kicking them until they got them into the police car waiting for them outside the door.

SALEHA

Why did I love Mitsy so much?

Because she was nice and well mannered, and because Kamel loved her, and I loved anyone Kamel loved. Perhaps I liked the experience itself—that I should be friends with an English girl who spoke Arabic and wanted to learn all about Egyptian life. I never felt the passage of time when I was with Mitsy. We would chat and discuss things and laugh a lot. She insisted on helping my mother and me with the housework, asking about everything I was doing. She learned things I never imagined would interest any English girl. The moments we enjoyed the most were when we were having a cup of coffee together. We would sit on the balcony around the large brass table on which we would place the burner, the cups and the cold water perfumed with a few drops of rosewater.

One Wednesday after early evening prayers, as we were getting ready to drink our coffee, Mitsy took the packet of coffee beans from me and said, "I'll make the coffee today."

She was wearing a blue dress and had pulled her hair back into a ponytail, revealing her dainty ears. A few minutes later, Mitsy looked at me as I was sipping the coffee, and laughed, "Sometimes I imagine that we're two women living in an Ottoman sultan's court."

"Why at a court?"

With a wave of her hand, Mitsy dismissed my comment and said, "Oh . . . the sultan's wives generally didn't do anything. They spent their days in the bathhouse and making themselves beautiful.

We would look after our bodies and get ourselves ready, because the sultan might summon us to his bed at any moment."

"Would you like to play a role like that onstage?"

"Of course I would! But even if the chance never came, I could always enjoy fantasizing about it! An actor must be able to imagine lives outside his own."

Mitsy was silent for a moment and then asked me, "Do you believe in reincarnation?"

It was so typical of her to change the subject so suddenly.

"I've read about it," I said.

"Could it not be possible that our souls have lived previously in different places and circumstances and that we died and have been reincarnated into this life?"

"It's possible. But I'm a Muslim, and in my religion God tells us that our spirit is in His hands and that he has sole control of it."

"Well, I often feel that in a previous life, I was an Egyptian woman. Egypt feels so familiar to me that this can't be the first time I have been here. Even when I speak with you, Saleha, I feel that I have seen and heard you before."

Mitsy fell silent for a moment and then added, "I just hope you don't think I'm mad!"

We both laughed, and then she changed the subject again. "How are you getting on with your studies?"

"I'm trying as hard as I can, but it hasn't been easy."

"I'll remind you of that after you pass the exams with flying colors."

Then we suddenly heard two light taps on the apartment door: Kamel's signature knock.

"Come in!" I said.

I had never seen Kamel happier than he was at that moment. He shook hands with Mitsy, kissed me on my cheeks and then said nothing for a while, as if he was trying to control himself. He put his hand in the pocket of his waistcoat and took out a folded piece of paper.

"Congratulations, Saleha!" he said. "Here's your divorce."

I could not take it in immediately, but then I jumped up and threw my arms around him and kept repeating, "Thank God! Thank

God!" I started crying, and a few minutes later my mother came in to congratulate me. It occurred to me that the last thing I had expected when I married Abd el-Barr was that my marriage would turn into such a nightmare that we should all be celebrating the divorce.

My mother then asked Mitsy if she had ever eaten *fatta*.

"I've heard of it," Mitsy answered.

"Well, I'm going to make *fatta* with beef," my mother said.

"Mother!" Kamel laughed. "I have to warn you. Mitsy is English, and her digestion might not be up to Egyptian *fatta*!"

Mitsy dismissed his comment with a wave of her hand as my mother put her arm around her saying, "Nonsense. I'm sure that she'll love it."

We had a wonderful evening. I laughed like I had never laughed in my life. Mitsy looked lovely in a flannel galabiyya with her hair pulled back as she stood in the kitchen helping my mother with the *fatta*. We ate and then drank cup after cup of tea, celebrating until the dawn call to prayer. Kamel went off to his bedroom, and Mitsy went to mine. I did my ablutions, and my mother and I said some extra prayers of thanks before our morning prayers. I slept more deeply than I had done for a long time.

The following day, I woke up after the noon call to prayer and found another surprise. Mitsy was in the sitting room, her suitcase in front of her and Kamel sitting next to her. My mother told me that Mitsy was leaving our home because she had found an apartment. I was shocked. Without thinking, I said, "Even if Mitsy has found an apartment, she should stay on with us."

My mother kissed Mitsy on her forehead and said, "We'd like you to stay with us."

Mitsy looked at us with gratitude in her eyes and said, "I don't want to leave you either, but I have to. I'll visit you all the time. My apartment in Garden City isn't far away. Saleha, you can bring your books and study in peace and quiet."

I embraced her again, and Kamel said, "We have to be off now. I asked for an hour off work so that I can take Mitsy to her apartment."

It was an emotional farewell. Fighting back tears, Mitsy said, "Thank you. I will never forget what you have done for me."

Kamel picked up the suitcase as Mitsy dragged him by the other hand.

"Why all the drama?" he asked playfully. "Mitsy's new place is only ten minutes away by taxi. You can go and see her every day."

With my divorce, a new stage of my life started. I could see the light at the end of the tunnel. I decided to apply for university and realize my father's wishes. I studied my heart out, and my mother devoted herself to looking after me. She excused me from doing any housework. Kamel signed me up with two private tutors, and though I felt bad about his paying so much, he reassured me, saying, "Thank God our financial situation has improved. The most important thing is that you pass your exams."

I felt like a trooper plunging into battle. I would wake up at dawn, and after a hot shower and breakfast, I would sit down at my desk and study until midnight. I only took breaks to say my prayers, and my mother brought me endless cups of tea and sandwiches. I went to visit Mitsy in her apartment at least once a week, and she visited us a lot too. In spite of being exhausted from studying, I felt confident and optimistic. I no longer thought of what I had been through at the hands of Abd el-Barr.

Aisha told me, "Don't look back! Forget that snake, Abd el-Barr. I'll get you married off to the best man in Cairo. You'll see!"

"The most important thing," I replied, "is for me to pass my exams and get into university."

Aisha let out a resounding laugh and said, "Well, education may be really important, but in our society no woman can do without a husband."

My brother Said no longer visited us, excusing himself by saying that he had to stay close to his pregnant wife, but we knew that he was punishing us for my divorce. We learned from Aisha that Abd el-Barr had decided not to go into business with him. I tried to console my mother by telling her that Said could not do without his mother and siblings and that eventually he would come around. Unfortunately, deep down, I rather enjoyed his absence. We had a carefree existence for a while, although I don't even remember how long it lasted— three or four weeks maybe.

Then that night arrived. It was after three in morning, and I was in my bedroom engrossed in my mathematics problems when I heard a sound in the hallway. I thought it was Kamel coming home. The noise got gradually louder, and I heard footsteps. I realized that something strange was happening. I got up and listened through my closed door. The hubbub was getting closer, and then suddenly I heard my mother shout, "No one is to go near my daughter!"

40

The lights went out, and Mahmud could not see a thing. Alarmed, he called out, "What's going on?"

In the darkness, Fawzy laughed. "You frightened? Pull yourself together, Mr. Mahmud!"

"But what's wrong with the lights?"

"Didn't I just tell you that Tafida has got a surprise for us!"

"And is that surprise," asked Mahmud sarcastically, "leaving us in the dark?"

"Just be patient, man!" Fawzy laughed.

A few minutes passed in the pitch-black. Mahmud flicked his cigarette lighter, which gave off a dull light as he groped his way toward the front door.

"Look, Fawzy. You and Tafida can play around as much as you like, but I'm going."

"Just wait a moment!" Fawzy shouted back.

Mahmud hesitated, and before he could decide what to do, the lights suddenly came on. Mahmud shut his eyes, and when he opened them again, he saw a strange sight. Tafida al-Sarsawy was standing in the middle of the room dressed as a belly dancer. Two skimpy pieces of cloth decorated with beads and sequins covered her chest, and she had a piece of cloth tied around her waist as a belt, showing off her scrawny body. The sight of her, nearly naked, in the belly dancer costume was pitiful. Her tired face caked with makeup, her bony body with its sagging flesh and flat chest were all a rather sad memory of femininity. It looked as if she had not been able to find a costume in her own size and was swimming in this one. Mahmud was beset by conflicting emotions as he watched Tafida in her outfit. He let out a laugh, which Tafida interpreted as one of admiration as she continued her little show. She held her arms up and twirled around.

"What a temptress! You're such a tease!" Fawzy called out.

Mahmud burst out laughing, and Tafida looked at him.

"Do you like it?" she asked.

"It's beautiful," replied Mahmud, trying to suppress his laughter.

Fawzy got up and poured two glasses of whiskey, one for himself and one for Mahmud, then went over to Tafida, patting her on the backside.

"I want to watch you dance!"

Tafida walked over to the gramophone and put on a record, and Fawzy started clapping enthusiastically. It was a piece that Samia Gamal used to dance to, but as Tafida nervously quivered through it, it was as if she were in spasms. Fawzy was clapping in time with the music and looking at Mahmud, egging him on to join in. Mahmud clapped feebly, but he could not help sitting back in the chair and laughing. Tafida was now in the full swing of her show and kept dancing until the record was finished. Sweat was running down her face, and she was out of breath. Fawzy and Mahmud applauded as Tafida made a stagy bow and then turned the record over and started dancing again. Mahmud had stopped laughing and was starting to find the whole spectacle rather tedious. The music stopped, and Fawzy jumped up.

"Go easy on us, you naughty, naughty lady!" he said ironically. "You're killing us with your sex appeal!"

He took her in his arms, but she wriggled out of them.

"Darling, I'm a little sweaty from the dance," she said with all the femininity she could summon up. "Let me go and take a shower."

She darted off down the corridor to the bathroom as Fawzy poured himself another whiskey, which he downed in one go. He sighed and his face flushed. Then he picked up his packet of cigarettes and the lighter and smiled proudly at Mahmud.

"By your leave, Mr. Mahmud!"

Fawzy made his way to the bedroom to wait for Tafida. Mahmud's impression of the ridiculousness that had just transpired now turned to deep gloom. He was furious at Fawzy for having forced him to watch this nonsense. What did he have to do with Tafida? She was Fawzy's mistress. And why had Tafida left them sitting in the darkness before she appeared as a bag of bones in a belly dancer outfit? Watching that old hag flaunt herself had made him feel angry and humiliated. He was furious and cursed Fawzy silently but still managed to convince himself, "In spite of all the goings-on, I'll be a decent guy and won't walk out on Fawzy tonight. I'll wait for him, but I swear by God that it's the last time I come here."

Mahmud wandered around the sitting room, looking at the photographs on the wall. Tafida had been really beautiful when young, but how she had changed. In the old photographs, she looked like a film star. There was a picture of her at the seaside, another in a garden and one of her wearing an evening dress and sitting at a dining table with a group of glamorous men and women. Had he met Tafida when she was young, he might have fallen for her, but now she simply aroused his disgust. Mahmud went out onto the balcony, lit a cigarette and with his elbows on the railing stood there looking at the traffic below. Suddenly, he heard a strange sound. He turned around and found Fawzy standing there completely naked.

"Mahmud. Help! Come quickly!"

"What's happened?"

Fawzy did not reply but rushed back to the bedroom. Mahmud tossed his cigarette over the balcony and ran after him. They ran down the corridor. The bedroom door was open, and the light was on, but the moment Mahmud went into the room, he saw a terrifying sight. Tafida was sprawled on a corner of the bed, completely naked, her eyes closed, her head lying limp next to a pillow.

"What's the matter with her?" Mahmud shouted hoarsely.

"I was giving it to her," Fawzy answered in a state of agitation. "She was doing just beautifully, but suddenly she screamed and then this . . ."

"Do you think she has fainted?" Mahmud asked tremulously.

Fawzy muttered under his breath and went over to her. He placed her head on a pillow and then started tapping her on the cheek and calling her, "Tafida . . . Get up! Stop playacting."

Tafida didn't stir. She was supine on the bed, her eyes tightly shut. For the first time, Mahmud noticed the red nightdress lying on the floor. After a few moments, Fawzy tried calling her name again, but she remained silent and motionless. Fawzy leaned over her head and held his fingers in front of her nostrils for a while. Then, his face ashen, he turned to Mahmud and whispered, "I think she's dead."

"Oh, hell!" Mahmud cried.

Fawzy looked down and said nothing.

"Tafida, dead?" Mahmud started wailing. "We're both done for. We're done for."

Fawzy said nothing. Then he had an idea. He grabbed Mahmud by the hand and told him forcefully, "Pull yourself together and act like a man. Tafida was over seventy. Her time was up. What could we do about it? People don't live forever. When their term ends, they cannot live a single hour longer . . ."

But he could not remember how the verse from the Quran ended. Not only that, but he realized it was a strange moment to be relying on the holy book. Still stark naked, he continued speaking in a low voice, as if addressing himself, "She can't have been well to start off with. I think she exhausted herself by dancing, and then I was giving it to her so hard that she couldn't cope and just kicked the bucket . . ."

Mahmud stared at Fawzy, sweat running down his face. As he was picking up the nightdress from the floor, he called out, "Come on, help me. We have to get her into the nightdress and make it look like she was in bed as normal . . ."

Mahmud helped Fawzy to sit the corpse upright, and he held her by the shoulders so Fawzy could get her into the nightdress and lay her back down again. Fawzy then got dressed quickly and dragged Mahmud down the corridor.

"We can't leave any trace," he said as they reached the sitting room.

Fazwi took out a white handkerchief and started wiping any surface which might have their fingerprints on it. The glasses, the door handles and table. This activity, which was straight from the movies, only served to increase Mahmud's anxiety. He felt he had turned into a criminal like the ones he had seen at the cinema. Fawzy finished wiping down everything, put the handkerchief back in his pocket and started giving Mahmud precise instructions: throw the cigarette butts out of the window, wash the ashtrays, dry them carefully and put them back where they were, put the food back in the fridge, wash the plates and put them back on the rack in the kitchen.

The two friends busied themselves doing all that for about half an hour, and then Fawzy cast a beady eye around the room and said "The last step is the doorman . . . I'm sure that he didn't see us coming up here."

"Even if he didn't see us coming in," Mahmud said despairingly, "he'll see us going out."

"Would you just listen to me!"

Mahmud's feeling of terror returned.

"God sees everything," Mahmud cried. "I'm done for, and it's all your fault."

"If you carry on wailing like an old woman," Fawzy warned him, "the neighbors will hear, and they'll call the police."

The word "police" was enough to silence Mahmud immediately.

"The door of the doorman's cabin," he continued calmly, "is sometimes open and sometimes just a little ajar. We can't take the lift down because the moment he hears the lift, he will open his door. We'll go down the stairs, and if his door is open, we'll wait until he shuts it, but if the door is just a little ajar, we'll be able to slip out onto the street."

These details just went in one of Mahmud's ears and out of the other. He said nothing, becoming so overcome with terror that he could hardly breathe until he thought he was going to pass out.

"If you want to get out of this mess," Fawzy tried to encourage him, "do as I say."

At the front door of the apartment, Fawzy took out his handkerchief and wrapped it round the knob before opening the door. Then he did the same to shut the door behind them. The stairwell was dark, but Fawzy took care not to turn on the light. They walked slowly and gingerly downstairs in the dark, trying as hard as they could not to make a sound or trip. Tafida's apartment was on the fourth floor, and it was now past one in the morning. They had the luck not to bump into anyone on the stairs. Then they had another stroke of luck in finding the doorman's door open only a crack.

"God help us," groaned Mahmud.

"Now walk behind me and don't make any noise," said Fawzy.

Mahmud walked behind Fawzy as he headed to the front door of the building. Fawzy walked quietly past the doorman's cabin with Mahmud almost frozen behind him. The two walked across the wide lobby, and when they reached the front door, they realized that they had done it. Fawzy gave a huge sigh of relief.

"Thank God! Now just walk as if there's nothing wrong," he told Mahmud.

Mahmud nodded and walked along slowly, looking ahead as if just taking a stroll. They had only gone a few steps before they heard the sound of someone screaming behind them. Mahmud froze, but Fawzy turned to face him and shouted, "Run, Mahmud!"

The two start running as fast as their feet would take them as the shouts of their pursuers became shriller and shriller.

KAMEL

It was almost three o'clock in the morning as I made my way home . . . I had left work at the Club to go to a meeting at the prince's and then went to check on Mitsy. After that, I went to study with a friend in al-Rawda Street. I was exhausted. I had a splitting headache and could hardly put one foot in front of another. Dying for a hot shower and a good, deep sleep, I reminded myself that I was off work the next day.

Al-Sadd Street was almost empty. Before I had passed the tram stop, I was surprised to find a man I did not recognize standing in front of me, barring my way. He gave me a strange look and then took out a cigarette and placed it in his mouth.

"Can you give me a light?" he said.

I put my hand into my pocket to fish out my lighter. As he brought his head closer in order to get a light for his cigarette, I felt that something dodgy was going on. The man thanked me and went on his way. When I reached our front door, I climbed up the stairs, letting myself in with my key. I did not want to wake my mother. I took a shower, put on my pajamas and threw myself on the bed. I had hardly put my head on the pillow when I heard a knock at the front door. It was loud and incessant. I hurried to the door, and as I turned the handle, I was startled to feel the door being pushed open forcefully, almost knocking me to the ground. There were four of them: three men in plainclothes and behind them a uniformed police officer. He scowled as he gave me a cold, searching look.

"Are you Kamel Abd el-Aziz Gaafar?" he asked in a loud voice.

"Yes."

"We have an order for your arrest and to search the apartment."

"Do you have a warrant?"

"I don't need a warrant," he smiled ironically.

It was then I noticed that the man standing next to the officer was the very same one who had asked me for a light. I saw there was no point provoking the officer and asked him calmly, "What do I have to do?"

"Go inside and wake up your family members. Then we'll start the search."

The officer strode over to the sofa in the sitting room, sat down and lit a cigarette. I went down the corridor, followed by the secret agents. When I reached my mother's bedroom, I turned to face the agents, and they moved back a few steps. To this day, I do not know why my mother had not woken up from the knocking on the door. I turned on the light and sat at the edge of the bed. I stroked her face gently and she stirred and opened her eyes. She looked at me worriedly.

"Is everything all right, son?" she asked.

"The police are here," I said in a low voice. "They want to search the apartment and arrest me."

My mother looked down, and her breathing became labored.

"Have you done something wrong?" she asked hoarsely.

"No."

"Then why do they want to arrest you?"

"It's political."

Either she could not take in the answer, or she realized that it was not the moment to ask any more questions. She got out of bed and put a black galabiyya over her nightdress. She fixed a scarf over her head and glanced at herself in the mirror.

"Where do they want to search?"

"Your bedroom, and then Saleha's and Mahmud's."

For as long as I live, I will remain in awe of my mother's strength of spirit that night, of how she took the shock, regained her composure and behaved with determination. The agent came in, ransacked the room and went out again. They found nothing. That night, Mahmud was staying over at a friend's. I went into the corridor and found

Saleha sobbing. My mother had woken her up. The agents searched Saleha and Mahmud's rooms and then took a long time searching mine. They went over to the officer carrying the material they had seized. The officer looked at it carefully and then asked me, "Are you reading books on Marxism?"

"We are studying Marxism at the law college."

"And books on political agitation?"

"I bought them from the book stalls in the Ezbekiyeh Gardens. I like reading about lots of things."

The officer smiled and gestured toward the shredder, which one of the agents was holding.

"All right then, sonny. Perhaps you can explain the purpose of this machine . . ."

"A paper shredder."

"So you have to shred your lectures?"

He gave a sarcastic laugh and then stood up and said, "Come with us."

The man whose cigarette I'd lit came over to me, grabbed my hands and cuffed me. Saleha screamed, but my mother calmed her down. I did not resist, perhaps because it seemed as if I were watching this happen to somebody else. The agent pushed me along in front of him, with the others following behind, and my mother running along behind them calling out, "Where are you taking him?"

"We're inviting him over for a cup of coffee," the officer said.

"I think," I told the officer, "that my family at least have the right to know where you are going to be holding me."

The officer mulled it over for a moment and then told my mother, "Kamel will be held at the Sayyida Zeinab police station."

I looked at the two of them, my mother and Saleha, and tried to give them a comforting smile. At the very bottom of the staircase, I suddenly heard Saleha sobbing out my name as if she had managed to restrain herself until that moment. They took me off in a big black police van, with the officer sitting in front next to the driver while I was in the back between two plainclothes officers. The third had not got into the Black Maria with us. The second we started moving, one of them grabbed my head while the other put a blindfold on me. I tried to struggle but was subjected to a rain of slaps and punches.

"All right, motherfucker. We've got you now. You'll do as we say, if you know what's good for you."

I was already in a new state of mind. I could hear voices around me but could see nothing. After about a quarter of an hour, the Black Maria stopped, and they took me out. We went into some sort of building, up about ten steps and then down a corridor and into a lift. It felt like the second or third floor. We walked down another cold corridor and went into an office. An agent uncuffed me and then removed the blindfold. I felt dizzy, and it took me some time to be able to focus. I saw a bald, corpulent man in his fifties, smartly dressed but there was something unpleasant about his face.

"Nice to have you here, Kamel," he said quietly.

"By law," I retorted, "without a warrant I cannot be arrested and my house cannot be searched. Moreover, I will only answer questions in the presence of a lawyer."

The man laughed as if I had made a joke. He gestured with his hand, and the two agents standing on either side of me started punching me in the stomach and in the head until the man made another gesture and they stopped. Then they dragged me over and sat me down on a bench, sitting beside me on either side.

"So," he smiled, "would you like to contact anyone in particular?"

I said nothing.

"For example," he continued, "would you like to contact Prince Shamel, head of the organization? Sad to say, he's no longer in a position to save you. Prince Shamel himself has been locked up by royal command. All your chums have been locked up too. Abdoun, the Jewess Odette and that Communist Atiya."

He was trying to break me by intimating he knew everything. But I said nothing. I knew that a single wrong word might be enough to get me another kicking. The investigator leaned forward on his desk and asked sotto voce, "Tell me about your girlfriend, Mitsy."

"I will not talk about such things."

The punches started again. The man on my right was aiming his punches at my head. I started to feel dizzy.

"When did you join the organization?" the investigator asked.

"What organization?"

"Kamel. Wise up! Don't throw your future away. We have many means at our disposal. We can do what we want with you. If you make a confession, I promise you I will let you turn witness for the state, and you'll walk scot-free."

SALEHA

It would have been natural for my mother to break down and for me to comfort her, but the opposite happened. My nerves were shattered, and it was my mother who made light of the catastrophe. I could not stop imagining Kamel with his hands shackled and the policeman and security agents standing there with him. In the days that followed, I did not do a moment of studying. I just sat at my desk, unable to stop crying and unable to concentrate. I was astounded at how composed my mother managed to remain. I went with her to the police station in Sayyida Zeinab. The officer in charge took our names. He was a polite man and gave an embarrassed smile.

"Kamel was not brought to this station," he said.

"But the officer who arrested him," my mother told him, "stated he was taking Kamel to the Sayyida Zeinab police station."

"Look, madam," the officer replied, "it sounds like Kamel has been arrested by state security. They generally give out misleading information to the family of the accused."

He said nothing for a moment and then wrote something down on a sheet of paper. "I would advise you to go and ask at the directorate. I will give you the name of a friend of mine there."

I still remember the name of the officer at the directorate. Fathy al-Wakil. He made a few telephone calls and then told us that Kamel was being held in the foreigners' prison. It was far away, and they would not allow us to see him, but finally al-Wakil managed to wheedle permission for us to go and see Kamel on Friday, the weekly visit day. We went home and found Mitsy waiting for us in Aisha's apartment. My mother and I both hugged her. Then we went over to our apartment along with Aisha. We sat in the sitting room sipping tea. Mitsy was nervy and pale. My mother told her and Aisha what we had been doing that day.

"I'm coming along on Friday," Aisha declared.

Mitsy decided to sleep over with us that night, and then she started spending whole days with us, only going back to her apartment to sleep. As for Aisha, yet again she showed her devotion. She did not leave us for a single moment. She sent a lawyer called Gameel Barsoum to see Kamel. He was a kind-looking fat man who came to visit us that evening.

"Did you manage to see Kamel?" my mother asked him apprehensively.

He did not know where to look. He removed his glasses, took out a handkerchief and started wiping the lenses.

"I saw him, and I was present during the interrogation," he said.

"How is he?" Aisha asked him.

"He's all right, thank God."

"I've heard," she said tremulously, "that they torture them there."

Gameel looked down and then went on in a low voice, "Unfortunately, there are signs of bruising on his body, and I have verified this during questioning."

My mother mumbled a few words that I could not make out, and then Aisha shouted, "They'll answer to God, those criminals!"

"Unfortunately," Gameel continued, "torture is a matter of course with state security, but once I have shown the presiding officer evidence of bruising, the interrogators generally ease off."

"And could you tell me," Mitsy asked him sharply, "on what charge he is being held?"

The lawyer gave a wistful smile and said, "Kamel is accused of membership in a secret organization which aims to overthrow the government."

Aisha beat her arm against her breast, shouting, "He's done for! He's done for!"

My mother grimaced and seemed to be expending a huge effort to keep her composure. "My son," she enunciated carefully, "is an honorable man. He has never hurt a fly."

Mitsy gave the lawyer a serious stare, looking for all the world completely English at that moment.

"Has Kamel confessed to membership in this organization?" she asked him.

"No."

"Do you think his legal situation is bad?"

"Definitely. The accusation is serious, and he could get life. The person accused of heading the organization is Prince Shamel, the king's cousin. The king even had his cousin arrested. That's how grave the matter is."

"But you said that Kamel hasn't confessed?"

"Not so far."

"Even if he were to confess, wouldn't they have to take into consideration that it was extracted under duress?"

"Of course. But unfortunately, they have evidence against him. They can connect him to a paper shredder and books on political agitation, and I still don't know whether his colleagues in the organization have confessed or not."

We all sat there in silence, as if every last bit of energy had left us. Gameel tried to lighten the atmosphere a little by smiling and saying to my mother, "Please God, we'll see him on Friday, and we'll be able to see how he's doing then."

Although I was longing to see Kamel, I was afraid at the same time. I would not be able to bear seeing him in a prison uniform with bruises on his face. I could not sleep all Thursday night. I said the dawn prayers with my mother, and we started to get things ready for the visit—underwear, clothes, new pajamas, fruit and lots of food. Aisha had contributed the *mulukhiya* with rabbit that Kamel loved so much. Gameel and Mitsy joined us, and we took two taxis to the prison. We sat in the waiting room as Gameel went to the prison office. Then he came back for us.

I walked down the corridor trying not to faint. The frightening moment was getting closer. My brother Kamel. The best person I knew, the support of my life: now I was going to see him looking like a criminal behind bars. Tears welled up in my eyes, and I could hardly see.

Outside a door, the lawyer stopped and whispered to us all, "You need to control your emotions now. If you break down in front of Kamel, it will have a harmful psychological effect on him. You are his nearest and dearest and you need to keep his spirits up. Do your utmost to help him."

I excused myself and went to the bathroom to rinse my face and then went back to the others, and we went in. In the large room an officer sat at a desk at the far end. I looked to the left and saw Kamel. He was pale, and his eyes were sunken. I could see blue bruises on his face. Mahmud shook his hand and then stood there saying nothing. My mother ran over to him, hugged him and burst out crying. Then Mitsy and Aisha and I shook his hand, and we all sat down in a circle with him.

The officer cleared his throat and announced pleasantly, "I wish I could leave you alone, but prison regulations do not allow that."

My mother forced a smile and said, "It'll all turn out all right, Kamel. Mr. Gameel has told us so. Please God, you'll be out soon."

"Uncle Ali," added Aisha, "sends you his greetings and says keep your spirits up, lad!"

I just kept looking at my brother, trying not to cry.

"Kamel," said Mitsy, "never forget that you are struggling to achieve your country's liberation. We're proud of you."

Kamel was looking at us and smiling, but something in his smile made me want to cry, something oblivious, distracted, fragile. The visit lasted half an hour, during which we exchanged trivialities and spoke of nothing important. But our words were simply a cover for another silent and more honest exchange.

At the end of our allotted time, the officer announced, "I'm sorry. The visit is over now."

Kamel said good-bye to us the way we had greeted him, with hugs and instructions to look after ourselves. Aisha burst out crying as my mother hugged him and said, "Good-bye, my hero. Keep your spirits up."

Mitsy and Kamel held hands and stared at each other. When it was my turn, I shook Kamel's hand and he kissed me on the cheek and told me, "Don't forget to study, Saleha."

41

Despite having drunk so much that evening, thanks to their regular workouts, Mahmud and Fawzy still retained their agility, and their terror made them flee at full speed from the shouting doorman.

"Stop them! Catch them!"

A soldier on patrol appeared and sounded off a long wailing siren to let all other soldiers in the area know that a pursuit was taking place. The two boys kept running, almost tripping over themselves. Fawzy noticed the Seif al-Din Building, which he knew from other amorous adventures, and ran toward it with Mahmud following. They ran through the front door into the lobby, and as luck would have it, the doormen were either away or asleep. Fawzy stopped and grabbed Mahmud's hand.

"The building has two entrances," he panted. "We'll go out the other door."

They crossed the wide gloomy lobby and went out of the other door, finding themselves in Qasr al-Ayni Street. They ran toward Ismailiya Square, and then Fawzy stopped and instructed Mahmud, "Just walk normally now."

As usual, it was Fawzy who set the pace. They walked down the street and then made their way through side streets back onto al-Sadd Street. From time to time, Fawzy stopped and looked back to make sure they were not being followed. After half an hour, the front door of their building loomed into view. They ran inside and up the stairs. When they reached the front door of Mahmud's apartment, Fawzy whispered, "Come up to the roof with me. We've got to talk."

Mahmud was beyond the point of being able to argue. He was

trying slowly to understand what had happened, ending up with the sight of Tafida lying naked and dead on the bed. Fawzy unlocked the room on the roof and took out two chairs and a small table. They sat, as they always did, next to the wall that looked onto al-Sadd Street. Fawzy took a lump of hashish from his pocket and started rolling a joint.

"I need something to get my head back together. The alcohol has worn off."

That was the way he dealt with a difficult situation, but his cheeriness seemed forced and meaningless. Mahmud sat there saying nothing, looking straight ahead but seeing nothing and occasionally letting out a sigh and banging his fists against his thighs or holding his hands on his head. Suddenly, he stood up and shouted out, in a voice raucous and strange, "The police'll catch us and throw us in prison . . ."

"They'll never find us. The doorman doesn't know my name or yours."

"But he knows what we look like."

"Even if the police question us, we haven't done anything. Life and death are matters for God, may he be praised. Tafida's time was up. She would have died in any case, whether we were there or whether she was alone."

"Tafida died in bed with you."

"All right, we had a relationship with the deceased woman, but she died a natural death."

Mahmud gave Fawzy a look of anger.

"Don't say 'we'! You're the one who was screwing Tafida. I had nothing to do with it."

"We were both there when she died."

At this point, Mahmud could no longer control himself, and his voice reverberated in the silence of the night, "You were the one screwing her. I told you from the very beginning I didn't want the job, and it was you who said that we had entered into a sort of traditional, oral marriage with them and that they were like the concubines of the Franks. You got me into this mess."

Fawzy went over to Mahmud and put his hand on his shoulder, but Mahmud brushed it off.

"Get away from me. I'm going downstairs."

Mahmud turned to leave, but then he stopped as if he had just remembered something. He turned toward Fawzy.

"I don't want to see you again!" he shouted. "Understand?"

As soon as he got to his bedroom, Mahmud lay down on his bed and stared at the ceiling, thinking. After a while, the sound of the dawn call to prayer reached his ears from the Sayyida Zeinab mosque. He got out of bed, took a shower and washed his mouth out well to remove any remnant of alcohol before dressing in his white galabiyya and saying his prayers. Seated on the prayer rug, he started reading from the Quran, but then his massive body started shaking, and he gave himself over to a fit of violent sobbing. He was beset with regret and fear. The meaning of what had happened was clear in his mind. He had been committing fornication with Rosa and Dagmar, but God Almighty had been merciful with him and was protecting him. God had given him chance after chance to return to a righteous life, but that devil Fawzy had turned his head, and so he continued committing debauchery, and now divine retribution had fallen upon him. He was mixed up in the death of a lady of some standing. He would have to prove that he had not killed her. Tafida al-Sarsawy's family would now be able to ruin his future, not to mention the stain of scandal that would forever stick to his family. He stretched out, full of regret, before sinking into a worried sleep, in which he dreamed he was watching the naked Tafida running along behind him as he was trying to get away from her, screaming in terror.

He became aware of his mother's hand stroking him, and he opened his eyes and sat up in bed. She smiled and said quietly, "Good morning, Mahmud. Your friend Fawzy's here."

His face turned ashen, and he was about to tell her that he did not want to see him, but he said nothing and nodded. His mother left his bedroom, and a short while later, Fawzy came in, shutting the door behind him.

"What are you doing here?" Mahmud protested.

Fawzy spoke quickly. "I know you're angry with me. But by God, Mahmud, I haven't done anything wrong. How was I to know that she would drop dead? But listen, Mahmud, I'm warning you. Don't you dare say a word about what happened to anyone. If you say a word, we're both done for."

"You got me into this mess," Mahmud wailed. "So you can get me out of it."

"Don't worry. I'll take care of it."

"But if the police arrest us, I'll spill the beans."

There was fear on Fawzy's face and he muttered, "Keep your voice down. Your mother will hear. Haven't we agreed?"

"Agreed to what?"

"That you won't speak of it to anyone."

Mahmud did not reply. He sat there scowling and staring into space as if at a loss to express what he felt. When Fawzy left the bedroom, Mahmud's mother asked him to stay for breakfast, but he thanked her and told her he had to go. Mahmud took a shower and forced himself to eat some breakfast before going to work. He carried out his orders in a state of total absentmindedness. He looked so worried that at the end of the shift, Uncle Mustafa asked him to go and have a cup of tea with him in the Paradise Café. Choosing a table on the far side, Uncle Mustafa ordered tea and a water pipe. Taking a deep drag, he asked, "What's the matter, Mahmud?"

"Nothing."

"You look shattered. Talk to me."

Mahmud recalled Fawzy's admonition about keeping mum, but Uncle Mustafa's sympathetic and kindly demeanor got the better of him. He felt a strong urge to confess everything to this man. He trusted him. Uncle Mustafa listened to him attentively and then said, "God is our refuge. May God protect you."

Mahmud looked down and said nothing. He was waiting for Uncle Mustafa, who had just taken another long drag on the water pipe, to give his opinion.

Uncle Mustafa knitted his eyebrows and said, "I told you to keep away from women, but you didn't listen to me."

"The devil has clever ways, Uncle Mustafa."

"You've ended up hurting yourself by ruining your future, you unfortunate lad."

Mahmud nodded, and a shudder ran down his body. Uncle Mustafa seemed moved and put his hand on Mahmud's shoulder.

"What we have to do . . . is go and see a lawyer."

"A lawyer?"

"The police will uncover everything. Eventually, they'll come looking for you. Don't forget that Madame Tafida comes from a family with some power and influence. We have to find you a clever lawyer."

"I don't know any lawyers."

"Leave it to me," Uncle Mustafa replied. "I'll find one."

Mahmud thanked him and then went home. He felt the relief of having unburdened himself. Uncle Mustafa was on his side. Mahmud was too frightened even to think about how difficult it would be when the police came to arrest him, when he was put in prison with criminals, when his mother learned that he had been fornicating with old women, when his sister, Saleha, and Kamel and Said came to know that their little brother was a pervert, when they came to see him in his prison uniform. All these thoughts were going round and round in his head, but at least he could rely upon Uncle Mustafa and the lawyer.

The next day, when Mahmud went to the garage to start his shift, Uncle Mustafa gave him a scowl.

"Come out to the street with me, Mahmud. I need to have a word with you."

Mahmud followed Uncle Mustafa as he walked from the garage to the street corner and then turned and faced Mahmud.

"Do you realize what a mess you have created for yourself?"

"I do," Mahmud replied.

There was silence, and then Uncle Mustafa went on angrily, "I just can't believe that someone like you, from a decent family, could have been carrying on like that."

"May God punish the one who caused it all . . ."

"Anyone else would have applied himself to doing decent hard work and not running round fornicating. You ought to be ashamed of yourself."

Mahmud hung his head like a naughty child, but Uncle Mustafa carried on, "God has blessed you with a large body, strong muscles and good health. You should be counting your blessings and using your good health to do God's work, not to go against Him. God has looked after you and given you more than one chance to repent of your ways, but you insisted on sinning."

"Oh God, forgive me please," Mahmud sighed.

Mustafa looked into the distance as if mulling something over and then looked at Mahmud and said, "Listen, Mahmud. Whatever happens, even if they arrest you, do not turn to sin again."

"I have repented, Uncle Mustafa."

"Give me your word."

"I promise."

"Let's read the opening verse of the Quran together."

It was a strange sight to see the enormous Mahmud in the street mumbling the words of the *fatiha* and wiping his face with his hands.

Suddenly, Uncle Mustafa smiled, and with emotion in his voice, he told Mahmud, "Thanks to your good father, may he rest in peace, God has found it sufficient to issue you with a warning."

"I don't understand."

"It's turned out all right."

Mahmud gave him a perplexed look and shouted, "What are you getting at?"

Uncle Mustafa's smile spread across his face.

"Thanks be to God, Tafida al-Sarsawy isn't dead."

Mahmud stared at him uncomprehendingly and then hoarsely stated, "Tafida's dead, Uncle Mustafa. I saw her lying there, dead, with my own eyes."

"She had fainted."

"Can't be."

"I went to her building this morning to see."

"I can't believe it."

"Listen, son, would I lie to you? I saw her myself as she was coming out of the building. Do you need any more proof than that?"

Mahmud let out a loud whoop and shouted, "Thank God! Thank God!" Then he gave Uncle Mustafa a big hug and, unable to control himself, burst out crying.

KAMEL

I held out, refusing to confess. I put up with the incessant beatings until I had no idea of what was going on around me, until I could no longer stand up on my own and had to be helped along. It was odd. The men who were beating the shit out of me were the same men who were helping me to get up and supporting me as I walked. Their faces bore expressions of perfect normality, as if they were just doing the sort of routine work that required no particular concentration. They would throw me down on the cell floor, and I cannot describe how it felt as I hit the ground. Every part of my body hurt. The cell was tiny, with only one small window about a foot wide. It was winter, the floor was tiled, I had one threadbare blanket and insects crawled around everywhere. Meals were just two pieces of bread and some indeterminate stew. The toilet was a bucket unemptied for hours so that I could smell my own excrement. They had taken care to put me in a cell next to where they tortured the detainees, and I could hear the screams reverberating all night long, my heart ready to break as I listened. Sometimes, I lost control and shouted and cursed, banging my hands on the walls until, finally spent, I sank back down to the ground. I knew that my protests were in vain. After a few days, I developed a terrifying obsession: What if they decided to torture me like that . . . would I be able to bear it? No one, no matter how true to his cause, would be able to endure such torture for an extended period. My resistance would crumble, and I would confess to everything or else I might even go mad.

The investigator called for me again. This time, however, the agents did not beat me up. The investigator smiled and asked me with a sneer, "Have you wised up yet, Kamel?"

"What do you want from me?"

"I want you to tell me all about the organization."

"What organization?"

"Stop playing the fool, my lad!" he shouted as the agents started hitting and kicking me and I screamed. The blows stopped suddenly, and the investigator laughed.

"By the way, we have a most entertaining little performance for you to see. I'm sure you'll like it."

He gestured to the agent by the door, and he rushed out. A few minutes later I heard commotion and shouting. The door opened, and agents brought in a short man, badly beaten up, with blood caked all over his swollen face. I recalled having seen him before; he worked at the Club in fact. The Upper Egyptian woman who had been brought in was screaming, and the agents slapped her.

The investigator continued, "This is Samahy, who works as a waiter at the Automobile Club. He caused a lot of problems for us, so we've invited him and his wife, Zahra, to stay with us until he wises up."

Samahy gave a snarl, which led to his being hit again.

"Samahy, my lad!" the investigator said. "Your wife, Zahra, has complained to us that you're not fulfilling your husbandly duties. What do you think about us getting some of our rough Upper Egyptian soldiers here to help out in that department? I think she'd like that."

The woman let out a nerve-shattering scream, and Samahy could not stop himself lunging at the agents, which only ended up with his getting another good kicking.

"Don't play the coquette with us, Zahra," the investigator sadistically cajoled her. "I've got a good strong Upper Egyptian guy here who can satisfy you. Strip her and take her to Abd al-Samad. He'll give her one and, Samahy, you can watch and learn how it's done."

The woman screamed even louder, and Samahy shouted, "Shame on you, you heathens."

The investigator made a gesture, and the agents dragged Samahy and his wife off. I could not hold myself back.

"You'll pay for this!" I shouted.

"We're not doing anything wrong," the investigator smiled. "We're protecting the throne and defending the country."

"Torture is a crime punishable by law."

"The law," he said, "is something you study at college, my lad. You graduate and then you have to forget it. Let me tell you, Kamel, that if you were in my shoes you'd do exactly the same."

"I could never," I retorted, "be a criminal like you lot."

The agents gave me another round of kicks, and then the investigator said calmly, "Now, I would counsel you again to start talking. When did you join the organization?"

"I don't join organizations."

"All right, Kamel." The investigator shook his head. "I'm trying to help you here, but you won't help yourself."

That was a signal to the agents to set about giving me another beating, after which they returned me to my cell. I felt like I had hit rock bottom, used like a laboratory animal. Everything they did was directed at extracting a desired result. The spectacle of Samahy and his wife both screaming was seared into my memory, and I kept reliving the scene in my mind, replacing Samahy's wife with Saleha. What if they were to do the same to her? I put all my strength into not falling apart. That night, for the first time, the voices and torture stopped, no more screaming to be heard. Had one of the detainees died? It was quieter than I had ever known it there, and I fell into a deep sleep.

The following day, there was a slight improvement in my treatment. They emptied the slop bucket twice and gave me more food, disgusting as it was. The investigator called for me again, but this time he was wearing a smile, and I was astonished at how those bastards' moods could swing from one extreme to the other.

"Mr. Barsoum, your lawyer," he said in an affable tone, "would like to speak with you."

He gestured toward a stocky man, who introduced himself, "I am Gameel Barsoum, a lawyer. Mrs. Aisha Hamama has retained me to defend you. With your agreement, naturally."

"Good to meet you."

Gameel then asked the investigator, "Could I speak to him outside?"

The investigator gestured toward the door.

"As you like, Mr. Barsoum. I'll give you half an hour."

I followed Gameel out of the room, and we stopped in the middle of the courtyard, where he heaved a sigh of relief.

"It's safer here," he said. "His office will be bugged. Listen, Kamel. We don't have much time. Speak to me. I'm your lawyer, and I need to know the truth."

I recounted everything in detail, from joining the Wafd cell and the organization up to my arrest.

"Have you confessed," he asked me in a serious tone, "to membership of the organization?"

"No."

"Well, don't even think about it."

"They have beaten me up to within an inch of my life."

"I know, and we'll get that corroborated tomorrow during the questioning. Anwar Bey Makki, head of state security, is interested in your case and has taken personal charge of it."

"What do you think they'll do to us?"

"Actually, there are two investigations in the Automobile Club. The striking workers have been arrested and are also being tortured. The second investigation is that of the organization of which you are accused of being a member. I must inform you that your case is a difficult one, with rather dangerous implications."

"Has Prince Shamel really been thrown into prison?"

"He has been released. But his having been held three days while the investigations took place is a dangerous sign. Prince Shamel is the king's cousin and could only be sent for trial by order of the king. The fact that the king had his cousin thrown into prison will only serve to make the investigators and the judges deal more harshly with this case."

I looked at him and said nothing. I was thinking about my ordeal, wondering how this nightmare would end, when I would be able to go back to my home, my own bed and my books.

As if he could read my thoughts, Gameel smiled sympathetically and said, "Whatever we do, I expect the directorate to try you in court. At that point, I will do whatever I can to get you out."

The next day, Gameel came to the interrogation with me and, pointing out my injuries, demanded my release, but I was ordered to be held for another two weeks.

On Friday, I had my first visit from my family. I tried to hold myself together. I told them that I felt optimistic and that I would soon be released, but their eyes told me they knew I was lying. My mother managed to keep her composure but then broke down crying. I was moved by Mahmud's teary eyes and Saleha's loving and sympathetic glances, Aisha's prayers and Mitsy's sad smile. I went back to my cell feeling slightly uplifted, comforted to know that I was no longer entirely alone in the hands of those bastards. At the very least, my family knew where I was and would be able to glean information about what was happening to me. But how was it all going to end? Was I nearing the end of the tunnel? Would I ever see the outside world again, or would I spend the rest of my years in prison?

42

The orders were plain enough: arrest the strikers with as little fuss as possible in order not to disturb His Majesty inside the Club. The soldiers succeeded in doing so and dragged the staff down the street, waiting until they had them in the police vans before raining down on them a torrent of punches and kicks. Those not detained remained busy at work, but some had caught a glimpse of the sorry scene. They would always remember their colleagues' futile attempts to wriggle out of the soldiers' grasp and would forever hear the screams and calls for help issuing from the police vans. Alku had sent orders to the staff not to go home after the end of their shifts, and so at four in the morning, they all assembled on the roof in their work caftans. As they stood there waiting, those who had seen the arrest operation told their colleagues about it in low impassioned tones. It had all been child's play until that night. Abdoun protesting the beatings and Alku's stance, his no-tips regime. It was as if all the foregoing events had been no more than a pantomime. All those who had opposed Alku were now under arrest, and no one knew what their fate would be. After a while, Alku appeared, followed by Hameed, and the staff all bowed and kowtowed. Alku stood there looking like a triumphant hero.

"Abdoun and that lot are getting what they asked for," he announced.

"Send them to the gallows!" some of the staff called out. "They can go to hell! Slit their throats! We don't want to see them again!"

Alku let them go on a little, allowing them to disown the strikers and declare their loyalty to him. He was staring into the distance as if gathering his thoughts. And then he asked them, "Does anyone here object to anything I do?"

They all stayed silent, so he asked again in a louder voice, "Speak up. Is there anything you're not happy about?"

"You are like our father, Alku," they started muttering submissively. "We're here to serve you! You're too good to us. May God bless you."

Alku scrutinized them, as if trying to make sure that he was back in control. Then he took two steps forward and announced, "From tonight, I am lifting your punishment. I am allowing you to have your tips again."

Shouts of joy rang out, the staff showering him with prayers for his well-being, and, when he turned to leave, clustering around him to express their gratitude. The next day, it was as if a new leaf had been turned over. They went to work with gusto, putting their all into the job, serving the customers as if performing for the camera, doing their best to show their loyalty and devotion, to affirm that they were the children and servants of Alku, who would never disobey him and who had nothing to do with those upstarts, already on their way to oblivion for their just reward, never again to sully the benevolent atmosphere of, or created by, their master, Alku, to whom they pledged themselves.

Their joy was boundless at having their former life back. After three months of hardship, finally they would be able to provide for their families. However pure their delight about the tips, about their arrested colleagues, they remained ambivalent, the way one feels when something awful happens to a close relative, with great sympathy for the one affected but, deep down, a guilty sense of relief to have been spared, a feeling of self-justified schadenfreude at the downfall of Abdoun and his bunch. Hadn't they made themselves out to be heroes, standing up to Alku and demanding their rights? Hadn't they accused the staff of being subservient and cowardly? Now the subservient cowards were getting their rights restored, not by rebellion or pretense to being high and mighty but by doing as they were told, by perfect subservience and acceptance of Alku's strictures and punishments, no matter how harsh. They had put up with the hard times, bent with the wind, and in the end, they came out on top. They

had their tips again, whereas that bunch of upstarts had ruined t̤.
futures and destroyed their families. The staff wanted to see Abdoun,
if only so that they could gloat. They would appear sympathetic to
him and then ask, "See, Abdoun? Are you happy with what you've
done to yourself and your colleagues? If only you'd listened to us, you
wouldn't be in this sorry state."

Days later, as they were sitting in the café, Abd al-Rasoul, who
worked as an assistant to Rikabi the chef, came and told them that a
relative in the Ministry of the Interior had confirmed to him that
the detainees were being subjected to horrendous torture and that
the state had even arrested their wives. The staff all started muttering
about the will of God, their expressions ranging from shock to glee.
They stammered out phrases of sham sympathy as they sipped their
mint tea and enjoyed their water pipes, as if the dire fate of their colleagues simply made them more appreciative than ever of the good
life, which they owed to a beneficent protector. They were safe and
could earn a living again, whereas those upstarts and their wives were
being beaten or worse, according to Abd al-Rasoul. He also told them
that charges were being trumped up against the detainees and that
they would spend years in prison. At the Automobile Club, their daily
work became more organized, and things returned to such a state
of normality that soon the incident became but a distant memory,
an anecdote to be recounted when a lesson seemed appropriate.
Abdoun was a deluded young idiot who had incited some of his colleagues against their master, and they all got what they had coming.
It became a cautionary tale.

Then one morning Hameed came to the Club on his own and
went to the telephone cabin. Labib jumped to his feet. "What can I do
for you, Hameed Bey?"

"Abdoun and the other guys are coming back at nine o'clock in
the morning," he said curtly and then turned and left.

Labib stood there dumbfounded for a time before rushing off
to tell his colleagues. The news spread like wildfire. The detainees
were coming back tomorrow? The news made everyone excited and
inflamed their dormant anxieties. Hameed had not elaborated. He
had just uttered one cryptic sentence: "Abdoun and the guys are coming back in the morning." Coming back where? Coming back to work

or coming home? And was the police van going to bring them and then take them away again? Had Alku pardoned them, or was he having them brought to the Club to parade them before the staff as a reminder of the wrong way before having them returned to prison? Gradually, the staff became convinced of one interpretation:

"Good God! Alku must have forgiven them."

"By God's will, they are being let out of prison so they can look after their families."

"They made some mistakes, that's undeniable, but they're still our brothers and didn't mean to do us any harm."

Thus they went on to each as if trying to form a new consensus, as if they were colluding to forget their former derision and abandonment of their brethren. They were rehearsing their new role for the following day—that of devoted colleagues who had not been able to sleep a wink out of worry and who were brimming with joy now that the whole sorry episode had come to an end. The next day, the day shift staff turned up early and were joined by the night shift staff, who had spent the early hours in the café before rushing back over to the Club. They all stood in the doorway, silently waiting. There was nothing to be said—they had already prepared themselves for the welcoming formalities. Each one had gone over how he would react when he saw the freed men, how he would shriek with joy and embrace them one by one, repeating the words prepared to express his happiness at seeing them again. They waited there for almost an hour with nothing happening and then started mumbling and whispering among themselves, wondering about the delay. Karara went over to Labib, who was sitting behind the glass window of his booth, and as if speaking on behalf of everyone, he asked out loud, "Any news, Labib?"

"They were supposed to turn up any second," the telephonist answered, smiling nervously. "I hope nothing has happened."

Karara turned around and went back to stand with his colleagues, when he heard a siren and some of the staff started shouting.

"They've arrived!"

The transport consisted of a black Cadillac carrying Alku and Hameed, followed by a blue police van, which was completely windowless apart from two small grilles. Suleyman rushed over to the car and opened the door for Alku, and Hameed jumped out of the other side. Alku looked serious and resolute, like a man about to carry out an urgent and delicate mission. He did not walk over to the entrance to the Club but strode slowly over to the door of the police van and gestured with his hand. As it was opened, the van door's hinges screeched, and the first person to appear was a thin soldier who jumped down the metal steps onto the sidewalk, and then, a minute or so later, the detainees started coming out. The scene was so shocking that the staff standing in the doorway were unable to take in what they were seeing. Coming out of the van were women, with black abayas covering their bodies and heads. They were moving slowly, with their heads held down. They walked toward the entrance of the Club, and gradually their faces could be made out in the light of day. It was at that moment that the reality struck the staff like a thunderbolt. Beneath the black abayas, they saw their colleagues: Abdoun and Samahy, then Bahr, Nouri and Banan, then Fadly, Gaber and Basheer. The staff were so shocked that not a single one could utter a word, so dumbfounded they could do no more than stare, as if hoping against hope that the scene was a hallucination. But it was the hard cold truth that they were seeing before them.

Alku took a few steps forward and shouted at the men, "Can't you act like men? I've brought you back to the Club, but you're all dressed up in ladies' clothing!"

They said nothing, standing there in their black abayas with their heads hung low. Alku laughed and then gestured with his hand.

"Go on up to the roof."

The procession formed spontaneously. The abaya-clad men went on ahead, followed by their colleagues, with Alku and Hameed bringing up the rear. They climbed the stairs in a silence broken only by the sound of their footsteps on the marble. They lined up on the roof, with the guilty men in black next to the wall and the other staff standing around them. Alku was in the middle of them and announced to the freed men, "There is no work for you today. You will stay here until the end of the day. I want everyone to be able to see you wearing your nice abayas."

Alku enunciated that last sentence as if savoring it. He turned around and cast a glance over the dumbfounded staff, then went downstairs, Hameed springing after him. With Alku gone, the staff now found themselves having to deal somehow with this supremely bizarre event. The colleagues, whom they had been waiting to welcome back, were now standing in front of them, heads bowed, faces emaciated and ghostly pale behind their abayas. Who would be the first to speak? What could men in abayas say? What could those who were supposed to greet them say? There was nothing to celebrate, and it seemed pointless to say anything. So no one said a word. The two groups of men stood there, rooted to the ground until Samahy wailed out, "Look! Alku has dressed us up in veils like women."

That sentence broke the ice and let the men vent the violent emotions which had initially been suppressed by shock. The staff rushed over to the freed men and embraced them. They tried to comfort them, but as they all started speaking at once, no one could make out exactly what they were saying. Tears ran down Bahr's cheeks, and Abdoun grimaced and bit his lower lip as if trying to suppress a sharp pain, the groans of the other men turning into shouts and wails.

43

Straight after the dawn call to prayer, and right on time, two taxis turned up on al-Sadd al-Gawany Street, and Umm Said, Saleha, Mitsy and Aisha all rushed down to the street and got into one of the cars. In the other, Gameel the lawyer sat with Fawzy and Mahmud and a man wearing a blue suit. Umm Said, sitting silently next to the driver, noticed Mitsy's face in the rearview mirror. Praise be to God. This was another of His miracles. An English girl, who had come from the far ends of the earth, to enter their life and live with them. As she looked out the window, she became aware of the constant whispering between Mitsy and Saleha and thought that these two girls, whenever they were together, would always have something to say to each other and could never sit saying nothing. Scenes from her life went through Umm Said's mind. She could see Kamel as a child and reminisced over what a happy and sweet boy he had been, what a sense of responsibility he had, unlike his selfish brother Said. She recalled the sudden death of her husband and Saleha's unfortunate marriage and divorce and the night of Kamel's arrest. His imprisonment was still like a deep wound gnawing away at her nerves.

"Kamel has been put in prison because he is a brave nationalist. I am very proud of him," she would always say to people trying to comfort her, but deep inside she really wished that he had never become involved in the whole affair. Her innermost self really wanted to rebuke him—but in the softest way possible. She would smile and tell herself, as if addressing him, "I'm not angry with you, Kamel. I could never be angry with you, whatever you do, but couldn't you have waited until you graduated before taking up the struggle?

Couldn't you have thought about us, son? There are thousands of young men to fight against the occupation, but how many of them provide for their family as you do?

After approximately an hour, the taxis pulled up in the courtyard of the foreigners' prison. Mahmud, Fawzy and the man in the blue suit stepped out, and Mahmud rushed over to help his mother and the women out of their taxi. They all stood in front of the building as Gameel quickly went through the entrance formalities. They walked through the massive doorway and down a long dark corridor until they reached the prison governor's office. Gameel opened his briefcase and took out a document.

"Please go and take a seat in the waiting room," he said.

They went through a side door into the waiting room. They all sat there, saying nothing, except for Umm Said, who kept muttering, "God grant forgiveness, great and merciful God."

A few minutes later, the lawyer appeared at the door and said, "Please come with me."

They all followed him, and as Umm Said headed for the usual visitors' room, the lawyer said, "Not that way. Please use the other door."

They looked at him in bewilderment, but he laughed and told them, "The governor is letting us use his office."

They trooped into the governor's office, and Kamel soon appeared. He was neatly shaved, his hair carefully brushed and even his blue prison uniform looked clean and pressed. His mother rushed over to him, embraced him and burst out crying. He leaned over to kiss her hands, and then Saleha gave him a hug. When it was Mitsy's turn, she laughed and shook his hand.

"You look well!" she chirped. "And I can confirm that you are still good looking."

The man in the blue suit went over to him and introduced himself.

"Muhammad Irfan. Notary."

Kamel shook his hand warmly. After a little while, they all sat down around the notary, who was sitting in the governor's chair and had placed in front of him a large file. He opened it, uttered the customary invocations of God's beneficence and power and started speaking of marriage in Islam. Then, taking Kamel's hand he placed it in Mitsy's and, covering them both with a white handkerchief, he went through the formalities of the marriage contract. Kamel looked happy, and Mitsy was emotional as they were congratulated. Aisha could not control herself. She raised her head and, putting her hand in front of her mouth, started ululating. The happy noise sounded odd in the gloomy atmosphere of the prison.

44

As he did every night, once Alku had made sure that His Majesty was fast asleep, he went over the next day's duties and just before dawn repaired to his own suite in Abdin Palace. This consisted of two large bedrooms, a reception room, a luxurious bathroom and a much plainer office. Alku was worn out and took a hot shower, then poured himself a whiskey, which he gulped down followed by two glasses of cold water before sinking down on his bed. He shut his eyes, rolled onto his right side and let sleep wash over him. Suddenly, he heard a noise in the room. He peered into the darkness and thought he could make out some shapes near the window.

"Who's there?" he barked.

No one replied. He sprang out of bed and reached out for the light switch but felt a hand grab him by the throat.

"Don't move!"

"Who are you, and how did you get in?" Alku shouted.

That was when he felt the first blow. Alku groaned loudly as if in protest, but the punches continued. They hit him on the head and punched and kicked him. He could just about make out their forms in the darkness. Two men pinned his arms apart while another stood behind and held his head up for more punches. The man in front of him, who seemed to be the leader, was holding a flashlight which gave out a small circle of light. The beating continued, violent and unabated, with Alku moaning and groaning loudly.

"Shame on you!" he managed to spit out.

The beating started anew, and the man in front kicked him in the shins. Alku started to plead, "I'm an old man and you're young enough to be my children."

The leader laughed, "So now you've become a gentle and caring father, you low-down bastard!"

"What do you want with me?" Alku managed to stutter out, terrified.

"We've come to settle the account."

"What account?"

"The bill for all the bad things you've done."

"If I've done something wrong, I apologize."

"It's too late for apologies now."

"Let me go and I'll do anything you want."

"We want our due. You have robbed us and treated us like filth."

"I'll do whatever you want."

"That's your problem all over . . . you think we're stupid."

"I swear. I'll do anything. Believe me."

"You're not going to trick us again."

"Give me one last chance."

"There isn't room for all of us. It's either us or you."

Alku called out for God's mercy. The flashlight went out, and the room was completely dark. Shots rang out followed by the sound of footsteps rushing away. There were shouts in the palace corridors and guards ran to Alku's suite. They switched the light on and found Alku, Qasem Muhammad Qasem, chief royal chamberlain, in his blue silk pajamas, stretched out on the floor with a bullet through his forehead, his mouth wide open and his eyes fixedly staring into the distance with a surprised look that he would wear for all eternity.